ST. MARTIN'S

MINOTAUR

MYSTERIES

GET A CLUE!

Be the first to hear the latest mystery book news...

With the St. Martin's Minotaur monthly newsletter, you'll learn about the hottest new Minotaur books, receive advance excerpts from newly published works, read exclusive original material from featured mystery writers, and be able to enter to win free books!

Sign up on the Minotaur Web site at:
www.minotaurbooks.com

"The dialogue crackles, and the Southern Colorado atmosphere astonishes, especially at night."

—*Publishers Weekly*

"Fans won't be disappointed . . . Doss pulls together an archeological dig, abandoned children, and a good, old-fashioned murder to pull off his latest success."

—*Chicago Tribune*

THE SHAMAN'S GAME

"Suspenseful and satisfying . . . Doss has reproduced the land of the Southern Colorado Utes with vivid affection."

—*Dallas Morning News*

"Doss could be accused of poaching in Tony Hillerman territory . . . but Doss mixes mysticism and murder with his own unmistakable touch."

—*Orlando Sentinel*

"Deft storytelling . . . Compelling . . . Ingenious . . . Intense . . . a richness of prose and plot that lifts it out of the expected ranks of mystery fiction."

—*Arizona Daily Star*

GRANDMOTHER SPIDER

"Propelled by fast-paced action and intriguing characters . . . like something out of Stephen King . . . with snippets from Dave Barry."

—*Chicago Tribune*

"Humor crackles through pages packed with surprises."

—*Albuquerque Journal*

ALSO BY JAMES D. DOSS

THE
WITCH'S
TONGUE

JAMES D. DOSS

St. Martin's Paperbacks

THE WITCH'S TONGUE

Library of Congress Catalog Card Number: 2004048180

ISBN: 0-312-99108-8
EAN: 80312-99108-1

Printed in the United States of America

St. Martin's Press hardcover edition / September 2004
St. Martin's Paperbacks edition / October 2005

St. Martin's Paperbacks are published by St. Martin's Press, 175 Fifth Avenue, New York, NY 10010.

10 9 8 7 6 5 4 3

For

Bob and Betty Eickleberry
Los Alamos, New Mexico

Julia Martin
Richland, Washington

Helen Randal
The Book Sleuth, Colorado Springs

ACKNOWLEDGMENTS

I wish to offer my thanks to these kindly folk:

Glen Raby, Chimney Rock Area Manager
USDA Forest Service, Pagosa Springs District

Administrative Sergeant Leon Mares
Southern Ute Tribal Detention Center, Ignacio, Colorado

Dick Hutson and Bob Newell
Los Alamos, New Mexico

Tom Elder
Arroyo Seco, New Mexico

PROLOGUE

NEARLY THIRTEEN THOUSAND SUMMERS HAVE PASSED SINCE that splendid morning when the first human footprints appeared between these towering canyon walls. But in all the years since that singular event, not one good thing has happened here. This being the case, hardly anyone visits this remote and dreadful place—though the rare exception is worthy of mention.

Consider Jacob Gourd Rattle.

Cloaked in twilight shadows, the solitary man holds a pointed stick in his hand. With the terrible intensity of a fanatic, the meticulous draftsman draws a coffin-sized rectangle in the sand. Satisfied with the length and breadth of his plan, he considers its depth.

The customary six feet is what he had in mind, but the soil is packed with stones and there will be tangles of roots to cut. The laborer balances rocks and roots against the weight of tradition. The scales hesitate, then tilt to accommodate his predisposition.

Four feet will be enough.

THE TRIBAL ELDER

DAISY PERIKA is a crusty old recluse, much preferring her lonely wilderness home to a more comfortable house in Ignacio. Because the dirt road to her small dwelling is treacherous even in dry weather, the Ute elder's flesh-and-blood visitors are few and far between. For the determined hiker, her dwelling is a three-hour walk from the paved road. For the motorized pilgrim blessed with fortitude and four-wheel drive, the journey can be completed in twenty-nine spine-jarring minutes. By the light of the waning moon, the amber-eyed owl wings her way from here to there in scarcely any time at all.

Whether locomoting by foot or wheel or wing, the traveler eventually encounters a collection of sandstone mesas rising above the arid prairie grasslands. Each of these isolated plateaus is separated from its neighbor by a deep, sinuous canyon. Three Sisters Mesa is bordered on the west by the narrow, meandering *Cañon del Serpiente* and on its sunrise side by *Cañon del Espiritu.* This latter chasm is, according to Daisy Perika, a place where the spirits congregate.

Perilously near the yawning mouth of Spirit Canyon, almost concealed among a cluster of juniper and piñon, is her modest house trailer. Resembling an oversized metal mailbox, the Ute woman's home stands confidently on stubby legs of cinder blocks. Scorched by decades of blistering sun, pelted by wind-driven sleet and sand, its once-glistening surface is now spotted and blotched by a sooty oxide pox. Now and then, a rivet pops. Beneath the thin aluminum skin, brittle steel bones fracture and crack. At sunrise and sunset, corroded joints expand and contract, making awful creaks and squeaks. When they work at all, electrical things sizzle and sputter. On her cookstove, blue circles of propane flame flicker and flutter. In the deep trough of night, the ghost in the thing utters painful groans and quaking shudders. The shaman's home should have collapsed long ago, and died a quiet death. But like its stubborn occupant, the structure remains. Moreover, it is a place where things tend to happen. Special things. And from time to time, distinguished visitors come to call. On this very day, for example.

In the small kitchen, seated at the table, see the kindly man of God—the tight-lipped woman.

THE PRIEST

HAVING COMPLETED his prayer, Father Raes Delfino opened his eyes, saw the Ute elder's prune-skin face staring at him.

Daisy seems upset. Perhaps she has already guessed what I am about to tell her. He had known the peculiar woman far too long to underestimate her powers. He hesitated, then got on with it. "I came to see you today—because I wanted you to be the first to know."

Daisy Perika held her breath, waited to hear the bad news. *He don't look healthy.*

The Catholic priest smiled at this meddling gossip, this wicked prankster, this seesawing backslider, this troublesome woman who persisted in her conversations with the dwarf-spirit—this most beloved member of his flock. "Just this morning, I posted a letter to the bishop. I am asking his permission to retire."

Oh, God—I knew it. He's dying! She laid one trembling hand over the other. "When?"

"It is not for me to say." The cleric stirred his coffee. "But I expect it will take at least six months—perhaps a year—for the ecclesiastical wheels to grind their grist."

He must have a cancer. "You're sick."

"Oh no, I am quite well." He chuckled. *Far better than I have ever been.*

"Then why . . ." The old woman's words trailed off down the path to nowhere.

He reached across the table, took her hand in his. "Because, dear lady—it is time."

Daisy brushed away the single tear coursing its way down her face. "Where'll you go—to one of them old priests' homes?" She snorted. "Sit in a wheelchair with a bib over your shirt while somebody feeds you oatmeal from a tablespoon?"

This produced a belly laugh. "Gracious me, I hope not."

Her tone was accusing. "But you'll move away from the reservation." *A long way away. And I'll never see you again in Middle World.*

He gave her a thoughtful look. "If God is willing, I will find a quiet place to rest." *And pray.*

I know what it is! The elder screwed up her courage. "Some people in Ignacio say you've been acting funny lately." She added darkly, "They claim you haven't been paying attention to church business—that you go around all day mumbling prayers and psalms. And singing to yourself."

"God forgive me, it is true." The holy man put on a repentant expression. "Now you see why I must be replaced by someone younger. A practical no-nonsense priest, who will get things done."

Daisy was not fooled by this evasive response. "There's even some that say you've had some kind of a *religious* experience." Her tone was distinctly accusing.

Father Raes arched an eyebrow. "Do they now?"

She nodded, pierced him with a flinty look. "Some say you saw an angel in the church one night. Others say you saw—" But *that* could not be repeated. "Is that why you're bailing out?"

He frowned. "Now, Daisy—do you really believe I'd let a bit of gossip drive me away?"

"You know what I mean. Are you retiring because you had a vision?" Daisy Perika encountered astounding apparitions once or twice every month, and the old shaman was not thinking about retiring.

The priest assumed his severe persona. "We will not discuss such rumors." Having done his duty, he softened his tone. "But I assure you—I am not retiring from the active priesthood because of anything I have *seen*." This was literally true. It was, in fact, what he had *heard*. But this would never be revealed to another mortal. Especially not to this Ute Catholic, who was a shaman on the side. Or was it the other way around? *God have mercy on our souls.*

The subject was thus dismissed. They talked for a while of other matters.

About Daisy's nephew, tribal investigator Charlie Moon.

About God and his Son. And the Holy Spirit.

Stern admonitions were given. And sweet blessings.

Promises were made.

And finally, good-byes.

ADRIFT

DAISY PERIKA stood on the wooden porch attached to her trailer home, wrinkled hands gripping the pine rail. The sounds of the priest's automobile were lost in the winds. Thick mists billowed and rolled out of the wide mouth of *Cañon del Espiritu*. The old woman felt as if her feet were slipping on the deck of a small ship tossed by a heaving, unseen sea. As the porch began to creak and sway beneath her feet, she craned her neck forward—straining to get a glimpse of that familiar landscape that must be out there still. It was not. For a terrifying moment, she was almost convinced that the pale blue sky, the piñon-crested mesas, the sinuous brown canyons—had never been. But in the pocket her mind, she had kept them, and could perceive them there. As she held on to the rail of the rolling craft, the elderly Catholic meditated on the Captain of her Soul.

Presently, the sea mists thinned.

The little porch became steady again.

The Ute shaman squinted at the massive stone figures waiting patiently on the crest of Three Sisters Mesa. Could those petrified women see through the mists of time and space? And the *pitukupf* who lived far up *Cañon del Espiritu* in the abandoned badger hole—could the dwarf reveal when the priest would leave her, and where Father Raes would go? This thought gave the old woman some slight sense of confidence. Everything would work out. One way or another, it always did. Maybe no replacement would be found for the priest. Then the bishop in Pueblo would tell Father Raes he had to stay for a few years more.

At least until I am gone from Middle World . . .

Daisy rubbed a sore hip and sighed. *I'll go inside, heat up the chili stew.*

But not so very far away, where a man had drawn four lines in the sand—a blacker pot had already begin to brew.

CHAPTER ONE

REGARDING THE WITCH'S BODY PARTS

TO THE TYPICAL OBSERVER, THE TRIO OF MUTE ONES DO NOT resemble human beings. Not in the least.

This being the case, it could hardly be expected that they would look anything at all like three Pueblo women who had been petrified (depending on the version of the legend) by either a feat of malicious sorcery or an act of supernatural mercy. To the uninformed eye, the massive monoliths appear to be merely three huge humps of weathered sandstone that were squatting atop the mesa aeons before saber-toothed tigers and majestic mammoths roamed the foothills of those mountains that would eventually be christened "San Juan" by the Spanish invaders. According to the tale the Ute shaman told—and Daisy Perika would not tolerate the least hint of skepticism—after fleeing to the top of the mesa to escape an Apache raiding party, the trio of Pueblo women had prayed for deliverance from their ruthless pursuers. Their bodies had been turned to stone, their spirits set free to enter Upper World. Daisy also asserted that the sandstone women were not quite nine hundred years old and that before the remarkable event, the top of the canyon had been as flat as a billiard table. Local geologists dared not contend the point with the hard-eyed woman.

Whatever the ages of the sandstone towers, the deep canyons that snaked and twisted and turned and twined along the edges of Three Sisters Mesa were ancient beyond imagining. And being so very old, there were some rather odd *things* that lingered between their walls. According to Daisy, some were wispy remnants of material bodies. There were others (so she said) that had never occupied a house of flesh. The shaman knew this to be true; she had encountered a score or more of them and often chatted with those who were lonely. Daisy's knowledge was not limited to the spirits. Because she prepared medicines, the tribal elder knew every plant that grew in this wilderness. She begged their pardon for harvesting flowers, berries, leaves, stems, and roots. She was acquainted with all the animals, too, and greeted each of them by name. Some returned the compliment. But there were a few odd features in these shadowy depths that even Daisy Perika knew little about.

For example, consider that canyon stretched out closest to the sunset.

The shaman did not know that ages and ages ago, halfway up the cliffs, a thick basaltic layer had bridged the chasm. Though having little utility except for the occasional lizard or mouse or fuzzy caterpillar who wished to cross over the shady depths, it was nevertheless a wondrous thing to behold. Or would have been, had human beings arrived in time to see it. Alas, the marvelous formation collapsed a hundred millennia before the most recent ice age. In the bottom of the canyon, portions of the fallen bridge have cracked and weathered and washed away in seasonal floods. Even so, some evidence remains. A few black basalt slabs are still half buried in the sandy floor, and there are lofty remnants of the ancient span. Opposed on the sheer cliffs are a pair of dark projections. Well above the Three Sisters side of the canyon, a black basaltic shelf juts out prominently from crumbling sandstone. On the wall across the way, a smaller sibling mimics its mate.

In the early autumn of 1883, a Scottish prospector on the way to Fort Garland happened by, riding a fat black ginny mule, leading a gray donkey. This European was cursed with a touch of superstition, blessed with a wry sense of humor.

While sipping black tea by his campfire, the traveler named the larger protrusion the Witch's Tongue, and made note of this small bit of vanity in his diary. Across the canyon, the smaller shelf cried out for similar recognition. And so the pliant pilgrim from Portnacroish dubbed it the Witch's Thumb, and penned this also on the yellowed page.

The seeker after gold was murdered six months later in Los Ojos by a swarthy prostitute who appropriated the Scotsman's poke, his Winchester carbine with the silver-inlaid maple stock—even his little writing book. Because she could not read, the sporting woman traded the dead man's diary to a U.S. Army cartographer for three Havana Provincial cigars. Sadly, the unfortunate prospector's name has been forgotten.

The Witch's Tongue and Thumb have not.

It may have been due to a few unfortunate references to *brujos*, or recurring tales of hunters and trappers who had fallen into that twilight crack in the earth, never to surface again—or it may have been a more subtle hint of evil sensed by tribal elders. But the canyon was always known to the Utes as a *bad* place. So bad that in the mid-twentieth century the Tribal Council had (in its collective wisdom) officially pronounced the six-mile-long crevasse off-limits except to members of the tribe. But there were, as there must always be, exceptions to the rule.

From time to time, a privileged few were granted special passes. These hardy souls were typically archaeologists, anthropologists, biologists, or geologists—and always *matukach*. The reckless white-skins did not believe in the People's legends, and so had some measure of protection from those unspeakable things that haunted the canyon.

The more sensible folk among the Southern Utes would not have thought of visiting this forbidden place; even the braggarts and scoffers and show-offs generally came up with an acceptable reason to avoid its dark recesses. And so it was that human beings—particularly tribal members—were not to be found in this particular canyon.

Except for the exceptions.

THE EXCAVATION

BETWEEN THE canyon walls, beneath the cloud-shrouded slit of sky, the lonely soul attended to his solemn business. He was confident that in this forbidden place, his enterprise would be safe from prying eyes.

Vain are the thoughts of men.

Jacob Gourd Rattle was already being watched.

OPPOSITE THE Witch's black Tongue, perched on the Witch's black Thumb—reclines the cougar. Her unblinking yellow eyes are focused on the man on the canyon floor. She does not wonder about what the peculiar biped is doing down there—such complex thoughts are not in her nature. The hungry feline licks her lips. Imagines how his warm flesh will taste.

THE BUSY man was unaware of the mountain lion's pitiless stare—or even the fact that she was there. As Jacob Gourd Rattle removed earth and stones from the hole in the ground, he concentrated on the happy thought that the troublesome woman was not with him.

Kicks Dogs would return, of course. She always did.

But, Jacob hoped—not until the appointed time.

Not until his work here was done.

CHARLIE MOON would have been quite interested in Jacob Gourd Rattle's clandestine activities, but the tribal investigator was a long drive to the north of the Southern Ute reservation. And like the man digging the grave in the canyon, Daisy Perika's nephew was also engaged in important business.

CHAPTER TWO

THE PLAYERS

THE THREE SERIOUS MEN WERE IN THE ANTIQUARIAN'S STORage room, seated around an unusual table.

Charlie Moon—intent on the delightful task of fleecing his friends of their currency—hardly noticed the furniture.

Scott Parris had already described the card table as "kinda sissy for a man's game of gut-bucket poker."

The mildly miffed owner—who made his quite comfortable living buying and selling fine antiques—informed his gaming companions that they had the distinct honor to rest their elbows on a genuine George II demi-lune mahogany card and tea table with a two-fold top, baize-lined surface with wells. Not to mention club legs and pad feet—thank you very much.

Ralph Briggs's semibrutish guests had not been impressed.

On the mantelpiece, a Victorian brass lantern clock twirled its delicate hands in the slowest of motions to measure the flow of that indefinable river called Time. When it chimed once to announce the eleventh hour, it so happened that Scott Parris was the dealer. The broad-shouldered, sandy-haired, blue-eyed chief of Granite Creek PD was also the heavy loser.

Charlie Moon was down by eight blue chips, but not defeated. The Indian was lying low, waiting for his chance to ambush this mismatched pair of *matukach*.

Ralph Briggs, banker of the game, was nearly twelve hundred dollars up. Hoping to get away while the getting was good, he faked a yawn. "Last hand?"

Scott Parris took a sip of black coffee from a china cup that was almost as translucent as the antiquarian's ploy. "Okay," he said. "But how about we switch to Leadville stakes and White Mule rules."

The Ute nodded his assent.

Ralph Briggs considered protesting, saw the flinty look on the white policeman's face, thought better of it. "Very well."

Parris rubbed his hands together. "Then let's play poker, gents."

Each of the gamblers anted in a white chip.

The chief of police shuffled, offered the cards to the player on his right.

Charlie Moon cut the deck, passed it back to the dealer.

Scott Parris dealt five rectangles to each of the players, pulled his own hand close to his chin. *Garbage*. He looked to the antiquarian. "Okay, Ralph—how many do you need?"

The smallish man pursed his lips. "Two will do."

The dealer dealt the pair.

Ralph Briggs looked at his new hand. *Well, now. Look at that*. Parris eyed his best friend. "Charlie?"

Moon wore a mask that grinned. "I am happy with what I'm holding."

Parris snorted at the Ute. "Dealer takes three," he said, and did. *More garbage!* He squinted over his pitiful cards at the antique dealer.

Ralph Briggs raised a thin eyebrow at the crafty Indian, eyed his Hearty flush. *I shall demolish Mr. Moon*. On the pretense of miserly caution, he started to push four white chips to the center of the table, hesitated—withdrew half of the pale quartet.

The Ute sniffed the air and smelled the musky odor of deceit. "I'll see that pitiful wager." He offered up two whites. "And raise—this much." The tribal investigator baited the pot with four red chips.

Parris folded. "I hate this game. I hate it more than dentist drills and cod liver oil and income taxes."

As if some dark magic might have transformed the cards since his last furtive glance, Briggs examined what he was holding with exaggerated care. *Moon is bluffing.* "I shall see you," he offered a quartet of matching reds, "and raise you—thusly." The antiquarian sent two blue chips to join their lesser friends.

The Ute called and raised again. Six blue chips.

The dapper little man in the tweed suit did the same. Six and six more.

"You are a bulldog, Ralph." Charlie Moon pondered his next move. "But I am feeling reckless. So I'll see that and raise you . . . hmm . . . how much? Oh what the hey, a greenback dollar means nothin' to a fella like me. I will risk all I've got." He pushed a multicolored pile of chips to gorge the pot.

The folded chief of police stared goggle-eyed at the players.

As a matter of civilized principle, Ralph Briggs firmly refused to sweat. In lieu of this means by which common men cool their skin, his high forehead beaded with tasteful pearls of unscented perspiration. *The Indian is bluffing. I know it!* He opened his mouth to call, but his churning stomach had the last five words. *But if he is not* . . . His fingers refused to touch the last of his chips. The antiquarian choked. And folded.

The Ute placed his cards facedown, raked in the red-white-and-blue pot, offered his surly adversaries the consolation of a melancholy sigh. "You fellas are the lucky ones. After you've hit the hay tonight, you'll only think about how bad you played for maybe an hour or two or three. But before the sun comes up, you'll finally get worn out from all your moaning and groaning, and drift off to a troubled sleep. But me—I'll be up all night long." He flashed a toothy smile. "Counting my winnings."

Scott Parris shook his head, glanced at the other beaten man. "Ralph, don't you just *hate* it when he does that?"

Ralph Briggs glared at Charlie Moon. *Yes. Indeed I do.*

While the winner was donning his fleece-lined denim jacket and black John B. Stetson hat, Briggs counted and recounted the meager remnant of his chips. He mumbled, "I just *know* Charlie was holding trash—I should have called."

Parris leaned close to Briggs and whispered, "That Ute never bluffs."

Ralph Briggs desperately wanted a reason to feel better. "Never?"

The town cop shook his head. "Never. If you'd have called, he would've cleaned you out."

After the chief of police had departed for hearth and home, the antique dealer followed the Indian into the display room of his expensive, exclusive shop. *I should not ask, but—* "Charles, just between friends, and just this once—I wonder if I could impose upon you to tell me what—"

The seven-foot Ute stopped in midstride, looked down at the smaller man. Charlie Moon shook his head in a gesture that suggested a mix of sadness and disappointment. "Ralph, it is one of Nature's fundamental laws—if a player wants to see the hand a man is holding, he has to lay his money down. But you did not call my bet."

"You are absolutely right, of course." Briggs looked away and had the grace to blush. "I do not know what came over me. It must be the lateness of the hour."

"Don't worry about it." Moon clapped him on the back. "Because you and me are buddies—I have already forgot you asked."

"I am eternally grateful—and you are very gracious."

Moon took a look around. "I might want to make a purchase from your store."

The vulgar reference to a *store* made the pale man wince. "Do you have something particular in mind?"

"I will know it when I see it. Or maybe the other way around."

The businessman made a halfhearted gesture. "Feel free to browse." With a greedy glint in his eye, Ralph Briggs watched Charlie Moon examine this and that. He wondered about a number of things. For instance—on top of his winnings, how much more hard cash did the full-time rancher, part-time tribal cop have in his hip pocket? And how much would he be willing to part with?

As it came to pass, the Ute was separated from the white man by a rift of cultures and a finely crafted walnut display case. The latter barrier was glazed with brittle Venetian glass that cast the contents in a pale bluish hue. On the top shelf, a remarkable assortment of collectibles was laid out on a plush carpet of purple felt.

An 1857 French Army dental kit, neatly packaged in a small wooden box that presented a silvered mirror on the open lid.

An ivory crescent of walrus tusk, delicately engraved with the ghostly form of a four-masted Boston whaling vessel, sails still billowed by phantom winds.

Representing the Yankee invasion of the Confederate States of America, a corroded assortment of powdery-white lead bullets, silver medals, brass buttons, bronze belt buckles.

A diamond-studded bracelet and magnificent emerald ring worn by the lovely young heiress of the Flint Hill and Nacogdoches Oil Company on the very night she drove her black 1949 Packard convertible into Attoyac Bayou.

The centerpiece of the display was a .45-caliber Colt Peacemaker with ivory grips. According to the information card, the single-action revolver had been presented to Chief Ouray by his first wife, Black Mare.

The proprietor of The Compleate Antiquarian observed his potential customer with intense professional curiosity. Though the Ute had a glance for each of the fascinating objects, Moon's gaze was invariably pulled back to that *special item*. Of course. Now Ralph Briggs thought he understood what the Indian was doing here. The proprietor allowed himself a knowing smile. "See anything you fancy?"

Charlie Moon pointed at the item that had caught his eye. "How much do you want for that?"

The owner of the establishment unlocked the case. "The Colt Peacemaker?"

The Ute shook his head, tapped his finger on the glass.

"Oh, *that*." He arched an eyebrow at Moon. "What on earth would a hardcase cow-pie-kicking cowboy like you want with—"

"How much?"

After a perfectly timed dramatic pause, Briggs told him how much.

Charlie Moon swallowed hard.

CHAPTER THREE

THE SHAMAN SLEEPS

AT ABOUT THE TIME THE POKER GAME IN GRANITE CREEK WAS coming to an end, Daisy Perika had turned out the lights. On the morrow, she was expecting her nephew for breakfast and Charlie Moon's arrival generally echoed the crack of dawn. The elderly Catholic got into bed, pulled the quilt to her chin, whispered a hurried Our Father, drifted off toward that gray land where dreams are born.

If she had known what was happening just up the canyon from her trailer home—and the astonishing events that would transpire there before the sun came up again—she would not have slept a wink.

But Daisy Perika was quite ignorant of all that wickedness. Sleep came quickly. The shaman dreamed her dreams. The phantom sights and hollow sounds were ripped from the ragged edge of sanity.

A TALKATIVE owl flies beside the shaman. They discuss a recipe for squash-and-sandstone stew, the bitter taste of dogbane tea, and how Sunflower Woman got her name. Daisy soars over the ruins of a foreign city. Rows of fluted granite columns stand above a cerulean sea painted on bone-dry sands. On the crest of a whitewashed tomb, a pregnant wolf raises her head, howls at a moon that was never there. In an alley of ice and cinders, ghosts of ragged old men dance and sing ribald songs.

Being late for a previous appointment, the owl takes her

leave of the Ute elder. The dreamer twists and turns through time and space. She hears a coarse, humming sound— "Voooom . . . vooooom!"—a giant hornet darting about in search of someone to sting?

She hears a sonorous voice: "In respect of the soon-to-be deceased, let us pause for a quarter-second of silence. Well done! You may dispose of the remains."

Daisy plummets from the sky for eleven heartbeats, strikes the earth hard enough to rattle her teeth. She is on her back, in a narrow pit. A knobby elbow of juniper root pushes up under her left shoulder, the smell of freshly turned earth settles into her nostrils. A glistening snow drifts down, decorating her dark skin with six-sided silver ornaments. An indistinct figure materializes above her, mouths a slow chant in a guttural tongue that is alien to the Ute shaman. The ritual ends.

Sand and stones are falling on her face.

She cannot breathe.

UNEXPECTED THEATER

CUTTING THE empty silence with feathered whispers, a red-tailed hawk wings its solitary way through the meandering canyon. Happily for an unwary rodent, the hungry raptor passes without noticing the jumping mouse perched in a clump of dead rabbit grass—its long, naked tail coiled around a brittle twig. With a blissful mix of suspicion and curiosity, the beady-eyed little mammal watches the labors of a human being. Also entranced by the unusual spectacle is a nervous chipmunk, whose rural life offers little in the way of entertainment. And of course the hungry cougar is counted in the audience.

The muscular Ute, stripped to the waist and sweating, was on his knees.

Jacob Gourd Rattle was not praying.

He was hacking maliciously at the earth with a U.S. Army surplus foxhole mattock. The grunts of the worker and the dull thump of the steel implement were perfectly synchronized. And so it went until the canyon was awash in moonlight. Bone-weary from his labors, Jake Gourd Rattle tossed the mattock aside. The trench was more than a yard deep. He got to his feet, pulled on his shirt.

In the secretive manner of a miser checking on his treasure, Jacob removed a precious object from his hip pocket. It was a thin blade of polished bone, wrapped in a sturdy leather cord.

A dozen times he had tried, with no effect. He would make another attempt.

After muttering the old incantation, the Ute called to the Thunder. There was no answer. He called again. He heard it. Not the Thunder.

Up the canyon, where the steep trail wound its crumbling way down from the mesa, someone was singing. It was a woman's voice.

Jacob Gourd Rattle's wife called out when she was still a hundred yards away, "Jaaa-aaake . . . Jaaa-aaake. I'm baa-aaak." A pause. "Jaaa-aaake?"

Her footsteps crunched on the sandy canyon floor. Closer now.

Kicks Dogs had a canvas knapsack strapped on her back, a spindly walking stick in her hand. Like a hound sniffing him out, the white woman walked back and forth, looking this way and that, finally stopping within two paces of her man. "Jaaa-aaake," she screeched, "where *are* you?"

The response came from behind her: "Here."

She whirled around, clasped a hand to her throat. "Oh—you shouldn't go scaring me like that!"

He took a quick step forward, backhanded her across the face.

The woman dropped the walking stick, stumbled back two steps—but did not fall.

"Stupid white trash," he growled. "I told you *four* days—and you come back in three!"

Intimidated by the bully, the woman looked at her feet.

"Say it," he snarled.

She mumbled the required response.

"So I can hear you!" He raised his hand to strike her again.

Her lower lip trembled. "I'm sorry, Jake. You know how I am—I just can't keep track of time."

It annoyed him that she was not weeping. Kicks always bawled when he hit her.

Not very much later, the curtain had fallen on the small melodrama. This being so, the furry audience dwindled one by one. The jumping mouse found a cracked acorn under a dwarf oak, gnawed on it. The chipmunk darted off into the recesses of a hollow log. The cougar on the Witch's Thumb stretched her tawny limbs and yawned. On this night, perhaps the predator would sleep. Dream otherworldly feline dreams. Perhaps not.

ONE CRYSTALLINE perfection at a time, the snow jewels began to fall from heaven.

SOME NINETEEN miles northwest of the dismal canyon, and just beyond the boundary of the Southern Ute reservation, the curator of the Cassidy Museum was tucked snugly under his patchwork quilt. He had tried counting sullen llamas, noisy guinea hens, even a long line of ancestral black sheep—but Bertram Eustace Cassidy could not find sleep. Finally, in the wee hours, he thought he heard something. The insomniac propped himself up on an elbow, shuddered as he stared into the black mouth of a horror barely held at bay by the fragile windowpane. For all the darkness and dead silence, he might have been on the far side of the moon. *Fiddle-dee-dee—it must have been my imagination.* No, there it was again—the sharp, tinkling sound of glass breaking. *Oh dear me—I do believe we are being burgled!* Bertie fell back on the bed, pulled the covers over his head.

CHAPTER FOUR

IN THE SHAMAN'S DEN

HIS POKER WINNINGS NESTLED SATISFYINGLY THICK IN HIS wallet, Charlie Moon arrived at his aunt's trailer home with the first stirring of smoky-gray light in the east. He jackknifed his long, lean frame into a straight-backed wooden chair, eased his knees under Daisy Perika's kitchen table. The tribal investigator stirred several helpings of sugar into a mug of scalding coffee, noted with approval that the brew was coal black even in the spoon.

The Ute elder, who had risen well before daylight to have a meal of warmed-over posole and saltine crackers, fussed around the propane stove to prepare a proper breakfast for her nephew.

The fifty-year-old vacuum-tube radio was tuned to KSUT—the tribe's FM radio station. The paper diaphragm of the permanent-magnet speaker vibrated to reproduce the haunting voice of a long-gone Hank Williams. The unspeakably sad soul wailed a melancholy lament about his lover's cheatin' heart.

Moon looked at the old woman's back. "Good snow we had last night."

"Good for you, maybe. This cold, damp weather makes my bones ache." Daisy Perika cracked three brown-shelled eggs into a cast-iron skillet where a half-dozen pork sausage links soaked in a blistering bath of popping grease. The cook was startled to discover that the third egg was abnormal. "Uh-oh."

Moon raised an eyebrow. "What?"

"This cackle-berry's got a double yolk." She scowled at the thing. "I don't remember right off if that's a good sign or a bad one."

Her nephew saw the opportunity and seized it by the neck. "It depends."

"On what?"

"It's good luck if one yolk is bigger than the other one. But if the other one is the biggest, that's serious bad news."

Daisy glared back at the offensive double-eye floating in the skillet. "That doesn't make no sense at all."

He was very pleased with himself. "It's just my notion of a yolk."

The old woman sighed, shook her head. "There was always rumors of insanity on your father's side of the family."

Moon grinned. "If I recall correctly, you are my father's oldest sister."

She did not miss a beat. "It was only the men that was affected." The tribal elder remembered the significance of cracking a double yolk. This was a double omen. Unexpected company was coming, and trouble was not far behind. Daisy Perika was not surprised. Bad news was always knocking at her door.

THORN BUSHES reached out hooked talons to rake her naked arms, tear at her cotton skirt. Terrified that her heart might stop beating—or that something far *worse* than death might embrace her soul—Kicks Dogs hurried along through the snow, stumbling over juniper roots and jagged pieces of stone. Though trembling with fear, she was immensely relieved to be out of that horrible canyon. Despite her unhappy night, the woman had an iron-willed determination to survive. She also had a particular destination in mind—the old Ute woman's home, which was out there somewhere. Over and over, the thought raced through her consciousness:

All I have to do is get to Daisy's little trailer . . . then I'll be all right.

Though she did not know why, she knew this was a lie.

She would never be all right again. *Never.*

• • •

AS IF bent on the complete and utter destruction of the eggs, Daisy Perika selected a delicate three-tined fork, stirred viciously at the yellow-white puddle.

Charlie Moon, who had his heart set on sunny-side-ups, grimaced. "Scrambled, huh?"

"This ain't no fancy restaurant." The cook did not bother to look at the hungry man. "The rule here is you take what you get and you like it."

He raised his nose to sniff at the sausage scent. "It smells almost good enough to eat."

The old woman muttered a phrase that was pointedly profane and, fortunately, unintelligible.

Moon turned his attention to the weekly tribal newspaper.

Daisy Perika raised her voice so he could hear her complaint: "I didn't sleep very good last night."

He took a taste of the sugary coffee, waited for the rest of the story. It would be because of the cold winds that moaned all night or a noisy coyote or some spicy leftovers she ate right before going to bed or bad dreams or—

"I had some bad dreams."

Aha.

"Somebody was throwing dirt in my face." She flipped a sausage. "And there was an owl on a tree limb right out there"—Daisy pointed a dripping spatula at the wall—"that hooted for hours and hours." She glared at the small, curtained window that looked out onto the pine porch. "At least a dozen times I thought about hauling myself outta bed, loading up my old twelve-gauge, blowing that big-eyed screecher into a splatter of guts and feathers."

Her nephew's mouth made a wry half-smile. "So why didn't you?"

She gave him a poisonous look. "You know why." *Big smart aleck.*

Charlie Moon put on an innocent, perplexed expression. "You fond of owls?" The old woman could barely tolerate any of God's creatures.

"Owls are messengers—they come to tell us when somebody's going to die." She twisted a knob on the propane stove, lowering the ring of blue fire under the iron skillet. "Any fool knows that."

"Oh yeah." The specified fool nodded. "I'd forgot to remember."

Ignoring a hint of amusement in the unbeliever's voice, she assumed a pious tone. "It'd be wrong to harm one of God's hardworking creatures when they're just going about their job in this world." And it would certainly summon up the very worst kind of bad luck. The human being foolish enough to kill a messenger owl might very well be selected to cross that dark, deep River before their appointed time. Daisy opened the oven door, pulled out a tray of made-from-scratch lard-and-buttermilk biscuits.

Charlie Moon watched Daisy hobble about her small kitchen, wondered how long it would be before the Owl called her name. Life without the superstitious, cantankerous, unpredictable old woman was unthinkable.

"I don't know why you bother to come out here," she grumped. "You with your fancy big ranch to run."

Moon winked at his aunt. "Must be the free food."

She held back a smile, slammed a plate on the table. "Well, here's your grub, so shut your mouth and eat!"

He nodded a happy assent to this contradictory order, and got right into the job.

The old woman sat down to watch her nephew enjoy his breakfast.

KICKS DOGS thought she could see the old woman's trailer, yonder just below the slope of the long, sinuous ridge. *All I've got to do now is keep on putting one foot in front of the other.* She tried to smile. *And keep my wits about me.*

The snow fell harder.

MOON GAZED out the window toward an invisible Three Sisters Mesa, watched the snow scatter in a light breeze. It was peaceful here, near the mouth of *Cañon del Espiritu.* Aside from the occasional groan of restless west winds, or the calls of night creatures scurrying about, the quiet in this place was more than the mere absence of sound. The silence was a palpable, intense medium that issued from the cool depths of Snake and Spirit canyons. It had a way of hushing those troublesome noises in a man's soul.

Daisy frowned at his faraway expression. The elder knew this look. It could come upon a man when his spirit was about to slip away from his body. Or when his mind was occupied by idle, foolish thoughts. As far as she was concerned, the former state was highly undesirable—the latter an outright affront. "Charlie!"

Mildly startled, he turned to focus on the old woman's wrinkled face. "What?"

Having nothing in particular to say to her nephew, Daisy was momentarily befuddled. She fumbled around for words. "You—uh—want some more coffee?"

Coffee? "Way you yelled, I thought maybe I had a six-inch centipede on my neck."

"What you had was a more-than-usual stupid look on your face. Now do you or don't you?"

"Coffee will be fine." He flashed a smile. "In all my life, I never shunned a second cup of stimulant or a lady's well-meant compliment."

Daisy poured a thin stream of ebony liquid.

He stirred up a small whirlpool in the mug. Watched another storm brewing behind the old woman's black eyes.

She tried to think of just how to say it. "How's you-know-who?"

"Could you be more specific?"

"That woman."

"Miss James?"

"When are you gonna tell me her first name?"

"I'll let her tell you."

Daisy snorted, swiped a damp dishrag across the oilcloth. "And when'll that happen?"

"When I bring her to see you."

She paused in midswipe. "You intend to bring that white woman to my home?"

"The thought had crossed my mind once or twice."

Daisy frowned, shook her gray head.

"Is she not welcome?"

"You men don't understand nothing." Daisy scrubbed at a sticky jelly spot. "I'm your closest family. You bring your white-eye sweetie pie out here to see me, she's liable to get ideas." She left the unsettling thought to curdle in his mind.

Charlie Moon watched his aunt rub a hole in the oilcloth. "I see what you mean."

Daisy sighed with relief. "Then you won't be bringing her."

"On the contrary."

She sat down, stared across the table. *Well, he's a grown man. It had to happen sooner or later.* "You goin' to ask this *matukach* woman to share your bed?"

He raised an eyebrow. "I had thought about proposing something a bit more formal."

Daisy closed her eyes. "Oh, God."

He smiled, reached across the table to touch her hand. "But if she says yes, we'll want your blessing."

Daisy got up, stomped off to the stove with the coffeepot. She tried very hard to think of some suitable response to this thunderbolt from her nephew. Something to say that she would not regret until her dying day. *Which, the way I am feeling, could be tomorrow.* She was distracted by the sudden sense that someone was *out there.* The tribal elder went to the window, pushed a curtain aside just a notch, groaned as she saw the bedraggled woman hurrying toward the trailer. "Oh no—it's Kicks."

Her nephew cocked his head. "Who?"

"Kicks Dogs."

"Oh. *That* Kicks."

Daisy rubbed her hands on her apron. "Before she married Jacob Gourd Rattle, her name was Frieda Something. I told Jacob he should've never taken up with a white woman." She shot a wicked look at her nephew, was annoyed that he took no offense at the sideways reference to his own pale-skinned girlfriend. "But you know how stubborn and know-it-all a man can be. Jacob told me that he didn't plan to raise no family with her, that he just needed a woman to take care of his house. And warm up his bed."

"Is Jacob out there with her?"

Daisy moved to the other side of the window. "No. And I don't see his rusty old van." She performed a bit of elementary logic. "Kicks must've walked in."

The tribal investigator considered this. "It's a long way from the paved road. Maybe her car broke down on the lane."

Daisy continued with her commentary: "I don't know why that paleface gal stays with Jacob—he's got a nasty temper. Last November, the Ignacio town police arrested him for whacking her on the head with a tire iron. But after she come to her senses—what little senses she's got left—Kicks wouldn't make any charges, so the police had to let Jacob go. Can you believe that?"

Charlie Moon could believe it without half trying. The former tribal policeman had seen it happen time and again. He buttered a biscuit, added a double dollop of chokecherry jelly. "How'd she get that name?"

"Her husband gave it to her."

"Does she really kick dogs?" He firmly disapproved of this.

"I don't know." Still peeking though a crack in the window curtain, Daisy muttered, "You can ask her yourself—here she comes up the steps."

There was a sudden pounding.

The Ute elder jerked the door open, glared at the wild-eyed white woman. Jacob Gourd Rattle's wife was teetering back and forth like she might collapse. "What is it, Kicks?"

"Oh, thank God you're home." The woman was a sight to be pitied. A floppy felt hat was squashed over a moppy shock of yellow hair; a tattered poncho almost covered a faded cotton blouse; a soggy canvas knapsack hung over one shoulder. Her gray cotton skirt was dirty and torn. The woman's bare arms were scratched and streaked with tiny lines of coagulated blood.

There was a crescent-shaped bruise on her right cheek.

Daisy raised her chin to point at the purple mark. "What happened to your face?"

At this remark, Charlie Moon got up from the table.

Kicks' lower lip began to tremble. Tears flowed from her pale blue eyes. Slowly, at first, then twin gushers. Enough, it seemed, to wash the spray of freckles away.

Daisy cringed at the pathetic display. "Oh, don't start bawling like a sick calf."

Having appeared at the door behind and above his aunt, Moon grimaced at the battered face. *Looks like Jacob has been at it again.* "How'd you get hurt?"

"Hurt?" Her hand went to the bruise. "I don't know. Must've bumped into something. A tree, most likely." She stared at the tall man. "You must be Daisy's nephew—Charlie Moon."

The Ute confirmed this suspicion.

Kicks pushed past Daisy to enfold the startled fellow in a hug.

Moon, a longtime member of Alcoholics Anonymous, noted that the white woman's breath smelled sweetly of whiskey.

Daisy slammed the door, muttered her complaints: "I might as well live in town. Way our here, you'd think I could keep my distance from the lunatics and riffraff. But does it help? No, it does not—the crazies walk for miles and miles, just so they can annoy me."

Gently, but very deliberately, Moon disengaged himself from the tightly entwined woman. He eased her onto a chair at the kitchen table. Kicks put the knapsack in her lap; tears continued to drip from her chin. He searched his jacket pockets, found a spotless handkerchief to offer the unexpected guest. He could not help but notice that Jacob's wife was a good-looking woman.

After wiping her face with the linen square, Kicks focused her watery blue eyes on the man. "I'm sorry to barge in like this and act such a silly fool. But it's been just *so* awful. . . ." The white woman's words drifted off into a pitiful sigh before she inhaled deeply. "I am just all worn out."

"What you need is a stiff dose of caffeine." Moon found a

cup in the cupboard over the sink, filled it with coffee, offered it to the distraught visitor.

The white woman accepted the hot beverage. "Thank you." *He is so sweet.* She took a drink of the black liquid. Made a horrible face, looked cross-eyed at the cup.

He grinned. "Ute Mountain Java. My aunt picks and roasts the beans herself, and adds a dash of paint thinner to give it character."

"No I don't," Daisy muttered. This white woman might be just dumb enough to believe such foolishness.

"But don't take big gulps," Moon warned. "It's a delicate brew, meant to be sipped."

Daisy plopped down in a chair, groaned.

The new arrival almost managed a smile. "Charlie—it is all right if I call you Charlie? I mean, I don't want to be too familiar or presumptuous or anything—"

"You can call me Charlie. And I'll call you Mrs. Gourd Rattle." Now that she was moderately refreshed, Moon inquired about what the matter was.

She stared blankly at the coffee cup. "I want to make sure I tell it just like it happened, but I don't know quite where to start."

"Start with something simple," he said. "Like what you're doing here."

She took another deep breath, brushed a wisp of wet hair off her bruised cheek. "It all started about this time last month. Jake—poor fella—he got so he was tired all of the time. I'm sure it was on account of those strange dreams he'd been having. That was what made it hard for him to get enough sleep."

At the mention of dreams, the Ute elder narrowed her dark eyes.

The white woman kept her gaze fixed on Charlie Moon's friendly face. "Jake told me he'd been having this same peculiar dream over and over. He was always at a particular place in that big canyon"—she pointed at the window—"so last week, he made up his mind he'd go there and stay a few nights. That way, he figured he might be able to find out what his dream was trying to tell him. On Monday, we drove out to the mesa. I left him in the canyon with his camping gear and drove the van back home. Then last night, I came back to get him." She looked at her hands, flexed her cold fingers. "But Jake had decided he wanted to stay for an extra night, and he asked me to stay there with him so I did."

"Spirit Canyon is no place to be staying all night," Daisy muttered. "Especially not in this kind of weather."

Kicks pointedly addressed Charlie Moon: "Would you like to hear about Jake's dream?"

"I'm sure it'd be real interesting." He said this with a slightly pained expression. "But first I'd like to find out why you're here, and where Jacob is now—"

"I'm here because I didn't have no other place to go." She dropped her gaze to the silver bear paw on the Indian's bolo tie. "And I don't know where Jake is."

Moon did not like the sound of this. "When was the last time you saw him?"

The white woman paused to wipe at her red nose with the loaned handkerchief. "This morning—around daybreak. Jake was walking off with his buffalo robe. It was foggy and snowing, so I thought he was going to look for a dry spot." She picked at a loose thread on her blouse. "I thought he might come make his bed with me, but he just walked off up the canyon."

Daisy drilled the woman with a gimlet eye. "You two wasn't sleeping together?"

Kicks shook her head. "Jake was camped out in the middle of the canyon—I'd bunked under one of those overhangs." The white woman frowned as she yanked the stubborn thread. "After he left, I laid there for a while, wondering where he'd gone. Finally, I got out of my blanket, hollered his name a few times. When he didn't answer back, I kinda got panicky. I worried that maybe he'd had a heart attack or something, so I went looking for him." Kicks rubbed her hands together briskly, as if hoping to produce some warmth. "I kept on yelling for him, but all I heard was my own words coming back at me. I got really scared. It was something about that awful, spooky place—it was quiet as a graveyard. And those clouds was a-billowin' up like smoke from Lucifer's chimney." Getting a blank look from the man, she turned to Daisy. "Do you know what I mean?"

Surprising herself, the Ute elder nodded.

The tribal investigator attempted to ease the distraught woman onto a track that went somewhere. "But you didn't find Jacob?"

"No." Kicks Dogs gave him a wild-eyed stare. "And that was when I got *really* scared. I started running. I don't know how long I run, but I finally got outta that terrible canyon. And I found Daisy's trailer house." She turned her head to smile at the old woman.

Moon chose his words with care: "Mrs. Gourd Rattle, where did you park your car last night?"

She pointed. "It's up there on the mesa."

"This morning, did you go back to your vehicle?"

Kicks gave him an odd look. "Why would I do that?"

"Well—to see if your husband had gone to the car."

She seemed perplexed at this suggestion. "Why would Jake do that?"

Charlie Moon felt his face getting warm. "Maybe to find a dry place to get out of the rain and snow." *Maybe to drive away.*

She shook her head briskly, whipping stringy strands of yellow hair through the air. "That's silly—he'd never go back to the van without taking me. No, Jake's wandered off somewhere in that canyon. He's hurt. Or dying. Maybe he's already . . ." She clasped her hands, gave Moon a big-eyed look. "Somebody has to go look for him."

The tribal investigator used his cellular telephone to dial the SUPD number he knew by heart. Charlie Moon had a brief conversation with a recently hired morning-shift dispatcher he had never met, requested that a search be initiated for a tribal member who had apparently wandered off alone in Spirit Canyon. The dispatcher informed him that Chief of Police Whitehorse would have to authorize a search, and the chief was currently tied up in a meeting with tribal chairman

Oscar Sweetwater. On top of that, there were no officers immediately available to take part in a search.

He reminded her that a tribal member might be lost in the snow. Moon doubted this, but it was a possibility. The dispatcher asked him to hold for a moment. She returned after a long absence to inform Moon that SUPD officer Jim Wolfe had reported in from the graveyard shift and was about to go home, but had agreed to drive his unit out to Three Sisters Mesa. He would meet Mr. Moon in Spirit Canyon.

CHAPTER FIVE

THE SEARCH

AS THE TRIBAL INVESTIGATOR ENTERED THE MOUTH OF *Cañon del Espiritu*, snow floated about him like goose down. A shallow river of blue-gray mists washed along the bottom of the broad canyon. A wispy, whispery fog imposed an eerie silence, transfigured familiar objects into nightmarish props. Jutting boulders stood like alien creatures frozen in instant death. A symmetrical, snow-covered juniper took on the appearance of a giant, frosted toadstool. A prickly yucca pretended to be an icy sheaf of two-edged swords—whose malignant purpose was to impale the unwary pilgrim.

Though endowed with considerable imagination, Charlie Moon was largely immune to these sinister portents. His practical mind was occupied with how best to complete this thankless task. And so as his boots crunched along a snow-packed streambed, the tribal investigator focused on the job at hand. He had already passed the easy way to the top of Three Sisters Mesa, which was near the mouth of the canyon. That path was used by his aunt on her occasional herb-gathering trips to the crest of the mesa. The more challenging trail was a mile and a half into Spirit Canyon. Based on Kicks Dogs' report, her husband had made his camp near the foot of this steep ascent.

A SLENDER, gray-eyed, sandy-haired six-footer, SUPD officer Jim Wolfe was a sturdy product of the Oklahoma hills. Weather of all kinds pleased the enthusiastic man—especially when it was wet. Outfitted in waterproof boots, a heavy black raincoat, and a broad-brimmed black canvas hat, he was sorry that the snow had not amounted to an all-out blizzard. As he watched the tall figure coming up the canyon in long strides, Wolfe removed the hat, waved it at the tribal investigator. "Hey—Charlie."

The Ute, who had seen the *matukach* first, waved back.

Moon approached, pumped Wolfe's outstretched hand. The white man's eyes were bloodshot; he looked to be badly in need of some serious sack time. "Dispatch didn't have any day-shift officers available. I'm glad you felt up to putting in a few more hours."

"No problem. I can use the time-and-a-half pay." Wolfe jerked his thumb upward. "My unit's parked up on Three Sisters Mesa."

"Was Gourd Rattle's van up there?"

Wolfe shook his head. "If it was, I didn't see it."

The fog was lifting, exposing the sandstone walls of *Cañon del Espiritu*. If even the bare essentials of Kicks Dogs' tale were to be accepted, they must be within a few hundred yards of the spot where her husband had set up camp. Moon squinted, examining the mesa rim. "You seen any sign at all of Jacob?"

"Nope." The paleface tried to smile. "So what's the scoop?"

The tribal investigator gave Wolfe the boiled-down version. "Mrs. Gourd Rattle dropped her husband out here on Monday, headed back home, then drove the family van back yesterday to pick him up. But Jacob wanted to stay another night, so she stayed with him. He slept somewhere near the middle of the canyon floor; she found a place under an overhang. The woman woke up early this morning, saw her husband walking away with his buffalo robe. She thought Jacob was looking for shelter from the snow."

The white man's eyes narrowed. "What was Jake Gourd Rattle doing in the canyon?"

The tribal investigator shrugged. *Following his dream . . .*

Jim Wolfe stared up at the place where the Three Sisters were still shrouded in clouds. "His vehicle might still be up there. But if his wheels are gone, then he's gone, too."

High on the cliffs, there was a harsh call from an unseen raven. It was answered by a raspy echo from the opposite wall. As if summoned, a low, moaning wind swept down the broad canyon. To Jim Wolfe's superstitious ear, it was the soul-wrenching sound of a ghostly woman wailing for her dead children. This was followed by a deep belly-rumble of thunder, a diffuse flash of lightning.

Moon wondered how much evidence had been covered up by the drifting snow. That was an odd thought. *Evidence of what?* "We'll look for his van later. But as long as we're down here, let's check things out."

Wolfe nodded. "You want to head up canyon?"

"Might as well."

The lawmen got to work, trudging doggedly along in the wet snow.

Every few paces, Moon would put his hands to his mouth, bellow the missing man's name.

As the spirit moved him, Wolfe would do the same.

The calls were invariably answered—by mocking echoes off the canyon walls.

Another boom of thunder was followed by a stinging sleet that peppered the snowy floor of the canyon. The sleet changed to a fine-grained snow. This was converted to heavy, wet flakes. It snowed hard for an hour, covering the canyon floor with several more inches of soft, feathery carpet.

During this time, the men did not exchange a word.

The snowfall finally ceased, and with it, the obligatory search.

Having backtracked, the searchers headed for the only trail that led out of this section of Spirit Canyon. The slippery snow made the winding path more hazardous than usual. The climb was steep until they reached the trail's upper portion, where the rocky path zigzagged to the crest of Three Sisters Mesa.

As if to celebrate their arrival, the clouds parted in a narrow slit. Sunlight spilled down from the cleft heavens like a waterfall of molten gold.

The tribal investigator followed the SUPD officer to his

coal-black Blazer, where Wolfe shared a Thermos of steaming coffee with him. Thus refreshed, the lawmen walked along the rutted lane. Even the heavy-treaded tracks the Blazer had left a short time ago were concealed under the new snow. While the white policeman watched, the tribal investigator climbed a six-story tower of sandstone—the lesser of the legendary Three Sisters.

Having reached the craggy shoulder of the Pueblo woman, Charlie Moon pulled the brim of his black Stetson down to shade his eyes. He had an unhindered view of the mesa and beyond. Unless Jacob had taken considerable trouble to hide it, there was no van. Convinced that he had done his duty and more, Moon descended the skirts of the petrified woman.

They returned to the SUPD officer's four-wheel-drive unit.

Moon listened while Jim Wolfe contacted dispatch, reported negative results on a preliminary search for Mr. Jacob Gourd Rattle and his vehicle, and requested that a second unit be sent to pick up Mrs. Gourd Rattle at the Perika residence.

Dispatch informed him that Officer Danny Bignight would transport the woman to tribal police headquarters for a formal statement, then take her home.

The call completed, Jim Wolfe rolled himself a sad-looking excuse for a cigarette, touched the tip of the drooping cylinder with a flame sprouting from a plastic lighter. He sucked carcinogenic fumes into his lungs, puffed a pair of smoke rings. "What do you think about all this, Charlie?"

Wolfe's cigarette was reduced to a butt before the Ute responded. "I think I'm ready to call it a day."

"It's a long walk to your aunt's place."

The Ute did not deny this.

"Hitch a ride with me," Wolfe offered.

Moon tipped his hat to salute the notion. "Let's hit the road."

CHAPTER SIX

THE MOONBEAM CLIMBER

JACOB GOURD RATTLE'S *MATUKACH* WIFE WIPED A CRUMB OFF her chin, cast a hopeful glance at the Ute woman's propane stove. "You sure do know how to make good biscuits."

Daisy Perika had baked a second batch. She opened the oven, brought the blackened pan to the table.

"Oh, thank you!" The guest snatched the largest of the flaky pastries. "Can I have some butter?"

The old woman plodded over to the small refrigerator, returned with a plastic tub of margarine, banged it on the table beside the biscuit pan. "Is there anything else I can get for you before I sit myself down?"

"Thank you kindly, but I don't think so. I expect this'll hold me for a while." Kicks pried the biscuit open, smeared a generous helping of the yellow spread into the warm interior. She tried to hide a yawn. "I don't know why I'm so sleepy."

Daisy seated herself across the table from the peculiar woman. "You probably didn't get enough rest last night." The old woman's tone suggested that she was merely making polite conversation.

Kicks Dogs' head bobbed in a nod. "That's the truth. Even after I had me a little sip of my sleeping tonic—which is one part whiskey and ten parts water—"

More likely, the other way around. Daisy's eyes twinkled.

"—And plenty of sugar, well—what little sleep I got, I kept having these crazy dreams. One of 'em started with this weird sound. It was something like this. . . ." She drew in a deep breath.

"*Vooooom.*"

Louder: "*Vooooom*"

Louder still: "*VOOOOOM!*"

The Ute shaman, whose dream was lost in the mists of her mind, squinted at the white woman. *Why does this sound familiar?*

Jacob Gourd Rattle's wife snapped off a chunk of biscuit, chewed. "Sometime later on, I dreamed I saw Jake's legs."

His legs? Daisy cocked her head. "Where was the rest of him?"

Kicks Dogs looked up, as if seeing the vision again. "I guess it must've been up there with his legs."

Daisy joined the narrator in gazing at the dusty plastic light fixture on the ceiling.

Kicks returned her attention to the biscuit. "He was up above me, in those smoky clouds. At first, all I could make out were his legs and his feet. Well, I couldn't actually see his *feet*—I mean I could see Jake's *boots*. And then after he kept on climbing, I couldn't see anything at all."

"Climbing?"

Kicks nodded. "That's what it looked like." The white woman had a vacant, dreamy look as she waved a hand over her head. "He was just sorta floating up there in the air. But I thought to myself: Jake's visions has come true—he is actually climbing up a moonbeam!"

The Ute elder leaned closer to the storyteller. "Did you say *moonbeam?*"

"Oh, did I forget to tell you about that? Jake had been dreaming for weeks that he was in that awful, scary canyon—climbing up a moonbeam." She finished off the biscuit, licked her fingers. "Mmmm. That was good." She regarded the Ute woman with pity. *I hope when I get that old I don't look like a wrinkled old toad.* "You want to hear about my other dreams?"

Apprehension was all over Daisy's face. "There's more?"

"Oh, sure. When I start to dreaming, it's just one after another all night. I had this one about these rootin'-tootin' cowboys having this knock-'em-down, drag-'em-out brawl. And then I saw King Kong fall off of the Empire State Building." She hugged herself. "I wish I could have fun dreams like that every night of the week."

I wish this wild-eyed matukach *woman had knocked on somebody else's door.*

"It all seemed so real at the time," Kicks said. "Even the part about King Kong falling off the skyscraper." She gnawed at her lower lip. "But when I woke up this morning at first light and saw Jake walking away from his camp, I knew it'd all been just a bunch of crazy dreams."

The Ute elder grinned. *Either that or he shinnied back down that moonbeam.*

Kicks Dogs reached for another biscuit. "These are really scrumptious. Do you have anything sweet to smear on 'em— maybe some homemade preserves?"

CHAPTER SEVEN

CONTRIVED ENTERTAINMENT

CHARLIE MOON HAD NOT BEEN IN AN SUPD UNIT FOR QUITE some time, and it was very pleasant, having a chauffeur. The tribal investigator spent his time watching interesting things pass by at a velocity slightly in excess of seventy miles per hour. Lots of things.

Her neck hanging over a barbed-wire fence, a fat red mare munching grass that *was* greener.

A chugging Farmall tractor, with a rusty hay rake attached.

A small pond, floating an empty rowboat.

Telephone poles.

Trees.

A roadside sign: 60 MPH.

Officer Jim Wolfe also saw it, let up slightly on the gas.

Charlie Moon was enjoying the absence of words flitting about. He was grateful that Wolfe was apparently not one of those *matukach* who cannot bear silence. The kind who must fill up a peaceful quiet with "small talk."

Wolfe wrinkled his brow. "What do you think—"

I shoulda known it couldn't last.

"—about Jacob Gourd Rattle leaving his wife out there in the canyon? And during a snowstorm!" The driver shot the tribal investigator a half-angry look.

"I don't."

"Don't what?"

"Don't think about it." *Now he'll tell me what he thinks.*

"Well, I think he left her out there to die from exposure." Wolfe scowled at his blurry reflection in the sandblasted windshield. "He's beat that woman half to death three or four times already." The driver set his jaw. "This time, he must've figured she'd freeze to death."

Charlie Moon calculated that it was almost an hour to his aunt's home, and thought he would give Wolfe something to think about. If he were thinking, maybe he'd be quiet. "I can imagine five or six ways to explain what happened."

Wolfe made a tight-lipped smile. "Okay, why did Gourd Rattle leave his wife in the canyon?"

Moon's tone hinted at a sinister notion: "Maybe he didn't."

The driver waited for a few seconds, then: "You surely don't think he's still there."

"In the canyon?" The tribal investigator pretended to roll this over in his mind. "For all we know, he might be." The more improbable the theory, the better. "Try this on for size— the little woman had enough of Jacob beating her up. Sometime last night, she stopped his clock for good."

Wolfe's mouth fell open. "You don't actually *believe* that."

Moon managed to look as if he just might.

The SUPD cop shook his head. "But that don't make any sense. If Jake is dead in the canyon, why ain't his van still on Three Sisters Mesa where his wife parked it?"

"Maybe she never left it on the mesa." After a pregnant pause, Moon added, "Could be she didn't even drive it there."

Wolfe snorted. "Then how'd she get back to the canyon— on foot?"

"That can't be entirely ruled out." The tribal investigator scowled, as if at an image of scandalous skullduggery. "But it's more likely that somebody drove her there."

"Who?"

Moon was enjoying himself immensely. "Her boyfriend." He turned to stare at the white man, watched the muscles in Wolfe's neck tense. "Go look it up. Nine times out of ten, when a good-looking young woman makes up her mind to kill off a husband who's twice her age, she's already found herself a brand-new hairy-leg to take his place. The replacement is always a good deal younger than her old man."

Wolfe was shaking his head. "That seems pretty thin to me—"

"But mainly, she picks her new fella because he is willing to lay it all on the line to help the pretty lady dispose of her husband. Which is another way of saying that the new fella ain't all that bright. This is why twelve times out of eleven, John Law will nail the both of 'em."

One of the Blazer's front tires hit the shoulder at sixty-six miles per hour, kicked up a spray of snowy slush. Jim Wolfe jerked the steering wheel, brought the vehicle back onto the blacktop.

Charlie Moon pretended not to notice.

The driver blushed pink. "This old rust bucket is a death trap. I need to get the steering checked."

The next sixteen minutes were devoid of conversation.

Presently, Chimney Rock loomed up on the south side of the highway.

When the SUPD Blazer topped the final hill before the turnoff at Capote Lake, Wolfe hit the brakes. There was a minor traffic jam at the intersection where Route 151 stemmed off in a southwesterly direction, following the willow-studded bank of Stollsteimer Creek. Officer Wolfe groaned. "A roadblock." His thoughts spilled out of his mouth in a mumble: "Prob'ly because of that burglary."

The tribal investigator's ears pricked. "Burglary?"

The white cop shrugged. "It wasn't in SUPD jurisdiction."

"So where was it?"

Wolfe stared straight ahead. "The Cassidy Museum was broke into last night."

The thirty-acre Cassidy estate was near the reservation boundary. "What'd the thieves get?"

"Ah—some old coins, I think." Wolfe scowled at the clutter of traffic. "Why didn't dispatch alert me about the roadblock?"

Moon was eager to get back to Aunt Daisy's trailer, say his good-bye, and aim his Expedition north toward the vast open spaces of the Columbine. "Jim, you're a police officer, you're

on duty, and you're driving a four-wheel-drive Blazer with
snow tires. You can whip right around this traffic."

Wolfe eyed the steep, narrow shoulder to his right and found
it not entirely to his liking. "I don't know—maybe I should
have a word with the state cops before I go barging through
their operation." The SUPD officer pulled halfway off the
pavement, shut off the engine, pulled on his long black raincoat, left his unit to have a powwow with a young state trooper
who was working the westbound lane from Pagosa Springs.

Resigned to the delay, Moon went along for the walk. He
wondered whether Danny Bignight had shown up at Daisy's
to take Kicks Dogs home. If not, Jim Wolfe could take care of
that task. The Ute preferred to avoid another encounter with
Jacob Gourd Rattle's distraught wife. The memory of how he
had pictured the meek little woman to Jim Wolfe as her burly
husband's murderer brought a smile to his face.

THE ENCOUNTER

HAVING FLIRTED with a pretty blonde in a sleek red convertible, the state police officer regretfully waved the Caddy on.

"Tough duty," Charlie Moon observed.

Lieutenant Staples turned to see the tall Ute and the uniformed SUPD officer. "Hey, guys—what brings you here?
You gonna give us a hand with traffic?"

Wolfe looked embarrassed. "Uh, I was wondering if it
would be okay if I drove my unit around the—"

"Just a minute. Let me get some of these good citizens on
their way." The trooper gave his attention to the next vehicle.
It was not shiny, the occupant was anything but pretty—and
also the wrong gender. The dark-skinned man in the 1957
Chevy pickup was trying very hard to look like he was not
alarmed about being stopped. This raised the trooper's suspicions. *Wonder what this yahoo's hauling. Drugs, maybe.*

Wolfe and Moon waited.

Officer Staples put on a counterfeit smile, made a circular
motion with his finger to indicate that the driver should lower
his window.

As he cranked the window down, the man in the old pickup wondered why the Indian cops were backing up the state police. He recognized the uniformed SUPD officer as Jim Wolfe—a real tough guy, not a man to cross. The tall one was Charlie Moon, the legendary Ute cop who had gone off to be some kind of cowboy. Felix Navarone stuck his head halfway out of the window, tried to smile back at the spiffy-looking state cop. "Wassup, bro?"

Officer Staples leaned close to the pickup, caught the faint scent of whiskey on the man's breath. He peered into the cab through shades that concealed sharp gray eyes. "Sir, may I see your driver's license?"

Felix Navarone produced a goat-hide wallet from his hip pocket, offered it to the trooper. A twenty-dollar bill was folded under the Colorado driver's license.

Staples lost the smile. "Sir, please remove your license from the wallet."

"Right." Navarone made a sickly grin, passed the plasticized card to the policeman.

A glance verified that the license was not expired, that the licensee was not required to wear optical correction, that the color photo was a good match to the anxious man behind the wheel. "Sir, please show me your vehicle registration."

There was a blank look from the driver, then: "Oh yeah. I think I know where it is." Navarone leaned toward the driver's side, fumbled with the chrome button on the glove compartment. When the curved door fell onto its hinges, a pint of whiskey was exposed. It was about half full. Which made it—in a legal sense—an open container of alcohol.

Lieutenant Staples grinned. *Gotcha.* "Sir, give me the ignition key, then get out."

Felix Navarone's dark eyes grew large. "What?"

"Give me the ignition key and—"

The driver's hand was moving toward his jacket pocket.

He's going for a piece! Staples crouched, reached for his automatic, yelled, "Put your hands where I can see them—right *now*!" His pistol had barely cleared the black canvas holster when the driver of the old pickup made a dive for the passenger side of the cab, burst through the door, hit the ground running, leaped over a ditch, sprinted across an open area toward a pine thicket.

While Charlie Moon and Jim Wolfe watched, several other state policemen abandoned their posts to help Officer Staples give chase.

Moon smiled at his good fortune to have happened on the scene just in time for the entertainment. Moreover, the tall Ute felt a wager coming on. "Jim, I'll bet you twenty bucks he'll make it into the piney woods and they won't catch him . . ." he glanced at his wristwatch, "for at least ten minutes."

Wolfe had no interest in the bet. "I think we should help 'em grab this guy."

"Not a good idea," Moon said. "For one thing, these Smokeys already got him outnumbered six to one. And for another, I have not been an SUPD cop for quite some time—my days of chasing drunks and crazies are over for good." He clamped a firm hand on Wolfe's shoulder. "Of course, if you want to go a-running after this knot-head, I would not try to talk you out of it. But I don't see why you'd even consider such a thing."

Wolfe told him why: "That fella they're chasing is Felix Navarone—a Mescalero Apache. And I'm sure you know that all Indians arrested in these parts fall under Southern Ute PD jurisdiction."

"I know who he is; but let these fellas cuff him. *Then* tell them he's a 'Pache and they'll turn him over to you for deposit in our tribal jail." The Ute pointed with a jut of his chin. "Looks like these law dogs already got this outlaw treed like a three-legged raccoon. You should've taken my bet."

Wolfe stalked off toward the cluster of state-police officers who had an isolated cottonwood.

Moon followed his enthusiastic comrade up the snow-packed grade, staying several paces behind.

LIEUTENANT VIRGIL Staples looked up at the man sitting on a branch twelve feet above the ground. The lunatic did not have a gun. Not in his hand. *Might be in his pocket, though.* "Sir, please keep your hands where we can see them." As an after-thought, he added in a hopeful tone, "You might as well climb down."

The climber shook his head.

Another state trooper pointed out the obvious: "There's no way you can get away, mister. We've got you surrounded."

Felix Navarone's eyes darted from one uniform to another. "I'm not comin' down."

The troopers exchanged glances. Muttered among themselves about who should climb up to get the man. There was a general consensus that Staples should do the climbing—by right, this was *his* prisoner. Officer Staples, who did not wish to soil his immaculate uniform on the bark of the cottonwood, opined that it would be best to chop the tree down. An older trooper quipped that Staples should just shoot the citizen off the limb—if he thought he could hit him at this range. All in all, the encounter with the tree climber was becoming a quite jolly event.

Startling everyone, the Apache threw back his head. Howled.

One trooper offered the opinion that this was a fair-to-middling imitation of a gray wolf.

Another argued that it was more like the sound of a red-bone hound.

The treed man howled again.

THE MORE crafty motorists used this unexpected opportunity to slip through the abandoned roadblock. A few more curious souls parked on the shoulder to watch the circus. Unnoticed by the police, one of these was focusing a brand-new video camera.

JIM WOLFE cleared his throat.

All eyes turned to the SUPD officer.

Wolfe pointed at the escapee on the tree limb. "That fella is an Indian. An Apache."

An old trooper grinned, flashing a gold tooth. "Good. Then you can climb up there and get him."

Wolfe studied the cottonwood, suddenly wished he had taken Charlie Moon's sage advice. He tried to think fast, and did. "The suspect is north of the highway, which is not within the boundaries of the Southern Ute reservation, so he is not in my jurisdiction. But when you take him into custody, he must be transferred to the tribal jail at Ignacio."

This produced a round of chuckles among the state troopers. "Hcy!"

The shout came from above the lawmen's heads. They looked up at the object of their pursuit.

Officer Staples took off his shades, focused his hard eyes on the Apache. "You ready to come down?"

Felix Navarone shook his head. "Not so long as any of you white cops are under the tree."

Staples grinned. "You prejudiced against Anglos?"

"You was gonna shoot me," Navarone said. "That's why I ran."

"That's a crock," the trooper barked.

The man out on a limb pointed at Jim Wolfe. "You state cops back off, leave the Indian cop here. I'll negotiate with him."

This produced appreciative laughter. Someone pointed out the fact that Officer Wolfe was not "a genuine Indian." He was merely a white man who worked for the Southern Ute PD. It was also noted that a real Indian was present. Maybe the man in the tree would like to have a powwow with Charlie Moon.

Navarone took a wary look at the seven-foot Ute. "I'll talk to Officer Wolfe."

The state troopers convened a quick conference. In the huddle, there was unanimous agreement that if they gave this Apache slicker half a chance, he'd hit the ground and run like an antelope. As he was apparently not armed, shooting him in front of several witnesses was out of the question. If the fleet-footed son of a gun made it into the underbrush, it was a three-to-one shot they would not catch him before dark; it would be necessary to bring in the dogs. And so they agreed on a plan. Leaving Wolfe under the tree, the half-dozen lawmen drifted away—forming a wide, loose circle around the cottonwood. It was unlikely now that the tree climber would be able to make an escape. But on the slim chance that he did, they could blame the White-Indian policeman. All was well.

Or so it seemed.

Wolfe looked up at the treed Indian. "Well?"

"I got something I want to tell you," Navarone said. "And I don't want them state cops to hear." The Apache took one hand off the cottonwood limb, gestured that the SUPD policeman should come closer.

Jim Wolfe stepped directly under the limb. "What's on your mind?"

Felix Navarone grinned. "Did you know that I can soar like the crow?" He raised both arms as if he might be about to fly away.

Wolfe tensed. *What's he up to now?*

Standing well outside the circle of state troopers, Charlie Moon watched it happen. The Apache dropped off the branch onto Jim Wolfe, flattening the SUPD officer onto his back. The men rolled in the dust, grabbing, gouging, grunting. There were shouted curses from the covey of state cops who were dancing around the entangled pair of men. At first, Jim Wolfe, who'd had the wind knocked out of him, was getting the worst of it. But after the SUPD officer sucked in some oxygen, he began to hold his own and more. When Wolfe bit him on the nose, Felix Navarone yelled for help. The state policemen took their time, but eventually the white cop was plucked off the Apache.

Felix Navarone had a hideously bloody nose.

Jim Wolfe suffered more from injured pride than from his minor physical injuries. Snarling, he made a lunge at Navarone, which was blocked by a pair of beefy state troopers. Denied his vengeance, the white man bellowed, "Next time I get my hands on you, Navarone—you are a *dead* man."

There was no doubt of the soul-felt sincerity of this threat.

Moon shook his head. *Jim, Jim—you should have listened to me.*

CHAPTER EIGHT

BAD MEDICINE

HAVING CONCLUDED THAT OFFICER JIM WOLFE WAS IN NO condition to drive, Charlie Moon had commandeered Wolfe's SUPD Blazer. Since leaving the scene of the melee, neither man had uttered a word. The tribal investigator was maneuvering the vehicle around the worst of the potholes that blighted the muddy road to his aunt's remote home.

Filled to the gills with regret, Wolfe cleared his throat. "I have to say it."

Moon kept his eye on the crooked lane.

"Back there at the roadblock—I should've listened to you. Let those state cops take care of that Apache."

The Ute gritted his teeth as the right front wheel slammed into a foot-deep pit concealed by the snow.

Wolfe's voice was full of self-pity: "I've always been dumb."

Charlie Moon wondered whether that last pothole had terminated a shock.

"Dumb as a stump," Wolfe muttered. "Dull-witted as a barnyard turkey, stupid as a . . . a . . ." He strained with concentration, then looked at the driver. "You can jump right in whenever you're ready."

"Sack of dirt?" Moon offered this in a helpful tone.

"You misunderstand." Wolfe managed a smile, which sent a sharp pain through his swollen lip. "This is where you're supposed to give me a pep talk. Tell me how I'm not half as dumb as I feel right now."

"Nah. It'd be wasted on a stubborn fella like you." Moon braked when a coyote darted across the lane in front of the Blazer. He tried to think of something to raise his comrade's spirits. "Felix Navarone got the worst of it. In fact, I think you almost bit that 'Pache's nose off."

"I bit his *nose*?" Wolfe made a horrible grimace.

"I thought it'd cheer you up—knowing you caused him seriously bodily harm."

Officer Wolfe felt like gagging. "I had that guy's *nose* in my *mouth*?"

"'Fraid so, Jim-boy. Your regular rough-and-tumble rhubarb ain't a pretty thing to see. Eyes get gouged out, ears and noses chewed off. But I doubt Navarone carried any more germs than your average run-of-the-mill, lice-infested, drug-popping bum who don't take a bath except when he passes out and falls in the gutter." He shifted to low gear. "All the same, I hope you've had all your shots."

"Excuse me for not laughing, but that ain't very funny."

Moon pulled into the yard by his aunt's trailer house, parked Wolfe's SUPD Blazer beside his Expedition, the flagship of the Columbine Ranch. A new set of tire tracks in the snow was evidence that Danny Bignight had already been here and gone—which meant that Kicks Dogs was on her way back to Ignacio. He turned off the ignition, turned to have a look at his passenger. "Jim, your lower lip has swole up like an inner tube. You'd better come inside, let my aunt check you out."

Wolfe gave the shaman's trailer a long, doubtful look. "Ah . . . thanks but I don't guess I should. She might think it was an imposition."

"I'll go talk to her." Moon got out of the Blazer, headed for the trailer porch.

Wolfe opened the passenger door, shouted. "Hey!"

Moon turned to see what the matter was.

"You took my car keys."

The tribal investigator pulled the Blazer keys from his pocket. Stared at them. *Funny how we get into habits.* He pitched the keys back to the SUPD cop.

Daisy met her nephew at the door, squinted at the SUPD police unit, asked who was in the car.

Moon told her.

She knew about the white man. "Oh, him."

"Didn't think I ought to invite him in." He lowered his voice: "Jim Wolfe is acting kinda peculiar today."

Daisy gave her nephew a wide-eyed look.

"Not an hour ago, and for no good reason I could see—he went out of his way to bite a man."

The Ute elder scowled at the report of such barbarism. "He *what?*"

"Well, I guess it'd be more accurate to say he *gnawed* on a man. But no matter how you put it, it amounts to the same thing—Jim Wolfe chomped right down on the poor Apache's nose—"

"He bit an *Apache?*"

Moon nodded. "Officer Wolfe recognizes the cultural diversity of our society. When it comes to gouging and biting and kicking, he don't show no favorites."

She squinted up at her nephew. "Charlie Moon, are you lying to me?"

"Cross my heart and hope to ride a spotted pony all the way to Steamboat Springs and back—Jim chomped down on that 'Pache's nose like he was bobbin' for a crab apple. Dang near took it off, too."

The Ute elder stuck her tongue out. "Ugh."

He felt the sudden need to exaggerate. "I expect it'll take twenty-six stitches to fasten the snout back betwixt Felix's eyeballs."

The shaman grimaced. "Felix Navarone?"

"The very same." Moon frowned at his aunt. "You acquainted with the man?"

She nodded her gray head. "I know all about him and his big brother, Ned. There's some disagreement about which one is the meanest, but Felix is the smartest of the two." Daisy assumed a tolerant look. "I don't have nothing against Apaches. I figure the best of 'em are almost as good as a Ute. But Felix and Ned—those two are bad all the way down to the marrow." She squinted at her nephew. "Did you know their own mother threw 'em both out of her house last year—told 'em to never come back?"

Moon admitted that he had not heard about this.

Daisy looked to the south, from where the Navarones had come. "I'd have felt better if the both of those yahoos had stayed down in New Mexico, but from what I hear nobody wanted 'em on the reservation. So they come up to Colorado, rented a place over by Pagosa." There was no point in telling her nephew that Felix dabbled in bad magic, because Charlie Moon did not believe in such things. And some of the reports were hard for even the shaman to swallow. Felix had made his brag around Ignacio that neither knives nor bullets could kill him. And if that were not enough, the Apache also claimed he could fly! Such foolishness. Daisy took another look at Jim Wolfe in the SUPD Blazer. She supposed that those sickly pale *matukach* folk must have their ups and downs, just like regular people. "Did he get hurt any by the Apache?"

Moon had been waiting for this. "He got bunged up a bit."

Daisy Perika raised an eyebrow. "How bad?"

"Don't let it worry you. It's not like he'd expect *you* could do anything for him." She did not take the bait. "What Jim needs is to see a *real* doctor—"

"You go get him," she snapped. "Bring him in here."

OFFICER WOLFE shook his head. "I don't think I should."

"It's up to you," Charlie Moon said.

"I wouldn't want to put the old lady to any trouble."

The Ute gave him a knowing look. "If you're afraid of Aunt Daisy, it's nothing to be ashamed of."

Jim Wolfe glared at the smug-looking Indian. "Charlie, I know you don't believe in any of that witchin' stuff." He nodded to agree with some unspoken conviction. "But I know of them that've been hexed, and them that've been cured by counterhexes. More than once down in Navajo country, I have seen it done with my own eyes." The SUPD officer touched a fingertip to his swollen lip, stared at the shaman's trailer home as a terminally ill man might regard an open grave.

Moon leaned closer to his victim, dropped his voice to a hoarse whisper. "You don't have to go inside, I could ask her to put some of her homemade medications in a plain brown envelope, then I could bring it out here, just drop it on the seat beside you, and—"

"Go ahead, Charlie—make fun of a brother lawman."

"Okay, if you're sure you don't mind."

"Anyway, the old lady's probably just being polite."

Moon grinned. "I think we can safely rule that out. But if you don't let her have a look at you, it'll hurt her feelings."

This seemed to alarm the prospective patient. "Well, I wouldn't want your aunt to think I was an ingrate."

HAVING INTRODUCED Jim Wolfe to his aunt, Charlie Moon stood just inside the kitchen door—waiting for the fun to begin.

Wolfe meekly obeyed the old woman's snappish order to sit down at the dining table. Unconsciously, he clasped his knobby hands in prayerful fashion. "Ma'am, it is real nice of you to help me like this. You are a real Good Samaritan."

There was no response from the feisty old Philistine.

The SUPD officer licked at his bulbous lip, which pained like it had been stung by a dozen wasps. He was certain it was infected with billions and billions of the Apache's virulent nose-germs. "If you don't have the right medicine on hand, that's all right. I'll be fine."

Daisy turned to stare at the white man, as if she wondered how such a pitiful specimen had gotten into her kitchen.

Wolfe tried to avoid the peculiar old woman's eyes, but was unable to resist the hypnotic gaze.

Daisy turned to Charlie Moon. She pointed at the door. "Out."

For Wolfe's sake, Moon assumed a worried look. "Maybe Jim would feel better if I hung around and made sure you don't use the wrong potion—"

Daisy pointed the finger harder. "Out *now!*"

Wolfe stared imploringly at the tribal investigator. *Charlie, please please please don't leave me here with her.* . . .

The tribal investigator understood the silent communication perfectly. He put on his hat. "See you later, Jim." And so it was that Charlie Moon took his leave. *This will be a great experience for Jim Wolfe. Give him some good stories to tell.*

CHAPTER NINE

THE FULL TREATMENT

FEELING DESPERATELY LONELY FOR CHARLIE MOON'S COMpany, Jim Wolfe stared at the closed door. After the sound of the Expedition had faded in the distance, he felt the need for conversation. "I'm a good friend of Charlie's." *So don't do nothing to hurt me.*

"I'm glad to hear it." Daisy snorted. "That big jug-head needs all the friends he can get."

Wolfe managed a sickly smile.

She glared at him. "What's so funny?"

"Oh, nothing." The smile slipped away. "Nothing at all, ma'am."

He had the lean, hungry look of a West Texan. "Where're you from?"

"Cherokee County, Oklahoma." He said this with a faraway look. "It's real nice."

"I was in Tulsa one time back in 1935. Ate some bad pork, got food poisoning." Daisy Perika disappeared into her small bathroom, returned with an ancient bottle of Mercurochrome. "I don't work for nothing. But if you're short on greenbacks, I might accept something in trade." She glanced at his wrist. "Like maybe that watch."

He pushed his cuff over the expensive timepiece. "What will I owe you in cash money?"

"Fifty dollars."

He squirmed under her avaricious gaze. "I don't think I've got that much on me."

The old woman's mouth twisted into a wicked grin. "How much *have* you got?"

Wolfe checked his wallet. "Twenty-six dollars."

"That'll do for a down payment." She shook the small brown container, unscrewed the cap.

He stared suspiciously at the bottle. "What's that?"

"A special potion. I make it from horny-toad livers, green grasshopper vomit, and salted hummingbird tongues."

"That sounds pretty . . . uh . . . potent."

"I learned the recipe from a blind Hopi sign painter who drives a school bus down by Shungopavi. Now hold still if you don't want your eyeball painted too."

Wolfe clamped his eyes shut, gritted his teeth.

The shaman poked the glass applicator at the split lip, leaving a scarlet streak of Mercurochrome.

"Ouch!"

"Don't be such a sissy." She muttered a few words in the Ute tongue, spat on her fingers, rubbed them across the patient's forehead three times. "Get up," she commanded.

The wary man stood.

"Now don't move a whisker." The old woman picked up a broom, made a swing, slapping the linoleum near his boots.

What was that all about? But the alarmed patient dared not ask.

"I swatted your shadow," she said. "That scares away any bad spirits that might be pestering you."

"Oh—thanks."

"Now sit down again." Having completed her surprise assault on his shadow, Daisy Perika stood with her eyes closed, teetering back and forth on her heels.

Wolfe stared at the performance. *I hope she don't fall down.*

Presently, the shaman opened her eyes, observed her patient's lip. "That'll be better by morning. Now I'll tend to your other cuts."

Worried that the notorious woman might be about to do some more spitting, Wolfe thought he might steer her off on another course by changing the subject. "Ma'am, I was just wondering. Do you still mix up them . . ." He could not make himself say it.

The shaman capped the medicine bottle, scowled at the impertinent fellow. "Do I still mix up them *what*?"

He wilted under her searing gaze. "Oh, nothing."

Having bullied her patient into submission, she dropped the Mercurochrome bottle into an apron pocket. She went to a cabinet over the sink, removed a black shoe box, placed it on the table. Under her patient's watchful gaze, she removed the lid, rummaged around in the assortment of jars and bottles half-filled with viscous liquids, bits of dried roots and seeds and leaves, a lumpy tobacco sack that looked like it was filled with pebbles. "I was hoping there might be something here good for healing cuts, but I don't see what I was looking for." She removed a plastic sandwich bag that contained a gritty, yellowish gray stuff. Daisy turned it in her wrinkled hands, muttered something in the Ute dialect, placed it ever so carefully on the table beside the shoe box—as if it contained a few grams of well-aged TNT. To add to the effect, she covered it with a paper napkin. Pretending not to notice Wolfe's interest in the small ritual, Daisy found a squat blue jar in the shoe box, opened it, and applied a soothing white salve to cuts on his face and neck.

Now that's more like it. "What's that?"

This time she was truthful: "My own special bee-weed ointment."

"Oh."

But that's not what you really wanted to know. Daisy waited for curiosity to get the better of the white man.

Wolfe knew with every fiber in his body that he should not ask. "Uh . . . what's in that plastic bag?"

"What plastic bag?"

Like a small boy standing at the end of a diving board thirty feet above the water, he hesitated. "The one under the napkin."

"Oh, *that* plastic bag." The old woman's expression was unreadable. "You sure you want to know?"

He nodded himself straight into the abyss.

She stared at the man as if appraising whether he was worthy to share the dark secret. "If I tell you what it is—you have to promise me you won't never tell a living soul." *Especially Charlie Moon.*

The policeman's voice was raspy with apprehension. "Yes ma'am. I mean, no ma'am. I mean—I wouldn't never breathe a word to nobody."

Daisy continued to stare at her patient. The interlude stretched into the longest moment of his life. Finally, she removed the napkin and said, "It's *corpse powder.*"

Wolfe's back flattened against the chair. He could not pull his gaze from the transparent sandwich bag. "You don't actually mean . . ."

She nodded. "Sure I do. It won't work if it ain't got some parts from a dead person in it."

Oh my God. "Like—a sliver of fingernail?"

She dismissed this optimistic guess with a grim expression, a slow shake of her head.

Fearing that the old crone was about to reveal the grisly ingredients, he hurried to divert her from this course. "So what do you do with the—uh—preparation?"

"It's only used for one ailment—ghost sickness."

It had not occurred to Jim Wolfe that ghosts ever got sick, and he barely stopped short of saying so.

Taking note of the perplexed expression on the white man's face, the shaman explained, "Sometimes, spirits of dead people come back to torment the living. That's what Indians call ghost sickness."

The light was slowly dawning. He nodded at the plastic bag. *I bet they have to swallow some of it. . . .* "So you treat the haunted person with that concoction?"

"That ain't no concoction, that's a medicine. A *powerful* medicine."

"Sorry, I didn't mean to—"

She fixed him with the sort of gaze a gray fox uses to mesmerize a cornered chicken. "If someone was to come to me, needing protection from a ghost, I'd sell 'em some of that medicine. They'd take it to where the dead person's mortal remains was, and sprinkle the corpse powder over the body."

He tugged at his shirt collar. "And that'd work, would it?"

"It has never failed." She got another gob of bee-plant ointment on her finger. "If you want me to doctor those other cuts, take off your shirt."

He did.

And the old woman was stunned by what she saw.

Suspended on a leather cord around his neck was a marvelous lump of turquoise. The crescent-shaped stone was the deep blue of the western sky on a cool October morning. Moreover, it was wonderfully marbled with silver veins—suggesting a multitude of glistening streams. So very beautiful. And so familiar. The shaman knew that this was more than a bauble—this was a very powerful object. *But where have I seen it before?* As she pondered this question, Daisy applied the bee-weed balm to a laceration on his arm.

Noting the old woman's interest, Jim Wolfe tapped his finger on the turquoise pendant. "Couple of years ago, I bought this in a pawn shop down at Farmington. Cost me three hundred bucks. It's a good-luck charm, but only if you to wear it next to your skin."

She took another look at the lump of blue stone. And the old woman who could not recall what she had for supper yesterday, suddenly remembered a day more than seventy-seven years ago. It seemed unbelievable, but there could be no doubt. This was the very pendant that had belonged to Hasteen K'os Largo, the famous Navajo medicine man who had done a sing for Daisy's father, when Daddy returned from France after that terrible War to End Wars. Its appearance here and now was nothing short of a miracle—and it was far too sacred and powerful an object to hang around the neck of this know-nothing *matukach*. Thus it was that the corrosive sin of covetousness took firm hold of Daisy Perika's heart.

Jim Wolfe watched her face, wondered what was going on behind the mask. *I think she likes it.* He removed the pendant, offered it for her inspection.

She backed away, raising her hand in a protective gesture. "No—I'd never touch that thing."

He blinked at the eccentric woman. "What's wrong?"

The shaman shook her head. "I shouldn't say." But of course, she did: "That's a bad piece of stone. *Very* bad."

"Oh, I don't think so." Jim Wolfe dangled the stone in her face. "This is where all of my good luck comes from."

She fairly hissed at him. "It'll make you sick."

He frowned at the turquoise lump. *What's she talking about?*

All that was required was a seed of doubt. "For a while, you won't notice nothing much." The man had bloodshot eyes. "Then you'll have trouble sleeping." She had seen a pouch of tobacco in his shirt pocket. "And you'll get a cough."

"I feel fine," he said hoarsely.

There were hints of fingernail marks on his dry, flaky skin. "And sooner or later, there'll be the itching."

He valiantly fought the urge to scratch.

Daisy looked immensely sorry for her unhappy patient. "And then you'll start to worrying all the time."

The worried patient nodded.

"I hate to tell you, but when it's almost too late—there'll be heart palpitations."

The thumping pump under his sternum missed a beat.

"And finally—" She interrupted herself with a sigh. "No, I'd better not talk about *that*."

He leaned forward. "What?"

"Trust me. It's better that you don't know."

His complexion now resembled chalky eggshell. "You saying this little piece of rock can do all that?"

"All that and lots more." She shrugged. "Of course, I could be wrong." Her confident expression was testimony that this had never happened. "But if it was me, I wouldn't keep that thing next to *my* skin."

Absently, the victim scratched at his chest.

"I wouldn't even want it in the same house where I slept," she added. "Not unless it was . . ." She let the suggestive words hang in the air.

"It cost me a lot of money." Wolfe laid the cursed thing on

Daisy's kitchen table, gave her a hopeful look. "Isn't there some way it could be fixed?"

The shaman stared longingly at the lump of turquoise. "It all depends."

"On what? Soon as I get my next check, I'd be glad to pay you whatever—"

She silenced him with a wag of her finger and a saintly expression. "I don't charge money for taking dark spells off people—or their things."

His eyes were wide with hope. "Look, anything you could do—I'd sure appreciate it."

"I might be willing to give it a try," the sly old woman said. "But it could be dangerous."

"Dangerous?" Wolfe's mouth went dry. "What could happen?"

"Maybe nothing at all." Daisy pointed at the subject of their discussion. "But if it's been witched real good—it might sizzle like a sausage in a skillet. Or go *boom!*"

His forehead furrowed into a puzzled frown.

She explained, "It might *explode*."

The wretched man's mouth fell open. He drew a raspy breath.

"Do you have a clean handkerchief?" She had seen it in his hip pocket.

Wolfe produced the folded piece of linen.

Daisy gave him an order: "Take that turquoise off the string." She went to a small table under a window, removed a cracked saucer from beneath a potted geranium. She pointed with a jut of her chin. "Put it on the saucer."

He hesitated. "Wouldn't it be better if you—"

"I'm not laying a finger on that thing." She appealed to reason: "You've had it against your skin all this time. One more touch won't matter all that much." She watched as he fumbled to disconnect the leather cord.

"You can throw the rawhide string on the floor. I'll sweep it up later."

Wolfe did as he was told, and laid the blue stone on the saucer.

"Now put the handkerchief over it."

He did.

The shaman closed her eyes. Passed her hands over the shrouded stone. Mumbled a few words in the choppy Ute dialect. Cracked one eye to check on the white man. His fists were clenched, his eyes wide open.

Daisy looked at the ceiling.

His gaze followed hers.

She shouted, "Hah!"

Wolfe jumped halfway out of his chair. "What?"

"You can take a look at the thing now. If it's still in one piece, you should be able to wear it without any problem."

He removed the handkerchief. In the center of the white saucer, where the lump of turquoise had been, was a pinch of dark powder.

The shaman groaned. "I was afraid of that."

The white man's voice quavered: "What happened?"

"That stone was witched, all right—when I took the spell away, it turned to poison stump dirt."

This is absolutely astonishing. He reached out a fingertip to touch the residue of his three-hundred-dollar investment.

"Don't!" Daisy snatched the saucer out of his reach. "It'd rot the end of your finger off."

He opened his mouth to speak, was interrupted.

"Don't thank me," she said in a kindly tone. "You're a friend of my nephew, so it was only right that I help you." She added, with a wag of her finger, "It would be better if this bad business wasn't talked about." *Especially to Charlie Moon.* "And you can give me that twenty-six dollars now."

Wolfe emptied his wallet, pulled on his blood-spotted shirt, thanked the tribal elder for her services. He left in a daze.

Daisy Perika stood on the rickety pine porch, watched the pale-skinned policeman drive away in the mud-streaked SUPD automobile. *This has been a very good day.* The tribal elder had not had so much fun since the last time she had put one over on her long-suffering parish priest.

Jim Wolfe stuck his arm out of the dusty black Blazer, waved to the old woman.

Daisy raised her right hand to wave back.

With her left, the shaman clutched the legendary K'os Largo turquoise pendant to her breast. Later on, she would dump the "poison stump dirt" back into the geranium pot.

CHAPTER TEN

THE VISITATION

PLUMP AS A PLUM, FIVE-TWO IN HER BOOTS, WANDA YERBA had the look of a shy schoolgirl. This impression was misleading. Sergeant Yerba was a senior SUPD jailer and a plenty tough customer. Last July, a Santa Clara Pueblo man on her work detail had made a run for it. Wanda bested him in a thirty-yard sprint, tackled him in the middle of the street. When the disgruntled would-be escapee made a crude reference to a female canine, the jailer punched him square in the nose. This had taken all the fight out of the foul-mouthed felon.

But she loved the job. "Every day," she would tell her mother, "there is something new and interesting."

On this particular day there was a visitor for the tree-climbing Apache. Wanda stared at the scar-faced Navajo, whose head was wrapped in bandages. "What happened to your head, Eddie—and your face?"

"I had an accident," Eduardo Ganado said. "I'd rather not talk about it."

Poor Eddie; he's always having accidents. "I'll have to check your briefcase."

Ganado opened the case for the jailer's inspection.

She stared into the gaping mouth of the shiny cowhide satchel. "There's nothing inside."

He offered her an embarrassed grin. "I don't have no legal papers to tote around yet—it's mostly just for looks."

She shrugged, led the lawyer's employee to the cell block.

"Hey, Navarone—somebody's here to see you. I'll take you to the library." Visitors were not allowed in the cells.

Halfway between his neatly made bunk and the stainless steel toilet-sink unit, the Apache sat cross-legged on the painted concrete floor. Felix Navarone had his back to the cell door, his gaze fixed on a narrow window set with a single horizontal bar. He did not respond.

Wanda was not offended by the silent treatment. At least this prisoner had made no attempt to spit on her. "It's a guy from your attorney's office—you want to see him or not?"

Felix Navarone closed his eyes. "I don't need no lawyer to spring me. I can leave this place whenever I want to."

The sergeant glanced at Ganado. "Navarone claims to be a big shot medicine man."

"*Góchi'*," the sullen prisoner muttered.

Though Wanda's Apache vocabulary was limited, it included that one. "It is not nice to call your friendly neighborhood jailer a pig."

Brand-new at his job and unsure how to proceed, the Navajo legal aide waited to see what was going to happen.

The Apache raised his arms, began to chant:

You will see it—steel blades cannot cut my flesh.
   Bullets cannot kill me—I will dance with the lightning.
You will see it—iron bars cannot keep me captive.
   The earth cannot hold me—I will fly with the Thunder People.

"Before you start flapping your wings," Wanda said, "you want to say hello to Mr. Ganado?"

Felix Navarone turned. "Who?"

"Eddie Ganado," the legal aide said.

The prisoner got to his feet, smiled crookedly at the Navajo. "You really working for my lawyer in Durango?"

Ganado held up his new briefcase for Navarone to see. "Started just this morning. She asked me to come down here, see how you're being treated." The visitor glanced at the jailer. "It's a part of my training."

"I'll tell you how they're treating me," Navarone snarled. "The plumbing stinks. The food stinks. This fat *Góchi'* jailer stinks!" Choking with hatred, he jerked a thumb at his stitched-up beak. "And that white SUPD cop tried to bite my nose off."

Wanda turned an earnest face to the legal aide. "We were very concerned about infection. So we made sure Officer Wolfe got his anti-Apache booster shots."

CHAPTER ELEVEN

THE FOREMAN

CHARLIE MOON PARTED THE CURTAINS TO HAVE A LOOK AT the dawning morning. And what a glorious new day it was. The sun was showing a crimson arc along the jagged crest of the Buckhorn range. The underbelly of a trout-shaped cloud was transformed to shimmering hues of turquoise and pink. As the great fish swam through the pool of heaven, there was an unspeakably lovely iridescence, hinting of rainbows in paradise. From deep in some place that he did not know, the man confined to the earthly world felt an inexpressible pang of melancholy.

In a heartbeat, the moment was gone.

Having things to do, the practical Ute got about his daily business.

Charlie Moon was preparing a breakfast of fried eggs, fried pork chops, fried potatoes, and baked biscuits when he heard the familiar rap-rap on the back door. "C'mon in, Pete."

The Columbine foreman pushed his bewhiskered face into the kitchen, sniffed. Approving of the scents, Pete Bushman closed the door behind him, clomped his dirty boots across the hardwood floor to have a look at what the Ute was up to at the kitchen stove.

Moon turned over an egg. "You want some eats?"

"Nah. My old woman's done taken care a that." To demonstrate the truth of this assertion, the scrawny old cowboy banged a fist against his chest, burped.

"If you'd like a dose of caffeine, help yourself."

Bushman took the sooty coffeepot to the table, pulled up a chair, poured a mug half full, squinted suspiciously at the tar-black brew. "Can't you make it any stronger?"

"Not without a special permit from the government." Charlie Moon put his plate on the table, took a seat across from his foreman.

For a minute or two, the crusty old man watched the boss eat. "You hear about old Joe Henry's spread to the east of the Columbine?"

Moon nodded.

"It's coming up for sale. The Big Hat only has a tad over eleven sections, but most of it's well-watered. And besides the prime grazing land, there's over nine hundred acres of good timber."

The Ute continued to eat.

Bushman wound up for another pitch. "There's some beef stock that goes with it, about two hundred and twenty head."

The rancher looked up from his breakfast. "Any horses?"

Bushman grinned under his whiskers. *All these Utes love horses.* "Maybe a couple dozen. And there's a Chevy stake-bed truck that's only three years old. Two good tractors. And a brand-new diesel well-drilling rig."

"Sounds like somebody'll be real happy with the Big Hat."

Bushman ignored this negative response. "Old man Henry set hisself up the best machine shop within a hundred miles. Power saws. Grinders. Welders. Cutting torches. Heavy-duty drill press. Even a metal lathe and a great big Detroit milling machine. You name it, that shop has got it."

Moon looked at his plate.

"With a setup like that, we could do all of our own repairs." Bushman put his elbows on the table. "And the price is right."

The boss gave him a doubtful look. "How right?"

The foreman told him.

Moon shook his head.

Bushman persisted: "That's a real good price."

"There's no use thinking about it, Pete."

"Charlie—in the ranchin' bidness, if you don't go full steam ahead, you go backerds."

The boss was unfazed by this pithy bit of stockman's wisdom. "The Columbine is just starting to turn a profit."

"You could take out a loan."

"I don't have enough in the bank for a down payment."

"There's more than one way to gut a moose."

Moon shook his head. "I know what you're going to propose. Don't bother."

"Look, boss—it wouldn't hurt us none to sell off some a that dry land on the far side a the highway to that developer in Granite Creek. It's fifteen miles away, we don't use it, and he'll pay us top dollar—"

"No."

When the boss used *that* tone, Bushman understood the discussion was over. But as he got up from the table, the old soldier took a parting shot: "If you don't buy the Big Hat, somebody else sure will." He gave the Ute a stern look. "And there's no telling who your new neighbor might be. You could end up with a buncha tenderfoot riffraff livin' right next door."

The Columbine's boundary with the Big Hat Ranch was a good twenty miles to the east. "Next door" was on the far side of the Buckhorn range.

The foreman was getting his second wind. "I'm talking about the kinda city folk that don't eat beef—that'd raise worthless critters. Llamas and ostriches and . . . and armadillos!"

Moon kept his grin inside. "I hear there's good profit in that kind of stock."

Pete Bushman slammed the door behind him.

THE FAREWELL

HIS FOREMAN having been properly disposed of, Charlie Moon washed the breakfast dishes, enjoyed a third heavily sugared cup of coffee, pulled on a fleece-lined denim jacket, popped the black John B. Stetson on his head, picked up the dog's crockery dish, closed the door behind him, and began humming the tune to "I'm Movin' On."

The homely hound appeared from nowhere.

The rancher put the dish on the porch. "Eat hearty, bub—I won't be back till way after dark."

Sidewinder sniffed at the victuals. Looked up at the human with undisguised reproach.

"What's the matter? That is beef." *Not* prime *beef, but good enough for the likes of you.*

The animal ignored the food.

"When you get hungry enough, you'll be glad to lap it up." Moon headed for his Expedition. Realizing that no one except the dog could hear him, he resumed the humming. And even if they could, the Columbine was his ranch. He could sing out loud if he wanted to. He thought he would. And did. Loudly.

The hound peeled a bile-tinted eye at the happy singer. Began to make a groaning sound.

Moon paused to address the ill-tempered beast. "What's wrong with you this fine morning?"

The music critic growled.

"Okay, you don't appreciate my singing. Well, I don't care one whit. Anything else you got on your so-called mind?"

Sidewinder glanced at the F-150 pickup truck, back at the human being he had graciously adopted.

The Ute shook his head. "The answer to your first question is no, I'm not taking the truck today. And to address your second inquiry, the answer is no again. You can't come with me."

A single bark from the hound.

"Well, since you ask, I don't mind telling you: I am going to pick up my lady. Me and Miss James will have a special dinner tonight. At which time I intend to make her a serious proposal."

Sidewinder barked twice. Cocked his head.

"I cannot dispute that; the woman does not have good taste. But she likes me lots better than a bumblebee up her nose."

Another bark, in the form of a question mark.

"Well, how should I describe her?" The man rubbed his

chin. "She's got this long, black hair. Pretty eyes big as saucers. Lots of nice curves—"

The hound muttered something.

"Her background? Well, there's not much to tell. Her folks died when she was just a little pup."

Orphaned himself at six weeks, the dog looked to be saddened at this news.

"But you might as well know this—if Miss James says yes to what I ask her, she will be coming to live at the ranch." The Ute gave the beast a warning look. "And you will treat her nice. Or else."

There was an odd, gurgling sound from the hound.

Moon patted the animal's head. "For someone who hardly ever has a word to say, you sure are full of talk this morning." He squinted at the sun. "I have enjoyed our conversation, but time's a-wasting and I got to hit the road."

Sidewinder followed the happy man to the Expedition.

Moon stuck his head out the window, grinned at the animal. "Try not to get in too much trouble while I'm gone. Remember not to eat any live rattlesnakes or prickly pears." A final jibe as he pulled away: "Did I mention that Miss James has two cats?"

Unfazed by this news, the hound trotted along behind until the automobile rattled the pine planks on the Too Late bridge. He stood, watched it go. After an interval, Sidewinder raised his head, began to howl.

AS CHARLIE Moon passed the foreman's house, Dolly Bushman appeared at the front window. The boss stuck his arm out of the Expedition, gave her an enthusiastic wave.

Dolly waved back, watched the big car top the crest of a low ridge, vanish from sight. She stood, listening intently.

The Columbine foreman was at the dining table, manfully attempting to balance the checkbook used for Columbine operating expenses.

The woman turned to her husband. "Pete, do you hear that?"

He looked up from his scribblings. "Hear what?"

The plump woman shuddered. "That dog."

Paperwork required all his powers of concentration; there was an edge of annoyance to his reply. "What about the danged ol' hound?"

She held her breath, then: "Just listen to him."

Her husband listened. "Yeah, I hear 'im." *So what?*

"It's kind of strange—the way that animal is carrying on."

He bulged his eyes at her. "There's nothin' *strange* about it. That peculiar old mutt is usually unhappy about somethin' or other. And when he's unhappy, he yowls his fool head off."

"No." Dolly shook her head. "That ain't it."

Pete shrugged, got back to his work. But the rows of numbers stubbornly refused to add up.

The telephone jangled.

Dolly Bushman pressed the instrument against her ear. "Columbine." She listened to a string of queries, followed each with a clipped response:

"Who wants to know?"

"Never heard of you."

"The boss isn't here."

"Sorry, I don't give out his cell phone number."

"Matter a fact, he just left."

"Maybe you can."

Dolly hung up.

Pete looked up from his laborious calculations. "Who was that?"

"Some fella wants to see Charlie."

CHAPTER TWELVE

THE HARD-LUCK KID

CHARLIE MOON PASSED UNDER THE MASSIVE PINE-LOG ARCH at the Columbine gate, turned east on the paved road to Granite Creek. Within a mile, he met a decades-old yellow Pontiac convertible with the top down. The automobile's headlights blinked half a dozen times before it went by him, screeched to a near halt, rolled up rubber on the road in a tight U-turn, resumed the headlight blinking—now accentuated by an urgent honking.

What's this all about? Moon slowed.

The Pontiac passed, cut in front of him, lurched to a halt.

The Ute pulled his Expedition to a stop on the shoulder.

A barrel-chested man got out, slammed the door, came limping along the pavement toward the Ute's car. He had a walnut complexion, wore an ill-fitting brown suit, a silver-dollar bolo tie—and had something on his head that resembled a white turban. Most remarkable of all, a black protrusion that looked like a pump handle appeared to be sticking out of his right ear.

The peculiar figure raised a hand to wave.

Moon recognized the odd figure as Eduardo Ganado, one of the more colorful characters in southern Colorado. The Navajo leased a small, run-down farm from tribal chairman Oscar Sweetwater. As he approached in his painful gait, it became apparent that the white turban on his head was constructed of surgical tape, the pump handle was his right braid, which protruded almost horizontally from the mummy wrapping. By all appearances, the left braid was but a memory.

Moon pressed a button to lower the window. "Hi, Eddie."

Ganado returned the greeting with characteristic cheerfulness: "Yo, Charlie."

The Ute eyed the beautifully restored convertible. "You must spend a lot of time keeping that Pontiac looking so spiffy."

The proud owner beamed at this compliment. "When a man has only got one automobile, he naturally takes good care of it." The odd character leaned forward, peered into the Expedition. There were ugly cuts and bruises on his face and forehead and several milky blotches on his dark skin that looked like burn scars. "Charlie, I appreciate you not asking about my injuries. Most folks, soon as they see me, say, 'What happened to your head, Eddie—and your face?' And I am *so* tired of explaining."

The Ute grinned. "What happened to your head, Eddie—and your face?"

The injured man gave him a bushy-browed scowl. "You don't want to know."

"That's true enough. But you want to tell me, so go ahead."

Eduardo Ganado did a grin-and-shrug. "Ah, you know how it is with me. One awful thing after another."

Charlie Moon did know. Among all the troubled souls on the res, Ganado was the one who most deserved the grim descriptor *accident-prone*. Wherever the luckless fellow went, bad things happened—mostly to him. Chimneys that had been solid for a hundred years tossed bricks onto Ganado's head. Windows that had never misbehaved fell on his fingers. And power tools of all varieties seemed to lust for a chunk of his flesh. If a sick vulture emptied its bowels in the sky anywhere over southern Colorado, the odds were nine to four that the putrid load would fall on the hapless Navajo. Eddie Ganado claimed he'd been struck by lightning six times, and no one doubted this. "Looks like somebody tried to scalp you with an ax."

This produced a chuckle. "No, but it was just about as bad."

"Grizzly bear peg you for a square meal?"

Ganado shook his mangled head, rotating the extended braid. "It wasn't no kind of animal."

"You got caught in a threshing machine?"

"Nope. But you're not far off."

"I'm all out of guesses."

Ganado leaned back, hooked his thumbs in his belt. This was his storytelling stance. "It was all because of a sickly old pine tree that was leaning toward my house. I figured, Next big wind, she'll come crashing down through the roof. So I get out my chain saw to cut it down, cranked 'er up, and—"

Moon could see it coming.

"—Got my hair caught in the infernal machine."

"You're lucky it didn't take your head off."

The Navajo nodded. "Don't I know it! My poor old melon was goin' bumpity-bump-bump against that chain-saw motor till I finally yanked off the spark-plug wire and shut 'er down." He tapped the left side of his head. "It pulled my hair out by the bloody roots—skin and all. And cut up my face."

Moon grimaced. "That must've hurt."

Ganado nodded solemnly. "You can say that again."

The fun-loving Ute manfully resisted the temptation.

"And just as I got the chain saw shut off, I tripped over it and fell down and banged my knee on a big rock. That's how I come to be all gimpy." He leaned to rub the painful joint. "This kinda stuff don't hardly ever happen to other folks. My mother was always saying: 'Eddie, you are a hard-luck kid.'" Eduardo Ganado nodded to agree with this assessment, which caused the pump-handle braid to rotate in the eerie fashion of an auger drilling into his bandaged skull. "Sooner or later, my knee'll mend. But I've lost half my hair. Maybe for good."

Moon offered the Navajo a thoughtful look. "Your hair'll grow back—if you use the right kind of medicine."

Well aware that Charlie Moon's famous aunt was a purveyor of marvelous curative potions, the Navajo took the bait. "What kinda medicine?"

"To start with, you have to drink at least six cups of strong black coffee every day."

"Hey—I practically do that already."

"Then you're already halfway there. But to make it work, you have to put a squirt of talcum powder in your java." He noted that the Navajo barely flinched. "And two tablespoons of castor oil."

That did it.

"Castor oil?" The scalped man's lips started to pucker. "How long will it take to get my hair back?"

Moon looked infinitely sorry for the unfortunate man. "Three or four years—whichever comes first."

Ganado's face drooped in despair. "If it don't grow back, I'll just shave off the hair that's left."

Having had enough fun, Moon cut the Expedition ignition. "What brings you out here—you in the market for some prime beef?"

"Uh, no, I don't need no beef—that ain't it. I'm here on accounta my new job."

No employer in his right mind would hire the trouble-plagued man. "So what're you doing?" *Ophthalmic surgery can safely be ruled out, and any task that requires the handling of high explosives.*

"Right now, I'm a legal aide—but I'm on a work-study program to become a paralegal."

"What's the difference?"

"A paralegal gets paid more money."

"Makes cents to me."

"And when I get all my paralegal studies done, I'll be certified."

Feeling generous, Moon let this opportunity pass. "Who are you working for?"

Ganado could not recall his employer's name. "Uh—that woman lawyer in Durango. The one who defends Indians."

Moon knew the lady from his time with the SUPD. *She must be hard up for help.* "She keeping you busy?"

Ganado nodded. "I mostly run errands. Sometimes I visit her clients that're in the jailhouse, other times I deliver legal papers. Today, she sent me up here to see you."

Uh-oh. "This about one of her clients?"

"Yeah. Let me see . . ." The legal aide thumbed through a small notebook. "It's about Mr. Navarone—that Apache who got treed by the cops over near Capote Lake." He gave the tribal investigator a challenging look. "This lawyer I work for wants to talk to you about it. But she says you ain't been returning her phone calls."

"I returned the first one, left a message on her machine. Told her if she wanted to talk to me about tribal business, she could either get permission through the tribal chairman to interview me in his office, or subpoena me for a deposition. I guess your employer wasn't pleased with my response." He took a hard look at Ganado's lemon-colored Pontiac. "That must be why she sent you up here to run me off the road."

"Don't get all bent outta shape, Charlie—I was just doing my job." Squinting at the notebook, Ganado continued. "According to our information, Mr. Navarone was arrested by one of your tribal cops—Officer James Wolfe." The Navajo rolled the distasteful words around in his mouth before spitting them out: "A white man."

Moon looked down the long highway, wishing he were miles away. "Felix Navarone shouldn't have been carrying an open container in his pickup. And he shouldn't have resisted arrest or assaulted an officer."

The Navajo's dark eyes narrowed. "Mr. Navarone swore up and down that he not only hadn't taken a drink outta that whiskey bottle—he didn't even know it was in his truck. That same morning, he'd picked up a hitchhiker from Dalhart. Mr. Navarone figures that sneaky Texan must've left the bottle in his vehicle."

Moon did not respond to this foolishness.

Wrongly sensing that he was making progress, Ganado plunged ahead. "That state trooper chased Mr. Navarone up the tree. After which, that white-faced SUPD cop bullied our client, harassed him, and beat the stuffin' outta him." Feeling the steel in the Ute's gaze, Ganado shifted to a more conciliatory tone: "And besides, Mr. Navarone needs to go visit his mother down in New Mexico."

Moon smiled. "I imagine the poor woman is not well."

"That's right. She's got a bad case of gout or distemper. Somethin' like that."

Charlie Moon set his jaw. "Look, Eddie—I did not participate in the pursuit or the arrest of Felix Navarone. And I am not a Southern Ute police officer anymore—haven't been for quite some time now."

Eduardo Ganado's mouth worked its way into a knowing smirk. "But you're a big-shot tribal investigator who's got the tribal chairman's ear. And Wallace Whitehorse—that Northern Cheyenne ex–Air Force military cop you Utes hired for a chief of police—he does whatever the chairman tells him to."

"I've got a pretty full plate today. Say what's on your mind."

"Okay. Here it is. You was there at the roadblock. You saw what happened." The Navajo's chest swelled like a tree toad's throat. He shook his finger at Moon. "Our client got a raw deal. That state trooper chased him up a tree"—he pointed the finger at the sky—"then Officer Wolfe shook him offa the limb—and kicked the daylight outta him. Then our client was charged with resisting arrest, carrying an open container of alcohol, and assault on a cop with intent to do serious bodily harm—boy, that's a laugh." To demonstrate this assertion he huffed out a "Hah!"

Moon stared at the peculiar man. Not known for his willingness to work, Eddie Ganado was taking his new job seriously.

Ganado kept right on going. "Our client suffered a severely dislocated shoulder."

"Serves him right for picking a fight with Jim Wolfe."

"The shoulder injury ain't all—that white SUPD cop bit him on the nose."

The tribal investigator shook his head. "That's not the way I see it."

"What?"

"Me and a half-dozen other witnesses are willing to swear that Felix Navarone bit *himself* on the nose."

The Navajo stared. "That don't make no sense."

Eddie never did have a sense of humor. "In a really wild

fight, strange things can happen. About seven years ago, down in Taos, I personally witnessed a scrap between two New Mexicans. Well, after it was broke up by the deputy, the massage therapist from Dixon was hauled off to the pokey—but the fortune-teller from Tres Piedras was so stewed up that he kept right on fightin' by himself—and chewed his own ear off."

This nonsense confused Ganado, so he chose to ignore it. "You tell the tribal chairman that if you people persecute our client on these humped-up charges, the lawyer I work for will sue you Southern Utes for more money than all your gas wells and casinos make in a year. And she'll see that Officer Wolfeman never works in uniform again. Not in Colorado, not New Mexico, not *anyplace*."

Moon pointed to his mouth. "Eddie, read my lips. You—are—talking—to—the—wrong—man. If Felix's lawyer wants to play Let's Make A Deal, she'll have to make her pitch to the tribe's legal counsel."

Ganado rapped his knuckles on the Expedition door. "Charlie, I'm going to do you a favor."

Moon closed his eyes. *God help me . . .*

The gossip looked to his right and left, as if some spy lurking on the empty prairie might overhear his next remark. "You should do some checking on Officer Wolfe."

"You think so?"

Ganado nodded the pump-handle braid. "That white man is one bad cop. Over the years, he's been taking bribes. Stealing. Beating up suspects. Even worse stuff than that. *He's* the one that oughta be in jail." The accuser touched a finger to his nose. "A word to the wise."

The Navajo was rapidly becoming a nuisance; Moon felt his face getting warm. "Thanks for the heads-up. I'll make a note of your slander against a tribal employee. And see that the appropriate legal authorities are informed."

"Now look here, Charlie, I was just trying to—"

Moon's cell phone warbled. For once the sound was a welcome interruption. The tribal investigator pressed the Talk button. "Hello."

Ralph Briggs's voice chirped in his ear: "Charlie?"

The Ute had hoped it might be Miss James. "Yeah, Mr. Briggs. It's me."

"You sound not a little nonplussed."

"I've been detained for a moment." He shot a look at Eduardo Ganado. "What's up, Ralph?"

"You know that special item you were interested in?"

Moon nodded.

"Charlie—are you there?"

"Yeah, I remember. In fact, I'm planning to stop by your place and—"

"I realize that you thought my price was—shall we say— slightly on the high side."

"Shall we say I could buy me a fine new registered bull for what you're asking."

"Then perhaps you should."

"Ralph, I've got places to go, things to do. State your business."

"I intend to do you a huge favor."

First Ganado, now you. "That'll be the day."

"Do not be such a cynic. I am perfectly serious."

"Prove it."

"How would you like to buy the object in question for say—one dollar hard cash."

Moon perked up at this. "Did I hear you right?"

"Uno dinero."

"I think it lost something in the translation, but you've got my attention."

"I will say it so you can understand. One government-issue engraving of President George W. And I am referring to the one who crossed the Delaware River in a small boat."

"Okay, I get the picture."

"There would be, of course, a quid pro quo."

"I thought so."

"Charles, I need your expert assistance with a certain matter. It has to do with the burglary near the tribal boundary. Where all those old coins were stolen."

"The Cassidy heist."

"The very same. How soon can we have a private conversation?"

The family museum had been burgled on the same night that Jacob Gourd Rattle had—at least according to his wife's account—disappeared from the canyon. The tribal investigator did a quick calculation. "I could be at your shop this evening—say nine o'clock."

"Done."

"Uh—hold on, Ralph." Moon cupped his hand over the cell phone, turned to Eduardo Ganado. "I've got five or six irons in the fire right now. Tell your employer if she wants my testimony, she can subpoena me. But I don't think what I'd have to say would do your client any lasting good. Officer Wolfe made a righteous bust."

"Okay, Charlie." Eduardo Ganado raised his hands in supplication to an empty sky. "I came to see you, tried my level best to make you see things our way. That's all the boss can expect of me." The comical man with the bandaged head limped away to the yellow car.

Moon resumed his conversation with the antiquarian. "You did say one dollar—that's the price?"

"You heard me right. All you have to do is provide me with a professional service."

Moon watched the Pontiac convertible kick gravel off the shoulder, roar down the highway. "Hold it, Ralph. Before you describe the job you have in mind, I would like to point out—for the benefit of any law-enforcement authorities listening in on a tapped line—that I do not commit murders for hire, or any other felonies. Or for that matter, petty misdemeanors."

"You are such a card, Charles."

"And I won't give you a kidney or lung. I need all my organs."

Ralph sniffed. "The task I have in mind cannot be discussed in detail over the telephone—but I assure you that it is not only legal, it serves the cause of justice. And the American Way of Life. Mom and her apple pie will thank you."

Pie is good. "I'm all for that."

"I knew you would be. When the deed is done, sweet little

rosy-cheeked children will sing songs about your derring-do, and those who had formerly pined to become astronauts or antiquarians will hence dream of growing up to be overly tall, joke-cracking tribal investigators."

"That's just a little over the top, Ralph."

"You are right, of course." A wistful sigh. "I never know when to stop."

"Last thing I want to know is—do I have to get myself horribly maimed or killed?"

"Only if you are determined to be a tragic hero."

AS CHARLIE Moon rolled on down the blacktop ribbon toward Granite Creek, he concentrated on pleasant thoughts. Like picking up Miss James. And finding out precisely what Ralph Briggs wanted in exchange for the *item*. After that, he and the lady would have a late dinner. A *romantic* dinner. Then, if he could work up the nerve . . .

AT THE COLUMBINE

SIDEWINDER DID not leave the rough plank surface of the Too Late bridge. The singular beast was still howling when the sun slipped into Dead Mule Notch, and a blood-red moon surfaced over the snowcapped Buckhorn range.

CHAPTER THIRTEEN

SUNDOWN

WHEN TWILIGHT DROPS ITS GRAY VEIL ACROSS THE FACE OF the land, the fabric of reality sometimes takes on an oddly pitched web and weave. Charlie Moon was not a superstitious man, nor given to fanciful imaginings, but the oddest notion kept running through his mind—that the woman at his side was not made of flesh and blood. The lady was composed of something less tangible. At any moment, she might simply . . . go away. As he piloted his automobile along a sinuous road lined with dark rows of spruce and pine, the Ute made an effort to banish the absurd idea from his mind. But every few minutes, he felt the urgent need to glance at the passenger seat—just to make sure the lovely, dark-haired woman was actually there.

She was. Miss James's delicate hand reached out. Touched his arm.

This got his attention.

Her dark eye caught his.

The happy man smiled.

His sweetheart had lost track of precisely where they were. As if someone might overhear, she whispered, "Is the restaurant way out here?"

"No," Moon said, adding in a casual tone, "I have a stop to make."

Miss James studied his dark profile. "Stop? What for?"

He shrugged. "Just some business."

She persisted. "What sort of business?"

"The kind it's better not to talk about." Moon managed an adequate poker face. Inside, he was grinning from ear to ear.

The woman made a pretense of being annoyed. "Very well. If you must be mysterious."

Better tell her something so she doesn't get overly curious. "I'm stopping at an antique store."

A doubtful look creased her brow. "I did not know that you were interested in antiquities."

"I like all kind of old stuff. Rusty pickups. Broken-down horses. Eighteen-year-old hounds." He grinned. "And—ah—mature women."

This earned him an elbow in the ribs.

"Ouch."

"I am almost sorry." Miss James reached out to caress the back of his neck. "Which antique store?"

His skin tingled under her touch. Suddenly, he could not remember the name of the business. "Belongs to a fella by the name of Briggs."

Her hand stopped halfway down his neck. "Ralph Briggs—owner of The Compleate Antiquarian?"

"Yeah. That's the place." He watched the painted white line slip past the car. "You know Ralph?"

"I met him once, at a party." She frowned at the Ute. "I understand that he shows his private collection only by appointment. To special friends."

"Well, me'n Ralph are old buddies." It went a bit deeper than that. Once upon a merry time, Charlie Moon and Scott Parris had done an interesting piece of work with Ralph Briggs. The process was not entirely legal, but, with the assistance of the antique dealer, a modicum of justice had been done. That had been back when he was still an officer with the Southern Ute Police Department—a long time before he'd gotten the title to the Columbine, and let the Southern Ute chairman Oscar Sweetwater talk him into doing part-time work as tribal investigator. He slowed the Expedition as they neared a blind curve, switched the headlights to low beam.

Miss James flashed a smile at her man. "I am terribly impressed that you are acquainted with Ralph Briggs." She clasped her hands like a child about to look under the tree on Christmas morning. "I can hardly wait to see the inside of The Compleate Antiquarian. There are rumors that Briggs has three priceless Tiffany lamps from the collection of—"

"Sorry, you can't come in."

"What?"

"You'll have to wait outside."

There was a taut silence before she said, "Charlie—tell me that you are joking."

Moon shook his head. "This is serious personal business. Between me and Ralph. But I'll see if I can get you inside next time."

"Golly gee, thanks a bushel and a peck."

"Sounds like you're a little upset."

"I am not a little upset." She pouted. "I am severely miffed."

"So what do you do when you get severely miffed—throw a fit?" He reached across the seat.

She took his hand in hers. Put it on her knee.

Moon swerved, hit the shoulder, came within inches of taking out a Do Not Pass sign before he got the big car back onto the blacktop.

"You really should concentrate on your driving." She offered this sober observation in the prim tone of a maiden who has very nearly been taken advantage of.

Moon was surprised to find both hands on the wheel. He remembered that it had been hilarious when SUPD officer Jim Wolfe had run off the road. *Guess I had it coming.*

The woman smiled. *Charlie is such a darling man—and so terribly cute.* "I still cannot believe you are such a brute. The very idea—leaving me sitting outside in the dark while you browse around in a fabulously exclusive antique shop with your old chum."

It took him a few heartbeats to find his voice. "I won't be doing any browsing. And it'll only be for ten minutes, tops." He took a deep breath. "Then we'll go have a fine dinner."

Miss James leaned over and whispered in his ear, "You still have not told me where."

He adjusted the rearview mirror until he saw the oval of her face. "How about the Blue Light?"

"That sounds very nice."

He had no doubt that it would be. It was a first-class joint. No one had been murdered there for almost a year.

CHAPTER FOURTEEN

SERIOUS BUSINESS

RALPH BRIGGS WAS SEATED ON A BALLOON-BACK ROSEWOOD chair, his knees under a Chippendale mahogany desk. The antiquarian was nattily attired in his customary work clothes—a three-piece gray wool suit, a pale blue linen shirt. A black bow tie was skillfully knotted at his collar; simple platinum links pinned his cuffs. He was quite the elegant figure—a fashion plate suitable for the cover of *American Antique Dealer's Monthly Journal*. Except for one detail: Like Huck Finn lolling on the riverbank on a muggy August afternoon, Ralph Briggs was barefoot. This very deliberate man did nothing without a purpose; there was a sensible reason for the naked feet. The meticulously neat housekeeper had removed his shoes to avoid soiling the fabulous Kilim prayer rug under the chair. Likewise his socks, because he enjoyed the pleasantly rough texture of the carpet on his toes. Behind him, tastefully displayed on a splendid John Goddard tea table, a Matthew Norman carriage clock nibbled away the seconds. Taking no thought of the diminishing number of ticks and tocks allotted to him, Ralph Briggs inked numbers into a leather-bound ledger. He attended to his accounting as if time could be purchased like bread or wine. Presently, the task was completed. He raised the lid of a cherry box that concealed a small control console, pressed an ivory button. Within two beats of his heart, waves of the Budapest Strings began to wash over him in great, soothing sweeps. The enchanted dance of Schubert's *Ständchen* carried him off to a distant, peaceful land.

Losing count of the golden minutes, Ralph Briggs sat with his eyes closed.

His reverie was interrupted by the throaty rumble of a V-8 engine, the crunching of seventeen-inch tires on gritty white gravel. He removed a priceless Abraham Louis Breguet timepiece from his vest pocket, stared at the elegant chronometer. *Eight fifty-nine. It must be Charles. The droll Indian chap is a full minute early.*

CHARLIE MOON switched off the ignition.

Miss James flashed a smile at her man. "You promise not to be too long?"

"I'll be back before you know I'm gone." He tarried for a moment, holding her hand.

THE FRONT of the antique shop was dominated by a fifteen-foot-wide plate-glass window. On each side of the large glazing was a narrow crank-operated ventilation window; each of these had been opened to allow a whiff of fresh air into the musty interior. Before the Ute had a chance to push the doorbell, Ralph Briggs opened the door. "Good evening, Charles."

"Hi, Ralph." Moon looked at the white man's bare feet. "Business been that bad?"

"Do not be snide." Briggs sat down on a nondescript three-legged stool, slipped on a pair of comfortable deer-skin moccasins, then got up to peer past the towering Ute. "Your major hug is in the car?"

"That's *main squeeze*."

"Do forgive my grammatical shortcomings. I must make a note to start hanging around pool halls and shopping malls so that I may master the vernacular."

"You are forgiven. And by the way, Miss James is my *only* squeeze."

"She is not coming in?"

"That's right."

"She doesn't know what you're up to, eh?" Briggs did not

wait for a reply. "Well, I suppose she will find some way to amuse herself during your absence." A twisting breeze stirred up the darkness. He squinted at the shuddering shadows cast by a congregation of quaking aspens, locked the door with a key.

Moon followed the proprietor of The Compleate Antiquarian past a carefully orchestrated array of furniture and glassware that suggested a posh Victorian parlor. Briggs stopped at a display case in the rear of the showroom, pointed. "There is the piece you have been lusting after. Allow me to say that I am both amazed and gratified that you exhibit such good taste."

The Ute was quite familiar with the small treasure, but he leaned to get a closer look. Among a dazzling array of glistening pearls and bejeweled butterflies was The Ring. The eternal circle was purest gold, the setting a brilliant green oval.

"I have never seen a finer emerald." Briggs said this in a reverent whisper.

Moon shot a sideways look at the fussy little man. "Ralph, I can't afford to get in trouble with my sweetheart, so I gotta ask—you dead sure that's the real McCoy?"

"No. I am a total charlatan, the setting is a piece of medicine-bottle glass, the ring is common brass." Briggs arched an eyebrow as he removed the item from the case, placed it on a small square of black velvet. "Frankly, I doubt you would know the difference. Though perhaps your fiancée would."

"She's not my fiancée yet." Dismissing the worrisome thought that she might say no, Moon focused his attention on the ring. "You really gonna let me have this for a dollar?"

"That is correct."

"And I don't have to kill anybody?"

"That is optional. Your choice." Ralph Briggs did not smile.

The tribal investigator searched the man's face and found nothing there. "What's this all about, Ralph?"

"During our telephone conversation, I mentioned the burglary of the Cassidy Museum."

"Right. According to the newspaper account, the night crawler got away with a bunch of rare coins."

"As well as a number of antique cameos. Though not of enormous monetary value, these baubles were very precious to Jane Cassidy. If you have kept up with the newspaper reports, you know that the wealthy lady has offered a reward of twenty thousand dollars for the return of the stolen goods."

"That did catch my eye."

Briggs's smile curled the tips of his neatly trimmed mustache. "Here is a piece of information that was not reported by the media: Only a few hours after the theft, and perhaps thirty minutes after the public announcement of the reward, I received a most interesting telephone call. It was in regard to—"

The Ute raised a palm. "Wait—don't tell me. Let me guess."

"You have my express permission. Guess away."

"Here's what happened," Moon said. "The masked guy with the bag called you, said he'd be glad to turn over the loot in exchange for the reward money."

"That is precisely what happened."

"Did you get a phone number on your caller ID?"

"Yes I did. It was a pay telephone in Pagosa Springs, a fact of which I have already informed the authorities. There were no useful prints found on the equipment—it had been wiped clean."

"But he figured that a well-known dealer in old stuff like yourself would be just the right fella to arrange an exchange."

Briggs sniffed. "To demonstrate the near-miraculous extent of my self-control, I will not express my overwhelming resentment of the phrase *old stuff*. But the caller evidently was aware of my reputation in the field of fine antiquities."

Moon noted the scowl on the antiquarian's face. "And this made you unhappy?"

"Please try to understand. While it would be quite a feather in my cap to facilitate the return of the stolen goods to the rightful owner, I did get a mite piqued when the rogue offered me ten percent of the reward as payment for arranging the exchange."

The tribal investigator grinned. "You wanted a bigger cut?"

"Please, Charles, do not be flippant."

Moon cocked his head. "You expect me to believe that for helping the rich lady get her stuff back—you would not accept a single greenback dollar?"

"I do indeed expect you to believe it. It is the unvarnished truth."

"Try and convince me."

"Charles, a man in my line of work cannot be seen to profit—even indirectly—from the commission of a felony. It would do irreparable damage to my reputation." A smirk twisted his lips. "You, on the other hand . . . well, I suppose one need not state the obvious."

MISS JAMES stared at the fascinating picture framed by the store window. *Charlie and Mr. Briggs seem to be having a rather serious discussion. What could they be talking about?*

MOON WATCHED the antiquarian's eyes. "You want me to deal with the burglar. Set up the exchange of the loot for the reward money."

Briggs nodded. "I do."

"I can see why you don't want to take a cut of the burglar's payoff—but I expect you'll want a split of whatever fee I might collect from the Cassidys."

"Certainly not. Under no conditions would I accept a thin dime."

The tribal investigator looked doubtful. "You really wouldn't?"

Briggs shook his shiny-bald head.

"Not a buffalo nickel?"

"Not a ha'penny, my friend."

"It makes me nervous when you call me 'friend.'"

"I am deeply hurt by that remark."

"Okay. I take it back. But tell me, Ralph—what's in this for you?"

"Well, if you must know, Jane Cassidy uses a significant portion of her considerable wealth to purchase antiques. Alas, I have collected very little in the way of commissions from her over the years. Virtually all of her trade is directed to an odious fellow in Boston who shall remain nameless, and a similar upstart who runs a rather pretentious South Broadway shop in Denver. But if I could get in Jane's good graces by seeing that her valuables are returned—well. Having refused any direct monetary remuneration for my services, I expect I would become Jane Cassidy's fair-haired boy. Which might very well translate into annual profits in the five-figure range for many years to come. And with no risk whatever to my reputation. Quite the opposite, in fact."

"Ralph, you are one clever guy." Moon glanced at the small man's moccasins. "And ethical all the way from the soles of your shoes to the skin of your feet."

The canny businessman was about to make a tart reply, thought better of it.

"But I bet getting on the rich lady's Christmas card list isn't all you want."

"You are surprisingly perceptive, Charles. What I want most of all is to see the thief rendered up to justice."

Moon frowned at the antiquarian. "Aside from offering you ten percent to set up the exchange, this presumed burglar has done something else to offend you?"

Ralph Briggs hesitated, then said, "When I informed the caller that I would not act as an intermediary between himself and Jane Cassidy, the blackguard *threatened* me."

The lawman adopted a professional tone: "What was the nature of the threat?"

"It was truly *hideous,* Charles. The scoundrel had the gall to suggest that if I did not assist him in this matter, he would see that the police got an anonymous tip—suggesting that *I* was implicated in the theft."

Moon managed not to laugh.

Briggs glared at the annoying man. "You are smirking. Say what's on your mind."

"It occurred to me that maybe this thief knows you. By reputation."

The little man bristled like a terrier about to make a lunge for the big dog's throat. "And what precisely does *that* mean?"

"Well, Ralph—you have been known to purchase an item without worrying much about where it came from."

Briggs closed his eyes, made a valiant effort to calm himself. "Not being so wonderfully perfect and pure as yourself, I may have occasionally made a slight error in judgment. But if I did, it was due to excessive enthusiasm when I was faced with the opportunity of acquiring a rare treasure, never with the conscious intent of professional misconduct. And I must add that it is unkind of you to make such allusions."

"Sorry. I didn't mean to hurt your feelings."

"Apology accepted." Briggs sniffed to show his displeasure. "Now let us proceed with the business at hand." He rubbed a finger across his immaculate mustache. "You can surely understand why I am determined to do everything in my power to see that the stolen property is returned, and the burglar dealt with. Severely."

Somewhat chastened, Moon turned the thing over in his mind. "Okay. I think I see the lay of the land. But why would this rich lady agree to hire me to act as middleman between her and the guy who's holding the loot?"

Briggs allowed himself a supercilious smile. "Aside from the twin facts that I trust you implicitly and am prepared to recommend you to Jane Cassidy as the right man for the job?"

"Despite the fact that I'm flattered senseless by your confidence, I'd like to know why I am Mr. Right."

Briggs leaned on the display case. "What if I told you that it is highly probable that the burglar is someone with whom you are acquainted?" It was apparent from the sparkle in his eye that he was highly pleased with himself. "In fact, I am virtually certain that I can *name* the person who called me."

"Ralph, I've always been of the opinion that *virtually* is one of those fuzzy cocklebur words—hiding out there somewhere in that big weed field between *dead sure* and *wild guess*. So give me a probability—is this a seven-to-three shot, or something better?"

"Oh very well, if you insist on being so boorishly quantitative." The antiquarian looked across the room, fixed his gaze on a magnificent ormolu candelabrum. From his pained expression, it was apparent that Briggs was involved in a difficult mental calculation. "Okay. I am *ninety-seven percent* certain that I can tell you the caller's name."

"Ninety-seven is a very agreeable number—in fact, I would go so far as to say it is prime."

"Then I have your undivided attention?"

"I am hanging on your every word."

"You will surely agree, my NBA-sized chum, that with the identity of the caller in your vest pocket, it would be a slam dunk for you to recover the Cassidy's stolen property and collect the entire twenty-thousand-dollar reward. Think of it—where else can you get a deal like that?"

"There is a minor issue that causes one to pause."

"Dear me, I hope you are not going to nitpick."

"What if your caller doesn't have the loot? This slicker may be holding an empty bag."

"Even if this person is a hoaxter, you cannot lose." Briggs pointed at the emerald ring. "To enlist your aid, I will have already sold you this fabulous piece of antique jewelry for the paltry sum of one dollar." He removed a spotless handkerchief from his breast pocket, polished away a thumbprint Moon had left on the glass display case. "The trouble with you is that you worry too much."

"Tell me why I shouldn't worry, Ralph."

"Because I am not a moron. I am well aware that it is a common practice for a person who has no connection to a burglary to cook up a scheme to collect the reward. This being so, I demanded proof that the presumed burglar was actually in possession of the Cassidy valuables." The antiquarian folded his handkerchief into a perfect square, pocketed it. "The caller described one of the coins burgled from the Cassidy collection. And the list of stolen coins was not made public until several days after he made the call."

"Aha—now we're getting somewhere. What did he describe?"

"A cent. More particularly, a large Liberty Cap cent."

The Ute was mildly disappointed. "A penny?"

Briggs snapped irritably. "This 'penny,' as you call it, was one of approximately one hundred and twelve thousand copper cents minted in the year seventeen hundred and ninety-three. And the condition of the Cassidy cent is Very Fine."

The Ute was unmoved. "So what's the very fine cent worth in common greenbacks?"

"Somewhere in the neighborhood of seven thousand."

"That is a pretty nice neighborhood. And there's no way anybody but the burglar or one of his pals could have known this particular Liberty Cap was part of the loot?"

"It is possible, but quite unlikely. The caller would have needed immediate access to the confidential list that was provided to local law-enforcement authorities." Briggs inspected his reflection in the display-case glazing, adjusted his bow tie. "Now are you satisfied that this is a rock-solid deal?"

"Nailing this guy who ruffled your feathers—this is really important to you?"

"Extremely. I will be quite satisfied if the snake ends up in the clink. Or severely injured. Or stone-cold dead, if the need for self-defense should require you to see to his demise." He enjoyed a dramatic pause. "So what say you, stalwart defender of truth and justice?"

"I say who is this guy who called you?"

"Not so fast, my crafty Indian friend. First, we shake hands to seal the deal."

This sounds too good to be completely on the level. But I can't see a hole in it. And Miss James will like the engagement ring. Charlie Moon grasped the white man's extended hand.

"Done," the antiquarian said, and gave him the emerald ring.

Moon reached into his pocket, paid the man with four shiny new quarter dollars.

Ralph Briggs beamed, stacked the quarters on the display case. "You know, when you first started sniffing around this display, I naturally assumed you were lusting after Chief Ouray's pistol."

The Ute eyed the .45-caliber Colt Peacemaker. "How do you know it was really his?"

"There is a rather unusual marking Ouray carved on the left grip," Briggs said. "Here, let me show you." He removed the heavy, single-action revolver from the display shelf, was passing it barrel-first to Charlie Moon when several things happened.

From outside, a terrified scream.

A splitting, cracking sound.

A bright red spot appeared on Ralph Briggs's shirt.

As the Peacemaker slipped from the antiquarian's hand, the tribal investigator went into a crouch, turned toward the window, instinctively reached for a pistol that was not strapped to his side. One thought flashed like lightning in his mind: *She's out there.*

THE PLATE glass exploded into ten thousand shards as the dark form of the Ute shattered the window.

The shooter was momentarily transfixed. The revolver slipped from cold fingers, clattered onto the ground.

COMING SO abruptly from the bright display room into the outer darkness, Charlie Moon was effectively blind. He took a few uncertain strides, bumped headlong into a porch pillar, stumbled down the steps. He attempted to shake off the effect of the encounter. The buzzing in his ears was gradually replaced with another sound. Whimpering. Now he could see the outlines of a grove of aspens, the peaked roof of the antique shop—and the form of someone on the gravel driveway only yards away.

In an instant, Charlie Moon was at her side.

She refused the comfort of his arms, fell into a fit of uncontrolled sobbing. Ignoring her protests, Moon scooped the woman up, carried her to his Expedition, deposited her on the rear seat. Having placed Miss James in the relative safety of the heavy automobile, he snatched his revolver and cell phone from the glove compartment, cocked the hammer, dialed 911.

CHAPTER FIFTEEN

DUTY CALLS

THE GRANITE CREEK CHIEF OF POLICE WAS ENJOYING A DE-
lightful dinner with a charming lady. And so far, it had been—
by Scott Parris's method of calibrating such encounters—a
100 percent perfect evening. Which is to say that he had not
dribbled clam chowder onto his new silk tie, or said anything
to offend the damsel's delicate sensibilities, or belched. Being
quite satisfied with his faultless behavior, the sandy-haired,
broad-shouldered man smiled across the linen-covered table
at the fetching woman who had a master's degree in something or other—and the *bluest* blue eyes that sparkled like she
knew a wonderful secret.

She was saying that she had been rereading *Lilie Lala*.

With a disarmingly earnest expression, Parris informed
her that the story was one of his favorites. *Why do I say things
like that?*

The pretty woman seemed surprised. "You are an admirer
of de Maupassant?"

He had gone too far to back down. "You bet your boots. I
buy all his new books—soon as they hit the street."

She leaned across the table, touched his hairy hand.
"Scott—you are just *precious*."

She likes me! His happy smile slipped away when he felt
the urgent vibration of the cell phone in his vest pocket. Hoping it would be a wrong number, Parris smiled apologetically

at his date, stuck the plastic thing against his ear, snapped, "Parris."

The GCPD dispatcher was abrupt and to the point: "Sir, we have a shooting."

The chief felt the expensive meal churn under his belt buckle. "Where?"

"That antique store out on Blackthorn Road."

Parris's hands went ice-cold. "Yeah, I know the place." *Please, God—don't let it be Ralph.* "What's the situation?"

"One down, male. The vic is the owner of the business, a Mr. Ralph Briggs. According to our caller, his condition is not good."

He closed his eyes. *Please, God—don't let Ralph die.*

"A male reported the shooting; there's also a female at the scene. Far as we can tell, neither suffered serious injury."

"Do we have the shooter?" *Or shooters?*

"No, sir."

"Do we have a description of the shooter?"

"Negative on that, sir."

Scott Parris shouted, "Well what in blue blazes *do* we have?"

His startled date dropped her dessert spoon.

The dispatcher's reply was delivered in a sullen monotone: "We have a gun, sir."

"Well at least there's *some* good news." He grinned reassuringly at the lady across the table. "Sorry, dispatch. Didn't mean to snap at you."

No response from the harassed dispatcher.

"Uh—who do we have on scene?"

"Whole evening shift. Officers Martin, Knox, Slocum. Plus some state cops. Captain Leggett is on the way, ETA about five minutes. An ambulance and two EMTs are already there."

Parris avoided looking directly at the attractive woman, who was twisting a napkin in her hands. "Tell Leggett I'll be there in fifteen minutes."

PUSHING THE aged red Volvo to its limit, the chief of police roared down Blackthorn Road just ahead of a spray of blue-gray exhaust that soaked up moonlight. A half mile away, he saw an alarming number of red and blue lights flashing. As he drew closer, Scott Parris estimated five units. *Looks like three of ours, couple of the state Smokeys.* He made a hard right, aimed the Volvo hood ornament up the long gravel driveway leading to The Compleate Antiquarian, where, according to the elegant sign, merchandise was SHOWN BY APPOINTMENT ONLY. The ambulance had already departed for Snyder Memorial. *I wonder if Ralph Briggs made it to the hospital alive.* He prayed for the twentieth time that the peppery little man would survive.

Scott Parris launched himself out of the Volvo, stalked past a pair of grim-faced state troopers. He likewise ignored officers "Rocks" Knox and "Piggy" Slocum. Knox, who lurched about on a wooden leg, was an absolutely fearless cop who could pass as a borderline lunatic six days out of seven. Piggy had a heart of pure gold and the mind of a slow ten-year-old. Lieutenant Alicia Martin, one of his ablest officers, was in a black-and-white with a dark-haired woman who was huddled in a blanket. The citizen did not appear to be injured, but Parris thought her face looked vaguely familiar. The chief was relieved to see Captain Bill Leggett, his second in command. Though Leggett was not gifted with an excess of imagination, he was a by-the-book cop who knew every page by heart. In addition to a flawless memory and an unflappable manner, the man had an IQ in the high 180s. "What've we got, Bill?"

Captain Leggett raised a rubber-gloved hand to display a revolver sealed in a tagged plastic bag. "One shot fired."

"Smith and Wesson?"

"That it is. Twenty-two caliber, two-inch barrel. And it's a fairly old one. May be a hard piece to trace."

Parris stared at the weapon. The standard-issue grips had been replaced with polished wood. Not walnut, though. And the custom grips, which were not checkered, looked to be relatively new.

Leggett looked toward the unit where Officer Martin was attending to the woman. "I guess you already know we've got a man shot. Mr. Briggs—owner of the establishment—took one in the chest. He's been transported to Snyder Memorial ER. The woman . . ." Leggett seemed to blush, though it was impossible to tell in the garish mixture of moonlight, head-lights, and red and blue flashes, "uh—we got us a small prob-lem with the female, who is a potential witness."

Parris squinted painfully at his subordinate. "What kind of problem?" *I hate problems.*

"The witness is almost incoherent. From what we've been able to get out of her, she can't ID the shooter. But she was scared out of her wits—apparently thought her boyfriend was going to be shot."

The chief of police struggled to keep an even voice. "Who's the woman?"

The embarrassed lieutenant avoided the boss's stare. "She hasn't given us a name."

"Where's her boyfriend?"

Leggett pointed his flashlight at a vehicle. "Over there."

Parris glanced at the trees, saw the Expedition, the tall, slender man. "Captain Leggett—is that who I think it is?"

"Yes, sir. I would say so."

The chief of police approached the Ute. "Charlie, you all right?"

Moon nodded.

"What happened here, partner?"

"Miss James wasn't hit." Charlie Moon's face flashed red and blue. "Ralph wasn't so lucky."

"I know." The chief of police clapped his hand on the Ute's back. "He's at Snyder Memorial."

Moon heard the dreaded question come out of his mouth: "Will he make it?"

Scott Parris looked up to the heavens. Summed up his total knowledge of the universe. "I don't know."

CHAPTER SIXTEEN

THE CONUNDRUM

HUNCHED FORWARD IN AN UNCOMFORTABLE SWIVEL CHAIR, Charlie Moon looked across Scott Parris's desk at the Granite Creek chief of police. "I went to the hospital to see Ralph. He's still in intensive care. Surgeon took the slug out, but he's got a collapsed lung and a couple of blood vessels severed. Floor nurse says he's in critical condition."

"Yeah, I know." Parris pressed the Hold All Calls button on his desktop telephone console. "He's been in a coma since the surgery."

Moon clasped his hands together, making a massive fist. "So what've we got on the shooting?"

Parris waved his arms in a gesture of futility. "I could talk for hours about what we *haven't* got." The sandy-haired man turned his head to look out a second-story window at the rocky creek whence the silver-mining settlement had taken its name in the early 1870s. "We haven't got a suspect. Despite Ralph telling you that he got a call from an unknown person who *claimed* to have the Cassidy Museum loot, I don't have a motive I can hang my hat on. And between you and Miss James, we don't have a witness who saw enough of the shooter to tell me whether the suspect is fat or thin, tall or short, male or . . ." He picked up a massive glass paperweight, turned it in his hands, stared at the object without seeing his distorted reflection on the curved surface. "Nobody even saw the perp drive away."

Charlie Moon stared at his scuffed boots. "Which would suggest that he was on foot. Or maybe he had his wheels parked a couple of hundred yards away—probably in that grove of pines down by the highway."

"Yeah," Parris said. "He could've cranked the engine, drove off without turning his lights on."

This wasn't going anywhere. "What about the weapon?"

Parris reached into a desk drawer, laid a transparent plastic bag on the polished oak surface. Hermetically sealed and tagged—along with the flattened slug recovered from Ralph Briggs's chest—this was the only significant piece of physical evidence in the shooting of the antiquarian.

Moon got up from the chair, leaned to study the deadly instrument. It was a .22-caliber Smith & Wesson revolver. Blued steel, custom rosewood grips. Two-inch barrel. Small enough for a man to drop into his hip pocket.

The chief of police smiled at the sidearm. "Pretty little thing, ain't it?"

"I guess it'd be too much to hope for some prints."

"There were some smudges. Nothing useful."

Moon grasped at another straw: "Any chance of tracing the owner?"

"State crime lab's working on it. FBI forensics also has a complete set of photographic data, serial number, and some sample slugs we shot into a barrel of water." Turning again to the window, the chief of police watched a small boy dangle a fishing line into Granite Creek. The ardent angler wished he were down there on the bank, casting one of his handmade mayfly lures onto the rolling waters. "This six-shooter was manufactured about sixty-five years ago. There have probably been at least a half-dozen owners over the years." He sighed. "But sooner or later, we'll turn up something." *And sooner or later, the Cubs will win the World Series.*

The tribal investigator reached out to touch the plastic bag, feel the steel surface of the precision machine beneath the 3-mil polyethylene film. "It's hard to believe this shooting was premeditated."

Parris replied, without taking his gaze off the stream,

"Yeah, I know what you mean. If I was going somewhere intending to pop lead at a fella I wanted dead—this little peashooter would not be my weapon of choice. Not even if I could stick the barrel in the guy's ear." He swiveled his chair to face the Ute. "So what does that suggest?"

Moon thought about it. "Try this on for size. What we're dealing with is a break-and-enter artist, like the guy who carted off the Cassidy valuables. The .22 is the burglar's pocket gun. It's not intended for any serious shooting—he packs it because it gives him a feeling of security. He shows up at Ralph Briggs's antique store after dark, hoping to conduct some business. The small windows on the porch are open. He comes close, hears Ralph telling me all about how some lowlife had called him about unloading the loot from the Cassidy burglary, how Ralph wants me to set up an ambush, put the arm on the felon when the stolen goods are exchanged for cash. The burglar took a dim view of this."

The chief of police propped his elbows on the desk, stared at his hands, made a peaked roof with his fingers. "But this shooter only plugged Ralph." He looked up at the Ute. "He never even takes a pop at you."

Moon wondered what was bothering his moody friend. "Bad guy knows Ralph can ID him, so Ralph is naturally his first priority. Burglar's first shot gets Ralph in the chest. I would've been his second target, but my sweetheart is screaming bloody murder, so he decides to call it a day."

The lawman allowed himself a thin smile. "I can imagine when you came crashing though that plate-glass window like a mountain gorilla on steroids, it must've unnerved the shooter some little bit. So he scrams without firing a second shot." Parris allowed his finger tent to collapse. "But aren't we lucky that he drops his piece."

"Fits with the burglar personality," the tribal investigator said. "The guy's a sneak thief—not a professional assassin. He panics, drops his pistol when things get out of hand." Moon frowned at the chief of police. "Scott, would you feel better if he'd shot me, then carried the gun away with him?"

Parris considered the last half of the question with some care.

The Ute assumed a hurt look. "I was hoping you'd speak up right away and say, 'No, pardner—why, I'd feel real bad if things had turned out that way.' "

"How's Miss James doing?" The chief of police played with a ballpoint pen. "She remember anything yet?"

"There's nothing to remember," Moon said. "I figure she heard the shot, yelled, got out of the car to come help me."

"Right. How is she holding up?"

"Under the circumstances, pretty good, I guess."

I guess? Parris grabbed this little thread, pulled on it. "You haven't seen her lately?"

Being of the firm opinion that this was no one's business but his own, the tribal investigator avoided a direct answer. "I'm having dinner with her tonight."

"Where? Sugar Bowl? Blue Light?"

Moon grinned. "None of your business."

"Well, I was only asking as a matter of—"

"Last thing I want is for the local chief of police to just happen to drop by our table, invite himself to a seat, start telling my lady long-winded lies about his many harrowing adventures as a Chicago cop in the pursuit of preserving law and order."

Parris snorted. "I can understand how a bumpus like you would not want any competition from a class-A ladies' man like myself."

"That's right. Not even when that ladies' man is old enough to be my father."

"Father is a little much." Parris seemed genuinely hurt by this remark. "I always thought of myself more like . . . well, an older brother."

Moon put on his hat. "Well, older brother, I'd like to hang around all day and keep you from getting any useful work done. But I got places to go and stuff to do."

The Granite Creek chief of police watched the tribal investigator depart. When the click of Ute's boots down the stairwell was but an echo in his memory, Scott Parris picked up the bagged firearm. He examined the Smith & Wesson .22 for the ninety-ninth time. And wondered whether Charlie Moon had noticed that this revolver was one of that special line manufactured for and marketed to a particular gender. It was, in point of fact—a LadySmith.

CHAPTER SEVENTEEN

THE LADY

THE RESTAURANT DOOR WAS MADE FROM TWO LAYERS OF aged spruce planks. These were fastened together with corroded one-inch brass bolts salvaged from steam engines and pumps abandoned eleven decades ago at the Orphaned Burro silver mine. Charlie Moon pushed the heavy door open for the lady. "You didn't need to drive. I could have picked you up."

"That's very sweet of you." Miss James gave him a quick, brittle smile. "But I'll be needing my car. I have an errand to run later."

In the center of the dining room, bathed in the soft glow of a honey-colored lamp, a bald, hawk-nosed pianist fingered the ivories on a massive Steinway. The twilight atmosphere vibrated with Chopin's Prelude in D flat major. Musical raindrops fell sweetly upon the few patrons.

An hour later, Charlie Moon was slicing succulent chunks off a twenty-ounce prime rib. The rancher silently computed the cost per pound at Phillipe's Streamside Restaurant—wished he could get 10 percent of that for his prime Columbine beef.

Having hardly touched her trout amandine, Miss James patted her lips with an embroidered cotton napkin. "It is an absolutely lovely place." She glanced at her date. "But terribly expensive."

Charlie Moon shrugged in a manful attempt to convey the impression that money meant nothing to him. In truth, the wallet he sat on felt tissue thin.

The pretty woman sipped at her iced tea. "Do you come here often?"

"Oh, sure. Me 'n the boys from the Columbine drop in here most Saturday afternoons to whoop it up during happy hour." There was a smile in his eyes. "That's when Moon Pies and RC Colas go for half price. And best of all," he nodded to indicate the pianist, "the ivory tickler dinks out the good stuff. Like 'Orange Blossom Special.' And 'She Don't Hear a Word That I Say.'"

"Yes," she said absently. "That sounds nice." The woman was looking past him. At a ghostly something only she could see.

A waiter in razor-creased black slacks, a pink silk shirt, and an immaculate white jacket materialized at Moon's elbow. Luis gave the couple dessert menus, promised to return in a moment, and vanished as magically as he had appeared.

Miss James made it known that she had no interest in dessert.

Charlie Moon took her hand in his, made it known that he had no interest in any woman but her.

Her hand was like ice.

The Ute had not been so scared since the ninth grade, when he asked Rachel Lopez to go to the movies with him. His throat was as dry as the high-plains dust blowing past the window. Moon put his free hand in his jacket pocket. "There's something I need to say."

The lady looked at her plate. "Charlie—please don't."

Moon tried to smile. "Don't what?"

She almost managed to meet his eyes. "I know what you're going to ask me."

He blinked. "You do?"

She nodded. "I would rather you did not." A single tear traced its way down her face.

He pulled his hand from his pocket. It was empty. He was empty.

She wiped the tear away, cleared her throat. "May I tell you a story?"

"Yeah," he croaked. "But make it a funny one. Right now I could use a good laugh."

"I'm afraid I cannot oblige you." She took a deep breath.

"This is a very, very sad story." Ever so slowly, ever so gently, she withdrew her hand from his. "Once upon a happy time, I had a wonderful man. Christopher. He was a police detective. We were very happy, and engaged to be married on the first day of June. It happened on the twenty-ninth of May. Chris went into a pawn shop to pick up something . . . something very special for me. But he—" She could not go on.

The tribal investigator nodded. "I believe I know the rest of the story." He'd heard it too many times.

Miss James forced the words from her mouth: "It was all so absurd. So . . . so needless." She put a hand over her eyes. "One minute he was alive and happy; the next moment he was dead." Her lips twisted into a bitter smile. "It was insane."

Moon didn't have to ask what this had to do with him. He knew.

But she told him. "The other night, when I thought you were going to be—" She shook her head as if to dispel the hateful memory. "It all came back to me." She gave him a pleading look. "Charlie, I could not go through that again. When Chris was shot and killed, I . . . I almost lost my mind."

Enough had been said. They dispensed with words.

After a six-minute eternity, Luis returned. Hands clasped behind his back, the waiter glanced meaningfully at the dessert menus on the table. Inquired what the lady wished.

Miss James's whisper, directed to no one in particular, was barely audible. The lady wished to go home.

Charlie Moon wished to be in another century. One with a smaller number. He asked for the check.

After he closed her car door, Moon leaned on the white Mercedes. "I'll call you in a couple of days. Or," he added in a hopeful tone, "maybe I'll drop by."

Her white-knuckled hands gripped the ivory steering wheel as if it were a life preserver. Miss James looked straight ahead. Toward a long, lonely road. The destination was hidden in darkness. "No."

Moon felt a numbness creeping along his limbs.

She raised her chin in a pathetic gesture of defiance. "I will not be there."

He tried to smile; it felt like his face might break. "Where'll you be?"

"Far, far away." She inserted the ignition key, cranked the engine.

He stared at her delicate profile. "When'll you be coming back?"

Miss James mouthed the words like an automaton: "I will not." She stepped on the gas pedal.

The tires kicked up gravel, pelting the Ute like a hail of bullets.

The wounded man watched the sleek automobile slip away. The taillights stared back at him until they disappeared over a distant rise in the prairie.

CHAPTER EIGHTEEN

THE BETTY LOU PRESCRIPTION

MORNING'S WARM BREATH SIGHED WITH THE WEEPING WIL-lows. Ripples skimmed across the face of the glacial lake, glittering reddish copper in the rising sun. The Columbine hound was curled up on the sandy bank, sleeping his life away. Charlie Moon sat on a cottonwood log, his gaze fastened on the water. He had achieved that state of being in which he was barely aware of his own existence.

Sidewinder awoke suddenly, raised his head in a jerking motion. The old dog blinked bloodshot eyes, rumbled a low growl.

Charlie heard the distant footsteps in the dry grass, recognized the measured gait. He did not turn to look.

The dog got to his feet, stretched a hind leg, yawned.

Scott Parris stopped at the shoreline, stared at a redwood sign. "Lake Jesse, is it?"

The silent Ute watched a ruffled-looking raven land on the charred limb of a lightning-killed ponderosa.

The Granite Creek chief of police seated himself on the log beside his friend. "Mild day for this time of year."

No response.

"Kinda makes a man want to just go somewhere and sit beside a lake."

"Yeah," the rancher muttered. *Where he don't have to put up with pointless conversation.*

Parris picked a smooth gray stone from the sandy beach, rolled it in his hand. "I sense that you're in a tetchy mood."

"I'm in tiptop temperament, thank you."

"No you ain't, Charlie. You just think you are."

"Thank you for setting me straight."

"You're welcome. And not only do I see that you have got the bluest kind of blues—I know *why* your guts are all tied in knots. Why you can't sleep a wink. Why you don't have any appetite. Why you—"

"If I was to suffer from any of those maladies, it might be because certain folks come around from time to time and annoy me half to death."

Distracted by a fat rainbow trout breaking the surface of Lake Jesse, Parris frowned at empty space. "Where was I?"

"You were about to tell me you can't stay but a minute because—"

"Oh yeah, I remember now. You want to hear why your guts are all tied in knots?"

"I would rather eat a cactus sandwich."

"Okay, if you twist my arm." Parris put on a satisfied expression. "You're all messed up because your woman left you."

Moon gave him a hard look. "Left me?"

"Aha—then you admit it!"

"I don't admit nothing."

Parris patted his best friend on the back. "Let it all out, pard."

"Okay. Here it comes—you are beginning to get on my nerves."

"Now that's the ticket. Heap abuse on your best buddy. Hey, I don't mind bein' bad-mouthed if it'll help my suffering friend. That's what I'm here for."

The Ute rolled his eyes.

Parris threw the stone, skipping it six times across the water. "When you was with her at Phillipe's overpriced hash house—did you pop the big question?"

"How'd you know we were at Phillipe's?"

Sidewinder came to sniff at Parris's knee, was rewarded

with a pat on the head. "I am the chief of police—I've got spies everywhere. But you didn't respond to my inquiry. Did you pop the question, or did you not?"

"That is none of your business."

"Everything in this county is my business." Parris gave the tribal investigator a sly look, tried to sound like he was making small talk. "You know where she's gone?"

"Ask one of your spies."

I bet you don't know. "It's just as well she dumped you. It would've never worked out between you and her."

"How do you figure that?"

"I'm a world-class expert on woman problems."

"Right."

"And I'm just the guy to tell you—you must not mope about." Scott Parris waved his hand to indicate the vast panorama before them. "There are plenty more women out there."

The Ute shaded his eyes from the sun and gazed at the empty prairie. "Amazing. I do not see a single one."

"Don't be a smart aleck. You know what I mean—you can't afford to get depressed about one solitary example of womanhood."

"She was one in a million."

Parris snapped his fingers. "That just goes to prove my point."

"Is this where you make a futile attempt to explain what you're talking about?"

"Of course—now listen close. You know well as I do that there's no use playing against a pat hand. So grit your teeth and look the odds straight in the eye. You said so yourself— Miss James is one in a million. But it is a known fact that not one woman in *eleven* million ends up married to a man who is seven feet tall in his bare feet."

Moon attempted to skip a flat pebble across the lake. He was shooting for at least a seven count. The stone sank after three feeble hops, did not rise again. "You are certain of this statistic?"

"Certainly. I looked it up in a book."

The hound scratched enthusiastically at his neck.

Charlie Moon had to say it: "I have to admit it—I was feeling fairly bad before you showed up."

"Thank you."

"Now I feel five hundred percent worse."

"Charlie, you are always jumping to conclusions. Like right now—you are wrong to assume that my work here is done. Fact is, I have not even got started."

"Somehow, this news does not encourage me."

Parris continued with an air of unshakable confidence. "Describing what your problem is—that's just the diagnosis. Me, I'm not one to point out a big ugly boil on my pardner's neck without being prepared to *lance* it." He reached into his pocket.

Moon cast a wary eye on the unpredictable white man. "If you pull a sharp-pointed knife outta your britches—"

"Try to remain calm." Parris produced an object strung on a steel ring. "Do you know what this is?"

Moon squinted at the display. "A car key?"

Parris shook his head.

"No?"

"Nay and negatory, my lovesick friend. This is Dr. Parris's prescription for what ails you." The chief of police got up from the log with a grunt, grinned down at his reluctant patient. "Let's ooze on back toward your big house. I got something to show you."

Knowing where they were going, the dog trotted along in front of the men.

IT WAS fire-engine red, streaked with glistening chrome, sitting confidently on big knobby tires. And it was parked right next to Charlie Moon's tired old F-150. *For the added advantage of contrast,* the Ute thought. *The way a pretty girl likes to sit beside a homely one.* He stared.

A satisfied grin split the white man's face. "You know what that is?"

The rancher frowned with intense concentration. "A pickup truck?"

Disappointed by his friend's lack of imagination, Parris shook his head. "That is not even close."

Moon shrugged. "Well, if I'm wrong I'll be the first to admit it." He pointed at the vehicle. "But you have to admit—it sure *looks* a lot like a pickup truck."

Parris threw his hands up in an eloquent gesture of frustration. "Charlie, this is not a pickup truck—this is *the* pickup truck. There ain't a four-wheel-drive buggy in the whole state of Colorado like this one."

This claim piqued the Ute's interest. "There ain't?"

"Or for that matter, in the whole United States of America. And I'm not just talking lower forty-eight." Parris tapped a blunt finger on the fender. "This here F-350 is a *bad* machine."

Moon reached out to touch the massive chrome bumper. "It does look like a woolly-booger all right. But I already got me a pickup."

Parris shook his head sadly at the beat-up F-150. "That thirty-year-old box on wheels was all right in its day. But the era of carburetors and manual chokes is long gone." The white man patted the bright red fender. "This is the twenty-first century."

"Don't remind me." The Ute was longing for an earlier, simpler time.

"Charlie, you just don't get it. This ain't just another beefed-up pickup—what we have here is practically the same thing as a Ford *concept* vehicle."

The rancher rested his boot on the bumper-mounted winch. "So what's the concept?"

"Bigger is better. More is macho. Traction is where the action is." He flashed a toothy smile at his friend. "Horsepower is what makes a man happy."

"Right at the moment, I'm not in the mood to be happy."

"Now there's the crux of your problem. This latest woman has left you like all the others. Sooner or later, you'll be prowling coffee shops, trying to pick up some cheap floozy who lives on green tea and organic prunes. But by and by, it'll all come to nothing. Like as not, you'll end up an old, lonely, cranky bachelor—with no friends at all except me." Parris glanced at Sidewinder. "And your dog will die."

Moon seemed untroubled. "Before or after you do?"

"You should take care not to hurt my feelings." Parris beamed at the pickup. "I brought this fine machine out here from the Happy Dan's Custom Trucks and Vans just for you. If you like it, Happy Dan will set you up with a killer deal. No money down, no payments for several months, zero percent interest."

"What's the gas mileage?"

Parris shook his head. "You know what's wrong with you, Chuck?"

"Is that what they call a rhetorical question?"

"What's wrong with you is you got a *attitude* problem."

"Maybe so. But I also got a bank account problem."

"Piffle."

"What?"

"*Piffle* is one of them fancy French words. It means you should not worrify yourself about the financial aspects of acquiring a vehicle of this singular nature."

"Do you intend to explain that remark?"

"Charlie, you are a rancher. A bona fide businessman who *needs* a truck like this to run his cattle operation." Parris knitted his brows into a frown. "In five words or less—you can write it off."

"Well, I depreciate that—but it'd still cost me a barrel of bank notes to—"

"Ol' buddy, you keep coming at this from the wrong direction. You should not think about the money. You should think about *accessories*."

For the first time since Miss James had left him, Moon grinned. "Loaded, huh?"

"Consider that winch you got your big muddy boot on. It's got two hundred feet of five-sixteenths-inch-diameter steel cable. And you know what else?"

Moon waited to hear what else.

"It's got remote control." He noted a flicker of interest on the Ute's face. "And I don't mean hardwired thirty feet from the dashboard. I'm talking radio control." Parris reached into the cab for a small plastic box. "You know what this is?"

Charlie Moon nodded. "I expect that's the remote-control unit."

"You are smarter than you look." Parris pressed a green button. "Watch this." The winch began to turn, unwinding a yard of shining cable. He pressed a red button to rewind the steel braid. "And that's just for starters." He pointed the small box at the pickup. "It's got GPS navigation system, with a nine-color map display."

"I thought four colors was enough."

Parris snorted. "A real red-white-and-blue American consumer don't settle for *enough*."

Unable to resist, Moon kicked the toe of his boot against a massive all-terrain tire.

"And don't forget the all-wheel ABS. A remote starter for those below-zero mornings—while you're sitting in your warm kitchen eating flapjacks and bacon, you press the button, fire up your supertruck. It'll be warm as toast before you finish your first cup of coffee. And the windows'll be defrosted."

"Bacon is okay, but I'd rather have pork sausage with my flapjacks."

"Then go ahead, that'll work just as well." Having been infected by the Ute's bad example, Parris also kicked a tire. "This baby is snowplow ready. It's completely set up for towing a ninety-foot trailer. And it's got plenty of gawr. Not to mention—"

"Wait a minute—what the heck's *gawr*?"

"Dang it all, Charlie, I don't know—but it's important." He had lost his place in the list of truckly virtues. "Did I mention heavy-duty air-conditioning for those sizzling summer days?"

"I don't think you did. But here at the Columbine we only have about six days of summer, so—"

"And a tilt steering wheel with speed control. Six-point-eight-liter Triton engine with three hundred and ten horsepower, four hundred and twenty-five pound-feet of torque at thirty-two hundred and fifty RPMs."

"Impressive numbers."

"You better believe it. Do you want me to tell you more about creature comforts?"

"Could I stop you?"

"Not unless you stuff a rag in my mouth. You got leather everywhere, heated front-seat cushions. You not only got standard AM-FM, you got high-tech satellite radio with one hundred and sixty-two channels. A ten-deck CD with wraparound sound like you never heard in a work truck before. Just imagine Johnny Cash rattling the windshield."

The Ute imagined it, and it was good.

"And on top of all that, an under-the-dash scanner that'll pick up police chatter a hundred miles away, even on a rainy day."

Moon nodded his approval.

"And besides all that, Betty Lou is—" Parris clamped his mouth shut.

"Betty who?"

The white man blushed to his ears.

Moon's face split in a grin. "You named the truck after your latest girlfriend."

"I did not," Parris snapped.

"Childhood sweetheart?"

"It's none of your business."

"Bet she was a high-school cheerleader."

The white man chewed on his lip.

"I am not going to let this go. You might as well tell me and get it over with."

"It was in the sixth grade. Betty Lou McWhorter was my first girlfriend." He mumbled, "Sort of."

Moon laughed. "Didn't much care for you, did she?"

Parris glared at the Indian. "Let's just drop the subject."

"Okay. But it occurs to me that a man does not name a horse unless he owns it." Moon looked in the cab. "This is *your* truck, ain't it?"

Parris shrugged. "Sort of."

"How long've you had it?"

"It was delivered last week."

"Worried that you can't make the payments, huh?"

The chief of Granite Creek PD pulled the brim of his felt hat down to shade his blue eyes. "The mayor of our unfair city promised me an eight-percent raise. Sad to say, the town council didn't come through. Claimed they needed every spare cent for sewer repairs and new schoolbooks." *Those morons have got their priorities all wrong.*

"Why not let the dealer take it back?"

"Charlie, I am a well-known public figure—I cannot be seen to welch on a deal with a local businessman. I got my image to think about. Besides, I've already named her." He patted the F-350 hood, "Giving Betty Lou back to Happy Dan now—why, it'd be like giving him my favorite dog."

"You don't have a dog."

Parris responded somewhat curtly, "I was speaking figuratively."

"So, figuratively speaking, you want me to take over the payments."

"I was kinda hoping . . ."

"I don't know if I could drive a truck that went by the name of Betty Lou." Moon frowned at the he-man machine. "I have to call it somethin' like Columbine Locomotive or Buffalo Hog or Big Red Chief or—"

"No!"

Moon stared at the white man.

"Once a man has named a dog or a horse or a pickup—the name *sticks.*"

Moon gave his best friend a doubtful look. "Well, I don't know. Betty Lou is kind of a sissy name for a muscle truck."

A hurt expression hung on Parris's face. "Do you want her or don't you?"

"I'll have to think about it." Moon thought about it.

"Well?"

"Maybe." Moon studied his warped image in the waxed sheen of a glistening fender. "Maybe not."

"Charlie, I know how to settle the issue." Parris smirked. "Without thinking about it, tell me this right away—what's her name?"

"Whose name?"

"Aha—you see? Just ten minutes with Betty Lou and you can't even remember her."

"Her name," the Ute said evenly, "is Miss James."

"What's the color of her eyes?"

"They're—"

"Don't bother making wild guesses. Admit I'm right."

The Ute assumed a pained expression. "Betty Lou." He sighed. "Every time I got behind the wheel, I'd be thinking about that pretty little McWhorter girl in the sixth grade. The one who detested you. And on top of that, you wouldn't even have your fine red pickup to take your mind off all the other women that've left you. That'd make me awfully sad."

Parris avoided the Indian's gaze. "There is one thing."

The Ute nodded. "You don't have to say a word. I know exactly what you want."

He eyed the unpredictable Indian. "You do?"

"Sure." Moon patted the pickup fender. "From time to time, you'd want to take Betty Lou out for a spin. Listen to some sad old songs on the CD about how My Sweet Baby's Left Me and All Kathy Gives Me Are Candy Kisses. Then you'll have to check the truck's coordinates on the GPS. Use that remote-control box to crank Betty Lou's winch back and forth a few times."

Scott Parris rubbed at his eye. "If you wouldn't mind."

"I'll have to think about it."

LATE THAT evening, shortly after Charlie Moon had returned from driving Scott Parris home in the magnificent red pickup truck, the rancher was seated by the fire. His eyes were closed as he listened to Mozart on the FM radio. Despite the fact that Miss James was gone, life was tolerable. No, it was better than that. For this moment, at least, life was *good*.

Too good to last.

The telephone rang.

It'll be Pete Bushman. The foreman called at all hours with reports of sick cattle, marauding cougars, cowboys that needed bailing out of jail, miscellaneous other calamities and a multitude of minor gripes and complaints. The owner of the ranch had decided to ignore the summons when it occurred to him—it might be *herself* calling. Without opening his eyes, Moon fumbled around on an oak stand by his rocking chair, found the offending instrument, said softly into it, "Columbine."

The voice of the tribal chairman barked in his ear. Oscar Sweetwater was in a highly agitated state.

Moon let the torrent of words sweep past him. "Okay. I'll be in your office tomorrow morning." The tribal investigator hung up the phone.

The complex strains of Mozart had been interrupted. A male announcer was reading a special weather alert.

A storm was moving in.

CHAPTER NINETEEN

SHIRLEY

CHARLIE MOON DECIDED TO DRIVE HIS "ON APPROVAL" PICKUP to the Southern Ute reservation. Not that he had any serious intention of spending scarce dollars on such a fancy machine. *What a working ranch needs is a rough-and-tough pickup. I'd be crazy to pick up the payments on something like this—what do I need with a nine-color GPS map and a ten-CD deck and all that other fancy stuff?* As he was passing through Granite Creek, Moon saw the neon sign at the drive-in where he habitually stopped for a tall cup of coffee, and instantly felt the need for caffeine. He pulled into the Chuckwagon Drive Up, found a vacancy at station 6. He pushed a button on the intercom, heard a garbled inquiry, requested a large coffee. Black with six packs of sugar.

The incoherent response might have been an urgent warning of an imminent invasion from the planet Zorp.

"Okay by me," Moon said. "Bring 'em on." He was a man who lived on the edge.

A long-legged, gum-chewing blonde emerged from the drive-in restaurant. A tray was balanced precariously on her palm; in the precise center of it was a super-size Styrofoam cup. She wore a crisp white blouse and a short red skirt. Though acutely missing Miss James, the Ute could not help but notice that this young lady was quite good-looking and then some.

She stopped chewing to gawk at the flashy F-350, flashed a saucy smile at the driver. "Wow—this is a real *tomcat* truck."

He grinned back at her. "You like it?"

"I just adore it."

"Then let me introduce you to Betty Lou."

Blondie did not see another passenger. "Who's that—your girlfriend?"

Moon shook his head, explained that Betty Lou was the truck's start-up name. And that a girlfriend was something he was minus.

The carhop was obviously relieved to hear this latter testimony. "Really?" She stroked the gleaming chrome side-view mirror, gave the gum an enthusiastic chew. "I'd just *die* for a bad set of wheels like this. Red is my favorite color."

It had not escaped Moon's attention that the truck's paint was a close match to her miniskirt.

She pointed a long crimson fingernail at the front bumper. "And that is just a *killer* winch."

"It's got remote control." His mouth was running on autopilot.

"No *kidding!*"

The driver felt a mind-numbing surge of foolish pride, then remembered that the vehicle was not his property. Not quite. Not yet.

She batted enormous glued-on eyelashes at him. "Uh—I almost forgot where I'm supposed to take this order. You *are* the coffee with extra sugar, aren't you?"

"That is what they call me."

The eyes blinked again, got bigger. "Just how much sugar do you like, sugar?"

He mumbled something, wondered what he'd said.

She gave the inside of the cab a once-over, passed him the cup. "Fancy truck like this must've set you back . . ." she paused to make a computation, "a good forty-five thousand, six hundred bucks."

She was within twelve dollars of Happy Dan's price. "You must know a lot about trucks."

"You must be rich." A sly smile. "That'll be a dollar twenty-five."

The land-poor rancher gave her a crisp new five-dollar bill, felt a sudden impulse to show off. "Keep the change."

"Wow—thanks!" Blondie stuck her head inside the window to peer at the dashboard, then locked eyes with the Ute. He could smell bubble gum on her breath. "I don't believe it—you actually got the nine-color GPS navigation unit."

"Sure I did. This is a serious pickup."

Her eyes sparkled with mischief. "What's the GAWR rating?"

Ohmigosh. That must be the gawr Scott was muttering about. He put on a virtuous look. "That's the sort of thing a real truck-driving man don't go around bragging about."

The carhop smirked. "You don't know, do you?"

This stung. "Well, I don't have it right on the tip of my tongue."

She assumed a superior, know-it-all look designed to annoy the lesser informed. "GAWR is the gross axle-weight rating—which is the maximum load for a single axle."

"Everybody knows that." *Smart aleck.*

"The GAWR number is on your truck's SCCL." The gum-chewing lass blew a small pink bubble that popped. "That's the Safety Compliance Certification Label, which is usually on the driver's door. If you'll open it, I'll show you where to look."

"I guess some fellas who pull in here like to look at labels and such." In an attempt to affect a rakish look, he pushed the Stetson back on his head. "But me, I'd rather look at you."

"I get off at two." She pulled his hat brim down over his eyebrows. "Why don't you drop by and take me for a ride."

"Uh . . ."

"What is it, honey pie—am I too forward?" She pouted prettily.

He adjusted the hat, shook his head. "It ain't exactly that."

"What then?"

Moon gave her a puzzled frown. "Well, I don't know

whether it's me you like—or my red pickup truck, which is loaded with every accessory the laws of economics allow."

The pretty girl laughed. "It's mainly your killer truck, sweetums." She looked him over. *Kinda skinny.* "But I think I could learn to like you too. If you was to be *nice* to me."

Moon was at a loss for words.

"Bobcat got your tongue?" She batted the synthetic lashes again. "My name's Shirley. Shirley Spoletto." She reached in to touch the leather-wrapped steering wheel. "What's yours?"

He grinned like an idiot. "Charlie."

Shirley Spoletto gave him a soul-searching look. "You might as well know—I got a weakness for tough-lookin' men who drive big, expensive pickup trucks. But I got to know something, Charlie-babe. And you tell me the honest truth— are you attracted to trashy women?"

He stared back into the big, green eyes, wondered how to avoid the trap. There was nothing to do but take a run at it. "No I don't—I prefer classy ladies like yourself."

She giggled.

That was a close call.

TWENTY MINUTES later, Charlie Moon was heading out of Granite Creek. South toward Durango and Ignacio.

He concluded that driving a brand-new truck had a way of encouraging a man to think brand-new thoughts. *A remote-control winch would come in handy when a cow falls into one of them deep arroyos. And if I ever got lost in a blizzard, that nine-color GPS gadget would come in real handy. Scott might be right—this truck could turn out to be a sensible investment. And I could write it off.*

CHAPTER TWENTY

THE POLITICIAN

SEATED ACROSS THE OVERSIZED DESK FROM THE TRIBAL CHAIR-
man, Charlie Moon noted that Oscar Sweetwater appeared
somewhat uneasy. The tribal investigator waited for the supreme
elected representative of the Southern Ute tribe to speak.

Oscar cleared his throat. "I guess you're wondering why I
asked you to drive all the way down here."

"Nope."

This response seemed to throw the old man off. He scowled
at Moon. "You must be in a hurry to get back to that big ranch."

Moon shook his head, glanced at his wristwatch. "You've
been paying me almost fifty cents a minute ever since I left the
Columbine. Plus expenses. The longer this takes, the bigger
the paycheck."

The chairman grunted. "Tribe's not made of money."

The contract employee grinned at the grumpy politician.

Oscar toyed with a handsome reproduction of an ancient
Mesa Verde black-on-white mug. It was filled with pencils,
ballpoint pens, paper clips, other odds and ends. "We got
some things to talk about." He projected a dark look at Moon.
"All highly confidential."

Moon's eyes twinkled with mischief. "Don't worry about
me blabbing. By the time I hit the street, I won't remember a
thing you said."

*Someday you'll make one crack too many and I'll fire you
on the spot.* The chairman removed a silver-plated mechanical

pencil from the Anasazi-style mug. "This thing about Jacob Gourd Rattle leaving his wife in *Cañon del Espiritu*. What do you think? I mean, why would the man do a thing like that?"

"Maybe Jacob and his wife had a fuss. He got mad, drove off."

Oscar nodded slowly. "But why was Jake in the canyon in the first place?"

"Is that a rhetorical question?"

"That's a question that wants an answer."

Moon dodged by posing his own question: "Does the SUPD have any leads on where Jacob is hiding out?"

The tribal chairman hesitated. "I've told the chief of police *not* to go looking for Mr. Gourd Rattle. His wife hasn't filed a complaint about his unexplained absence."

Moon understood. Jacob Gourd Rattle was an influential man in the tribe. There had even been talk that he might run against Oscar Sweetwater in the next election, and some of the oddsmakers thought Jacob had a fair chance of unseating the older man. Oscar was a highly cautious politician. He didn't intend to open himself up to charges that he had used the tribal police to smear Gourd Rattle's reputation—such as it was—by fueling rumors that the man had abandoned his wife in the snowy wilderness.

Oscar pointed the expensive mechanical pencil at Charlie Moon. "Did you know that back in the eighties, Gourd Rattle served three years of a seven-year sentence at Folsom?"

"I heard something about that." The whole tribe knew the story.

"Word is, he was involved in some kinda robbery." Oscar shook his head. "Him and some Colombian thug knocked over a liquor store or gas station or something. And that ain't all." Oscar put on an outraged expression. "From what I hear, he's knocked his *matukach* wife around some."

"Maybe Kicks Dogs is glad he's gone."

The chairman nodded. "If she's got half a brain." He drew a childish stick-figure man on a yellow pad, penciled in a six-sided star on its skinny torso. "I figure Jacob'll show up sooner or later."

"Yeah. I suppose he will." *But you didn't bring me a hundred miles to talk about Jacob Gourd Rattle's family problems.*

Oscar Sweetwater twisted the pencil this way and that, watched the lead pop in and out. "What do you know about this white man we hired on to the police force?"

"Jim Wolfe?"

"Do we have another *matukach* on the SUPD payroll?"

He's a bit testy today. "I don't keep up with the new hires. Since the last time I talked to him, Chief of Police Whitehorse might've loaded up the roster with North Koreans."

The chairman drew a hat on the stick-figure man. "What do you think about Officer Wolfe?"

"I've got lots of cattle and cowboys to occupy my thoughts. Nine days out of ten, I don't think about Jim Wolfe at all."

Oscar Sweetwater gave his consultant lawman a stern look. "I understand you were with Wolfe during the recent—ah—incident."

Moon pretended not to understand. "Which incident was that?"

"At the state police roadblock, when they treed that Apache—Felix Navarone." Oscar opened a three-ring notebook, squinted at a copy of the arrest report. "Navarone was charged with carrying an open container in his motor vehicle, resisting arrest, flight to avoid lawful arrest, assaulting an officer, and disturbing the peace."

The tribal investigator chuckled. "Oh yeah—*that* incident."

The chairman's tone was dryly sarcastic. "Seeing as how you're too busy with your ranch work to be concerned with affairs on the reservation, I will remind you that we are currently providing Mr. Felix Navarone with free room and board over at the tribal detention center."

"I hope he's happy with our hospitality."

Sweetwater snorted. "Not overly much, from what his lawyer tells us."

"By the way, that reminds me. Felix Navarone's attorney has hired Eddie Ganado. Eddie's training to be a legal aide."

"I know." Sweetwater continued his doodling. "Being so

tied up with your cattle and cowboys, how did you happen to find out about this?"

"Eddie came to see me on behalf of Navarone's attorney. She wanted to find out what I know about the Apache's arrest."

He glared at Moon. "And you didn't bother to tell me about that?"

"It slipped my mind, Oscar. A few hours later, I dang near got shot."

"Oh, right. You was with that white man who sells used furniture and stuff."

Moon wondered what Ralph Briggs would think about this description of his top-drawer antique business.

Oscar drew a scraggly-looking tree beside the stick-figure man on the pad. "Tell me about what happened between this wild Apache and our *matukach* cop."

"There's not that much to tell. Me and Wolfe show up at the DWI roadblock. Felix Navarone gets there about the same time, in this fifty-seven Chevy pickup. State policeman checks Navarone out, spots a open container. The Smokey orders Navarone to shut off the ignition and give him the keys. Navarone makes a run for it, climbs a tree." Moon decided to skip over Wolfe's stubborn insistence on tribal police jurisdiction. "When it becomes widely known among the state lawmen present that the man who shinnied up the cottonwood is an Apache, they'll think it best to let Officer Wolfe arrest him. And it turns out that Felix Navarone is willing to talk to Jim Wolfe, but only if the other cops move away from the tree. So they do, leaving Officer Wolfe with the treed man pretty much to himself."

The tribal chairman was staring holes in Charlie Moon. "What happened then?"

"I'm sure Wolfe did his best, Oscar. But he wasn't able to convince Mr. Navarone to climb down from the tree in an orderly manner." Moon shook his head. "In fact, before our SUPD cop was able to exchange more than a few words with him, Felix jumped off the limb like he planned to fly far away from there. But something must've went wrong with his flight plan, because he landed right on Wolfe."

The chairman raised a heavily veined hand. "You say he *jumped* out of the tree?"

"You heard me right."

"Mr. Navarone's attorney claims his client was shaken out of the tree. And that Officer Wolfe did the shaking."

"Doesn't surprise me Felix's lawyer would say something like that. It's her job to twist the truth to make things look better for the yahoo we got in the lockup."

"There's more." Oscar Sweetwater produced a pair of remote-control units, gave them an anxious look. "I can never figure out which one's for the tape machine, which one's for the TV." He pointed both units at a console in the corner, began pressing buttons at random.

Presently, the television screen crackled with electricity, turned a bright cobalt blue. Moments later, the tape began to turn. There were a couple of minutes of jerky frames from a fishing boat that Moon thought was on Navajo Lake. Then, quite abruptly, there was a scene filled with police cars and running cops. Off in the distance, a tree. A zoom of the camera's telescopic lens revealed a man in the cottonwood. Beneath the tree, the backside of an SUPD officer—Jim Wolfe, of course. Wolfe was making impatient gestures at the dark-skinned man on the limb a few feet above him. The treed man shook his head, said something. Wolfe moved to the trunk of the cottonwood, put his hand out as if to lean on it. Navarone toppled off the limb. The scene was momentarily blocked by the out-of-focus figure of an overweight tourist. Seconds later, the camera had the tree in view again. Officer Wolfe and Felix Navarone were rolling on the ground; the state police were rushing to give aid to their brother officer. A gaggle of tourists moved in front of the video camera.

The tribal chairman pressed the Stop button on the VCR remote unit. He got up to eject the videotape, turned to wave the plastic cartridge at Moon. "One of our tribal members was stopped at the roadblock. She happened to have a new video camera in the car. I found out about it, used up some favors to get the cassette. From what I'm told, this is the original tape—but there could have been a copy made. If Navarone's lawyer don't know about the tape yet, she will before long. And if she finds out I've got the original, she'll demand to see it and the tribe will have to give her a copy." Feeling the weight of responsibility heavy on his shoulders, Oscar Sweetwater sat down behind his desk. "Charlie, you were there. You *saw* what happened. You claim that Apache jumped out of the tree on Officer Wolfe. I believe you. But if Felix Navarone's lawyer gets up in front of a jury and tells 'em her client was *shaken* out of the cottonwood like he was some kind of animal, and pounced on by a Southern Ute police officer—this videotape could be used to support that allegation. We see Officer Wolfe reaching out for the trunk of the tree, then we see Felix Navarone fall off the limb. After that, we see our SUPD cop rassling around on the ground with Navarone. And though it wasn't in his report—and you haven't seen fit to mention it—I have it on good authority that Wolfe made verbal threats to kill the Apache."

"That kind of talk don't mean anything, Oscar. Wolfe had just been in a fight. He had his dander up."

"That's just your opinion. What matters is that Felix Navarone heard the threat made, and he told his lawyer about it. And his lawyer says she'll file a suit against the tribe if we don't turn that wild Apache loose." He began to count on his fingers. "Unlawful arrest and physical assault. Navarone has a dislocated shoulder." He grimaced. "And did you know Wolfe bit that Apache on the nose?"

Moon nodded. Barely suppressed a smile.

"Where was I? Oh yeah—the charges that nasty woman is threatening against our police department." Sweetwater counted the third and fourth fingers. "Harassment. Verbal threats of deadly violence." He glared at the tribal investigator as if Moon were responsible for this mess. "She'll ask for ten million dollars."

Lawyers made those kinds of threats five or six times a day. Moon thought Oscar was taking this far too seriously.

The chairman's face was like chiseled flint. "And that's not all. She claims Officer Wolfe is a bad cop. And that she can prove it."

"Wolfe must have a clean slate, or Wallace Whitehorse would've never hired him."

"No matter what's in Wolfe's file, there could be something ugly in his past. Something that lawyer has found out about—and could spring on us if this Navarone business goes to trial." He stared at Moon. "Officer Wolfe has become a liability."

The former SUPD policeman could hardly believe his ears. "Felix Navarone's attorney is pressuring the tribe to fire Officer Wolfe?"

Oscar felt a sudden surge of heartburn. "And you know why—much as I might like to do that—I can't." The chairman sighed. "If the tribe fires Wolfe without due cause, *he* can turn right around and sue us."

Moon nodded. "And Wolfe'd probably win." *And ought to.*

The old man set his jaw. "So you see the spot we're in." He pitched the videotape onto his desk. "I haven't told our legal counsel about this evidence."

Moon understood. Once the tribe's attorney had seen the tape, it would be his duty to turn it over to Felix Navarone's lawyer.

Oscar glared at the cassette. "Take that thing with you. I don't want to see it again."

"I wish I could be sure you're not telling me to destroy physical evidence."

"Of course I'm not. I want you to keep it somewhere safe and sound, in case I ever get asked about it while I'm under oath." Sweetwater's face crinkled into a sly smile. "Of course, if our tribal investigator has misplaced the videotape by then—or accidentally dropped it in the river . . ."

This had gone far enough. "Forget it, Oscar. You want it misplaced or dropped in the river, do it yourself."

"Oh, all right, Mr. Straight Arrow."

"Are we finished?"

"I am, but you're not. You are going to pay a call on Eddie Ganado."

Moon slipped the videocassette into his jacket pocket. "Why would I want to do that?"

The tribal chairman ignored this tart retort. "Seeing as how

Ganado's been hired by Navarone's lawyer, I imagine the lazy bum hangs around her office most of the time. So he'll know the scuttlebutt. You go find out whether that Navajo good-for-nothing knows that the tribe has the videotape." The politician had an afterthought: "And whether that lawyer is actually holding any serious bad news on Officer Wolfe."

"Why would Eddie Ganado tell me anything?"

"That's your department, Charlie. I don't care how you get the truth out of him. Twist his arm. Break his bones. Kick him around till he spills his guts all over the ground."

The old man watched too many of those old hard-boiled detective movies. "I've got some urgent work to do at the Columbine, then—"

Oscar was near the end of his patience. "I don't want to hear about how you're too busy branding cows and mending fences and singing Whoopee-Ti-Yi-Yo with your band of cutthroat cowboys to do your job for the People." He shook his finger at the tribal investigator. "We pay you good money, so for once you'll do your duty without any griping."

The hired gun looked the chairman straight in the eye. "Oscar, you are not paying me half enough to take all this guff." Moon removed a small leather wallet from his shirt pocket. "If you would like to have my badge, just say the word."

The chairman looked as if he were about to have a cardiac seizure, apoplectic fit, and major anxiety attack all rolled into one. "What would I do with your badge?"

"I am sorely tempted to tell you."

For a painful moment, the tribal investigator's part-time job teetered on the brink. Finally, the chairman blinked. "Oh, don't be so touchy. Soon as you have the time to spare, handle this business any way you want."

Moon returned the badge to his pocket. "I will take that as a heartfelt apology."

Oscar Sweetwater had an acidic reply on the tip of his tongue, wisely decided to swallow it.

Not wanting to depart on a sour note, Charlie Moon thought he would sweeten things up with a dash of whimsy. "There's one last thing." The tall man put the black Stetson on his head, hesitated as if this was a difficult subject to bring up. "It's about a matter of professional pride."

Oscar Sweetwater never knew what to expect from this mercurial employee. "What?"

"I know it'll sound downright petty. But you have one, with your name on it. And so does Wallace Whitehorse." Charlie Moon looked out the window, to the spot where the big F-350 gleamed redly in the sun. "A tribal investigator should have a reserved parking space."

The chairman leaned on the desk, hands clenched over his face. "Please, Charlie—just go away and let me be."

CHAPTER TWENTY-ONE

THE NAVAJO TENANT

AFTER SEVERAL MILES ON A BAD ROAD THAT GOT WORSE WITH every jarring minute, Charlie Moon slowed the red pickup to a growling crawl, steered around a crater that appeared to be the result of either hostile mortar fire or a recent meteor impact. At a point where the road was petering off into a week-choked, boulder-strewn trail, he spotted a dented steel mailbox fixed to a fence post. The owner of the receptacle had used a Magic Marker to inscribe his name on it: E GANADO.

The rusty flag on the box looked as if decades had passed since it had been raised to announce the arrival of incoming mail.

Moon nosed the F-350 onto a narrow dirt lane that snaked through a drab little apple orchard. Scrawny limbs reached out to scratch at the truck. A fat raccoon waddled across the driveway, its rump disappearing into a clump of huckleberry bushes.

Eddie Ganado's rickety old house was hunkered down on a scrubby clearing between the orchard and a large bean field. The front windows of the rented home had no curtains, and the sun-yellowed shades were pulled more than halfway down, leaving the impression of sullen, heavy-lidded eyes— as if the derelict building had woken up with a bad hangover and wished to be left alone. The yard was dotted with a variety of hardy bushes that had sprouted from seeds sown by the winds—and a single, lonely, anemic-looking elm. An aluminum-paneled garage was set near the north side of the modest dwelling. Much farther from the house, a rusty-roofed barn leaned precariously, seemingly supported by a capricious enchantment that might be withdrawn at any moment.

The only sight to please the eye was Ganado's yellow Pontiac. But even this product of Detroit's glory days had lost its sheen. Parked under a fanlike branch of the elm, the sleek convertible was spotted from occasional spitting rains and intermittent dust-laden winds. Above the classic automobile, parched leaves chattered inanely with the breeze. Moon wondered whether the tribal chairman, who had rented the dismal property to Ganado, was looking for an excuse to evict him.

Having heard the pickup coming when it was almost a mile away, Eduardo Ganado stood at a window, waiting to see who his visitor would be—hoping it was not that person he least wanted to see.

Charlie Moon pulled to a stop behind the Pontiac, waited. After a full minute, he saw the door on the front porch open. Eddie Ganado emerged, a pump shotgun resting easily in the crook of his arm. Wondering what the eccentric Navajo was afraid of, Moon got out of the pickup. As he approached the porch, he instinctively crooked his elbow, placing his right hand a couple of inches closer to the .357 Magnum revolver strapped onto his hip.

This subtle move was not lost on the Navajo, who kept a wary eye on the tall Ute.

Charlie Moon smiled as he broke the silence: "You're well armed, Eddie."

"Thought I heard a prowler last night." He hesitated, then leaned the shotgun against a dilapidated chair. "Prob'ly just a bear, rustling around in my trash barrel."

Moon allowed his arm to straighten out by his side.

The cuts on Eddie's face were almost healed, but the small, circular white scars remained like a persistent pox. The bandages on his head had been replaced with a patch of dirty gauze secured with a piece of duct tape. "How's your scalp coming along?"

"Okay." Ganado limped a few steps, reached out to pump

the visitor's hand. "When I got tired of paying twenty dollars a pop to that nurse at the clinic, I started doctorin' myself."

From habit, the lawman scanned the shabby grounds. No sign of a dog. A pane in a loft window was cracked. The steel roof was rusted in several spots. A shiny new television antenna was mounted on a sandstone-and-cement chimney. A cord of firewood—all cottonwood logs—was stacked neatly against the side of the garage. It was not nearly enough for the long winter, and there was no propane tank in sight. "How long you been living here?"

"Almost three years now." Ganado's dark eyes followed the Ute's gaze with a curious, almost surprised expression, as if he were examining the rental property for the first time. He tried to think of a compliment to apply to this seedy estate. "It's quiet." He made a sideways nod. "Come on inside—I'll get you a cold brew." And then he remembered whom he was talking to. "Or a soft drink."

"Thanks anyway." Moon hitched his thumbs in his belt. "I won't be here that long."

"This a social call?" Ganado sounded hopeful.

"Wish it was. The chairman sent me out here to have a few words with you."

"What for? I ain't behind in my rent."

"This is not about your rent." Moon looked up at the thirsty elm, decided he might as well have some fun. "It's a legal matter." He paused to let that sink in.

It did. And hit bottom. "About what?"

"Eddie, you have attempted to influence a witness to a criminal offense."

"Says who?"

"Says me. You tried to talk me into lying about what I saw when Felix Navarone jumped out of that tree and assaulted Officer Wolfe."

"No I didn't, all I did was—"

"If your employer decides to sue the tribe over Navarone's arrest, I'll have to get on the stand and tell the whole truth and nothing but."

"Look, Charlie—I was just doing my job for that lawyer. I

didn't mean to suggest that you should say somethin' that wasn't true." His voice took on a whining tone. "Let's talk about this—maybe there's some way we can work it out."

"Under the circumstances," the tribal investigator said, "it is hard for me to do any serious talking."

Ganado's broad face mirrored his puzzlement.

"Before I can carry on a serious conversation," Moon explained, "I need to put my foot up on something." He looked around. "Like a sawhorse, a tree stump, or a keg of nails."

The Navajo stared at the eccentric Ute. "I don't have no sawhorse or nail keg—but I got a stump out back of the house."

Moon was cheered by this news. "Then let's go to it."

He followed the limping man through a space between the house and the garage.

Ganado pointed at a crumbly stump.

The Ute made a close examination. "I don't mean to be overly critical, Eddie—but this is not a good talking stump. It's sawed off too close to the ground, and it's rotten old cottonwood."

Moon's host wished it to be known that he was not responsible for this deficiency in his hospitality. "That stump was here when I rented the place from Oscar Sweetwater—and it was rotten then."

"I was hoping for a pine stump." With undisguised disappointment, the tribal investigator kicked at the offensive wooden corpse.

Ganado's tone took on an edge. "Well, I'm sorry as I can be, but that's the only stump I got." *Grandma was right—all these Utes have a crazy streak.*

Moon took a look at the lay of the land, pointed to a gasoline-powered irrigation pump at the edge of a ten-acre bean field. "I'll give that a try."

Relieved, the Navajo followed the Ute to the substitute for a stump.

Moon rested his boot on the pump. "These your soybeans, Eddie?"

Ganado seemed mildly amused by the notion. "Nah. Oscar

Sweetwater leases this field out to one of them stiff-necked Mormon farmers down by Arboles."

The tribal investigator made a small probe: "So how's your job going?"

"Oh, okay I guess. But I don't expect I'll stay there much longer." With minimal effort, he made an ugly face. "That lawyer wants me to take a class at the university—learn how to use a computer." To demonstrate his contempt for such a fool idea, he spat on a dusty bean plant.

"And you'd rather be a full-time unemployed person."

A listless shrug. "Till something better comes along."

Realizing that a subtle approach would be wasted on Ganado, Moon cut right to the bone: "Does that Apache's lawyer really think she can make trouble for the tribe?"

"Hey, she don't tell me nothing." Ganado hesitated. "But I think she's like to cut a deal to get Mr. Navarone sprung." He kicked at a clod of dirt. "Mr. Navarone says that white SUPD cop shook him outta the tree—and would've killed him if those state cops hadn't pulled him off."

The tribal investigator studied the irrigation-pump motor as if the rusty machinery held a special fascination. "On the way here, I stopped off at the junction of Route 160 and 151. Which is where Felix Navarone bailed out of his pickup, ran from the state cop, and climbed the tree."

Eduardo Ganado ran his hand through his mangled mat of hair, laughed. "That Felix—he always was kinda excitable."

Felix? This use of the Apache's first name surprised Moon. Up to now the jailbird had simply been "Mr. Navarone" to Ganado. "You knew the Apache before he was jailed?"

The Navajo squinted at the bean field. "Sure. That's what makes me so useful to the law firm. Within a coupla hundred miles, there ain't a dozen people worth knowing that I don't know. I can tell you the names of their kids. And dogs." He hurried on. "And I know lots of other stuff that comes in handy in the lawyer business."

Moon gave the man an appraising look. "What do you know about pi?"

Ganado blinked at the Ute. "What kinda pie?"

"The diametric kind." Moon put a hand into his jacket pocket, produced a paper tape measure. "That tree Navarone climbed has a nice round trunk that's thirty-one and a half inches around, which makes it ten inches in diameter. Give or take a smidgen."

Ganado continued to stare at the calculating man.

"That Apache climbed a sturdy tree. Even if he'd had a half-dozen state troopers helping him, Officer Wolfe couldn't have shook it hard enough to make one of last year's dead leaves fall off a branch. Let alone Felix Navarone, who was holding on like a leech—until he made up his mind to let go and jump on a trusted employee of the Southern Ute Police Department. Which amounts to deliberate physical assault on a sworn officer of the law."

Ganado performed his characteristic shrug, indicating that it mattered not to him whether Felix Navarone had jumped or fallen, or whether he ever got out of jail.

"And besides myself and the state police, there are some other witnesses that saw what happened." Charlie Moon watched the Navajo's flat black eyes. "There were quite a lot of travelers stopped on the highway, gawking at the show. And lots of tourists carry cameras with them. Maybe one of 'em took a snapshot that'll show Navarone jumping off the tree limb."

Ganado's face expressed his acute disinterest in picture-taking tourists.

Well, that's that. "Eddie, I'm going to offer you some sound advice." He watched Ganado's jaw muscles go taut. "Don't get on the wrong side of Oscar Sweetwater. The tribal chairman is a contrary old man. And he'll always find a way get even with a fella who crosses him."

"I'll keep that in mind." He looked pointedly at Moon's red pickup.

Moon took the measure of his shadow, which stretched two yards from his boots. "Guess I'd better be rolling on down the road."

Eduardo Ganado did nothing to delay his guest's departure.

THE SECRET SIN

DAISY PERIKA performed the secret ritual once every twenty-four hours, always at the appointed time. The marginal Catholic would wait until her home had fallen into the deep trough of night. In the darkness, it seemed less likely that God would notice what she was up to. He would be busy keeping track of those millions of Chinese on the sunny side of the world.

After making certain that the windows were tightly curtained, the aged woman would take the black shoe box from the kitchen cabinet, put it on the dining table, and remove the lid. Among the potions and herbs and odds and ends and this and that was the object of her special affection. Hands trembling, Daisy would withdraw the K'os Largo horned-star pendant that she had *liberated* from SUPD officer Jim Wolfe.

This midnight was much like the others.

Daisy alternately gazed at the lump of turquoise, pressed it against her wrinkled face, imagined how she would use the magic in the stone to find lost objects, heal deadly diseases—even see through that heavy veil that cloaks the future from the eyes of ordinary mortals. The shaman could *feel* the power in the silver-marbled stone. She also felt something else—a nagging sting of guilt.

The tough old warrior struggled valiantly with her conscience. Daisy's weapons were a characteristic stubbornness combined with an inventive flair to rationalize her banal theft into an act of unparalleled virtue. After all, it was not like this pendant had actually belonged to that silly white man. Those *matukach* think they can buy anything with money, but the People know it isn't so. The treasure had once belonged to Hasteen K'os Largo, but the Navajo medicine man was dead and gone. Daisy assured herself that if she knew who K'os Largo's grandchildren were, she would certainly return the precious object to them. The tribal elder piously imagined a simple ceremony down at Window Rock, where she would present the horned star to the dead man's grateful descendants. She would make a brief but stirring speech about how the Utes and Navajos should forget past disputes and work harder to get along.

But that ugly old Navajo man probably never did find himself a woman who'd give him any children. So until I hear he's got some family still alive, it's up to me to take good care of his property.

CHAPTER TWENTY-TWO

LUNCH WITH OSCAR

IT WAS MIDAFTERNOON AT ANGEL'S CAFE, A SLOW TIME WHEN a single waitress could tend to the few patrons. On this particular day, the hash slinger assigned to this duty had taken the afternoon off, to drive her mother to the dentist in Durango. *Or so she claimed.* Made hard and cynical by his three decades in the restaurant business, Angel Martinez did not believe his employee's tale for a microsecond. But the harried businessman had no alternative but to act as cashier, cook's helper, dishwasher, and waiter.

And so it was that Angel headed for a corner table where the Southern Ute tribal chairman was seated with Charlie Moon. The Ute politician had already expressed his wish for privacy; Oscar Sweetwater had even had the gall to direct the owner of the establishment not to seat other customers anywhere near him and Charlie Moon—this was a business meeting. It was mutually understood that the restaurant counted on tribal members for a large proportion of its business, so the proprietor had promised that the Utes would not be disturbed. Now, Angel signaled his approached by clearing his throat, and inwardly winced as the conversation between the Indians stopped. The hardworking Hispanic forced a bright smile, rubbed his hands on a dish towel tucked in his belt. "You fellas ready to order?"

The crusty old Ute picked up the plasticized menu, pointed his forefinger at the soup of the day. "With crackers," he said.

"You want your usual glass of milk?"

Oscar Sweetwater nodded.

Angel smiled hopefully at the younger man, who was always polite.

Charlie Moon selected the catfish dinner with great northern beans, home fries, and coffee. And an extra side of hush puppies.

Angel inscribed each detail on his order pad with the exquisite care a nineteenth-century journalist would have used to record the Gettysburg address.

Moon pointed to the tribal elder. "And don't bring two checks—Oscar's buying."

After the restaurateur had hurried away to shout instructions at a sweating cook, Sweetwater took half a minute to unwrap a paper napkin that enfolded the stainless steel flatware. He gazed with childish fascination at his distorted reflection on the convex side of a spoon. "So you went to see Eddie Ganado—what did you find out from that lazy Navajo?"

The tribal investigator watched a pretty girl pass by the cafe window. "Ganado may not be working for Felix Navarone's lawyer much longer. He said he was thinking about quitting."

The tribal chairman scowled at his part-time employee. "More likely, he'll get fired for stealing stationery."

"And I don't think Navarone's lawyer has any dirt on Officer Wolfe," Moon said. "I expect she's throwing a bluff."

Sweetwater nodded halfheartedly. "Maybe. But if Navarone goes to trial, she'll claim our cop shook the tree and made that crazy Apache fall off the limb."

"Officer Wolfe didn't shake Navarone off a limb. That cottonwood's almost a foot thick. A nine-hundred-pound gorilla couldn't shake that tree hard enough to—"

"I don't care whether that *matukach* cop shook the tree or not," Sweetwater said. He looked around the empty restaurant, lowered his voice. "What about the videotape—does that Apache's lawyer know about it?"

Moon took his time stirring six teaspoons of sugar into the black coffee. "If she does, Ganado hasn't heard anything about it."

Sweetwater was fascinated by the tribal investigator's methods. "How did you figure that out?"

"I mentioned that maybe one of the tourists at the roadblock had taken a snapshot while the Apache was up the tree. If Ganado had known about the video, I would've seen it in his eyes." Moon sipped at the sugary coffee.

Sweetwater closed his eyes, massaged the lids with his thumbs. "I still don't feel good about that tape. She's threatening to sue the tribe big-time."

"Oscar, you want my recommendation?"

"Say what's on your mind."

"Call that lawyer's hand. Watch her fold."

Sweetwater eyed the tribal investigator. Charlie Moon had good instincts. "How sure are you?"

Moon stared at the shimmering surface of the coffee. "Ninety percent."

Angel brought their food to the table. As he hurried away from the secretive Utes, he amused himself with a frivolous thought: *They're probably planning a horse-stealing raid against the Arapahos.*

Oscar Sweetwater ate his mushroom soup with considerable deliberation, taking sufficient time to enjoy each mouthful. He watched the younger man wolf down the oily catfish, gas-generating beans, and deep-fried potatoes. The tribal elder—who had a tricky gallbladder and all sorts of colonic complaints—would have given a month's salary to be able to eat just one or two of the grease-soaked hush puppies on Moon's platter. He waited until the tribal investigator had wiped his mouth with a paper napkin, then prepared to announce a decision he had made hours earlier. "You're the best poker player for a hundred miles."

A hundred? Charlie Moon thought this faint praise indeed, but on account of excessive modesty he did not protest.

Oscar Sweetwater turned the empty milk glass in his hands, watched the blue neon script of the *ANGEL'S* sign reflect off the cylindrical surface. "So if you say the lawyer is bluffing, I expect you're probably right." Sweetwater heaved a heavy sigh. "But I can't afford to get the tribe involved in a lawsuit—even if there's just one chance in ten the Apache might win. We're bringing in good money off the gas wells and real estate and the casino, but we've got every dollar allocated. The risk is just too big to take."

Our tribal chairman is throwing in his hand before he sees what the lawyer is holding. Moon squinted at the desserts listed on a board over the lunch counter. *Blueberry pie and vanilla ice cream sounds good.*

"I'll going to make some calls," Sweetwater said. "Get that troublesome Apache cut loose, but without the tribe losing face. I don't want it looking like I caved in to his two-bit lawyer's threats."

Which is just what you're doing. "What about Jim Wolfe?"

Sweetwater's black eyes popped fire. "What about him?"

"Wolfe was the arresting officer."

"So?"

"So arresting officers have a peculiar habit of getting highly annoyed when they make a righteous bust—and somebody upstairs turns the bad guy loose on a technicality. And in this case, there's not even a technicality. Wolfe got Felix Navarone dead to rights."

"That white cop can get annoyed if he wants to." Sweetwater banged the glass on the table, sloshing milk on his thumb. "He has a complaint, he can take it to Chief of Police Wallace Whitehorse."

Moon had expected some such response. "Turning the Apache felon loose will make for bad morale in the whole Southern Ute Police Department. From Wallace Whitehorse down to the part-time janitor."

"I don't give a hooty-toot about morale," Sweetwater snapped. "Let them spoiled cops go suck their thumbs. I've got a responsibility to protect the tribe."

"I have a responsibility too."

"Which is?"

"Advising my duly elected tribal chairman about the likely consequences of the actions under consideration."

Oscar Sweetwater leaned forward in a mildly belligerent manner. "Okay. Advise. What would you do if you was me?"

"Keep the Apache in the clink. Report his lawyer to the state bar association." Moon grinned merrily. "Charge her with—oh, I don't know—slandering one of our officers. Overbearing barristry. Whatever's likely to rattle her cage."

The tribal chairman snorted at this. "I never mess with lawyers or rattlesnakes. The decision is made—Felix Navarone will be back on the street soon as I can make it happen."

"You're the boss." Moon waved at Angel, requested a generous serving of blueberry pie à la mode.

Angel removed a fresh pie from the display case. "Quarter cut?"

Moon allowed as how this would be just barely sufficient, then smiled at the tribal chairman. "Now that business is done, why don't you settle down and enjoy yourself. Order some dessert."

The dyspeptic tribal elder grimaced.

"Not even a little bowl of ice cream?"

Sweetwater laid two fingers on his jaw. "Cold stuff hurts my teeth."

"How about a slab of hot apple pie?"

"Hot stuff hurts my teeth too."

"I'm sure Angel would be glad to bring you some room-temperature pie if that would—"

"Stop tempting me, Charlie." The old man grinned in a most unpleasant fashion. "Besides, our business isn't quite finished."

"Uh-oh."

"I want you to have a powwow with that *matukach* cop."

"And what will me and Officer Wolfe pow and wow about?"

Sweetwater pointed his finger at the insubordinate subordinate. "The facts of life. Explain to him how I am the Big Chief. How he ain't even an Indian."

"That's pretty cold, Oscar."

"Try this for cold—just a few hours ago, Felix Navarone's lawyer filed papers for a restraining order to keep Officer Wolfe at least a hundred yards away from her client."

Moon assumed his poker face. *I should have seen that coming.* "It's a standard tactic prior to a harassment charge."

Beaming with pride at his cook's culinary craftsmanship,

Angel delivered 25 percent of a blueberry pie. Centered on a dinner plate, the succulent slab was cunningly flanked by four scoops of French vanilla ice cream.

Moon made appropriately appreciative remarks.

Angel discretely placed a check on the table, went away happy.

Oscar Sweetwater stared longingly at the dessert before glancing at his wristwatch. He mumbled something about being late for another meeting, got up with an old man's painful groan.

"Hold on," Moon said. "You're forgetting something." He pointed at the bill.

"Put it on your expense account," Oscar said. The old man walked away stiff-legged, but with a smile on his weathered face.

THE UTE had almost finished his pie when an old friend happened by. Father Raes Delfino leaned on the table. "Hello, Charlie. May I join you?"

Moon kicked out a chair. "Can I buy you something to eat?"

"Thank you." The Catholic priest seated himself, bellied up to the table. "A bowl of soup would do nicely."

The tribal investigator and the man of God discussed the comparable merits of green chili stew and chicken noodle soup. Father Raes settled on the latter. As he crumbled two crispy saltines into the bowl, the Jesuit frowned at his meal. "The bishop has approved my request for retirement. My replacement should be here within the month."

Charlie Moon could think of nothing useful to say. "Where will you be going?"

Father Raes polished his spoon with a napkin. "Someplace remote and quiet, I hope. I am looking at a small cottage in Maine. It will need some fixing up, but it should meet my needs."

The Ute waited while Angel filled his coffee cup to the brim. "This cottage close to the ocean?"

"Dear me, no." Father Raes smiled. "That is quite beyond my means. I shall be deep in the inland woods."

Moon shook his head. "Maine is a long ways off."

"Meters and miles are illusions of the mind."

The Indian presented another objection: "They don't get much sunshine in the wintertime."

"But it is very lush and green in summer."

"I hear the mosquitoes grow big as bats. And I won't even mention the gnats."

"I appreciate that." The priest tasted the soup, found it a tad too salty.

"Besides," Moon said, "they talk funny up there."

"I shall learn to like it."

And so they whiled away a small measure of the afternoon.

When the retiree's briny bowl was half empty, he could get no more past his lips.

Noting the cleric's hungry look, the rancher suggested something more palatable. A genuine cowboy recipe.

Father Raes nodded as he listened. "That sounds rather enticing," said he.

CHAPTER TWENTY-THREE

THE WARNING

JIM WOLFE WAS SEATED ON A CHROME-PLATED STOOL; HIS EL-
bows rested on a sour-smelling pine bar that pretended to be
seasoned oak.

The rheumy-eyed woman on the other side of the counter
pretended to be forty—the age of her daughter. She wiped
away a smear of beer suds, offered the off-duty cop a painted
smile. "So how come them Indians hired a white boy like you?"

Wolfe stared glumly at the small glass of amber liquid in
his hand. "For the promotion of cultural diversity, I imagine."

"What?"

"I am the token *matukach*."

"What's that?"

He pondered how best to communicate with the woman.
"*Matukach* is to Ute as Gentile is to Jew."

"Oh, I get it." The drink pusher filled a plastic bowl with
pretzels. "It's some kind of religious thing."

Wolfe helped himself to a twisted snack. "Your insight is
remarkably obtuse."

The barmaid nodded. "I was always the brainy one in my
family." She found a second bowl, filled it with salty beer nuts.
"It's just a matter of listening to what people say, then thinking things through. My daddy always said I was—" She
looked up from her task. An expression of alarm pinched her
pale face.

Jim Wolfe felt the presence behind him. Without knowing

how he knew, he knew it was the man who cast the long shadow. He turned on the stool, gawked at the tribal investigator. "How'd you know I was here?"

"I smelled your aftershave a mile away," Charlie Moon said. "And your Japanese horse is tied up out front."

"Ah, yes. My trusty Subaru steed." Wolfe raised the whiskey glass in a mock salute to the alcoholic. "Can I buy you a fizzy soda pop?"

"No, but thanks." Charlie Moon nodded to indicate a table in the rear of the Bear Claw Bar. "How about we talk."

It was not a question. Not even an invitation. This was a summons. A flash of irritation glinted in Wolfe's eyes. "I hope this ain't business."

"Why do you hope that?"

"I'm off duty."

"So'm I. This isn't official—more like a professional courtesy."

The muscles in Jim Wolfe's jaw and neck bulged. "I already know that Navarone'll get sprung today. And I know his shyster lawyer has filed for a restraining order to keep me away from that piece of trash."

"I thought maybe you'd heard, that's why I—"

Something snapped in Wolfe's alcohol-soaked brain. "And I am plenty tired of getting pushed around by lying Apaches, slime-ball lawyers—and big-shot Utes!" The white man got to his feet.

"I only want to have a civil word with you." Moon spoke softly. "But if you have something else in mind, I'll do my best to accommodate you."

Wolfe held his ground, looked the legendary Ute up and down. *I can take him. But I might need a club.* He eyed a whiskey bottle near at hand.

The woman behind the bar felt the tension in all of her limbs, wondered what was going to happen. Hoped it would be something terrible and bloody that she could tell gory stories about.

What happened was this: Charlie Moon began to unbutton his jacket.

Somewhat sobered by this development, Jim Wolfe coughed up a hollow laugh. "Hey, you want to do me a professional courtesy? Well, that's fine with me." He led the way to the table the Indian had selected, twirled a dirty chair backward, straddled it.

Charlie Moon seated himself across from the white man, back to the wall.

They were within spitting distance of the broken men's room door. An ammoniac stink of urine hung in the dank atmosphere.

"Great location," Wolfe said with a sniff. "Has a certain air to it."

Behind the door, a leaky toilet burbled a caustic response.

Moon stared at the belligerent white man.

The Ute's silence was unnerving. "Charlie, this conversation is highly stimulating. I'm not even sure I need this whiskey." Jim Wolfe tossed it down anyway, slammed the glass on the table. "I guess the decision to cut Navarone loose was just standard tribal politics."

"What's done is done," Moon said. "The less you know about the details, the better you'll sleep tonight."

"It's my own fault. I should've broke that tree-climbing thug's neck when I had the chance."

Moon shook his head. "That is not the right kind of attitude."

"Sure it is," Wolfe said with an air of unassailable logic. "If I'd of terminated Navarone when he jumped outta that tree on me, it would've been a clear and unequivocal case of self-defense. There'd be one less felon on the streets."

"You've already threatened to kill Felix Navarone," Moon reminded him. "And in front of a half-dozen cops. Cops who would be called to testify against you if Navarone's case went to court. And any one of those witnesses would be compelled under oath to repeat what you said."

Wolfe glared at the tribal investigator. "Including you?"

Moon nodded. "If I was in the witness stand, I'd tell the truth."

The SUPD cop rolled the glass between his hands, took a deep breath. "Is that what you dropped by to tell me?"

"I wish it was." Moon tried to think of a way to present the truth so it wouldn't look quite so ugly. But that would be like smearing lipstick on a warthog's snout. So Moon told Wolfe straight-out: "The chairman has been getting threats from Navarone's lawyer, and he's taking them seriously."

Wolfe glared at the man who was trying hard to help him. "What does that mean?"

"Here's the bottom line—from the tribe's point of view, you have become a liability." Charlie Moon took the empty shot glass from Wolfe's hand, turned it upside down on the filthy table.

The white cop stared at the thing.

Moon watched the man's bloodshot eyes. "You got any change in your pocket?"

Officer Wolfe attempted a grin. "You want to play the juke?"

The Indian waited.

The puzzled SUPD cop found a few coins, dumped them onto the table.

The Indian selected a shiny nickel. He balanced it on the upturned bottom of the shot glass.

Jim Wolfe squinted at the aristocratic profile of Thomas Jefferson.

Moon nodded at his construction. "You know what this is?"

The subject of the inquiry studied the display. "Well, this is just a wild guess—but it bears a striking resemblance to a nickel on a whiskey glass."

Moon shook his head.

"No?"

"The nickel is your job. Maybe even your future in the law-enforcement business. One careless little bump from you . . ." He left the rest to the white man's fertile imagination.

Mesmerized by the delicately balanced coin, the SUPD cop held his breath. Finally, he exhaled. "So how'll it fall, Charlie . . . heads or tails?"

"Don't matter," Moon said softly. "Either way, you lose."

"Then I guess I better be careful not to shake the table."

Moon smiled at his pupil. "You're beginning to get the gist of the situation."

Jim Wolfe watched the Ute get up, walk across the barroom floor, and disappear through the swinging doors. He muttered a curse, banged his fist on the table. In that agonizing slow-motion where pink roses blossom and wither, billowing clouds form and vanish, the off-duty cop watched the nickel roll off the inverted shot glass. Onto the filthy table. Off the edge. By the time it bounced onto the floor, Wolfe had emerged from the spell.

The waitress yelled, "Hey, you—what's wrong over there?" Getting no answer, she hurried to the dark corner.

The off-duty cop was under the table, clawing at the floor like a starving dog scratching for a buried bone.

This one's had too much to drink. "Whatta you think you're doing?"

Jim Wolfe found a folding knife in his pocket, flicked out the blade. "My nickel—it went in a crack." *And if I don't get it back . . .*

"Well, don't go cutting up the floor for it." *Cheap bum.* The hardworking woman reached into her apron pocket, where her tips jingled. "I'll give you another nickel."

"No!" He hacked wildly at the half-rotten wood. "I gotta have *this* nickel."

He's *drunk* and *crazy.*

MUCH LATER that night, when Charlie Moon should have been in bed, he was not. He was hunched in front of a television screen. He pressed a button on the VCR remote control, advancing the videotape frame by frame.

In the slowest motion imaginable, Felix Navarone spread his arms in tiny, jerking movements—and launched himself from the limb. There was no room for doubt. He definitely did not fall, he *jumped.* The Apache's leap from the cottonwood branch amounted to a deliberate physical assault on SUPD officer Jim Wolfe. Having been an eyewitness to the event, Charlie Moon was not surprised.

It was what happened *after* Navarone landed on the white man that fascinated the tribal investigator—there was something about this wrestling match that did not look quite right.

For the most part, it was a regular rough-and-tumble, grunt-and-gouge, give-and-take battle where each of the combatants seemed to be doing his level best to obliterate his opponent. But for just a moment—and in a most peculiar fashion—one man was either doing all the taking or all the *giving*. Charlie Moon could not decide which. Or why.

CHAPTER TWENTY-FOUR

THE OPPORTUNITY

NOT LONG AFTER CHARLIE MOON LEFT OFFICER JIM WOLFE IN the Bear Claw Bar, Felix Navarone was released from the tribal jail in Ignacio.

Despite Moon's stern warning to stay clear of the man he had threatened to kill, Wolfe felt compelled to follow the jubilant ex-prisoner's 1957 Chevrolet pickup out of town. From long experience, the policeman knew that tailing was an iffy proposition. Blink an eye, your ninety-year-old grandmother would lose you in a half-empty Wal-Mart parking lot. And if your target suspected he was being followed, you might as well forget it and go home. This being so, Officer Wolfe was properly cautious.

A few miles south of Bayfield, Navarone turned off the paved highway onto a gravel road. From time to time, the pickup's taillights would disappear over a ridge. This made Wolfe uneasy; he kept his distance at a good quarter mile. But when he topped a particular rise, Wolfe was confronted with an unexpected complication—a fork in the road. There was not even a distant puff of dust to indicate which direction the Indian had chosen. *Well, this is just dandy.* On a hunch, Wolfe took the right branch of the fork, goosing his Subaru Forester to speeds that were reckless on the gravel. *If he's up ahead, I'll spot him pretty quick.* But after several miles there was no sign of Navarone's pickup. Cursing his bad luck, Jim Wolfe did a sliding U-turn, raced back to take the other fork. He doggedly spent an hour searching for a trace of the ancient Chevy pickup. It was no use. The Apache had slipped away.

He considered the situation. The left and right branches of the fork had multiplied into a multitude of smaller lanes, and most of these ended at isolated dwellings or locked gates. As far as he could tell, there was no through road on either branch. Which meant that Navarone must eventually return to the split in the road. But when? Tonight? Tomorrow? Sometime next week?

Having nothing better to do, Jim Wolfe decided to wait for a few hours. He parked his car a few yards off the road in the concealment of a clump of willow bushes. He slipped a Judy Collins disk into the CD player, settled down, watched. There was only a dribble of traffic. When Ms. Collins had played out, he substituted Emmylou Harris. As twilight came and went, he watched the bloodred sun slip behind a distant mesa—then go in free fall to the bottom of the world. When the darkness was complete, he shut the CD player off. The occasional sound of an approaching automobile would arouse his interest, but mostly he listened to crickets chirp and wished a hundred times that he had taken the left fork.

Shortly past midnight, he decided to give it up. *Wherever that Apache is, he's holed up for the night. I might come back in the morning—*

He was startled by the whine of an engine. As the vehicle got closer, it began to take shape in the moonlight. Wolfe strained to see whether it might possibly be an old Chevrolet pickup. It was. Looked like a 1957. The off-duty cop laughed out loud and muttered to himself, "Navarone—you are dead meat." He cranked the Subaru's engine. Leaving the lights off, he slipped quickly behind his prey.

After a mile or so, the pickup in front of him slowed to a crawl.

FELIX NAVARONE leaned forward to look through the '57 Chevy pickup's sand-blasted windshield. He squinted to make out the little-used dirt lane that led out to the natural gas field near Butterfield Mesa.

• • •

JIM WOLFE adjusted his speed to match the Apache's truck. *What now, Navarone?*

The Chevrolet pickup came almost to a stop. Started again. Moved slowly, as if searching for something. Turned off the gravel road. Moved slowly into the brush. Vanished.

Wolfe passed the location where the pickup had turned, took a hard right, bumped down the shoulder into a dry streambed. He shifted to low, snailed along for a hundred yards. When he saw no sign of the pickup's headlights, it occurred to him that Navarone might have already stopped. *If he has, he might hear my engine.* Wolfe switched off the ignition, removed the bulb from the dome light. He checked his sidearm, opened the car door as silently as possible, did not close it. He walked slowly toward where he thought the pickup might be, taking care not to step on a dry twig that might snap. Juniper and piñon cast black shadows in the silvery moonlight.

What is Navarone up to? A possibility had been gnawing at the police officer. *He might have spotted me behind him and figured he'd suck me into an ambush. Well, my momma didn't raise no fools.* Wolfe dropped to his hands and knees, crawled to the crest of a grassy ridge. He scooted along on elbows and belly until he could see what lay beyond—an open, almost flat valley, bisected by a deep arroyo. Towering above the valley was a broad mesa, with a split chimney towering from its crest. There was no sign of the old pickup. He cursed. *I've lost him again!* But as his eyes gradually adjusted to the moonlight, he saw a hint of parallel lines in the sand. The tire tracks ran along a barely discernible lane that snaked through the low brush. Wolfe got to his feet, fell into a crouching run, crossed a shallow arroyo. He found the pickup's tire tracks but did not hear any engine sounds. And then he saw it—the truck was parked in a narrow neck of valley, between a gigantic pair of sandstone mesas. The Indian had taken no particular trouble to hide his wheels. Which could mean that he didn't expect anyone to follow him into this wilderness. Or that he didn't care if someone did. Someone whose name was Jim Wolfe. The troublesome thought pounded in his head.

Could be an ambush. I need to get to higher ground.

He selected a knobby hill sprouted with sage and piñon, made his way to the top, and took up his position by a pillow-shaped outcropping of sandstone.

Nothing moved around the Indian's truck.

Time passed without the ticks and tocks of mechanical clocks.

The lawman watched. Waited. Thought his troubled thoughts.

White-hot stars winked and sparkled. Unseen by the eye of man, a four-billion-year-old, pea-sized meteorite gleamed in the dark sky for one final glorious moment. Mindless of the mortal and his minuscule concerns, the Milky Way whirled ever so slowly—as spiral galaxies are required to do.

Somewhere out there in the faraway, a lonely coyote yip-yipped. There was an answering yodel from the crest of a craggy mesa. Then another.

An owl, hungry for her nightly mouse, began to hoot. She was joined by her mate.

A pleasant night breeze played with the juniper branches.

Presently, a heavy cloud skimmed across the heavens, cloaking the world of men in inky darkness.

Jim Wolfe was squinting, vainly attempting to see the pickup. *If I get my hands on that Apache, I'll give him the beating of his life.*

There was a sharp prod against his spine.

Wolfe felt his entire body go taut. *Navarone has slipped up on me. I'm a goner.*

The English words were spoken in the characteristic choppy dialect of an Indian: "I know you're packing, cop—so don't you even move a whisker."

The lawman felt the warmth of the man's breath by his ear, the clumsy fumbling of a hand against his side. *He's going to take my gun, then he'll kill me. But I ain't leaving this world without a fight!*

In one motion, the desperate man twisted to elbow the Indian on the chin, jerk the heavy revolver from its holster, and empty the cylinder into the shadowy figure that was stumbling, turning away. The first five slugs smacked the ambusher's thigh, hip, lower back, neck, and shoulder. The last hollow-point bullet entered the back of the Indian's head.

Jim Wolfe stood over the prone figure, trembling with rage and fear, pulling the trigger on empty chambers. Click. Click. Click. When he lowered the revolver, his world was perfectly silent.

A half-dozen coyotes had ceased their canine conversation. Unblinking owls held their breath.

Even the breeze was stilled.

All the off-duty policeman could hear was the rhythmic thump of the pulse in his temple. After a seven-second eternity, the dark cloud slipped away to unveil the pale face of the moon.

Jim Wolfe rolled the corpse over. The final .357 Magnum hollow point had done its job all too well. The top half of the Indian's face was gone. His mouth was twisted into a knowing smirk. It took Wolfe a long moment to get hold of himself. *I need to be glad that it's Navarone that's dead, not me.* And Navarone was certainly as dead as men ever get. *Not only that, I killed him in self-defense.* But a search for his assailant's gun proved fruitless. A horrifying possibility occurred to the lawman: *Maybe Navarone wasn't armed . . . maybe this harebrained Indian poked a stick in my back.*

In the startling manner of a suddenly rising tide, the cold truth began to wash around the SUPD cop. *I have just hunted down a man I was warned to stay away from—a man I swore I'd kill. I've shot him six times—in the back. And him with no gun. Oh, God—I am in serious trouble.* He took a deep breath. Tried to think. *I'll have to hide his body, then get out of here well before first light. If I keep my cool, I'll be fine.* But fear and fury were not to be so easily dismissed. Those hideous twins returned, hand in hand.

Wolfe shook his fist at the dead man and shouted, "Navarone—this is all your fault!" He spat on the corpse. The gesture of contempt was considerably more than a mistake.

It was a mortal error.

CHAPTER TWENTY-FIVE

HAUNTED

JIM WOLFE LOCKED HIMSELF IN HIS APARTMENT, PEELED TO
the skin. His hands trembled as he soaked his blood-splattered
shirt in lighter fluid, burned the fabric to ashes in the fireplace.
He stood under a hot shower for twenty minutes, used half a
bar of soap in a fruitless attempt to wash away the stench and
stain of his sins. The off-duty police officer dressed in crisply
clean khaki trousers and a white T-shirt, ground a handful of
Colombian beans, made a fresh pot of strong coffee, took a
few sips—grimaced. *This tastes like rotten eggs!*

He plopped onto the couch, turned on the television, stared
at the talking heads without comprehension. Finally, he turned
off the flickering screen, stretched out on the couch. Closed
his eyes.

Sleep would not come near; even rest was denied him.

As noon came and went, he paced about barefoot in his
small parlor, smoked a pack and a half of filtered cigarettes, re-
lentlessly relived the insane events of the previous night. From
time to time, he would stop to push a curtain aside, stare out the
second-story window at a neat row of Russian olives lining the
space between the parking lot and the sidewalk. The normal,
sunny world outside his window was like that unattainable left-
is-right realm on the other side of the mirror. Recalling what he
had done only a few hours ago, he shuddered, touched the
flame to another cancer stick, resumed his aimless pacing.

When the shadows had grown long and indistinct, he unlatched the door, went onto the porch. The air was fresh and clean. Crickets chit-chirped with others of their kind. Swallows flitted about in impossible accelerations. In Wolfe's shattered mind, they were vain pretensions, fleeting shadows from other dimensions.

For a few minutes, it was as if he were emerging from a nightmare. A mere dream.

But a gray twilight signaled the swift approach of night.

Wolfe retreated into his den, switched on all the lights.

The darkness in his soul returned full force.

Feeling weak and light-headed from lack of food, he searched the refrigerator. The bachelor folded slices of Polish ham and Swiss cheese between thick slabs of rye bread. He smeared the meat with mustard, the cheese with mayonnaise. It was his favorite sandwich. The taste was sour and metallic. He felt an overpowering surge of nausea, ran to the bathroom, vomited into the toilet. Caught in a sickening cycle of shudders and shivers and dry heaves, the policeman turned off the lights, stumbled to his bed, crawled in between the sheets, pulled the quilt up to his chin. He was convinced he would never, never sleep again.

But shortly after eleven he fell into that bottomless abyss of unconsciousness. All who go there leave sanity behind. Living things grow cold. Dead things become alive. The imagined horror becomes real.

HE WAS on a rocky hillock, alone in the wilderness.

No . . . not quite alone.

Someone pressed a cold barrel against his spine. Now your time is at hand.

No. I will not die. . . . *Wolfe turned, fired his weapon.*

The mortally wounded man bled buckets of blood, laughing all the while.

Wolfe looked down, beheld the human being he had killed. While he watched, the corpse withered. Turned to ash.

The ashes became a powder-fine dust.

A dark, funereal wind came from the west, sighed, blew the dust away.

The sleeper felt himself moving swiftly, to some distant upside-down place.

Now Wolfe was stretched out on a coarse straw mat. Bleeding. He looked up at the ghost of his victim.

The dead man's features could not be seen. There was only an outline of his body. Blackened corpse flesh on star-studded sky. The half-moon sat precariously on the spirit's shoulder.

The dreamer floated up from the depths. Toward something much like consciousness. Opened his eyes.

It *was still there.*

THE PHANTOM stood just outside the sleeper's bedroom window. Waiting for an opportunity to—

Wolfe made a muffled scream, instinctively raised his arms in a protective gesture. Looked again.

There was no one at the window.

Only an opalescent moon, floating in an arid, cloudless sky.

The sheets were wet with his sweat. Wolfe groaned. *I'm losing my mind. I've got to do something—anything but stay cooped up here.* The haunted man got out of bed, dressed himself. He stuck a fresh cigarette under his lip, pushed the revolver under his belt, went outside. He ambled aimlessly along empty sidewalks, across quiet streets, onto the cool grass of a small park, past a miniature playground, through a grove of cottonwood and willows, down to the rocky banks of a small stream. The eastern sky was flooded with a pale, frothy sea. On that faraway western shore, a million-million stars were washed away.

Wolfe sat on a rotting stump. Thought his sickly thoughts. *Maybe I'm not going crazy. Maybe Navarone's ghost has come back to torment me. If he has, that Apache will never let me be. But what can I do about it?*

At that moment the sun came up like lightning. Warming the land. Illuminating the man.

He knew exactly what he could do about it.

CHAPTER TWENTY-SIX

THE WAGES OF SIN

DAISY PERIKA'S HOAX ON THE HAPLESS WHITE POLICEMAN HAD backfired—it was the shaman who had been cursed by the lump of turquoise. All those invented afflictions she had warned Officer Wolfe about had come to plague her. Daisy could not sleep at night. She coughed. She itched. Now and then, her tired old heart would miss a beat or two. Worst of all, the Ute elder could not dismiss the gnawing worry that by some means, Jim Wolfe would discover what she had done. And the white man would return, full of rage—determined to have his revenge on a poor, helpless old Indian woman who had wanted only to protect a sacred Native American relic. It was so unfair.

Hoping it might help if she did not see or touch the Hasteen K'os Largo pendant for a week or two, she left the stolen object in the shoe box. This seemed to help. Day by day, Daisy's symptoms began to dissipate. Her troubles, it seemed, were in full retreat. Until one sunny afternoon.

JIM WOLFE tapped tentatively on the door. "Miz Perika—you there?"

She was not.

He twisted the knob. The door was unlocked.

The desperate man stepped into Daisy's small kitchen, called out again, "Anybody home?"

Silence.

The old witch is probably out gathering eye of newt or

something. But I can't wait around here all day. Maybe she won't mind if I just borrow what I need. Having made his decision, the lawman crossed the small room in three long strides, opened the cabinet door, found the black shoe box. When he lifted the lid, he was astonished at what he found there. He smiled. *Well, well—you sly old thief.* He pocketed his lucky pendant, then proceeded with the more important business that had brought him to this place.

DAISY PERIKA was prowling around on the narrow termination of Three Sisters Mesa, which towered above her home in the valley. The shaman had filled one of her apron pockets with wild buckwheat, another with seed pods harvested from dead stalks of spider milkweed. When she thought she heard the sound of an automobile in the distance, she was on her hands and knees, digging up the turniplike taproot of a storksbill. Daisy paused, cocked her head to listen. *I must have company.* Wondering who the caller might be, she hung the willow basket over the crook of her arm, hurried along a dusty deer path. She came to the end of mesa, looked down to see the aluminum skin of her trailer home gleaming in the sun. She squinted. There was no sign of an automobile.

Daisy was certain her ears had not played tricks on her. There *had* been someone there, but they were already gone.

Who would leave in such a hurry? Not her cousin Gorman Sweetwater. The silly man would have hung around till well after dark, in hopes of getting a free meal. And Charlie Moon would have called for her. Or, more likely, tracked her all the way up the trail to the mesa top. A happy thought occurred to the isolated woman: Maybe it was the UPS truck that had come and gone. Sure. *The man in the brown uniform has probably left me a package.* This possibility cheered the lonely soul. Aside from monthly checks from Social Security, Daisy did not get more than two or three useful pieces of mail in a month. And packages—well! Parcels with gifts inside were very rare treats indeed, usually appearing only on her birthday and Christmas. Why was there not an Aunt's Day? She solemnly promised herself to write a letter to the president of the United States.

After descending the trail down the talus slope, Daisy mounted the porch steps, put the basket down, leaned on a stout oak staff.

Her door, which was rarely locked, was not quite closed.

The visitor had been inside.

Maybe he still is. For a tense moment, she stood on the porch. *No, he must be gone or I'd have spotted his car from up on the mesa. Unless there was two of 'em and one stayed behind. But I can't stand out here all day.* Daisy Perika took a deep breath. *Well, here goes.* Grasping the oak staff in one hand, she pushed the door open. As soon as she was in her kitchen, she had a strong sense that there was no one in her trailer. She stood very still. Looked around to see whether anything had been disturbed.

On the linoleum she had swept just this morning, there was something that did not belong there. A little spot of yellowish white powder. With a painful effort and much pathetic grunting, the old woman got down on her knees. Touched the tip of her finger to the gritty stuff, peered at the sample. *It looks like . . .* Daisy touched it to her tongue. *It is.* Instantly, she understood what had happened. She went to the cabinet over the sink, opened the painted wooden door, reached for the black shoe box. Opened it.

The K'os Largo pendant was gone.

And that was not all.

LIFE WAS good for Charlie Moon. He had a fine red pickup under him, was rolling along south on Route 151 toward the jutting thumb of Navajo Lake. Off to his right, Chimney Rock tickled the belly of a low-hanging cloud. A handsome raven was perched on a telephone pole; it squawked and stretched a wing as he passed—as if to direct the Ute to the Promised Land. Grateful for all blessings, Charlie Moon tipped his Stetson to salute the helpful bird.

Another mile of his life slipped by, a well-spent minute passed into history.

He lowered the window. Sage-scented air wafted in, sweet with the promise of rain. He turned on the FM radio, heard an

NPR announcer in Washington, D.C. say something about trouble brewing along the border between China and North Korea, quickly poked the CD player button. LeAnn Rimes began to croon "Good Lookin' Man." *Yes indeed.* Moon hummed along. *Miss James beside me and this would be perfect. . . .*

But Miss James was not beside him.

Near-perfect moments are fleeting phantoms.

His cell phone made a burbling sound. *Like a fringed cockatoo choking on a peanut,* he thought. Just last year, Charlie Moon had witnessed just such a distressing event in an upscale Denver pet store. The magnificent, three-thousand-dollar bird had survived.

Again the cockatoo gagged.

Moon reached into his jacket pocket for the instrument. "Yeah?"

Aunt Daisy's brittle voice crackled in his ear. "Charlie—is that you?"

"Yup."

"Yup?" There was a derisive snort. "That's no way for a grown man to answer a telephone."

"Excuse me, please. This is Charlie Moon. To whom do I have the pleasure of speaking to—a shy lady admirer who'll only talk to me on the phone?"

"It's me, you big jug-head."

"That was my second guess. What's up?"

"Somebody has been snooping around in my house."

The lawman's smile faded. "Are they gone?"

"Long gone."

"You sure?"

"Car pulled away, oh—almost half an hour ago."

It would take about that long for whoever it was to drive the rutted dirt lane from Daisy's home to Route 151, and Moon was three miles from the junction. Once he encountered the paved road, the intruder might head south and get a good head start. Moon pressed the accelerator. "Look, I'm not far away. Maybe I can—"

"And the scoundrel messed around in my kitchen."

On the list of a hundred sure ways to get on the wrong side

of the old woman, "messing around in my kitchen" was right up there in the top ten.

There was an uneasy pause before she continued. "He took something outta the cabinet over the sink." As was her custom, she waited for him to ask.

"What was taken?"

Daisy would certainly not mention the famous Navajo shaman's pendant, and she hated to tell her nephew about the other thing. But something must be done about this outrage, and Charlie Moon was the man to do it. "A little plastic bag."

"What's in the bag?"

"Uh . . . about half a pound of yellow cornmeal."

Moon frowned at the long ribbon of asphalt stretched out ahead of the red F-350. "Cornmeal—that's all?"

Daisy's voice betrayed the fact that she was getting testy. "There was some baking powder in it. A pinch or two of salt. About a teaspoon of sugar. And just a little bit of paprika." She groaned. "My legs are hurting from all the walking I've done today."

"Maybe you'd better sit down and rest awhile."

She leaned on the small dining table, seated herself in a straight-back chair, groaned with relief. "Ah—that's lots better."

"Good. Now do you have any idea who might've—"

"Sure I do."

Silence.

Moon smiled at his reflection in the windshield. "Take all day if you want to. I got nothing important to do."

"It was that *matukach* policeman you brought out here a while back—the one who needed doctoring."

Charlie Moon thought this to be highly unlikely. "Officer Wolfe?"

"That's the one."

It seemed like a really dumb question. "Uh—here's what I don't understand. Why would Jim Wolfe—or anybody for that matter—drive all the way out to your place to steal a handful of cornbread mix?" He laughed. "Did he take some lard? Or a frying pan?"

"I am old and tired and cranky. Don't you get smart with me."

"Okay. But you have to admit, it seems like a pretty dog-gone strange thing for a person to do."

The old woman tried to sound as if her interpretation of the theft was the most logical response imaginable. "Maybe he thought he was stealing corpse powder."

Moon's pickup topped a steep hill, hurtled down the other side. "Would you please repeat that?"

"Maybe because—"

"Just the last part."

"Corpse powder."

Corpse powder? The tribal investigator attempted to digest this assertion. It still didn't make any sense. Unless . . . well of course. He smiled at a mental image of his aunt spoofing the superstitious white man. "I wonder—what would lead Officer Wolfe to believe you kept something in your kitchen like . . . ah . . . corpse powder?"

The shaman hesitated. "Who knows why these crazy white people believe all the peculiar things they do?" She sighed, shook her head. "Charlie, they are not like us."

Moon encountered a black-and-white Subaru Forester heading north. "I'll talk to you later." He jammed his boot heel on the brake pedal, did a skidding 180 on the two-lane.

CHAPTER TWENTY-SEVEN

THE SHAMAN'S REMEDY

JIM WOLFE PARKED HIS SUBARU HALF A MILE FROM BUTTER-field mesa, took exaggerated care to close the car door quietly, making a barely audible click. He stood quite immobile—a mere shadow-man, infected with a palpable emptiness.

A dry breeze rattled the pulpy leaves on a dwarf oak.

Wolfe turned his face toward that place where he had left the Indian's mortal remains. He stuck his hand in his jacket pocket, felt the reassuring lump of the plastic bag.

Might as well get the job done. He trudged off toward an uncertain destiny.

CHARLIE MOON stood on the bushy side of a ridge, his slender frame masked by juniper and piñon and the instincts of a thousand generations of painted warriors, stealthy mammoth hunters, sly prowlers of dark forests. The modern Ute raised a pair of binoculars to his eyes, turned the knurled focus knob. Jim Wolfe's wispy form jumped into startling clarity. The tribal investigator frowned over the eyepieces. Wolfe was standing by an oblong cairn of stones. Maybe this was not a fool's errand.

The white man stared at the pile of rocks, leaned over as if to pick up a stone, hesitated.

Moon watched through the excellent German optics.

Wolfe straightened his back, removed a glistening packet from his jacket pocket.

Okay. Give him enough rope to hang himself with.

The watched man poured a bit of gritty powder into his palm. Began to sprinkle it onto the stones.

Moon grimaced. *That's not the way.* Had Aunt Daisy forgotten to tell him the rules? Corpse powder had to be sprinkled directly onto the body.

As if he had heard Moon's thought, Jim Wolfe paused, assumed the stony-faced expression of one who must do the unthinkable. He squatted, began the grisly task. In no hurry, he removed one stone. Then another.

Moon was greatly relieved that Wolfe was doing the thing right. Not that there was any such thing as a magical powder that would keep a malevolent ghost from tormenting his enemy's soul. Haunts and magic potions—it was all old-women's talk, invented to frighten unruly children and relieve credulous folk of their money.

Jim Wolfe was making two neat piles of stones. One on his right, another on his left.

This could take a long time. But Charlie Moon had no option except to stay where he was, watch the white man uncover the corpse—presumably of some unfortunate he had killed. But one must not jump to conclusions. Though a sizable portion of homicides are cold-blooded murder, a few are accidental and others justifiable as self-defense. But violent deaths of human beings have this in common: Every one must be investigated by the legally constituted authorities. The tribal investigator would wait until Jim Wolfe began putting corpse dust on the body before he approached to make an arrest. He imagined how surprised Wolfe would be to see him.

It was the Ute who was surprised. Moon blinked, readjusted the binoculars. *What's going on?*

Jim Wolfe was on his hands and knees, flinging stones this way and that. From a hundred yards away, Moon heard the man screaming what seemed to be a mix of pleas and curses.

With a suddenness more eerie than his outburst, the white man fell eerily silent.

WOLFE GOT to his feet, reeled like a drunk, stared at the stones. He began to turn his head. The terrified man examined the twilight landscape of swollen ridges, arroyo scars in the earth's skin, mesas stitched like black patches onto a blue velvet sky. The white SUPD cop took another long, thoughtful look at the scattered stones. Feeling like a child caught in a nightmare, he tried to think straight. *This is crazy. It doesn't make any sense at all.* He turned to look down the broad valley, to the spot between the massive sandstone mesas—where the Apache had left his truck.

Felix Navarone's 1957 Chevrolet pickup was not there.

MOON WATCHED through the binoculars as the drama unfolded.

Wolfe had broken into a headlong run. He tripped over a twisted piñon root, tumbled down the bank of a dry arroyo, scrambled to regain his footing, ran like a man pursued by an invisible *something*. Wolfe disappeared from view. A minute later, Moon heard the off-duty cop's Subaru start up, tear off toward the highway.

TRANSFIXED WITH wonder, Charlie Moon tried to make some sense of what he had witnessed. Jim Wolfe was a pretty tough customer. What could such a man have found under the stones that would scare him half to death? As he made long strides toward the ridge that Wolfe had vacated in such haste, images of a rotting, half-human corpse flitted through the dark corners of the Ute's mind. Moments later, the tribal policeman planted his boots where Jim Wolfe had stood. He stared. There was no corpse. Only a scattering of stones.

SUMMONED

HIS FINGERS resting lightly on the leathered steering wheel, Charlie Moon maneuvered the machine along the gravel road, north into the gathering darkness. The truck engine hummed contentedly.

He mused about Jim Wolfe's peculiar behavior. *There's something going on here—something I should be able to see.* Despite the puzzle of a man who stole cornbread mix from an old woman, drove into the reservation wilderness, threw a bunch of rocks around, then ran off like a grizzly was snapping at his shirttail, Moon was not disturbed. On the contrary, the drive was soothing. This being so, he was relaxed and at peace with the world. Until . . .

The telephone called to him.

He pressed the black, antennaed bug to his ear. "Hello."

Though the fidelity of the connection was excellent, the gender of the caller was uncertain. "Am I addressing a Mr. Charles Moon?"

"Who wants to know?"

"This is Bertram Eustace Cassidy." There was an expectant pause, as if the name was expected to carry some weight. "I am calling on behalf of my aunt, Miss Jane Cassidy."

Cassidy. Sure—those people whose museum had been burgled. Those *wealthy* people. The sort who—after they paid their bills—still had piles of money left over. "Mr. Cassidy, what can I do for you?"

The caller's tone was mildly doubtful, as if he might have dialed a wrong number. "Is this Mr. Charles Moon—the Indian policeman?"

"This is Charlie Moon, the tribal investigator." *And all-around good fella.*

"Mr. Moon, my aunt would like to confer with you."

"Confer about what?"

"It is my impression that Auntie Jane would prefer to tell you herself. Do you know where we are located?"

"Sure."

"I suggest that we set up an appointment, here at our estate."

Estate? I can hear the cash register ringing. "How about tomorrow afternoon?"

Bertram E. Cassidy replied, in the self-assured tone of a man accustomed to calling the shots, "This evening would be much better."

"I'll be there in about an hour."

"Auntie Jane is somewhat finicky about appointments." A pained hesitation. "Could you be somewhat more precise?"

Moon calculated the miles between here and there, consulted Betty Lou's digital dashboard clock, which was synchronized with WWV. "I will knock on your door at eight-fourteen." He grinned. "And twelve seconds."

Bertram Eustace Cassidy did not bat an eyelash. "Eight-fourteen-twelve. That will be quite satisfactory."

Charlie Moon heard a click in his ear.

CHAPTER TWENTY-EIGHT

BERTIE AND JANE

CHARLIE MOON ARRIVED AT THE PERIMETER OF THE CASSIDY estate at two minutes past eight. Not wishing to be early, he parked the F-350 on the street. The grounds were shrouded in that tasteful silence which may be purchased by the reclusive rich. At the far end of the winding asphalt driveway, the white three-story mansion rose to imitate a mammoth tombstone. On the first floor, ten mullioned windows showed only hints of light leaking through folds of heavy draperies. He set his wristwatch to match the dashboard WWV clock.

At 8:14 PM plus twelve seconds, the Ute rapped his knuckles against the double-door main entrance.

The brass knob turned, the massive door swung on oiled hinges to reveal an elfin presence. The man of the house wore a black velvet robe over crisply ironed polka-dot pajamas. His size-6 feet were nestled in wool-lined felt moccasins. The face, like the rest of him, was of a roundish, plumpish quality. The diminutive white man checked the Rolex on his wrist. "Dear me—you are twenty-one seconds late."

"I hate to be argumentative right off the bat," the Ute said. "But I knocked on your door right on the dot. You better get your Oyster checked."

"As you say." The eyes were blue and merry. "You are Mr. Charles Moon, I may safely presume."

"Last time I looked in the mirror, this was me." The Ute removed his black Stetson. "And I'll lay five bucks to six bits—you are Mr. Bertram Eustace Cassidy."

"I am the very same." He stepped aside, indicated with a polite gesture that the Ute should enter. "But please call me Bertie."

Moon looked doubtful. "I don't know if I should—does that mean you get to call me Charlie?"

"It would seem equitable."

"Then I'll have to go along with it."

Bertie extended a pale hand that was light and lifeless in Moon's big paw.

The handshake was terminated by a shrieking call from down a dark hallway: "Bertie—is it Mr. Moon?"

"No, Auntie—it is my friend Charlie."

"What on earth are you babbling about?"

"Charlie Moon, my old chum. He is entirely here and accounted for." He lowered his voice to a whisper: "And waiting anxiously to be summoned into your august presence."

"Then bring him to me!"

Bertie gave his guest a nod, padded down the hall.

Moon followed.

The pale woman, who looked to be somewhere in her seventies, was seated stiffly in an overstuffed chair. Her gaunt form was hidden under a tasteful blue silk nightgown. Jane Cassidy had been listening to an opera; she switched off the CD player, turned to glare at the visitor.

During the appraisal, Charlie Moon waited patiently.

Finally, the woman arched a thin eyebrow at him. "My word, no one told me you were so tall." As if Bertie should have informed her, she shot her nephew an accusing look, then continued in the injured tone of the grande dame who must deal with half-wits, "I am tired. It is very late to be having a guest."

The nephew gave the Ute an apologetic look. "Charlie preferred to come on the morrow, but I told him that you would prefer this evening, so—"

"Shut up, Bertie." She flicked the lever on a gold-plated

antique cigar lighter, touched the flame to a skinny Turkish cigarette.

Moon looked down at her. "Miss Cassidy, I was up before the sun. I've had a full day, and I've still got a long drive home. If this is an inconvenient time for you, I'd just as soon say good-bye and—"

She pointed to a chair that matched her own. "Sit."

"No, thank you." He stood, hat in hand.

"Oh, very well then." She tapped the cigarette ashes into a crystal ashtray. "You are no doubt aware that the Cassidy Museum has been burgled."

"I heard something about it."

"Bertie"—she pointed the cigarette at her nephew as if Moon might not know whom she was referring to—"informs me that you recently had a rather dramatic meeting with Ralph Briggs."

"Auntie is referring to the terrible incident where Ralph was wounded and you—"

"Do not interrupt, Bertie." She gave Charlie a stern look. "I understand that Mr. Briggs was attempting to gain your assistance in recovering the items stolen from our temporary display in the museum annex. And that while this discussion was in progress at The Compleate Antiquarian, someone shot and wounded Mr. Briggs."

"That's what the newspaper reported."

"I never read a newspaper. Or watch the television."

Bertram Eustace Cassidy nodded. "That is quite true. Auntie depends entirely upon myself for news of the outside world. It is my duty to report events of any significance."

Jane Cassidy glared at the inoffensive little man. "Do be quiet, Bertie."

"Yes, Auntie."

Again she turned her attention to the Indian. "Now tell me what Ralph Briggs had to say."

"No."

Her eyes grew large with outrage. "I beg your pardon?"

Moon shook his head. "Begging won't help."

"Now see here—"

"It's a matter of professional conduct, Miss Cassidy. What was said between me and Ralph Briggs stays between him and me."

"But surely, if it has to do with the burglary of my museum—"

"Ma'am, that don't matter. Now if that's what you wanted to talk about, I might as well—"

"Please sit down," she said.

"What was that?"

She responded in a pleading tone that was patently false, "Please."

"Don't mind if do." Moon folded his long frame into an ugly chair, perched the dusty Stetson on his knee.

Jane Cassidy tapped the long cigarette against the back of a heavily veined hand. "I am pleased to know that you have professional scruples."

Moon's eye twinkled. "I am pleased to know that you are pleased."

Bertie snickered, was instantly impaled by a piercing glance from his aunt.

She forced a smile that exposed a marked gap between her front teeth. The mirthless expression could have passed for a reaction to acute food poisoning. "At my instructions, Mr. Moon, my attorneys in Denver have conducted some research into your background. I am informed that while you primarily work for your tribe, you are also a licensed private investigator. I also understand that, on occasion, you will work for a non-Indian client." She waved off his response with a flick of her wrist. "I require some expert help in recovering the precious objects that were stolen from the Cassidy collection. I naturally assumed that you would be interested in providing me with your services."

Charlie Moon thought about it for a full half second. "No."

"No?" She detested that word—it was so *negative*.

"Not a chance."

Bertie fell into a fit of giggles.

Jane clenched her teeth. "Shut up, you silly little oaf."

The nephew bit his lip in a valiant but mostly fruitless effort to stifle himself. He imagined what it would be like to have red-hot tenpenny nails driven under his toenails while being chewed on by a rabid wolf and forced to listen to rap music at 130 decibels. This self-inflicted vision sobered him somewhat.

Jane Cassidy raised her chin in a haughty gesture. "Why will you not work for me?"

He tried to find a nice way to say it: "You and me—we would not get along."

She curled her lip. "Why—because I am rude and demanding?"

And obnoxious. "Yes, ma'am."

A sly look crinkled her wrinkles. "I pay well."

Though momentarily tempted, Moon shook his head. "You could not afford me."

To demonstrate that she was hurt and insulted, the rich woman crumpled in her chair, dabbed a lace hankie at her eyes. "What a horribly offensive remark!"

"Even so, it's the truth."

She pitched the hankie aside. "Just out of curiosity, what is your hourly rate?"

Moon decided to put a quick end to this farce. "Two hundred dollars."

Jane's mouth popped open to display a number of well-maintained molars. "Astounding, I am absolutely flabbergasted."

This was good fun. "Plus expenses. And I get a thirty-minute coffee break every hour."

"This is simply outrageous." She slapped a palm on her chest. "I may have a heart attack."

Moon grinned at the rich woman. "I warned you."

She grinned back. "I accept your terms."

If the dark-skinned man could have paled, he would have. "You do?"

"Certainly. Keep a detailed account of your various nefarious activities on my behalf." She gazed at the chandelier, where a tiny red spider was weaving a delicate web. "I will expect you to submit your bills on a weekly basis."

The man who had stepped into his own trap felt a stinging surge of heartburn. "What, exactly, do you want me to do?"

"Do? What sort of question is that?" Jane banged her corpselike fist on a granite-topped tea table, toppling a small decanter of extremely expensive whiskey. "Do whatever it takes to recover my stolen property—every last piece of it!" She took a long draw on the Turkish cigarette, blew a wriggly string of smoke through the gap in her teeth. "I just *hate* it when the common riffraff comes creeping around the estate, dares to swipe my property." She gave her nearest of kin a saccharine smile. "Someday, of course, everything I own will belong to my silly nephew—over my dead body, as it were."

Bertram made a little bow. "You are the very soul of charity, Auntie Jane."

Moon shifted in the uncomfortable chair. "What about insurance?"

Jane's eyes turned to blue ice. "What about it?"

The tribal investigator struggled to come up with a response. "You probably think I burgled the museum for the insurance, is that it?"

"Uh, well—no. It's just one of the first things that comes up and—"

She aimed the cigarette at Moon. "You detest rich people, don't you?"

"No, ma'am. As a matter of fact I try to put a little money in the bank every chance I get so that someday—"

"For your information, Mr. Suspicious of His Betters, the collection was not insured. I saw no reason for it. We Cassidys have lived here for seven generations without any problem with common criminals. But recently I had become alarmed at the number of break-ins in the neighborhood. I instructed Bertie to contact several reputable brokers and secure bids for insuring not only the Cassidy collection, but every stick of furniture in my home. Within days of my decision, the burglar struck. Sadly, there was no coverage whatever. The theft represents a total loss." She paused. "Do you have any other insinuating questions?"

How did I let myself get sucked into this? Charlie Moon

stared at the willful woman. "I'll have to know everything about the burglary."

"Of course." She blew a puff of smoke at her nephew. "Bertie, call the state police, talk to Officer What's His Name—see that Mr. Moon is provided with a copy of the official report. And show him the scene of the crime, answer all his questions." She fell back in the chair. "Now please, you two—leave me alone." She sighed wistfully, allowed the blue-tinted lids to slip over her eyes. "I must get my beauty sleep."

Bertie grinned mischievously at the Indian.

Her eyes still closed, his aunt smiled cruelly. "I know what you are dying to say, Bertie. Go ahead—take the cheap shot. I'll squash you like the nasty little bug you are."

Thus chastened, the little man beetled away.

The Ute followed in his wake.

CHAPTER TWENTY-NINE

THE MUSEUM

CHARLIE MOON AND BERTRAM EUSTACE CASSIDY WALKED across a lawn that rolled gently, like small waves heaving upon the tide of night. Before the previous dawn, there had been a sweet, soaking rain. Beneath their feet, the spongy mat of grass would hold a record of their passing until a spray of sunlight washed it away. Above them, tiny water pearls and other priceless gems glistened on spruce needles and aspen stems.

Bertie approached a peak-roofed structure that was almost concealed behind a picket line of lodgepole pines. The red brick walls were matted with leafy vines that clung desperately with thousands of tentacled fingers. He looked up at the Ute. "This is where we house the old, moldy family treasures—known more widely among antiquarians and other eccentrics as the Cassidy collection." The small man allowed himself an odd half-smile, hinting that he knew a hilarious family joke that could not be shared with an outsider.

Charlie Moon wondered how difficult it had been for the burglar to get inside.

Anticipating the question, Bertie's tone was apologetic. "Aside from an outdated lock on the door and simple latches on the windows, I am afraid we didn't have a security system worthy of the name. The thief had no trouble at all gaining entry." He pointed. "The rascal simply broke through the glass window in the door, reached inside, unbolted the latch."

The shattered glazing had been replaced, though there were still a few tiny shards of glass scattered about that had been missed in the cleanup. The Ute noted that there was no indication that any type of alarm system had been installed. The same burglar could return tonight, break in the same way.

Bertie inserted a shiny brass key in the new lock mechanism, twisted until he heard an oiled bolt respond with a satisfying *thunk*. He opened the door, indicated with a sideways nod that his guest should go in before him.

Charlie Moon entered a dimly lit room that smelled of oiled woods, candle wax, and dust of ages long forgotten.

The last male of the wealthy branch of the Cassidy clan pressed an old-fashioned push-button switch. On the acoustic-paneled ceiling, a double row of fluorescent lights sizzled and popped before blooming to life.

A wee black mouse went lickety-splitting across the unpainted concrete floor, found refuge in a corner, under the bristles of a broom.

Now inside his habitual lair, Moon's host assumed the confident air of a professional guide who knows everything about his subject. "The building was constructed in 1939, just as the war was heating up in Europe. When I am in one of my whimsical moods," Bertie said this almost to himself, "I refer to this old crypt as the Cassidy *Mausoleum*. This makes Auntie Jane quite furious." He snickered.

The tribal investigator waited for his eyes to adjust to the light.

Bertie blinked at the flickering fluorescents. "We are in the display room, where I occasionally bring out a few items for viewing by selected groups. Years ago, when the family allowed drop-in visitors three days every week, we entertained everyone from mom-and-pop tourists to distinguished university scholars. These days, the collection is shown only by special appointment. Auntie Jane does not care to have curious erudites poking and prowling about the family treasures. She prefers to cater to senior citizens, church groups, Boy and Girl Scouts, and schoolchildren who have an interest in the Cassidy curiosities." He noted that the Indian policeman's gaze had been pulled to the steel door on the far wall. "That is the entrance to the secure storage space, where the most valuable items in the collection are generally kept locked away. It is a veritable vault. The walls are steel-reinforced poured concrete, there is no outside door, and the windows—which are primarily for ventilation—are just fourteen inches square and protected with two-inch-diameter steel bars. The burglar would have required dynamite or a cutting torch to gain entry to the inner sanctum."

"Interesting place," Moon said.

"Yes. Interesting." Bertram Eustace Cassidy sucked too much dust into his nostrils, paused to sneeze. He wiped his nose with a spotless silk handkerchief. "To be perfectly candid, the place does not deserve to be called a museum any more than I deserve my title as curator. This is merely a storage shed for a collection of old stuff. Some of it mere bric-a-brac, some quite hideous, some even quite valuable—but there is no theme to the collection, and I am little more than a caretaker."

The tribal investigator was only half listening. "Looks like the fella with the sack found what he wanted here." In the center of the room, a glass display case had been smashed, and was empty. No attempt had been made to tidy up.

"Indeed." Bertie indulged in a melancholy sigh. "Nine days out of ten, there would have been nothing in the display room but relatively common stuff. Sadly, I had been preparing for a visit from the Salida High School History Club. These precocious youths were to be bused in for my presentation—only three days after the burglary." Bertie shook his bald head. "If it were not for that unfortunate coincidence, the sneak thief would have gained access to very little that was worth hauling away."

Moon tried to remember what he had read in the newspaper. "The break-in, didn't it happen on the second day of May?" The same day Kicks Dogs had shown up at Daisy's home, reported her husband missing.

Bertie nodded. "At almost precisely two AM Auntie Jane was awakened by the sound of breaking glass. I also heard the sound, but thought I had imagined it." He turned to stare at the door. "I should have thought a professional burglar would have used a glass cutter—it would have made virtually no sound at all."

"Yeah. Sounds like an amateur. You or your aunt see anything?"

"Sadly, no. But she immediately called the police, then came to my bedroom yelling her head off. I went outside with a flashlight and a baseball bat, but by then the thief had fled."

Lucky for you. Moon surveyed the items left behind by the thief. There were unpainted pine shelves lined with jars and bottles containing biological specimens—slugs, snails, snakes, amphibians, and more than a few unidentifiable, monstrous things. An unbroken display case was filled with fossils of mollusks, mammoths, and mastodons. Another contained an assortment of obsidian and flint projectile points, beaded moccasins, Mesa Verde pottery. On the walls were reproductions of ancient maps of strange, mythical lands where dragons breathed fire, fathomless seas where scaled serpents appeared suddenly from the depths to crunch sailing ships in monstrous toothed jaws. More strange by far were a dozen frames of iridescent butterflies, giant moths, glistening blue-black crickets, mummified tree frogs, beetles both great and small—some with pincers raised high. All quite lovely, made perfect in death.

Charlie Moon rapped a knuckle on the broken display case. "What exactly did the bad guy take?"

"I will, of course, provide you with the detailed list we provided to the police," Bertie said. "But the scoundrel made off with the bulk of the Cassidy rare-coin collection, which included everything from Spanish pieces of eight to early American cents, many of them quite rare."

This matched the newspaper accounts. "What're the coins worth?"

Bertie shrugged. "It is impossible to be precise, but on today's market the collection would certainly bring three million dollars. Perhaps twice that much."

"That's a sizable pile of money."

"Indeed. Then there was Auntie Jane's three or four dozen antique cameos, probably worth no more than seventy or eighty thousand dollars—but of considerable sentimental value."

The cash-stretched Ute glanced at Bertie's face to see if he was joking. There was not the least sign of humor.

"The cameos were not all that remarkable." He blinked at the Indian. "But I thought the young ladies in the History Club would enjoy seeing them."

Moon was thinking about the rare coins. "And everybody loves money."

"Oh my, yes." The curator of the Cassidy collection chortled. "Even innocent children drool over disks of silver and gold. And copper, for that matter."

"Bertie, it strikes me that you're in an awfully good mood for a man who's lost a good chunk of his inheritance."

Bertie struck a Puckish pose, snapped his stubby fingers. "I care not a tra-la-la for this world's rubies and crowns and rings—what I want is angel's wings."

The Ute, who had taken several literature courses at Fort Lewis College, cocked his head. "Who said that?"

"I did, of course." Bertie giggled. "What do you think," he pointed at the ceiling—"there's a poetic pixie prancing in the loft?"

Moon grinned. *Not in the loft.* "How much trouble will the thief have when he tries to sell the stuff?"

As he considered this question, Bertie scratched at his hairless scalp. "It will not be easy. The list of coins has been posted on the Internet. Alarms would certainly go off among reputable numismatists if some lowlife attempted to sell even one silver three-cent piece on the legitimate market."

"But there are collectors who are more than willing to buy stolen goods."

Bertie nodded. "Sad but true. And in principle, every piece that was stolen could be sold on the gray market. But unless the thief took on the job specifically *for* such a client, he would have to be very patient, and enormously cautious. The most sensible option would be to sell the goods back to Auntie Jane. But even that approach has its obvious hazards. The thief would require a reliable go-between, an honest broker who could be trusted by buyer and seller alike. Which is why the thieving rascal contacted Ralph Briggs—a dealer who happens to be a trusted family friend." He studied the Indian's dark profile, wondered what sort of man this was. "Would you like the grand tour of the inner sanctum?"

In truth, Charlie Moon would not. But he did not know how to say no to his happy little host.

The curator of the Cassidy collection twirled a combination lock six times, opened the steel door, switched on another bank of fluorescent lights, led the tribal investigator along the aisles inside the massive vault. Aside from row upon row of shelves lined with meticulously labeled cardboard and wooden boxes, there was little to see other than a few magnificent Chinese spittoons, a silver-inlaid French crossbow, a Remington bronze of an Arapaho buffalo hunt, a small display of Mayan jade artifacts. The men's footsteps raised swirls of dust. When the tour was finished, Moon was happy to hear the heavy door close behind him. He was even happier to be outside, where the air was fresh and sweet, where crickets and frogs were chirping, and moths fluttered about electric floodlights.

They headed across the wet grass toward Moon's pickup, Bertie skipping two steps to the tall man's single stride. "Tell me the honest truth, Charlie—do you think you can help us recover the stolen items?"

The Ute ducked to pass under a mulberry branch. "I doubt it."

"Then you're merely in this for the money you can squeeze out of Auntie Jane?"

"Sure."

"Bully for you."

Moon stopped at Betty Lou, picked an elm leaf off the windshield wiper.

Bertie kicked the toe of his fuzzy slipper against the massive tire. "This is quite a remarkable truck." He heaved a long, wistful sigh. "If Auntie Jane was to see me driving a huge, vulgar vehicle like this around the neighborhood, the poor old thing would throw a hissing fit." Rubbing his fingers along the fender, he addressed the owner of the marvelous F-350: "I should not tell you this, which is the very reason I am determined to—but another law-enforcement professional is already working on the recovery of the Cassidy coins and cameos. And I'd bet a Morgan silver dollar to a Roosevelt copper dime that it is someone you know." He watched the Ute's face, expecting a reaction. "Does that worry you?"

"Not a smidgen," Moon said. "Competition is the American Way."

"Oh, fudge—I was hoping you would attempt to wheedle the details out of me."

He grinned at the odd little man. "If it'll make you feel better, consider yourself wheedled."

"Oh my, you are so intimidating—why, I feel compelled to tell you everything!" Bertie lowered his voice to a raspy whisper. "Your competition is a police officer who showed up several hours after the burglary—but just minutes after the gaggle of police who were investigating the break-in had departed."

Mr. Moon stared at Mr. Cassidy.

Bertie clapped his hands. "Aha—I thought that might get your attention." He continued in a conspiratorial tone, "This policeman—who said he'd been working all night at his appointed duties—claimed that he had a pretty good idea about who is responsible for the recent burglaries in our neighborhood. He said he couldn't work on it *officially* because the crime was committed outside his jurisdiction. But the cheeky fellow hinted that he might be enticed to help us get the stolen goods back if a suitable financial remuneration was forthcoming. This suggestion inspired Auntie Jane to offer the twenty-thousand-dollar reward for the return of the loot. She told him to contact us when he had something solid. So far, we have not heard from the fellow."

Moon considered the possibilities. "If your home isn't in his jurisdiction, it couldn't have been a state police officer. Must've been one of the fellas from Durango."

"Negatory." The pale face grinned. "This John Law was one of yours."

"A Ute?"

"I would not want to go so far as to say that he was a *Ute*." The tattler was highly pleased with himself. "But the constable in question did have a Southern Ute PD patch stitched onto the arm of his jacket."

Moon muttered to himself, "One of our officers . . . on the night shift." *Surely not.*

"You are an uncommonly sly fellow, Mr. Moon—do you think you can get the copper's name out of me?"

"Probably not." The Indian shook his head in a regretful manner. "The tribe has some new rules against staking folks out on anthills or sticking their heads in a basket of snakes."

Bertie feigned great disappointment. "Oh dear me, and I so wanted to pass on that one last tidbit of juicy gossip." He pondered for a moment. "If I shall not be forced to tell you the gendarme's name outright, would you object to a subtle hint?"

Moon wondered whether the peculiar man had fabricated the story for the sake of entertainment.

"Very well, I shall take your stony silence as a yes. Now here goes—think of a wild animal that howls at the moon. We're talking canine, but you can eliminate the fox, jackal, and dingo. This is the same big bad howler that et Little Red Riding Hood's aunt."

"Granny."

"Oh dear me, you are right—it was Red's granny that got et, not her auntie." Bertie giggled. "That must have been a Freudian slip."

A MILE down the road, Moon dialed Chief of Police White-horse's unpublished home number, waited through a recorded message.

"Wallace, this is Charlie Moon. We need to talk about Jim Wolfe. I'll be in your office at eight AM sharp."

OFFICER JAMES Wolfe was unable to eat, much less to sleep. The desperate man paced across his small parlor, his thoughts racing in maddening circles like a crazed dog attempting to bite its tail. *Felix Navarone has to be dead—I shot that*

Apache up enough to kill him half a dozen times. So why isn't he under that pile of rocks where I put him? Finally worn out from going nowhere, he paused, leaned on the papered wall. *This is a bad dream, that's all. I need to do something to wake myself up.*

This was the SUPD officer's most hopeful thought in several days.

I could leave Colorado, go someplace where nobody knows my name—get a brand-new start. Yeah—maybe I should just walk away with what I've got in my pockets—leave everything behind. His mouth curled into a childish grin. *That'd sure make Charlie Moon and the rest of those Ute cops wonder what in the world happened to ol' Jim Wolfe.*

This notion sounded better and better.

I could head down to Mexico. Sonora, maybe.

The question of travel was a sticky one. A man could get on a bus without attracting much attention. Or thumb a ride with a lonesome trucker. A better notion came to mind. *I could call my kid brother over in Alamosa. If I asked him, Dave would come and get me tonight.*

CHAPTER THIRTY

AN INTERNAL MATTER

CHARLIE MOON APOLOGIZED TO THE SUPD CHIEF OF POLICE
for calling the meeting on such short notice. "But I didn't feel
like I had much choice—Officer Wolfe has been doing some
peculiar things."

Wallace Whitehorse eased himself into the creaking chair
behind his desk. The Northern Cheyenne had never been particularly fond of the white cop who was the subject of this
meeting. But Jim Wolfe was *his* white cop, and Charlie Moon
had no official authority whatever in the Southern Ute Police
Department. But what the tribal investigator did have was the
ear of tribal chairman Oscar Sweetwater. And that carried
plenty of weight with the politically conscious chief of police.
He slapped his big hand on a stack of files and duty logs. "I
got all of Wolfe's paperwork here."

"Let's take a look at his work report for . . ." When had the
Cassidy Museum been burgled? "May second."

Whitehorse thumbed through the logbook. "Here it is." He
adjusted the spectacles perched on his big beak of a nose.
"What're we looking for?"

"I believe Wolfe was on graveyard duty."

The chief of police nodded. "One o'clock to nine AM. But
he ended up working some overtime later that morning. At
time and a half." He gave the tribal investigator a look. "Says
here, Wolfe responded to a call from somebody who goes by
the name of C. Moon."

"That was the morning Kicks Dogs showed up at my aunt's home, claiming her husband had walked off and left her in Spirit Canyon. I put in a call from to the dispatcher, requesting a search. Wolfe had just got in off his night duty, but he responded."

"So?"

"Can I have a look at his duty log?"

"Sure." Wallace Whitehorse slid the paperwork across the desk.

Charlie Moon squinted at the white man's neat print. There were entries every half hour or so. Mostly of routine patrol. Wolfe had been working the north central area of the res, which put him in the general area of the Cassidy property. At twenty minutes either side of two o'clock in the morning, Wolfe had made no entries. And there was nothing in the log about a visit to the Cassidy home after the museum burglary. Moon looked up at Whitehorse. "Did Wolfe request night duty?"

The chief of police nodded slowly. "He liked working at night. And alone." Whitehorse took a deep breath, his chest bulged under the blue cotton shirt. "Charlie, what's this all about?"

"I'm not entirely sure." Moon gave an abbreviated account of what Bertram Eustace Cassidy had told him about the only white officer in the employ of the SUPD.

Wallace Whitehorse listened without interruption until the Ute had had his say. "Okay, let me see if I understand what you're telling me. We got an alleged witness, the rich white woman's nephew, who claims Officer Wolfe showed up a few hours after that family museum was broke into. And Wolfe talks to the rich old lady—ah—What's-her-name . . ."

"Jane Cassidy."

"Right, Jane. And according to this verbal report from the nephew, Officer Wolfe hints that he has a notion about who the burglars might be—and if there was some money in it, he might be able to help the Cassidys get their stuff back. Which leads Jane to offer a twenty-thousand-dollar reward for the return of the stolen property. This is all according to the nephew, What's-his-name?"

"Bertram."

"Yeah. And this Bertram, he spills the beans to you about Wolfe."

"That's about the size of it, Wallace."

"Why does Bertram do that?"

"Hard to explain. You'd have to meet him."

Wallace Whitehorse scowled at the duty log. "Wolfe didn't write down nothing in his report about stopping at the Cassidy place." The top cop frowned at his mental image of the meddler who was accusing one of his officers of improper conduct. "This Cassidy guy, you think he could be mistaken?" His tone was hopeful. "Maybe it wasn't Wolfe that knocked on his door, maybe it was some other cop."

Moon felt sorry for Whitehorse. "Anything's possible. But it'll be easy enough to find out."

"Right." The chief of police snatched up a sleek black telephone, punched two buttons, barked an order. Waited. "You sure of that?" Whitehorse drummed his big fingers on the desk. "Okay. But send somebody over to his digs." He listened for a few seconds, slammed the phone down. "Wolfe didn't show up for work last night. Maybe he's sick or something."

"Yeah," Moon said. *Or something.*

"Danny Bignight is headed for Wolfe's apartment, so we should be able to sort this business out pretty quick." An expression of relief spread over the chief's face. "So I guess we're finished till Danny gets back here with Wolfe."

"Not quite yet."

The Northern Cheyenne groaned. "Please—don't tell me there's more."

"Sorry, Wallace—there's more." Moon gave a brief account of Jim Wolfe's apparent entry into Aunt Daisy's trailer.

"She actually see him in there?"

"No."

"Was the trailer door locked?"

"I'm not sure," Moon said. "But probably not."

The chief of police grasped at this slippery straw. "If it wasn't locked, Officer Wolfe wasn't technically breaking and entering. He might've just dropped by to see the old lady. She did doctor him after he got bunged up in the rassling match with that Apache we sprung, What's-his-name . . ."

"Felix Navarone."

"Right." Whitehorse scrawled the name on a pad.

Moon tried to get him back on track. "I think you're right. Jim Wolfe probably went out to Aunt Daisy's place expecting her to be at home. And when he didn't find her there, he went inside. And *borrowed* what he'd intended to buy from her."

Whitehorse was not sure he wanted to know, but it was his duty to ask: "What would Officer Wolfe borrow from your aunt?"

Moon had to work hard to say it. "Some . . . uh . . . corpse powder."

The Northern Cheyenne did not have to ask what corpse powder was. "She keeps stuff like *that* around?"

The embarrassed tribal investigator did not respond. For the moment, he preferred to let Wallace Whitehorse believe the old woman was dabbling in bad magic. When the time was right, he'd tell him the stuff was only cornbread mix.

Whitehorse suddenly realized that there was a far more pertinent question: "What would Officer Wolfe want with corpse powder?"

Moon shrugged. "As far as I know, it's only used for one thing."

"Yeah. To sprinkle on a dead body—so the ghost can't hurt you." Whitehorse made a face. "I sure don't like the sound of that."

"Me neither," Moon said. "That's why I followed Wolfe."

"Followed him where?"

"The canyon country over by Butterfield Mesa." The tribal investigator gave a detailed account of what had transpired.

Wallace Whitehorse had trouble believing what he had heard. "You actually telling me that Wolfe took the corpse powder to what looked like a grave? Dug up the grave—"

"It was just a pile of rocks," Moon said. "He took some of the rocks away—"

"And then he gets scared and runs like a scalded jackrabbit?"

Those had not been Moon's exact words, but he nodded.

"And you go check out the rocks, and there's no dead body there. So why does Wolfe take corpse powder where there ain't no corpse?"

"I'm hoping he'll tell us," Moon said.

SUPD OFFICER Daniel Bignight opened the Subaru door, conducted a superficial search of Jim Wolfe's automobile. He found nothing unusual in the glove compartment or under the seats. Bignight was not surprised that his brother officer had not bothered to lock his car. Wolfe, who was somewhat absentminded, was always worried about locking his ignition keys inside.

THE CHIEF'S telephone rang. Whitehorse slammed it against his ear. "Yeah?" His expression became grim as he listened. "Stay there. Me'n Charlie Moon'll be right over." He spoke to Moon: "Danny Bignight says Wolfe's car is in the parking lot at his apartment building. But Wolfe, he ain't responding to repeated knocking on his door."

The Ute got up, donned his black Stetson. "Let's go find out why."

THE APARTMENT building manager was an attractive, fortyish, Hispanic woman. She used her master key to open the door, watched across the threshold as the trio of Indian cops conducted a quick search.

It was immediately apparent that Jim Wolfe was not at home.

While Danny Bignight and Chief Whitehorse poked around the apartment, Moon stepped outside to speak to the manager. "Have you seen Mr. Wolfe in the past day or so?"

The manager nodded. "Last night, I saw him pass my window going up the stairs. My apartment is right under his. And the stairway light is always on."

"About what time would that have been?"

She replayed the previous evening in her mind. "I was watching a rerun of *Buffy the Vampire Slayer*, and it was almost over. So it must've been a few minutes before the ten o'clock news." The manager was startled by a recollection.

"You know what? I think Mr. Wolfe may've left two or three hours later."

The tribal investigator felt his pulse quicken. "Why do you think that?"

"I sleep really sound, thunder won't wake me up." The manager closed her eyes to concentrate. "But sometime last night, I woke up when I heard a car horn start toot-tooting out front. I thought it would never stop but then—"

Wallace Whitehorse materialized at Moon's side, addressed the Ute as if the woman were not present. "What's this about a car horn blowing?"

"Well, the lady says she—"

The chief of police barked at the woman, "Tell me about it."

The manager took her time. "It was late last night when that horn started tooting; I pulled a pillow over my head and tried to go back to sleep. Pretty quick, I heard Mr. Wolfe's door slam. A little while after that, the honking stopped." She opened her eyes to stare at Wallace Whitehorse. "Somebody came and picked him up—some jerk who didn't care if he woke up the whole neighborhood."

The SUPD police chief told the woman that he'd send someone around to take a detailed statement. She could return to her apartment now. The manager understood that this was a polite dismissal, but chose to hang by the threshold and stare into Wolfe's apartment.

Wallace Whitehorse gave Charlie Moon a nod. Moon followed him into the small apartment. Whitehorse shut the door in the manager's face.

"Looks like all of Wolfe's stuff is here," Wallace Whitehorse said. "His SUPD uniform is hanging in the closet with a rack fulla his clothes. And there's several pairs of shoes and a suitcase on the closet shelf."

Moon had a look at the closet. Over the years, he had learned to notice what was *missing* from the picture. "Did you find Wolfe's sidearm?"

Whitehorse had not thought of this. "Uh—I guess he must've took it with him."

Officer Daniel Bignight stomped into the small parlor.

"Look what I found under Wolfe's bed." He held something in his gloved hand—a plastic bag half filled with a coarse yellowish substance. The Taos Pueblo man had not heard the report of Wolfe's alleged theft of corpse powder from Daisy Perika's trailer. Bignight shook the grainy mixture. "It looks like cornmeal."

The chief of police was dismayed to see this physical evidence of Officer Wolfe's burglary of the old woman's home, but Whitehorse was a traditional Cheyenne. He had no intention of going near the least speck of corpse powder. "Danny, treat that as evidence."

Bignight wondered, *Evidence of what?*

Moon glanced into the bedroom, noted Wolfe's neatly made bed.

Whitehorse followed the tribal investigator's gaze. "He didn't sleep here last night. I imagine he was sitting up late, waiting for somebody to come pick him up." *And I'd give two weeks' pay to know who.*

The evidence suggested that Wolfe had left in the middle of the night with nothing but his pistol and what he wore on his back. Moon waited for the chief of police to reach the inevitable decision.

Wallace Whitehorse's leathery face had drooped several notches below its customary gloomy expression. The Northern Cheyenne mumbled a curse in his native language, switched back to English. "I'll have to notify the FBI."

Moon watched a bemused Bignight bag and tag the stolen cornbread mix. "Is Stan Newman still the Man in the Durango office?"

"Yeah," Whitehorse said. "And Stan's got a new partner." The SUPD chief of police pressed a button on his cell phone to dial the programmed number. He exchanged the customary pleasantries with his FBI contact, then proceeded to explain the reason for his call. Wallace Whitehorse's mumbled narrative was punctuated by brief silences that Charlie Moon knew from long experience were pointed questions from Special Agent Stanley Newman. Finally, Whitehorse said three words:

"He's right here." He seemed relieved to pass the telephone to the tribal investigator.

Moon held the small instrument to his ear. "Hi, Stan."

Newman got right to the point. "Wallace tells me he's got a possible rogue cop who left town last night with person or persons unknown. And what's all this nonsense about stolen corpse powder and empty graves?"

Moon smiled into the mouthpiece. "We reservation cops aren't smart enough to figure it out. That's why we're happy to call on the services of our nation's top law-enforcement agency. We need you to come give us a hand."

There was a braying laugh from Stanley Newman. "Maybe there really was a body in that grave, Charlie. I bet you just didn't dig deep enough."

"I would not even think about doing any digging at the scene of a potential crime where the FBI would have ultimate jurisdiction."

"Okay, smart guy—here's the drill. You and Wallace saddle up and head to the spot where the grave is. Me'n my partner will fly out in the Blackbird."

"Stan, I don't think you'll find anything, but if you really want to—"

"If there ever was a body, maybe we can find some something for a DNA ID. Hair. Blood. Saliva. Flakes of epidermis." His tone turned caustically sarcastic. "That's what we *do,* Charlie."

The tribal investigator was forced to admit that Newman was right. Technically. If there had ever been a body under the pile of stones.

"I am gratified that you see it my way, Chucky. So tell me where we're going."

Charlie Moon told him. "When we spot the copter, we'll use a cell phone to talk you in."

"You do that." Newman hung up.

Moon returned the telephone to Whitehorse. "Stan is determined to check out that pile of rocks where Wolfe went to sprinkle some corpse powder."

The chief of police nodded. "The one where there ain't no corpse."

"The very same."

"Charlie, I don't like the feel of this."

Corpse powder? Danny Bignight cleared his throat. "Excuse me." He pointed at the evidence bag. "Is this really . . . you know . . . what you just said?"

Moon and Whitehorse nodded in perfect synchrony.

The Taos Pueblo Indian stared at the doubled-bagged sample of cornbread mix with an expression of utter horror. *Oh God—I hope I didn't get any on me.* Bignight hurried to Wolfe's kitchen sink, washed his hands.

CHAPTER THIRTY-ONE

NEWMAN'S PARTNER

A MASSIVE BLACK THUNDERHEAD HAD BOILED UP IN THE west, casting chill winds and a threatening shadow across the reservation canyon lands.

Officer Danny Bignight sat behind the wheel of the four-wheel-drive Blazer. Like his boss, the Taos Pueblo man had a bad feeling about this outing.

A few yards away, Charlie Moon and Wallace Whitehorse held on to their hats with both hands as the FBI pilot expertly lowered the small helicopter onto a clearing near a defunct gas well.

ON THE aircraft, Stan Newman leaned to yell in his new partner's ear, "See that tall guy with Wallace Whitehorse?"

She nodded, shouted back, "Is that the man I've heard so much about?"

After the engine was shut off, the props slowed to a lazy *whoosh-whoosh,* finally stopped with a metallic clunk. Long black petals drooped as the mechanical flower wilted under the sunless sky.

Newman lowered his voice to accommodate the welcome silence. "Yeah. That's Charlie Moon."

A faint smile touched her lips. "Is Mr. Moon half of what he's cracked up to be?"

"I'll let you be the judge of that. But I can tell you this—

Charlie knows more about the res than all the rest of the Ute cops put together. And he's a lot smarter than he looks."

He looks smart enough to me. "He must be a useful resource for the Bureau."

"He could be if he wanted to," Newman said. "But none of us have ever gotten much from ol' Charlie—he holds his cards pretty close to the vest." He watched his ambitious partner's face, knew she was eager to stake out her claim and mine it.

CHARLIE MOON watched Special Agent Stanley Newman emerge from the helicopter hatch, the breeze whipping at what little hair he had left. Stan was muscular, round shouldered, pushing sixty, and had a round spot shining on the top of his skull. Newman was followed by a creature of another sort entirely. Moon raised an eyebrow. The woman in the dark blue jumpsuit was tall, slim, moved with the lithe, catlike confidence of one who has never slipped on the ice or stubbed her toe on a stone. Her black hair was done in a single braid, her face was oval, her eyes large. The Ute leaned close to Wallace Whitehorse. "That's Stan's new partner?"

The chief of Southern Ute police muttered something that Moon took to be an affirmation, hurried off to greet the mismatched pair of feds. Wallace Whitehorse shook hands with Newman, who immediately made a path toward Moon. Whitehorse hung behind to exchange a few words with the strikingly handsome woman.

Newman seemed to be in excellent spirits. "Hey, Charlie—what's going on, you Indians can't even keep track of your cops now?"

Ignoring the customary bluntness of the white man's hello-now-let's-get-down-to-business greeting, Moon pumped Newman's knobby hand. "Good afternoon, Stan."

"Good afternoon yourself." The FBI agent nodded to indicate the stunning woman. "How d'you like my new sidekick?"

"Until I get to know her a little better, I must decline to comment."

"Don't give me that malarkey."

Moon felt his mouth grin. "Okay. She is not hard to look at."

The fed snickered. "Don't get your hormones all heated up, Charlie. Special Agent McTeague is miles outta your league. And my new partner is very particular about who she associates with."

"This is too easy—but I feel obligated to point out that she is hanging around with the likes of you."

"On that matter, McTeague had no choice." Newman curled his lips into a nasty smile. "It was an assignment, and she is a pro—so she gritted her perfect teeth and got on with the job."

Her teeth are nice. "I see what you mean."

"Then we're making some progress."

"But just for the record, I merely remarked that she was easy on the eyes." Moon looked down his nose at the fed. "It's not like I had intended to ask her to share a strawberry milk shake."

"Well, if you did, chump—she'd laugh right in your homely face."

"She is that downright mean?"

"Mean? Why, that don't half describe McTeague. The woman is cold as a snowball and hard as an anvil. And she's smart, too. Which is another reason why she'd never waste a minute on a stumblebum like you."

Sensing that there might be an opportunity lurking here, Moon played along. "You think this federal cop would find me repulsive?"

"Your words, not mine. But since you put it that way, odds are ninety-nine to zero that she will gag when she gets within three yards of you. If she ever gets that close."

He walks right into it every time. "Pardon me, Stan—but that sounds distinctly like a challenge."

"You want to make a bet?" Newman shook his balding head and chuckled. "No, not even Charlie Bet-His-Whole-Wad Moon would be so lame-brained as to—"

"Name it."

The fed assumed a thoughtful expression. "A wager must be well defined."

"Define it."

The FBI agent thought about it. "Within a specified time from right now, you and her have to go out on a date."

It was Moon's turn to look doubtful. "A *date*?"

Newman smirked his most irksome smirk, knowing this would undo the Ute. "The real thing. With flowers."

"Okay." Flowers were no problem. "And I like the ninety-nine-to-zero odds."

"That was merely a figure of speech."

"Uh-oh. Looks like the suit is backing off."

The fed ignored this remark. "I say ten to one McTeague'll spit in your eye." He added quickly, "Figuratively speaking."

Moon tried not to look too happy. "Okay. I'll put up fifty bucks. If you think you can risk the other number."

An expression of unease passed over Newman's hawkish features. "Five hundred clams?"

"Unless they've changed the rules, ten times fifty is still five hundred."

"I dunno. On my salary, with my daughter in college, five hundred—"

"I sense a sudden lack of confidence on your part, Stan. A fellow less polite than me would say you are choking."

"It's not that, Charlie—I just can't afford to risk that much cash on a silly bet that—"

"Then you admit you might lose the bundle?"

Newman set his jaw. "Okay, smart guy. You're on. And now there's the matter of how much time you've got to get the job done."

"Okay. Let's say your partner and I will have our first date within . . . thirty days."

The fed's eyes popped. "An entire month?"

"Twenty-nine?"

Newman shook his head. "Three days."

"Twenty."

"Six days and that's absolutely my last word on the matter."

"Ten."

"Done."

She appeared suddenly with Whitehorse, startling the gamblers. "Agent Newman, are you going to introduce me?"

The senior agent jerked his chin to indicate the tall Indian. "Agent McTeague, this is ol' Charlie. From time to time, he pretends to do some police work for the Southern Utes. But thirty-two days a month, he's a bronc-riding, rope-twirling cowboy-farmer who don't know a felon from a melon and—"

"Charlie Moon, ma'am." The owner of the name removed his black Stetson. "What Stan is trying to tell you—in his own peculiar way—is that I'm a special investigator attached to the office of the tribal chairman." He produced the small breast-pocket leather wallet, flashed the gold shield. "And when I'm not doing Stan's work for him, I find time to run one of the finest cattle operations in the great state of Colorado."

"I have heard about your excellent law-enforcement work over the years, and your distinguished military service." The smile was a little more than Mona Lisa, the tint of her eyes outright violet. "And I have heard quite a lot about the Columbine Ranch." Special Agent McTeague offered her hand.

Moon accepted it. "From time to time—I hope we'll have the opportunity to work together."

McTeague's lips parted, her smile scintillated. "I'm sure we will, Mr. Moon."

"You can call me Charlie."

"You may call me Special Agent McTeague." The smile was teasing. "Or, if someday we meet on the street, Lila Mae."

McTeague's partner broke the spell. "There's not too many hours of daylight left. We better get at it."

Leaving Danny Bignight with the helicopter pilot, White-horse and the FBI agents followed the long-legged Ute along the edge of the massive red-sandstone slab known locally as Butterfield Mesa. Under the overhang of a rain-streaked cliff, Moon paused, stopped, turned to eye the pretty lady. "Agent McTeague, have you ever seen a woolly-mammoth petroglyph?"

Her big eyes got bigger. "Why, no."

He pointed. "Look right up there."

Wallace Whitehorse did not bother to look.

Special Agent Newman squinted himself cross-eyed. "I don't see no mammoth."

Lila Mae McTeague shaded her eyes with her hand. "Where is it?"

Moon addressed the woman. "C'mon, I'll take you where you can get a closer look."

She followed him up a crumbling embankment.

Newman made a move to follow his partner, felt the Northern Cheyenne's firm grip on his arm. "What?"

The chief of police gave him a fatherly look. "Sometimes young people need to be alone."

"*Young* people?" The fed watched Moon and McTeague climb the ridge. "Who am I—Great-granddaddy Newman?"

Wallace Whitehorse seated himself under the fanlike branch of a fragrant juniper. The sensible man found a wrinkled green apple in his pocket, wiped it off on his sleeve, took a bite. Like his life, it was a bit sour to the taste. He did not mind.

CHAPTER THIRTY-TWO

THE GENTLEMAN'S PROPOSITION

SPECIAL AGENT MCTEAGUE SCANNED THE OVERHANG FOR something that looked even vaguely like a curly-tusked elephant. "I'm sorry—I still don't see the petroglyph."

"Look again," Charlie Moon said. "Right up there, just to the left of that big black spot."

She squinted. "Is there really a woolly mammoth up there?"

"No."

McTeague turned to face the Ute. "Mr. Moon, what is this all about?"

He managed a sickly grin. "What happened to *Charlie*?"

"That was then." She was definitely not smiling.

This was not looking good. "Uh . . . here's the deal. I've got myself into a little bind, and I need you to help me out."

"I beg your pardon?"

These modern professional women can be kinda sensitive, so I'll have to be extra careful how I say this. "Agent McTeague, I want you to know that as far as I'm concerned, you're the same as a man."

"What?" The word was like a pistol shot.

He blundered on, stumbling straight into the abyss. "You know—one of the guys."

For the first time since Lila Mae McTeague had choked on a grape lollipop, she was at a loss for words.

Taking advantage of this apparent opportunity, he went

into free fall. "The fact that you're technically a member of the other gender—that don't mean a thing to me."

She made a partial recovery. "You are not interested in women?"

Moon was genuinely puzzled. "Sure I am—practically all the women I see interest me."

"But I am an exception." She put her hands on her hips.

Why is it so hard to talk to them? "Agent McTeague, when I said you were one of the guys, what I actually meant was—"

"That you consider me *masculine*?" There was a glint of outrage in her eyes.

"Uh—only in the *good* sense of the word." Like a possum caught sucking eggs, Charlie Moon foolishly thought he could grin his way out of this predicament. "Fact is, I am partial to ladies that wear baggy coveralls and big hobnailed boots. And pack automatic pistols."

"Well, make a note of this, Mr. Tact. I don't find you all that attractive either. You're way too . . . too skinny. And did I mention *weird*?"

It was apparent from his startled expression that Moon was stung by this remark.

She frowned thoughtfully at him. "Excuse me for asking, but are you on any kind of medication?"

He took a moment to think about it. "I am partial to caffeine, and need a dose every few hours."

"Caffeine—that's it?"

"Well, I do pop an aspirin a day. My doctor says it prevents heart trouble." *But it don't seem to be working right now.*

Briskly, as if attempting to dislodge an insect from her ear, Lila Mae McTeague shook her head. "What on earth is this all about?"

Moon was grateful for another chance to explain himself. "I got a proposition to make. But I don't want you to get the idea that I'd ever flirt with you."

"Thank you, Sir Galahad. This news does wonders for my self-esteem."

"Thing is, I have a serious illness."

She pretended to be surprised. "Mental?"

The tall man nodded. "You hammered that spike right on the head. I have what those high-priced brain doctors call a gambling compulsion. Why, I'll bet on anything. The very minute a big boulder will cut loose and roll down a hill, how many time's it'll thunder before sundown, which two ladies will get into the first fistfight at the Bear Dance."

"You do not sound that much different from a dozen other adolescent males that I have had the misfortune to encounter."

"That's because you have not heard the worst of it—I bet on things where I'm *bound* to lose. Now imagine there was sixteen fat magpies sitting on a barbwire fence."

The bemused woman concentrated. "Okay. I can see them now."

"See the third one from the left?"

"The scruffy one with the droopy wing?"

"That's the bird. Right here and now, I'll give you even money that she'll be the one to fly away first."

"I like the odds."

"Now imagine you and me was standing in downtown Durango."

"Could you be more precise?"

"On the corner of Seventh and Main."

"I know the spot. So what are we doing?"

"Just passing away the time of day. The sun is shining. Birds are chirping."

"Sounds wonderful. But must you be there?"

"Try and work with me on this."

She closed her eyes. "Okay. We are standing on the corner of Seventh and Main. I think I shall have lunch at the Strater."

"You can eat later. Notice all the traffic."

"I can practically smell the exhaust."

"I'll bet you the tenth license plate to pass by will be from Saskatchewan."

"You're on."

"And in four minutes flat, a snow-white pigeon will swoop down from the sky, land right at your feet, and start tap dancing and whistling Dixie."

"A little more of this, you will be flat broke."

"And therein lies the problem, Agent McTeague. With me, making wagers is a vice I just can't resist. And the longer the odds, the quicker I make the fall. Which is why with all my considerable income from high-paid investigative work and the lucrative beef cattle business, I can hardly ever lay up more than a few hundred thousand dollars in the bank."

"Mr. Moon, you are a mildly amusing man—borderline lunatics often are. And though I'm very sorry about your mental condition, I am not a qualified therapist."

The Ute heaved a great sigh. "Then I'm in deep trouble."

"And why should I care?"

"Thanks for asking. Just a few minutes ago, I let someone talk me into a bet. I stand to lose some serious money."

"That is what we women in hobnailed boots call tough cheese." Curiosity made an assault and got the better of her. "What was the nature of this wager?"

He hesitated. "Before I tell you, I want you to promise me you won't get mad at your partner. Even though Stan knows about my sickness, he doesn't really mean any harm when he suckers me into these bets and—"

"Special Agent Newman made a bet with you? About what?"

"It's kind of hard to explain."

"Try."

"Well, Stan told me right off the bat that you wouldn't like me."

"Well, think of that." She glanced downslope at her fellow fed. "Perhaps the man has more insight that I had given him credit for."

The Ute continued, "And Stan bet me a sizable sum that if I asked you out on a simple, innocent date—say to have a milk shake and see a picture show and get you back home way before midnight—he said you'd laugh. And spit right in my face."

"Date? Ha-ha."

At least she didn't spit.

Stan made a bet involving me? She scowled at her partner, who was standing fifty yards away.

Moon continued in a melancholy tone, "I knew Stan was

right. A fine-looking, stylish woman like yourself wouldn't give a homely face like mine a second look. Every bone in my body was saying, 'Charlie—don't you take that sucker bet. No way under heaven you can win.'" He gave her a downcast look. "But my sickness talked louder. So I laid my hard-earned money down."

She turned to smile at him. "And you think I'll feel sorry for you—and get you off the hook?"

"Well, I *was* kinda hoping—"

McTeague shook her head. "Absolutely not."

"It don't have to be a *real* date."

She studied this odd specimen with a detached, clinical air.

Moon sensed that he was making progress. "Here's the deal. When I ask you for a date—where Stan can hear—all you have to do is say somethin' like, 'Sure, Charlie—I don't mind if I do. You can pick me up about six o'clock.'"

"That's all?"

"Right. And o'course I won't show up—and you can go on doing whatever you was planning to do anyway."

She ejected the words through a quite lovely set of clenched teeth: "Not in a million years!"

"How about if I cut you in for half?"

This threw her. "Half of what?"

"Five hundred bucks."

She groaned.

"Two hundred and fifty dollars is not small potatoes."

The woman rolled her hands into knotty fists. "Let me get this straight—you thought I could be *bought*?"

Moon shrugged. "Thought it was worth a shot."

"You are just the most *exasperating* man!"

The gambler played his last card: "Five hundred dollars is a lot of money for a man to lose. Especially with a daughter in college."

She fairly shrieked. "I've read your entire folder—you don't *have* a daughter!"

"It's Stan that has the kid in college." He grinned. "So paying out will really make him grind his teeth." Surely she could appreciate that.

She did not. Special Agent McTeague turned, slip-slided down the crumbly bank.

He watched her go. Women were the most peculiar creatures. Feeling something staring at the back of his neck, Charlie Moon turned. Looked up at the cliff. For the briefest moment, he could have sworn that he saw—painstakingly pecked into the red stone—an ancient artist's sketch of a massive, curly-tusked, woolly creature. It smiled down at him. Seemed about to erupt in a mammoth belly laugh.

THE ODD quartet trudged on.

Moon marched in long, easy strides, thinking his disjointed thoughts. *This is a snipe hunt. We should be looking for Jim Wolfe. I bet he's halfway to Panama or Costa Rica by now. But at least I'm getting paid by the hour. I think McTeague likes me. I wonder where Miss James is right now.*

Newman stomped along at Moon's side.

Whitehorse and McTeague followed a half-dozen paces behind, the latter shooting odd looks at the gangly Ute.

Newman tossed an over-the-shoulder glance at his partner's grim face, muttered to the Indian. "Looks like you struck out with Big League McTeague. But don't blame me—I told you the lady throws spitballs."

"Your partner could not see the mammoth. I think she's a mite nearsighted, and this bothers her." Charlie Moon smiled in a manner intended to unnerve the FBI agent. "Besides, I have not yet walked up to the plate. I am thinking of asking her out to some fancy to-do. Maybe the opera, down by Santa Fe."

Newman knew a bluff when he heard one. "Don't slice me no baloney."

"Wait and see."

"I expect to see fifty of your greenback dollar bills lining my wallet."

Grandmother Wind roared around the edge of a butte, flung sand in their faces.

Newman muttered vile curses under his breath, spat a wad of grit out of his mouth, scowled at the Ute. "Okay, Chucky—where's this famous pile of rocks?"

"Right over there." The tribal investigator pointed with a tilt of his chin. "But it's not much of a pile anymore. When Officer Wolfe was here yesterday, he scattered 'em around quite a bit." Thirty paces later, Charlie Moon realized that he was wrong. There was indeed a pile of rocks. About eight feet long, a yard wide, knee high. And quite neatly assembled.

CHAPTER THIRTY-THREE

THE UNEXPECTED

THE OFFICERS OF THE LAW APPROACHED THE CAIRN OF smooth stones with due caution, but there was scant evidence of footprints on the rocky surface. In a hand-sized spot of sand there was a faint imprint of a boot heel, which might have been left the previous day by either Charlie Moon or Officer Wolfe. It might, of course, be the partial footprint of a third person who had been in this remote spot more recently. But who? An eccentric passerby who harbored an obsessive drive to create order out of disorder—to make a neat pile of rocks from those that had been scattered by Jim Wolfe in his inexplicable panic?

There was, at the moment, a more pressing issue.

While Charlie Moon and Wallace Whitehorse watched, the methodical federal officers—not given to musing about the possibilities—proceeded to uncover the truth.

Special Agent McTeague produced a fresh pair of latex gloves from one of the oversized pockets on her jumpsuit. Having donned these essential tools of the forensics specialist, the lady went about her task with quiet efficiency, removing stones one by one.

Stanley Newman stood close by with his digital camera, making certain the Bureau had sequential graphics to record this gradual process of uncovering something or other.

Wallace Whitehorse leaned toward Moon. "Whatta you think—will there be somethin' under those rocks?"

Not wishing to converse with the humorless Northern Cheyenne, the Ute shrugged under his denim jacket. Charlie Moon had already been dead wrong when he had predicted they would find nothing but a scattering of stones. But it made no sense that someone had gone to the trouble to come out here several miles past nowhere—just to cover up *nothing*. Moon turned the facts he had upside down and inside out, rotated the ensemble around its axis. In whatever dimension he viewed the construction, he came up empty. *But I must've missed something yesterday evening.*

A trio of ravens sat on a juniper, gawking and squawking at the human beings.

McTeague paused to examine a greenish lump of stone. She gave Newman a look.

He squatted. "What you got?"

She held the sample under his nose.

Newman squinted at what looked like black varnish on the glossy rock. "Blood?"

McTeague nodded, bagged the potential evidence.

Moon watched the work proceed, feeling more than a little incompetent. *I should've looked for blood on the rocks.*

Special Agent McTeague pried up a large, flat stone. Gasped.

Stanley Newman made a horrible grimace.

The Indians drew near for a closer look. There were precisely two things to see.

A dead man's head.

A Ruger .357 Magnum revolver.

A pale face looked up at them. The pistol barrel had been jammed deep into the corpse's throat.

SUPD chief of police Wallace Whitehorse found his voice. "It's Officer Wolfe. And that looks like his service revolver." He felt his legs tremble, leaned against a piñon snag.

To preserve the site for the human remains experts, Special Agent McTeague placed the flat stone back over the face of the corpse.

Newman asked Whitehorse to post a pair of uniforms at the grave site until a complete forensics team could be assembled, then gave Charlie Moon a flinty look. "You absolutely one hundred percent sure there wasn't a body here yesterday?"

"I'm sure." Moon stared at the pile of stones. "But there's something you may want to consider."

"Tell me."

"Before somebody put Jim Wolfe there, there might've been another dead body under those rocks."

The senior FBI agent started to speak but did not.

"When your experts check for traces of blood," Moon added, "you might want to ask them to be on the lookout for two types—"

Newman threw his hands in the air. "One dead cop ain't enough. There's got to be another corpse." The fed shook his head. "I don't suppose there's a relevant fact hiding somewhere behind this speculation?"

The tribal investigator spoke softly. "Stan, I'm sure Jim Wolfe came here to sprinkle corpse powder on somebody he'd put under the stones."

Newman snorted. "Corpse powder. Disappearing bodies. I don't buy it."

"I know it sounds pretty strange," Moon said, "but odds are—" *Odds.* Unintentionally, the Ute had said the magic word.

Newman's mouth split into a hungry-hyena grin. "Okay, Charlie. You're telling me forensics will find evidence of two corpses. But how sure are you?"

Moon stared. "What do you mean?"

Newman patted the wallet in his hip pocket. "Are you willing to put your money where your mouth is?"

It was a reflex action. Seeing McTeague give her partner a startled look, Moon instinctively set the hook: "Well, Stan—I s'pose I really shouldn't let myself get tempted into making any more bets. You know how I've been trying to get over my bad habit and—"

Annoyed half to death and bone-weary from the day's grim labors, Newman could not deal with this nonsensical drivel. He yelled, "What are you talking about?"

As one who finds himself the object of public humiliation,

Moon looked at his boots. "I've been trying to cut back on my gambling."

"You—quit making bets? That's a laugh." To emphasize this assertion, he added, "Haw-haw."

"It is not funny!" McTeague snapped.

Special Agent Stanlcy Newman gawked at his partner. "What?"

"Compulsive gambling is a serious disorder." She pointed at Moon, who presented his best poker face. "You should be *helping* this poor man, not making sport of his . . . his *disability*."

Newman took this assault with surprising grace. "Well, I didn't exactly mean to—"

Special Agent McTeague took Moon by the arm. Looked up at his innocent-as-a-newborn-babe expression. "Charlie, there's something I've been wanting to ask you."

"Yeah?"

"Are you free on Thursday evening?"

"Uh—well, I guess could be. Sure."

"Could you pick me up at six?"

Now the grin had to come out. "I'd be proud to." To properly punctuate this happy affirmation, he tipped his dusty Stetson.

"I want you to take me somewhere nice." She flashed him a smile that sizzled. "For a milk shake."

"The old-fashioned kind, with lots of vanilla ice cream?"

"Certainly. And gooey chocolate syrup. And chopped nuts."

"After that, could we go to a picture show?"

"If it's a tragic romance. I want to see something that'll make me cry."

"I promise to have you home by ten sharp."

"If you must."

Stanley Newman watched them walk away—into the crimson sunset, no less. He heard Wallace Whitehorse clear his throat. Say something corny.

"They make a nice-looking couple, don't you think?"

The fed made an ugly face. But underneath Newman's feigned expression, there was this happy thought: *That was so easy. Ol' Charlie even helped me. He is such a sap.*

· · ·

WHEN THEY were far enough away not to be overheard, Moon spoke to the pretty woman. "That was real nice of you—what you did for me back there. But you don't have to worry, I won't hold you to it."

McTeague squeezed his arm. "Oh yes you will."

"I will?"

"You will show up at my place, Charlie Moon. Thursday, six o'clock sharp." She blinked the Big Violets at him. "Or I will be very, very annoyed."

This was an unexpected complication. Miss James was somewhere back East. It was a thousand-to-one shot that she would ever come back to Colorado. Even so, he had an obligation to wait for a while for the bird in the bush. But not forever. And this bird in the hand was armed and dangerous. "Well," the Ute said, "we sure wouldn't want you to be annoyed."

"No," she said. "We would not."

SPECIAL AGENT Stanley Newman punched in the Granite Creek number. After the customary greetings were exchanged, and the grisly discovery of Officer Wolfe's corpse was described in some detail, Newman got to the reason for the telephone call. "And you're gonna love this—the Ute and Long Tall Lila Mae are practically an item."

"Stan, you are the Man."

"You are right about that. Poor ol' Charlie had no idea I was setting him up with McTeague. And my partner—well, that kid's so green she bleeds chlorophyll."

"I love it."

"And get this—it was McTeague that asked Charlie for the date!"

The man on the other end of the line laughed. "This plan was just brilliant."

"Well, you'd naturally think so—it was mostly your idea to steer Charlie toward a new girlfriend." Newman paused. "There is a downside."

"Break it to me easy."

"It's gonna cost us two hundred and fifty bucks apiece."

There was a slight hesitation. "But it'll be worth every penny."

Newman tried to sound nonchalant. "You're right about that."

There was a ring of hope in the other man's voice. "You think those two might hit it off?"

"Hey, Moon and McTeague are made for each other." The FBI agent grinned. *The woman is tall enough to bite a giraffe on the ear.*

The Granite Creek chief of police's smile could be heard in his voice: "Once Charlie's got himself a new lady, he'll quit stewing about the one that's dumped him."

"You said it—we did the right thing for our old buddy." *And Charlie, being the sort of bumpus he is, will help his new sweetie solve the Gourd Rattle disappearance and the Wolfe homicide. Which will help me get promoted right out of Indian country and back into the real world.*

"Thanks for the call, Stan."

"You're welcome. G'night, Scott."

CHARLIE MOON spoke to his aunt about the weather. He told her that some rain was already falling in northern Arizona, how it might slip up into La Plata County.

He thinks I'm a silly old fool. "It's late. Now get around to what you called me about, so I can go to bed and get some rest."

He said the words he'd been dreading to say: "Officer Wolfe is dead."

Daisy Perika clenched the telephone. "What happened?"

The tribal investigator could not tell his aunt the details of the murder. "I guess his luck ran out."

The shaman's hands turned clammy-cold. The white man had told her his luck depended on a piece of turquoise on the leather string under his shirt—the K'os Largo pendant she had stolen. Now the *matukach* was dead.

Shortly before midnight, the weary old sinner went to bed with her guilt.

Daisy was still awake when the sun came up.

CHAPTER THIRTY-FOUR

THE DATE

CHARLIE MOON AND LILA MAE MCTEAGUE STROLLED SLOWLY along bricked sidewalks, under the leafy branches of maple and oak, through dusky shadows and glowing moonlight. The night air was warm, sweet with the scent of flowers.

Her braid had been undone. Waves of coal-black locks fell to her waist. She stole a glance at his dark profile. "I liked the movie."

"Made you cry, did it?"

"Oh, when that poor girl died of tuberculosis . . ." Lila Mae wiped away a fresh tear. "That was just so terribly romantic."

Right. Like getting your liver chewed on by a grizzly.

For a few paces, there were no words.

Moon cleared his throat. "I'm still waiting."

"For what?"

"You haven't said a thing about that four-dollar milk shake. It had lots of chocolate syrup. And chopped nuts to boot."

And about ten thousand calories. "The milk shake was very nice."

A low cloud slipped away, exposing a cosmic pasture blossomed with stars. An insomniac mockingbird trilled a few bars.

The attractive woman reached out to squeeze his hand. "This is Buttonwood Lane."

Charlie Moon realized that they had turned a corner. He

took a look around. "You know—I'm fairly sure I've walked on this street before."

"Really?"

"Sure—this street where you live."

She stopped at a cleft in an aromatic lilac hedge. "This is my house."

"Nice place." He followed her to the porch. "Right now, there's nowhere I would rather be."

Her eyes sparkled in the night. "You are in a whimsical mood."

"This is no mood. It is a permanent condition."

"Would you like to come inside?"

He cocked his head. "Is that a trick question?"

"Maybe."

"Then I'll pass."

"Then you pass." She pulled her hand away. "I am moderately impressed."

"With my combination of good character and iron self-will?"

"With the fact that not once all evening have you mentioned homicide, larceny, or even referred to a petty misdemeanor. Imagine—a cop who doesn't end up talking shop."

He looked down at the tall woman's pretty face. "Now why would I want to do that in the company of a charming lady like yourself?"

Her blush was but a shadow in the moonlight. "To pick my brain. Find out where the Bureau's investigation into Officer Wolfe's murder is going."

"Don't matter to me if it goes to South Dakota by way of Saskatoon."

"You don't fool me one bit, Charlie Moon."

"I'd never try, Lila Mae."

"Play coy if you want to." The rangy filly tossed her dark mane. "But you are bound to be just the least bit curious."

"Not me. I have a high regard for Uncle Sam's federal constabulary and their well-deserved reputation to get the job done. If Officer Wolfe is murdered, let the FBI take care of it, says I."

"Do you really mean that?"

He pretended to think about it. "As far as I can tell."

There was a lengthy silence before McTeague finally spoke. "Officer Wolfe was not shot. He died of a single blow to his left temple. Canonical blunt object. The pistol barrel was probably placed in his mouth as some sort of ritual."

Charlie Moon looked off into the infinite darkness.

"Do you suppose the Cassidy burglary has some connection with Mr. Gourd Rattle's disappearance—and the murder of Officer Wolfe?"

He nodded.

McTeague pressed on: "I am sure that my partner would be grateful for any information or assistance you might provide."

No response.

"Do you dislike Stan Newman?"

"I don't dislike him," Moon said. "He's almost my favorite FBI agent. In fact, on my list Stan is number two."

"But then why—"

"That is the wrong response."

"Okay," she said. "Who is your most favorite FBI agent?"

"You mean number one?"

The swirl of the Milky Way glistened in her eyes. "I do."

"It's a toss-up between Efrem Zimbalist, Jr., and that cute Scully gal."

"That was not very nice."

"And you, McTeague—you're number one and a half."

"Thank you."

"Don't thank me. I could see you were fishing for a compliment. It kinda made me feel sorry for you."

"Sorry enough to help me solve the Wolfe homicide?"

He gave her a long, appraising look. "How long do you expect to be assigned to the Durango FBI office?"

She looked away. "Hard to say. But there's talk of kicking Stan upstairs."

This was news to the tribal investigator. "And if he goes, you'll stay on as the senior agent in Durango?"

"If I do a good enough job." She gave him a moment, then added, "And if I have a good reason to stay." She waited for a response, got none. *He's still mooning over that James woman.* "Good night, Charlie."

After she closed the door, McTeague looked through the curtains.

The Ute had been swallowed up by the night.

CHAPTER THIRTY-FIVE

THE FILE

FBI SPECIAL AGENT STANLEY NEWMAN LOOKED ACROSS THE government-issue desk at his partner. "So how're you this fine morning?"

Agent McTeague did not look up from her work. "Good enough."

"Have a nice time with Charlie last night?"

She turned a page on the Wolfe homicide report. "What I do on my personal time is none of your business."

He snorted. "Well, *excuse me.*"

"Very well, Stan. You are excused." *Now please go away.*

He grinned at the handsome lady. "Do you know that Charlie has a girlfriend?"

"If you are referring to the James woman, of course I do." *But she is a* former *girlfriend.* McTeague turned to file the folder. "The lady was waiting in Moon's car when the antique dealer got shot. Now she's back East somewhere."

"Baltimore."

She gave him an odd look. "You have been checking on her?"

He nodded. "I don't think she's coming back to Colorado."

Good. McTeague rummaged through her beaded purse, found a platinum compact. "I suppose being present at the shooting of Mr. Briggs must have been terribly traumatic for the poor woman."

"And seeing her boyfriend about to get perforated probably

didn't help." He watched his partner inspect her face in the compact mirror. "Especially because of what happened sometime back."

She found a hair that had gone awry, tucked it neatly back into place. "Which was?"

Newman wore a deadpan expression. "Approximately five years, one month, and six days ago, Miss James witnessed the shooting of her fiancé."

McTeague stared at the silvered glass without seeing her startled reflection. "What were the circumstances?"

Newman's face was grim. "The fiancé was an off-duty detective, Baltimore PD. One fine day, he went into a pawn shop while she was sitting in his car at the curb. The owner of the establishment spotted the automatic pistol under the detective's jacket, thought he was about to be robbed for the third time that month, pulled a pistol out of the cash register and shot the off-duty cop five times. Death was instantaneous."

McTeague snapped the compact shut, dropped it into her purse.

"As a result of witnessing this incident, Miss James consulted a shrink for quite some time."

"Does Charlie Moon know about this?"

Newman shrugged. "Not unless she told him."

"Are you going to tell him?"

"Of course not, McTeague. This information is part of a confidential Bureau file—it is none of Charlie's business." *The more interesting question is—are you going to tell him?*

CHAPTER THIRTY-SIX

A SMALL SURPRISE

HAVING PROMISED THE CATHOLIC PRIEST A DOZEN TIMES OR more that she would not visit the dwarf, Daisy Perika was hesitant to break her word to Father Raes Delfino. The shaman was worried that by one devious means or another, the clever Jesuit would find out if she wandered into *Cañon del Espiritu,* just happened to pay a call at the abandoned badger hole where the *pitukupf* had made his home for ages. But the tribal elder was unsettled about the strange goings-on up in Spirit Canyon, and thought she might make an exception. The canyon was, after all, practically her backyard—and Daisy was consumed with curiosity about what had happened to Jacob Gourd Rattle. Had he really abandoned his silly white wife in *Cañon del Espiritu,* or was Jacob still lurking up there in some dark little tributary of the main canyon—or were his bones moldering under the ground? Since that morning when Kicks Dogs had last seen her husband walking away with his buffalo robe—or *said* she had—there had been no sighting of the man.

Daisy Perika was at the small kitchen window that looked over the porch toward the mouth of the canyon. She leaned against the wall, closed her eyes, felt like dozing. But it was too early in the day for a nap. *I'll just stand here, think about things.* It was so very quiet. So very still.

Until.

Something tugged hard at her skirt.

"Yaaaaaa!" Daisy lurched forward, bashing her forehead against the window. Ready to do battle, the game old woman turned to face the intruder.

It was the little man.

She gasped, found a raspy voice. "You did that on purpose—to scare me to death!" Daisy took a kick at him. Missed by a millimeter, lost her balance, almost toppled.

The knee-high *pitukupf* looked up at the Ute elder, his homely features feigning innocent curiosity at her peculiar antics.

The furious woman shook her fist. "Don't give me that baby-face look, you nasty little imp!" She grabbed a fly swatter, made a vicious swipe that would have knocked his floppy hat off—had not the little man managed some fancy footwork in a tactical retreat.

Knowing she was too old and slow to catch the elfin creature, Daisy hobbled over to a chair, fell on it with a grunt, emitted a long, wistful sigh. "All these years, that priest has been warning me about you. God knows—I should've listened to Father Raes."

At the mention of the holy man's name, the dwarf made an ugly grimace. But he kept himself safely outside the old woman's reach.

Having caught her breath, she laid the fly swatter aside. "What do you want?"

The *pitukupf* blinked, looked around the kitchen.

"Food, I imagine." She hammered the dwarf with a hard look. "And tobacco."

His hopeful expression suggested that she was right on both counts.

"Well, you can't have neither." Daisy clamped a hand on her chest, felt the thumpity-thump of her tired old heart. "Not after what you did to me." She shook her head. "If you was starving to death, I would not give you a single pinto bean. And if they lined you up at dawn to shoot you, I would not give you a cigarette butt."

The dwarf scurried over to the pantry, reached out his hand—

Daisy flung a pepper shaker at the annoying little man.

He jumped when it whizzed by his ear, turned to give the shaman a glinty-eyed glare.

"This ain't no Salvation Army handout-kitchen," she croaked. "You want to get something from me, you'll have to earn it."

At this news, he became quite downcast.

"There'll be no peppermint candy for you," the canny old woman said. "No homemade serviceberry pie. No coffee beans to haul back to your dirty little den." She saw the hateful glint in his slitted eye. "And that big red can of Prince Albert tobacco I got in the cupboard, it'll stay right there on the shelf." It seemed there was no limit to shaman's cruelty. "Even if I have to smoke it myself."

The dwarf snarled. Bared yellowed teeth at the tribal elder.

"Save that for scaring little children." Daisy cackled. "You don't bother me none, you half-pint of warm skunk-spit."

It seemed the little man had never been so insulted, or so angry. For a flesh-tingling moment, he crouched as if about to pounce on the old woman.

Daisy motioned for him to come right on. "Make your move, runt—I'll reach down your throat, grab you by the guts, and jerk you inside out!"

Apparently sensing that he had met his match, the dwarf became docile as a baby lamb. He climbed onto a chair, ascended from there to the kitchen table—where he sat with spindly legs dangling over the floor. He eyed a biscuit pan.

"Just you try," she said. "And did I also mention that you can't have no beef jerky?" Daisy waited for this to sink in.

It did.

In the archaic version of the Ute tongue the little man always used, he made a plea to the hard-hearted old woman. All he wanted was a cold biscuit.

Daisy shook her head. "I meant what I said."

He muttered again, made a grudging offer.

The shaman made a show of thinking about it. "No, I don't think we can set up a trade. There's nothing you've got that I want." But to demonstrate an inner reservoir of selfless charity, she pushed the biscuit pan toward him.

The *pitukupf* snatched three, stuffed two in his pockets, began to gnaw on the other.

The tribal elder waited until he had swallowed it all, then said: "Maybe there is a little something you could do for me."

Her small visitor waited to hear what this might be.

"There's been some odd stuff going on up in *Cañon del Espiritu*." The shaman knew how to slip the knife under his skin. "But I doubt you'd know anything about it." She gave the visitor a pitying look. "You're getting old and tired like me. I expect you've been sleeping away your life in that badger hole—and wouldn't have heard a herd of wild buffalo stampeding down the canyon, tromping all the trees and bushes down."

He made a tart reply to this.

The shaman pretended not to recognize the archaic expletives directed at her ancestry. "I imagine that you didn't even notice—about the time of that last big snowstorm—when Jacob Gourd Rattle and his *matukach* wife were camped out in Spirit Canyon."

A sly grin creased the little man's thin face. He mumbled his mumbles, conferring the intelligence that he knew all about the white woman and her Ute husband. But having offended him with her insults, the Ute elder must now demonstrate her good faith. The *pitukupf* licked his dark lips, looked toward the pantry.

Having had many unsatisfactory dealings with the little man, Daisy was wary. But the crafty old woman sensed that she had gone about as far as she could go. She agreed to the deal.

Minutes later, the little man had the handles of a plastic grocery-bag linked over his skinny shoulder. In it was hard candy, half a berry pie, three strips of rancid beef jerky—everything except the Folgers coffee and Prince Albert smoking tobacco. These would be rendered up after he had provided certain information.

"Okay," the shaman said, shaking a finger in his face. "Now tell me what happened with Jacob and Kicks Dogs in Spirit Canyon."

The *pitukupf* told her immediately. Someone was still up there, he said—pointing a crooked finger more or less toward Three Sisters Mesa. But he would not say who. And more curious still (if the little trickster was to be believed) neither Jacob nor his pale-skinned wife had set foot in *Cañon del Espiritu.* Having kept his side of the bargain, her guest pounded a tiny fist on the table, demanded the promised coffee and tobacco.

The shaman stared hard at the *pitukupf's* face for any sign of deception. It was like trying to read a matchbook cover at fifty yards. The little scamp always found a way to hold something back, or confuse her, or conceal a kernel of truth in the husk of a riddle. And she had no doubt he could lie a blue streak with both hands on the Bible, though the act would probably scorch his palms.

But a deal had been made and a debt must be paid. She presented two red cans to the little man, secretly hoping the combination of caffeine and nicotine would do him in.

CHAPTER THIRTY-SEVEN

A MODEST RECOMMENDATION

JANE CASSIDY'S GAUNT FORM WAS CLAD IN FADED JEANS, A man's white cotton shirt, black rubber boots, a tattered straw hat. Armed with a two-foot-long pair of shears, the aggressive woman had mounted a determined attack on her garden, snipping viciously at this and that. Having tired of the shears, she now wielded a hand sickle, happily lopping the heads off orange mallow, yellow dandelions, blue grama, and a host of other undesirable emigrants.

To the man who watched, it seemed that the rosebuds and geraniums cringed as this comical version of the Grim Reaper passed by. Charlie Moon leaned against the trunk of a red willow. Waited for the fuming woman to take a cut at him.

He did not have to wait long.

Jane Cassidy deftly nipped off a sprig of hedge that had exhibited the unseemly ambition to rise up from among its fellows. "You took your time getting here."

In response to her frantic telephone call, the tribal investigator had left his foreman worrying with half a dozen sick cows. Moon had also driven ninety-two miles without breakfast—only to be met by a woman who did not have the common courtesy to offer him a cup of coffee. In spite of this, he held his tongue.

She paused, attempted to point the steel crescent at the taciturn Indian. "I want a progress report."

"Sometime back, Mr. Bell invented a wonderful machine."

"I dislike conducting personal business over the telephone wires." She raised the sickle, made a wicked slash at a passing bumblebee. Except for unsettling her hat, this effort was without effect. The plump bee went bumbling on its way. "Face-to-face is what I prefer. So tell me, Mr. Moon—what have you discovered about the burglary of the family museum?"

"Not nearly as much as I'd like to."

"Then we are in full agreement on that point."

"But I have got a notion."

She adjusted the straw hat, taking care not to muss her hair. "About what?"

"About who stole your stuff."

"Tell me."

He pinched off a delicate willow twig, braided it into a circle. "Not till I can prove it."

She rolled her eyes. "What am I paying you for?"

The big man took her hand, gently put the ring on her thumb. "You haven't paid me a nickel yet."

"Do not be impertinent." She stared in childish wonder at the primitive ornament. "When will you recover my valuables?"

"Don't know that I ever will."

She turned the willow circle on her thumb, felt a lump in her throat. "Is that the best you can do?"

"You want to fire me, I wouldn't blame you."

I like him. "I may just do that."

"It would be the smart thing to do."

She gave him a thin-lipped look. "Mr. Moon, you are a most irritating man."

"You are a very gracious lady. I feel fortunate to be in your employ."

"Sarcasm does not become you." She threw the sickle on the ground near his feet.

"No, I am dead serious." He retrieved the curved instrument, deftly cleaved a dead branch off the willow. "Even though I don't get paid, the fringe benefits are enormous. Where else could I associate with a remarkable person like yourself?"

Jane Cassidy plopped down on a wrought-iron bench,

shook her head wearily. "It is this dreadful waiting that I cannot bear. If there were only some way to *make* things happen."

"There is." The tribal investigator seated himself beside the woman. "But I doubt you'd do it."

She removed the twig ring from her thumb, placed it on her index finger. "Why do you say that?"

"You are like most rich people."

"What do you mean by that snide remark?"

"You really want to know?"

She raised her nose a notch higher. "When you use that tone, I am not sure that I do. But go ahead—hurt my feelings."

"Ma'am, you hold a penny so tight—old Abe gets a headache that lasts all night."

She turned her pale blue eyes on Charlie Moon. "It is true that I do not cast greenbacks into the wind. But I am willing to spend serious money to get serious results. If you have an interesting proposal, I will certainly consider it."

"There's just one thing."

"What's that?"

"If you don't take my advice—I will tender my resignation."

"My, my." Her smile was without warmth. "I did not realize that you were such a sensitive man."

He leaned close, whispered in her ear, "Please don't tell anyone. Aside from excessive humility, being overly sensitive is my only shortcoming."

"I promise to keep this intimate knowledge of your shameful faults to myself. Now tell me what is on your mind."

"You must be willing to spend a barrel of money."

The wealthy woman winced at this image, held her breath for a moment. "Give me the particulars."

He told her precisely what she must do.

She listened with keen concentration. Nodded at each particular. Decided that this red Indian was the sort of man who did not dillydally around a problem. Mr. Moon went right to the root of the thing.

CHAPTER THIRTY-EIGHT

THE BROADCAST

THE DUSTY, MUSTY, FOUL-SMELLING ROOM WOULD HAVE been totally dark had it not been for the television screen, which cast a sickly bluish hue on the meager furnishings. The single human occupant of the dreary space was watching the late evening news out of Denver. Electronic snow drifted across the face of the cathode-ray tube, horizontal lines zigged and zagged along the handsome announcer's face.

"And now we have an up-to-the-minute exclusive News-Cam story from La Plata County. Jane Cassidy, well known for her philanthropic activities in the world of fine arts and theater, will make a statement about the burglary of the Cassidy Museum." He turned to view the scene on a life-size monitor.

The wealthy woman was standing outside the family mansion, her slender frame hidden under a buttoned tweed overcoat. She cleared her throat. "Just six weeks ago, an unknown person or persons broke into that building." She turned to point; the camera panned the grounds to frame the museum. Her off-camera voice continued, "A number of valuables were taken. The theft has been covered rather thoroughly by the media, so I shall not repeat the details." The camera found her face, zoomed in. She was reading from a document that had been prepared by her Denver law firm. "I am hereby offering a reward of one million dollars in cash to any person or combination of persons who will provide information that shall result in the return of the stolen property." She paused to take a deep breath. "Such person or persons will not be presumed to be guilty of the burglary. Furthermore, in the unlikely instance that such person or persons should ever be indicted by any legal authority for the burglary, I will provide sufficient funds to defend said persons." She stopped, glared at the papers, then at the camera. Jane Cassidy pitched the legal document aside. "Oh, can that lawyer gibberish. If the weasel who ripped me off is watching—prick up your pointy little ears. Here's the deal. You have two options. Number one, you contact an attorney of your choice, make arrangements to return the stolen property. You have my personal guarantee, you will be paid the full one million dollars for the return of what you stole. You do that, far as I'm concerned, it's over. I will not make any attempt to determine your identity or have you arrested." Her eyes became slits. "But hear this, night crawler—you've got thirty days from right now. If you do not return my property during that period, you will have automatically selected the second option, which is this: I will spend the million dollars and more on the best private cops, bounty hunters, and knuckle-dragging mercenaries my money can buy. There won't be anyplace on earth you can hide. You will be hunted for the rest of your miserable, rotten life. Even after I'm dead and gone, you won't be able to rest. I have made a stipulation in my will that funds will be set aside in a trust to pay the hounds that will dog your trail till you're run to ground." She stopped, took a breath. "So there it is, lowlife. Your call." She turned and walked away.

The wide-eyed face of a local stringer appeared on camera. "Well, Howard, that was quite a dramatic statement by a very determined lady."

The Denver anchor's face filled the television screen. "It certainly was, Bud." He grinned at the unseen audience. "If I was the burglar, I'd be making plans right now to get the stolen property back to Miss Cassidy and collect the million bucks. It is obvious that the lady means business."

The thief got up, walked across the room, switched off the television. *I can't believe it—a million dollars in cold hard cash.* That was a sizable pile of money. And the second option was extremely unattractive. *What a nasty old witch!*

CHAPTER THIRTY-NINE

DREAMING WOMAN

HEARING THE SOUND OF THE V-8 ENGINE, KICKS DOGS SHUT off the television set, parted a tattered curtain to take a peek out the window. She watched the tall, lean man get out of the pickup. On the way to the door, the woman paused before a mirror, made a hurried attempt to pat her wild hair into place. She stared glumly at the result. *Wonderful. I look like I've just been electrocuted.*

After she had led Charlie Moon into the kitchen, Jacob Gourd Rattle's wife stomped around, wringing her hands, looking this way and that. The pale woman's eyes were wide with an expression of alarmed curiosity, as if she had never been in the room before this moment. A gray cat leaped onto the cluttered table, mewed at her mistress.

She stared blankly at the animal, then: "Oh, Bitsey—it's you."

The cat sniffed at a saucer. The dish was encrusted with a black smear that might have been the fossilized residue of King Tut's chocolate cake. The animal licked at the sugary remnants with all the enthusiasm a haughty feline can be expected to demonstrate.

Kicks Dogs plopped herself onto a pine chair, propped her elbows on the table, cradled her chin in her hands. As if suddenly aware of the Ute's presence, she cocked her head at him. "What brings you out here?"

Moon, standing with hat in hand, returned the peculiar

stare with a patient smile. "I thought it was time we had a talk."

"Talk?" The pale face assumed a suspicious expression. "About what?"

"About that night Jacob left you in the canyon."

The woman watched a tiny yellow moth dart about above the table. "I'll help you if I can. But these days, I have a hard time remembering anything that happened more than a few minutes ago."

"I was hoping you could—"

Kicks Dogs pointed at a straight-back chair. "Siddown there, if you want to."

Moon seated himself across the dining table from the woman.

She waited until the silence began to crush her like a vise. "What do you want to know?"

"I'd like to ask you some questions about your husband."

Kicks snorted. "What husband?" She pointed at the bedroom door. "If I had me a husband, why would I be sleeping by myself every night? Can you answer me that?"

"No, ma'am." He made another try: "When you showed up at my aunt's place during that big spring snow, you said you and Jacob had spent the night in the canyon."

Kicks patted her matted hair. "Did you know that I used the last of my savings to pay off the mortgage on this place?"

Moon shook his head.

"Sure you didn't. And I bet you also didn't know that I paid over eleven hundred dollars to put a new crank case in Jake's clunky old van."

Moon admitted that he was ignorant of that fact too.

"If Jake don't come back pretty soon, all of his sneaky Indian relatives'll swoop down on this place and take everything that ain't nailed down. And most of the furniture is mine."

"I'm sure you don't need to worry about anyone taking your possessions. But if someone bothers you, you call me and I'll see to it that—"

"You know what I need?"

Charlie Moon thought he should not respond to that.

"I need me a lawyer."

"Uh—could we get back to what happened when Jake left you during the snowstorm?"

"Oh, I guess so." She folded a soiled napkin into a small, thick triangle. "What do you want to know?"

"You said Jacob left you in Spirit Canyon."

"Is that what they call it—Spirit Canyon?" She frowned, as if trying to remember. "I don't think Jake ever mentioned the *name* of the canyon we was in." The cat leaped off the dining table, came to lick at a sore on the woman's ankle.

Moon continued politely, "About an hour after you reported Jacob missing, I met an SUPD officer in the canyon. We not only didn't find your husband, Jacob's van wasn't parked on the mesa where you told us you'd left it. After the snow melted, the tribal police organized a thorough search—brought in about forty volunteers. They combed Spirit Canyon for three days. Never found a trace of Jacob."

She pushed the cat away with her foot. "If nobody fund Jake, then he must've not been there. Which is not all that amazing, since I saw him walk away from his camp."

He said it slowly: "The search didn't turn up any trace of Jacob's camp."

Unfazed, Kicks Dogs found a blob of something sticky on the oilcloth, scratched at it with her thumbnail. "Maybe they didn't look hard enough."

The tribal investigator stared at the faint greenish yellow remnant of the bruise on her cheek. "Why did you stay with a man who knocked you around so much?" It was a highly personal question, but pertinent to his investigation.

She shrugged. "Jake wasn't all that bad."

He tried another approach: "Can you think of any reason why your husband would have gone away?"

"Men are always going away." She flicked this particular member of the gender an angry look. "That's just the way they are."

The tribal investigator watched her eyes. "What was Jacob doing in the canyon?"

The pale woman curled her fingers, examined the chewed nails. "He was there because of those dreams he'd been having."

"He went to Spirit Canyon because of a dream—that's all he told you?"

A slight shudder rattled her thin shoulders. "Jake—he said what he was doing in that canyon wasn't for a woman to know—it was *men's* business. And I wasn't supposed to tell anybody he was there." She darted a glance across the table at her guest. "Would you like something to eat? I got some prunes in the fridge. And some candied yams."

"That's very kind of you, ma'am—but I'll pass."

"Something to drink then? I could brew up some herbal tea."

Moon shook his head. "Is there anything about that night you could tell me about?"

"What night?"

"When Jake left you alone in Spirit Canyon."

"I already told the police and the FBI everything I can recollect." Her face brightened. "Would you like to hear about what I dreamed that night in the canyon?"

The tribal investigator looked at the ceiling. Suspended on a brass chain, swinging slightly in a draft, was a blackened sixty-watt bulb. It wore a cone hat of greasy white plastic that was cocked at a jaunty angle. Anchored between the corroded chain and a dusty pine beam, a ragged spiderweb billowed like a macabre sail. *If I wait for a little while, maybe she'll forget about the dream.*

This was wishful thinking.

She followed his gaze. "I dreamed about those demons and things up there on the ceiling, hanging over me while I tried to sleep."

"Demons?"

"Oh yeah. I spotted 'em with my little flashlight."

He heard himself mumble. "You saw demons with your flashlight."

"Sure. I had a fresh set of double-A alkaline batteries. And you can bet your eyes that after I fell asleep—" She bit her lip. "I'm sure it was the spotted lizard that put the double whammy on me."

Charlie Moon tried to appear interested. But as her nasal voice droned on, he drifted away to that perfect refuge, the Columbine. He imagined himself a mile south of the ranch headquarters. Standing on the pebbled bank of the glacial lake. Casting a feathered lure onto the mirrored surface. As he was strictly a bait fisherman, this was odd. But there—just under the mirrored surface—the darting form of a twenty-six-inch rainbow flashed in the sunlight. He tensed. *Attaboy. Take it and run.* From far away, he heard someone call.

"Hey!"

Moon jumped, blinked at the woman.

"When a lady is talking, you should pay attention."

"Uh—yes, ma'am."

"Do you want to hear my dream?"

"Sure I do." *Forgive me, Father, for I have lied.*

"Okay then." Kicks Dogs tugged at an unruly ringlet of corn-yellow hair; an expression of certitude glinted in her watery eyes.

Surreptitiously, Moon glanced at his wristwatch.

The cat rubbed her spindly ribs against his boot, a fine-tuned purr rattled in the feline throat.

"I was laying there on my back." She looked up at the lightbulb, her pupils shrunk to tiny black dots. "It seemed like the clouds was all yella, kinda glowing. And I thought I heard somebody talking, only not in any earthly language." She gave him a knowing look. "It sounded like *aliens.*"

"Aliens, huh?"

She bobbed her head in a jerky nod. "But I want to be perfectly honest and tell you that I'd had just a little sip of my sleeping tonic—which is a little-bitty, teensy-weensy dab of whiskey in a pint of hot water. With lots of sugar."

Moon wondered how much better his life would be if he resigned his appointment as part-time tribal investigator.

In a mildly theatric gesture, Kicks Dogs put her hand over her eyes. "Anyway, through the mists, I see Jake coming. He stops just a little ways off. For a minute or so, he just stands there, looking up into those clouds."

Moon watched the cat chase a cockroach across the linoleum. *I should check the oil in my fancy new truck. And rotate the tires.*

"Then up he goes." She frowned at the Ute. "Are you listening to me?"

"Sure."

"Then what'd I just say?"

Uh-oh. "You were telling me about . . . your dream."

She seemed satisfied with this response.

That was a close one.

Kicks returned her gaze to the lightbulb above the table. "Then Jake starts climbing."

He thought it best to show some interest. *Once she gets past the dreaming, maybe I can get something useful out of her.* "Climbing what?"

She presented a little-girl smile. "Now that's the sixty-four-dollar question. In my dream, I couldn't hardly see what it was my old man was climbing. But I'm sure it had to be something that was magical." With her finger she drew an invisible line on the tablecloth. "Do you know what I mean?"

He knew a trap when he saw one. "Uh . . . more or less." *Mostly less.*

"I believe Jake was climbing a *moonbeam* in my dream." An expression of intense self-satisfaction brightened her face. "And it was the spotted lizard that caused me to have that dream." She fluttered her eyelashes as if she knew a delicious secret. "Do you want to hear the rest?"

The defeated man nodded.

"Right after I had that vision of Jake climbing the moonbeam, I had this other dream. I was a sassy dance-hall gal all decked out in a shiny red dress and I was working in one of them old-timey saloons. All of a sudden, these wild and woolly cowboys came roarin' in—they was half-cocked and loaded for bear." She paused and squinted at nothing in particular. "If I remember right, two of 'em was John Wayne and Gabby Hayes. Well, this bunch started to yellin' and sluggin' it out with the other customers, which included

Teddy Roosevelt—who is my most favorite president. First thing you know, there's this big free-for-all brawl. A real knock-down-drag-out."

Charlie Moon gave her a glassy-eyed stare.

"Well, I ran outta the saloon and then I dreamed that I saw old King Kong get hit right in the snout by a little airplane and fall off of the Empire State Building—*thump!* And I do mean to tell you, when that big ape hit the street it sure did make the earth rattle and shake." She paused, as if recalling a pertinent detail. "It was all in black-and-white, like one of them old movies. I wish it had been Technicolor, like most of my dreams."

After an hour or more of patiently listening to the lady pitch fairy tale and fable, Moon finally got up from the table. He thanked the eccentric woman for her time, said his good-bye.

Kicks Dogs stood at a window, watching through a slit in the curtain as the Indian drove away into the gathering darkness. Her pale eyes squinted until the tail lights faded into the distance. *I bet he thinks I'm crazy.*

Sitting beside her mistress, Bitsey chewed contentedly on a cockroach.

CHAPTER FORTY

A GOLDEN OPPORTUNITY

PETE BUSHMAN SAUNTERED UP TO THE COLUMBINE HEAD-quarters porch, scratched enthusiastically at his unkempt beard. "Fine day we're havin'."

Charlie Moon nodded. Waited for the next scratch.

The foreman scratched his ear. "I was talkin' to old man Henry yestiddy mornin'."

"How's he doing?"

"Oh, his arthritis is kickin' up again." Bushman shot the boss a look. "He'd sure like to sell the Big Hat to you."

"I'd like to buy it, Pete. And if cow pies was greenbacks, I'd have the Big Hat deed in my hip pocket right now."

"He's come down on the price."

"How much down?"

Bushman told him.

Moon leaned against the porch railing, thought about it from six different directions. "That's still a lot more'n I could come up with."

Bushman chewed on a wad of Red Man Tobacco. "There's more'n one way of raisin' cash."

"I know," Moon said. "But robbing banks is risky business."

Ignoring the crack, the foreman reminded the boss that the Columbine acreage on the far side of the paved highway was of no use to them at all. "And I just happened to run into that hotshot land developer yesterday afternoon."

"Where did you just happen to run into him?"

"In his office in Granite Creek. On the third floor of the Goldman Building."

"Pete, you are a meddling busybody."

"Thank you—I work hard at it." Bushman chewed a few chews, spat tobacco juice into a scattering of pebbles under the gutter spout. "He'll give you twelve hundred dollars an acre for the land that's within a mile of the paved road. Eight hundred for that what's farther back. O'course, they'd have to have some water rights." He did not mention the developer's interest in building six three-story condominiums and a nine-hole golf course.

Despite his love for the land on both sides of the highway, the Ute was sorely tempted.

The foreman kicked a chunk of gravel toward a sandstone pillar that supported the corner of the redwood porch. Missed it by a yard. "Whatta you think?"

"I'll think I'll think on it."

"Don't think too long. At the price old man Henry's dropped down to, some know-nothin' city slicker'll snap up the Big Hat before you can say—"

"We'll talk about it later, Pete." Moon had seen a spot of dust in the distance. "I have company coming."

The foreman turned to squint. "Who?"

"Unless I'm wrong—and I don't think I am—it will be a representative of the federal government."

At this news, Bushman swore and stalked away.

AN OLD, SWEET SONG

CHARLIE MOON and Special Agent McTeague mounted a matched pair of copper-colored quarter horses. They rode under cottonwood branches on the bank of the river, then uphill past a creaking windmill that pumped cold water from a deep well and generated surplus electrical energy for the Columbine. The tall woman was decked out in trim khaki slacks, a long-sleeved white blouse, shiny new Roper boots. The Ute wore his workaday ranch clothes—scuffed cowboy boots, faded denim jeans, a blue cotton shirt. This ensemble was topped off by his black John B. Stetson hat.

McTeague cleared her throat. "I suppose you're wondering why I asked if I could stop by this morning."

"No. I naturally thought you desired the pleasure of my company."

The hint of a smile played at the corners of her mouth. "You were right."

"Not that I'm surprised." He patted the horse on the neck. "But right about what?"

"The burial where we found Officer Wolfe's remains— there were two blood types on the stones. Wolfe's A-positive and a John or Jane Doe with type O." She patted her mount on the neck. "My partner still doesn't buy your two-bodies-in-the-grave theory. Stan believes the person who killed Wolfe must've been injured during the struggle, and bled on the rocks while he was concealing Wolfe's body."

Moon had a look on his face she had not seen before.

She frowned. "What is it?"

"I am puzzled about something."

"Want to tell me what?"

"Not right now."

They passed by a sturdy corral attached to a small stock barn. The ensemble was shaded by a pair of knotty ponderosas. As they moved up a rise, their mounts crossed a narrow snowmelt stream on its way to the river. They topped a rocky crest, entered a thick glade of aspen and spruce. Shrouded in the midday twilight, a jungle of ferns, blueberry bushes, and curled lousewort sprouted from a carpet of bright green pyrola. The damp undergrowth was furiously alive with sounds of invisible creatures scurrying about to accomplish their daily business.

The pair came so suddenly into the sunlight that the woman lifted a hand to shade her eyes. The air was now crisp and dry. The lightest of breezes caressed them with perfume offered by wild pink roses, twining honeysuckle, purple lupine.

Farther out in the grasslands was the most exquisite lake she had ever seen.

Off to their left, nestled in a dark stand of spruce, was the sort of log cabin that a realtor would list as "rustic." The square-cut logs were chinked with concrete, the chimney was constructed of a dozen types of local stones, the pitched roof was painted a dark, rusty red. McTeague heard something, reined her mount to a halt.

It was an older man's voice, but sweet and pure—like the sun-drenched stream that splashed down the grade to feed the lake.

Sweet hour of prayer—sweet hour of prayer,
that calls me from a world of care . . .

She looked to her companion for an explanation.

With the barest nod, Moon let her know that they must ride on.

When they were near the edge of the lake, Lila Mae McTeague got off her horse.

The Ute also dismounted, took the reins of both animals.

She turned her pale face, looked up at the silent man. "Charlie?"

He looked down at the big eyes. *This woman gets prettier every time I see her.*

"Shall we walk around the lake?"

Spaces out here could easily deceive the inexperienced eye. He looked at her stiff new boots, then at the distant shore and beyond. "It's a lot farther than it looks."

"I'm not in any hurry."

"All right then."

"One more thing. While we walk, will you hold my hand?"

He said that he would. And did.

Minutes passed without effort, as did a mile. And then two.

"I want to ask you something." She had slowed her pace to a meander. "Something important."

A virginal bride lightly veiled in a diaphanous mist, the pristine lake filled his eyes. He waited for the question.

"Are you happy?"

Surprised, he played for time. "You mean right this minute?"

"Yes."

He pondered this weighty question for so long that she thought he was not going to respond. After a hundred heart-beats and then a dozen more, he said, "I'm not sure."

A shadow passed over her face.

"But if I'm not entirely happy, this'll do just fine."

It was an acceptable answer. Lila Mae McTeague squeezed his hand. "Let's not talk." *Let's just walk.*

And with the man leading the horses, the woman at his side, so they continued. It seemed a shorter way than it was. They strolled past a field of granite boulders that resembled patient old soldiers waiting for that final battle to begin. Through an exclusive neighborhood of straight-spined aspens, all with their heads in the air. Along the edge of a dry arroyo, where the fossilized ribs of an ice-age bison were exposed.

Far off in the distance, toward the highway miles away, there was a lonely wail. A mournful whistling. It might have been the wind.

Or one of Daisy's friends.

It reminded the lovely woman of something quite pleasant. A happy experience from her childhood. "Have you ever ridden on a train?" She smiled at a hummingbird darting about a cluster of purple asters. "I mean—one of the really old ones. With a steam engine."

"Yes I did," he said. *Sixteen coaches long . . .*

"When?"

"About three years ago." *While I was dead.*

She saw the faraway expression, knew she should not ask.

The breeze was against their faces, the edge of the lake at their feet. Charlie Moon looped the horses' reins over the delicate arm of a white-barked aspen. As they stood watching sunlight dance and glance over the waters, their shadows stretched along the narrow beach. It may be that some word-less communication passed between their palms. Or perhaps it was a whisper between two like souls. However it was managed, they knew precisely when it was time to turn back. And without exchanging a word or a glance, they mounted the muscular horses, departed from the lake.

As they approached the log cabin, the man was still singing. But now he sang a different song.

The Ute's sharp ear picked up the words before the city-bred woman heard the sounds. He listened with unusual intensity.

As they came closer, McTeague heard the man's voice.

Sinner do you—love my Je-sus

His hour of prayer seems to be over. The slender woman turned in the saddle, fixed the violet eyes on her companion. "May we stop and say hello?"

Moon looked toward the cabin. "Most of the folks on the Columbine are here because they don't like living in town. This one likes to spend his time alone." Seeing the disappointment on her face, he quickly added, "But I'll ask him if you can drop by next time you're here."

"Very well." *That sounds very much like an invitation*. She turned away to smile.

As they rode past the cabin, the haunting challenge of the Negro spiritual followed them.

If you love him—why not serve him

Loath to depart from the hymn singer, McTeague slowed her mount to a walk.

Charlie Moon seemed lost in a trance.

His pretty companion began to wonder what sort of man she was riding with. "Shall we go by the stream again?"

He nodded. Somewhat vacantly, she thought.

They turned their mounts toward the fragile willows and gnarled cottonwoods clustered along the rocky riverbank.

They rode slowly beside the rushing, rolling waters.

Charlie Moon dismounted, let his animal drink from the cold river.

The woman did the same.

From somewhere deep inside the man, a great laugh boomed out.

She considered this quite extraordinary.

He gave her a boyish grin. "Special Agent McTeague, I have a serious question to ask you."

"I'm listening."

"Are you on duty today?"

She did not quite like the look in his eyes. "Well—it is hard to say."

"Give it your best shot."

"This is my day off. But I'm always on call." She pushed a long strand of black hair off her face. "Why do you ask?"

He came close to her. "If you are on duty, what I'm wanting to do could get me in some serious trouble with the federal government."

She smiled at the unpredictable man. "Then perhaps you had better reconsider."

"*Perhaps*" *is good*. "It's way too late for that." He reached for her; ever so gently, ever so slowly, pulled her to him.

Lila Mae made no attempt to escape the embrace. Before she knew she had, she was hugging him back.

The river flowed on toward the salty sea.

After an eternal instant, he whispered in her ear. "I'm sure now."

She closed her eyes, sighed. "Sure about what?"

"What you asked me about."

The woman listened to his heart beat. "Please explain."

Charlie Moon laughed, lifted her off the earth. "I am a happy man."

CHAPTER FORTY-ONE

CAÑON DEL ESPIRITU

BEFORE THE FIRST WARM HINT OF DAWN, CHARLIE MOON parked the Ford F-350 on the crest of Three Sisters Mesa. By the time the tribal investigator made his way down the rocky trail into Spirit Canyon, the sun had shown its crimson brow over the fuzzy bulge of Burro Mountain. Now the blazing disk was halfway across the sky.

The Ute hiked up the big canyon until it was reduced to a dark, narrow cleft in the base of the mountains. He conducted as thorough a search as a man could make in half a day, but had found not the least evidence that Jacob Gourd Rattle—or anyone else—had camped in *Cañon del Espiritu* in recent times.

Moon found a seat on a variegated-sandstone outcropping, removed a thick ham and cheese sandwich from one jacket pocket, a pint Thermos of honey-sweetened coffee from the other, proceeded to eat his lunch.

The food was good, but he found no pleasure in his thoughts.

Kicks Dogs either had imagined the whole episode or was lying through her teeth. Or some of both. Maybe the woman had spruced up her visions and dreams with a few well-fashioned falsehoods. But that did not throw any light on the central question—exactly what was she doing in Spirit Canyon that morning? He took a man-sized bite of the sandwich. Smiled at the memory of the woman's strange ravings. Kicks Dogs had blamed her bad dreams on a *spotted lizard*. Moon was about to take another bite. He lowered the sandwich. Jacob Gourd Rattle's wife had said she'd slept under an overhang at the cliff's edge. Any decent rock shelter would have been used by the Anasazi. Maybe Kicks had turned on her flashlight, looked up at a smoked stone ceiling, saw a lizard petroglyph. But Charlie Moon had roamed Spirit Canyon as a boy and seen most of it ten times over—if there was a spotted lizard in Spirit Canyon, it would be news to him. So she had probably dreamed about a spotted lizard. Even so, something nagged at the murky depths of his consciousness, tried ever so hard to bubble to the surface.

A shaft of noonday sunlight moved across the canyon floor, illuminated him.

Of course.

When Kicks Dogs showed up at Aunt Daisy's home that morning, she had not said she had been in Spirit Canyon— Kicks had simply said she had been in "the canyon." Moon's aunt had assumed that the distraught white woman had emerged from the larger of the canyons, because the mouth of *Cañon del Espiritu* was closest to Daisy's home. And when the tribal elder had voiced this perfectly reasonable assumption, Kicks Dogs had not disputed it; she didn't know any of the canyons by name. It had never occurred to Daisy that a traditional Ute like Jacob Gourd Rattle would have little enough sense to set up camp in that *other* canyon—on the other side of the Three Sisters. That was a very bad place.

Moon hurriedly finished the remnants of his sandwich, gulped down the sweet coffee, headed for the trail that would take him to the crest of Three Sisters Mesa—that miles-long slab of sandstone that separated *Cañon del Espiritu* from *Cañon del Serpiente*.

In half an hour, the tribal investigator was on the floor of Snake Canyon.

Above him was a basalt formation that protruded rudely from the Three Sisters side of the narrow canyon. On the opposite wall was its smaller sister. Moon plumbed the murky memory of his childhood. What had the traditional Utes called it? The answer came to him. The larger was the Witch's Tongue, the smaller the Witch's Thumb.

Where had the white woman slept?

He approached an impressive overhang beneath the *Brujo's Lengua,* noted the sooty campfire coating that was evidence of occasional human habitation over several centuries, perhaps millennia. The Ute stood under the arching ceiling, gazed up at an assortment of stick figures. Human beings with arms outstretched. Four-legged animals that might have been deer and elk, a few horses added by more recent artists.

And in the center of the blackened canvas, a fat, open-mouthed lizard—with spots that gave it a comical polka-dotted look.

So Kicks had been telling the truth—at least about sleeping under the spotted lizard. She had, if her story could be believed, come to this place to take her brutal husband home. But what had Jacob Gourd Rattle been doing in Snake Canyon? Having no ready answer, Moon left the menagerie of fabled animals behind.

At the center of the rock-strewn canyon floor, he came upon something quite unexpected—a rectangular spot where not a sprig of grass grew. The tribal investigator estimated it to be about seven feet long, more than thirty inches wide. As he stared at the patch of sterile earth, the Ute had the beginning of a notion.

Within a yard of the patch that had the appearance of a grave was a dry streambed. On the off chance that something of interest had been washed away by the snowmelt, Moon walked along the rocky surface. *This is a real long shot.* But after a half-dozen paces, he knelt to get a closer look at the long, tangled strand of rawhide. Attached to one end of the leather cord was a thin blade of polished bone. It was not quite two fingers wide, and as long as his hand. Engraved on one face of the object were four wavy lines. On the opposite side were three deeply incised zigzags.

He touched his thumb to one of the beveled edges. It was as sharp as a butcher knife.

Charlie Moon stared at the singular instrument. *I should leave it here, let the FBI deal with it when they excavate the grave. But if I do, it might wash away with the next hard rain.* Having rationalized his way to where he wanted to be, the Ute wrapped the rawhide cord and sliver of bone in his handkerchief.

He continued to search for another hour, found nothing more.

When the shadow of the west cliff was slipping over the canyon floor, Moon's gaze swept up the wall of Three Sisters Mesa, past the Witch's Tongue. He recalled Kicks Dogs' dream about Jacob Gourd Rattle climbing a moonbeam into the clouds. But after she had awakened at dawn, Kicks had seen her husband walking away with his buffalo robe. Or so she said. *Maybe her dreams are closer to the truth than what she sees when she's wide awake.*

After a return hike up the trail to the summit of Three Sisters Mesa, he approached the cliff over Snake Canyon. It had been a highly productive day, and sunset was only a couple of hours away. He stood as still as one of the stone Sisters, staring down at the extended black basalt tongue, the sandy canyon floor. Charlie Moon considered many things—some quite odd, others mundane. It was like peering through a telescope at a past that was slipping in and out of focus while it receded. Though there was still a fuzzy patch here and there, portions of the image would occasionally become more distinct. The tribal investigator thought he knew why Jacob Gourd Rattle had come to Snake Canyon. Why the man had sent his wife home. Why there was something in the canyon resembling a grave.

One absurd image still nagged at him—Jacob the moonbeam climber. Sensible folk believed that what went up would generally come down again, though the reverse was not necessarily true. *How* to do it was the issue. By force of habit, the tribal investigator's gaze examined everything great and small.

Over and over again—the earth under his boots, the Witch's Tongue, the dry streambed meandering through Snake Canyon.

Without knowing why, the solitary man began to hum an old, familiar tune.

Then he began to sing it: *We are climbing* . . . He listened to the words fill his mouth.

In an instant, the truth dawned. For an electric moment, he was stunned. It was so simple.

As he recovered from the shock of discovery, the Ute began to consider what must be done. When the time was right, he would bring Special Agent McTeague to this place, show her the excavation one person had dug, another filled. But right now there was more urgent work to do. *Jacob used what he found that night. I'll use what I've already got.* It took a few minutes to formulate his plans in detail. *I'd better head back to the truck.* And a fine pickup it was—with all the bells and whistles. Every hardworking man ought to own one. Charlie Moon boomed out a hearty laugh.

The happy sound echoed off towering sandstone walls.

LONG BEFORE the weary man reached the Columbine, darkness had slipped across the high plains. A cold rain was peppering the F-350 windshield. He lowered the window at his elbow. The smell of wet sage and fragrant juniper refreshed him.

Sidewinder met the big truck near the Too Late bridge, plodded along behind to the ranch headquarters. Before Charlie Moon knew he was there, the peculiar old hound vanished into the night.

CHAPTER FORTY-TWO

THE CAMEL'S BACK

A WET NIGHT HAD YIELDED TO A DAMP, GRAY DAWN.

Charlie Moon pulled the red pickup onto the paved driveway, braked it to a stop at the main entrance to the Cassidy mansion. Sidewinder, who had hitched a ride, awakened, raised his head, yawned to display an intimidating array of yellowed teeth. The beast took a look out the window, rattled a low growl, turned to give the Ute a questioning look.

Moon cut the engine, patted the hound's shoulder. "Don't fret. I won't be gone long."

Overhead, thunder mumbled an ominous warning. A few fat drops plopped on the windshield.

The tribal investigator buttoned his denim jacket, took long strides toward the porch. A new door had been installed since his previous visit, presumably to deter burglars. Familiar with such equipment, the lawman knew there would be a slice of quarter-inch steel plate sandwiched between the heavy oak panels. Also new was the brass knocker. It was a smirking monkey's face, biting on a heavy ring. Ignoring the simian grin, he rapped his knuckles on the reinforced door. After a moment, there was a dry crackling of static behind a metallic grille, then Bertram Cassidy's high-pitched pixie voice on the intercom speaker: "Pray, who is it tapping on the manor door—some homeless soul in search of a crust of black bread, a mug of mulled mead?"

Moon heard the hum of a television camera hunting impotently for a target.

Bertie's voice took on a nervous edge as he mumbled to himself, "Oh parrot pimples and tadpole feathers—I cannot see a thing on this pathetic monitor."

Moon smiled at the monkey face on the door knocker, which bore a remarkable resemblance to Bertram Cassidy. He imagined the chubby man twiddling with the controls on his aunt's complex new protective system. "Try turning up the brightness control," he said. "And it might help if you adjusted the contrast."

There was a tone of hope in Bertie's response. "Charlie Moon—are you the owner of that disembodied voice?"

The rain began to fall in sheets.

The remote-controlled camera swiveled, a burst of ultrasound automatically focused a telescopic lens on the Ute's profile. "Ah yes, I can make you out rather clearly now." Quite pleased with his control over the high-tech toy, Bertie chuckled like a happy little boy. "What do you want?"

Moon turned to return the camera's cold, Cyclops stare. Water dripped off the brim of his black Stetson. "For starters, I'd like to come in outta the rain."

"Well, of course you would—great toasted marshmallows, where have my aristocratic manners gone? Just a moment; I must find the right button to poke." After a few muffled mutterings from Jane Cassidy's nephew, there was a heavy snap as a solenoid bolt was activated. The doorknob turned.

But it was Jane Cassidy's face that appeared in the doorway. Wrapped in a blue silk robe, the hatchet-faced woman carried a tumbler of amber liquor in her hand. She glowered through whiskey fumes at the Ute. "You might have called, Mr. Moon. I am not accustomed to entertaining unexpected guests at this hour of the morning."

Moon presented his most disarming smile. "I know just how you feel, but—"

"Do not interrupt me. I have something to say." She took a deep breath, aimed a bony finger at his chest. "Charles, I am highly disappointed with you. You made a recommendation that I offer a huge reward for the return of my stolen property, coupled with a stern threat. I took your advice. Not that I am entirely blameless—I should have known better than to be counseled by a half-witted country rube."

Moon opened his mouth to speak.

Jane raised a pale, vein-ribbed hand. "You will hear me out, Indian chap. Then you may have your say." She frowned at the whiskey glass. "Where was I?"

"Ah—if I could get a word in edgewise—"

"Oh yes, now I remember. Since making the one-million-dollar offer, the Denver law firm which represents my interests has been inundated with calls from a veritable horde of pests, lunatics, practical jokers, and outright hoaxters—and I must evaluate every one of these inquiries. I have lost my appetite, my ability to sleep, and my good humor." Her brow furrowed into a hateful frown. "You have let me down, Charles. I am sad to discover the ugly truth—which is that you are ineffectual."

"I can understand why you're upset, but—"

"Hush! I have come to the inescapable conclusion that your reputation for getting results is mere puffery. Therefore, you are no longer in my employ."

"I'm fired?"

"You are indeed. Sacked. Laid off. Made redundant. And retroactively to the very hour of that unfortunate day when you talked me into offering the thief—or thieves—a fortune for the return of my property, which I shall undoubtedly never lay eyes on again." She paused to take a sip of her strong drink. "And furthermore, I insist that you return the portion of your fees charged to my account since that date." She bared her gums, as if preparing to hiss through the gap in her capped teeth. "Otherwise you shall hear from my army of attorneys."

"But you've never paid me a thin dime."

"Do not bother me with piddling details, young man." She pointed at some imagined spot in the distance. "Now hit the road—and don't come back!"

A raw wind moaned the bluest kind of blues, blew rain horizontally across the porch.

"Miss Cassidy, if I could come inside for a minute, I'm sure I could—"

"Don't plead with me—it is highly unbecoming." Leaning to look around the tall man, Jane saw the pickup for the first time. She made a horrid face. "Where did you get such a hideously ugly vehicle?"

Moon glanced over his shoulder. "That's my new—"

"Dear me, I hope none of our neighbors sees that monstrosity parked on my drive. You must remove it immediately."

Sidewinder, big mouth gaping, tongue lolling over rows of teeth, stared out the truck window at the woman.

"And that horrible, filthy animal!" She started to cackle, sloshing expensive whiskey out of the glass. "I have never seen such an exquisitely homely creature."

The Ute, wet to the skin, looked down his nose at the drunken woman. "Excuse me—what did you say about my dog?"

"Are you deaf as well as dumb?" Jane Cassidy put a wrinkled pink palm beside her mouth, shrieked, "Your beastly companion is homely. Ugly. Hideous. Repulsive. Vile." She laughed in his face. "If you wish to hear more, I will instruct Bertie to fetch a thesaurus."

A bitter smile twisted his lips. "No need to go to all that trouble."

She backed into the spacious parlor, slammed the door.

The tribal investigator tipped his sodden hat. "Sorry I bothered you."

Jane Cassidy went to a mullioned window to peer through a slit in the heavy drapes. She watched the big pickup move down the long driveway, disappear. The wealthy woman turned to glare at her nephew, spilling what was left of the whiskey on his shoes. "How dare that cheeky fellow—I did not give him permission to leave."

"Yes, Auntie." Bertie barely suppressed a smirk. "The man's behavior is simply indefensible."

CHAPTER FORTY-THREE

THE CALL

IT WAS A FEW MINUTES AFTER 10:00 PM. CHARLIE MOON WAS
still awake when the telephone at his bedside made the usual
warble. He scooped it up. "Lila Mae?"

"So you have caller ID," she said. A heartbeat. "No. That
couldn't be it—I have an unpublished number."

"Don't matter, lady. I got your number."

"No, really—how did you know it was me?"

He grinned at the darkness. "None of my other women call
me this late."

"I imagine that's because they don't lie awake at night
thinking about—" *What am I saying!* "What I mean is—"

"I was thinking about you too, McTeague."

"Were you—really?"

"Cross my heart."

"Charlie, do you miss me?"

"Only when you're not with me."

For a dazzling moment, she was sixteen again. "When will
I see you?"

"I'll crank up the pickup, be at your place in forty-six
minutes."

"Don't be silly." *Not that I'd mind.*

"Okay. I'll drive the speed limit. Make it an hour."

The teenager faded away. "Charlie, I called on official
business."

He put his bare feet on the cold floor. "I hope this isn't bad news."

"I just had a call from Stan. The Bureau has some new information on the .22-caliber revolver—the one used in the Ralph Briggs shooting."

The tribal investigator waited.

The FBI agent dropped the hammer: "The weapon has been traced."

Sure. To a woman. From that day in Scott Parris's office, Charlie Moon had recognized the revolver as a LadySmith. He stared into the darkness. *Please, God.* "Anybody I know?"

"Yes. I believe so."

"Who?"

"Sorry, Charlie—I can't break the rules. No name until the potential suspect is either cleared or under arrest. I merely wanted to advise you that we are making progress in the Ralph Briggs shooting."

No response from the Ute.

"Look—I'll talk to my partner. Maybe Stan will let me stretch the rules."

The telephone felt cold in his hand. "That won't be necessary."

"It would not be a personal favor—merely a professional courtesy. You scratch my back, I'll scratch yours."

A long silence, then: "Is your back still itching, McTeague?"

"What have you got?"

"A riddle."

"I hate riddles."

"You'll like this one. A man owns a very nifty car. Why doesn't he keep it parked in his garage?"

She thought about it. "The garage is full of junk?"

"Wrong answer."

"There's another car in the garage?"

"Bingo, McTeague. You win the teddy bear."

"I already have a teddy bear." *I sleep with it.* "But if you have any information relevant to a Bureau investigation, you'd better tell me right now or I'll—"

"Break my arm?"

"We're talking compound fracture."

"Ouch."

"This fellow with the garage—who is he?"

"Sorry, McTeague. I can't break the rules."

"I hate and despise you."

"I know. Want to meet me somewhere for breakfast?"

Her voice softened. "Sorry. I have a seven-thirty appointment with my partner." She waited for a response that did not come. "Some of us have to work hard for a living."

"Better you than me, Lila Mae."

CHAPTER FORTY-FOUR

ENCOUNTER IN IGNACIO

THE TRIBAL INVESTIGATOR HAD PULLED THE COLUMBINE EXpedition into a gas station across the highway from the Sky Ute Casino. He was filling the tank when the stringy-haired blond woman saw him, came running across two lanes of traffic. As if he might not notice her approach, she waved and shouted, "Charlie—Charlie Moon!"

He tipped his black Stetson, smiled.

Kicks Dogs leaned on the gas pump, caught her breath. "Oh, I am *so* glad to see you."

He thought he knew, but asked, "What's the problem?"

Jacob Gourd Rattle's wife shook her head. "Oh God—my whole *life* is a problem. You would never guess who's been harassing me."

Moon watched a gray Ford sedan pass by. "FBI?"

Her eyes went round and large. "How did you know?"

"Years of experience."

Kicks Dogs pointed at his silver belt buckle. "They spent half the day at my house, practically accusing me of being mixed up in some kind of break-in. And shooting some man up in Granite Creek."

"Ralph Briggs."

She nodded. "That's the one."

"The FBI don't make a habit of questioning people for no reason at all."

The woman chewed on her lip. "The .22 pistol that was used to shoot that Mr. Briggs—it turns out it belonged to me." She looked away. "Sort of."

"Sort of?"

"Well, it's like this." Her pale blue eyes implored him to believe. "I had the pistol when I met Jake. But he liked it a lot, and used to carry it around in his coat pocket. Sometimes he would keep it in the van."

"That night Jacob left you in the canyon—did he have the .22 with him then?"

"I guess so." She shrugged. "I ain't seen it in months. And that's the honest truth."

"I can see how this is a problem." He tried not to sound too hard. "But why are you telling me?"

Her answer was frank, and totally disarming. "Because you are so nice and kind."

He did not know what to say.

"You are a man who really *cares* about people—I can always tell." Kicks rubbed a frayed coat sleeve across her nose. "And I think maybe you could help me."

I know I shouldn't ask. "How could I help you?"

"I believe the FBI is going to arrest me." Fear pulled at the pallid face. "Maybe you could talk to them, tell them I didn't have nothing to do with shooting that Briggs fella."

"I hate to admit this, but I don't have the least influence with the feds."

Kicks made a face, glared at the gas pump as if she might punch it right in the snout. "What I need is a good lawyer."

"That would be the right place to start."

She turned her head to look off in the distance. "If I had some money, I'd move miles and miles away from here."

"Where to?"

"Back home." The confused woman pointed west. "North Carolina." She looked as if she were about to cry. "But I don't have a job, or hardly any savings left. I got a fourth-grade education. Where is a person like me going to get more than a few dollars?"

• • •

THE GRAY Ford sedan did a U-turn, pulled into the broad parking lot at the Sky Ute Casino. The driver used a palm-size Japanese camera, adjusted the zoom lens, shot six digital images of the tribal investigator and the blond woman—who appeared to be listening very attentively to what the Ute had to say. From time to time, the suspect nodded. Finally, Kicks Dogs Gourd Rattle hugged the tall man, hurried away as if she was late for an important appointment. *So which one do I follow?*

MOON PULLED away from the gas station. As he had expected, the gray Ford was not far behind. He parked at the curb in front of Wiseman's Hardware. The FBI sedan pulled up beside him, the passenger-side window was lowered. He nodded at the occupant.

Special Agent McTeague gave him an unreadable look. "Want to go for a ride?"

"One way?"

"Depends on how you behave."

"Your wheels or mine?"

"Get in," she said.

He did. "Don't get the wrong idea, McTeague. I'm not usually such an easy pickup."

She was not amused. "You want to tell me what that was all about?"

"I cannot pass a hardware store. And once I'm inside, I'm liable to browse around for hours purchasing copper pipes and roofing paint and tin snips—"

"Can it."

"Oh—do you refer to my accidental clandestine meeting with Mrs. Gourd Rattle?"

"Talk to me."

"I thought we were going for a ride."

"That was what's commonly known as a figure of speech. Not to be taken literally."

"I literally wanted to go for a ride." Moon shook his head. "I am very disappointed."

"Look, cowboy—I haven't got all day."

"Neither have I. So start driving, Special Agent McTeague."

She gave him a suspicious glance. "Where to?"

"I'll tell you on one condition."

"Name it."

"This is between you and me."

She arched a pretty eyebrow. "You wish to act as an un-named informant?"

" 'Confidential source' sounds a lot better."

"You expect me to keep my partner in the dark?"

"Like a baby mushroom."

She shrugged. "I suppose it would be all right."

"You'll never regret it, McTeague."

"I doubt that. But tell me where we're going."

He told her.

AN HOUR later, she glanced at her passenger. "This pathetic excuse for a road is perfectly hideous and we're a dozen miles from no place—what are we doing here?"

"Don't get any ideas." He gave her a bashful grin.

She blushed. "Shut up and talk."

"You sound a lot like my aunt Daisy."

"I would like to meet the lady."

But would she like to meet you. That is the question.

"How much farther—"

"About thirty yards, on your left."

She braked the Ford to a crawl, squinted at the rusty mail-box. "Who is E. Ganado?"

Moon shifted his long frame in the small car. "An accident-prone Navajo who rents this splendid estate from our highly esteemed tribal chairman."

"Why should I pretend to be interested?"

"Because Eddie Ganado was hired by the attorney who represents Felix Navarone."

"That weirdo Apache who got treed near Capote Lake?" She turned the car into the weed-choked lane.

"That's the guy."

McTeague parked by the yellow Pontiac. Ganado's classic automobile was coated with rain-spotted dust and an assortment of sticky seeds and windblown leaves. She set the parking brake. "Okay, Confidential Source. What is this all about?"

"This is about the answer to the riddle."

She arched a pretty eyebrow. "The one about the man who has a snazzy car that he doesn't park in his garage?"

"Right."

She looked around the property. "Okay. The Pontiac is sitting out in the weather. Whose car is in the garage?"

"I'd like to tell you, ma'am—but my momma didn't raise me up to be an obnoxious show-off."

"Go ahead," she urged. "Just this once."

"All right." He assumed a pensive look. "But if I'm wrong, I will be extremely embarrassed."

For the first time that day, the pretty woman smiled. "Then for me, this is a win-win proposition."

"What we will find in the garage is the Dodge van that belongs to the missing Mr. Gourd Rattle."

Without another word, the federal agent got out of the car. He followed her.

"The garage door is padlocked." She frowned at the tribal investigator. "And I do not have a search warrant."

"Check the other side," Moon suggested. "See if there's another entrance."

McTeague walked around the garage, found no second door. When she returned, the Ute had the lock and hasp in his hand.

"Dang thing was loose." Moon grinned. "Poor installation, I guess. If I had not caught it, it would've fell on the ground."

The FBI agent rolled her big, beautiful eyes. "You are impossible."

"You are hard to please. But before we leave, I guess you'll want to check inside the garage." He took hold of the handle in the center of the garage door, lifted it shoulder-high.

McTeague stared at the rear end of the Dodge van. "Charlie—please tell me that you did not find the van somewhere, drive it here yourself."

"You are an unusually suspicious woman—even for a federal cop."

She sniffed. "Do you smell what I smell?"

He nodded. "I think you'd better open the van door."

She shot him a look. "Why me?"

"You're in charge, McTeague. I'm just an innocent by-stander."

With a handkerchief in her hand, the FBI agent turned the chrome-plated handle, opened the van's rear door. "Oh God."

A swarm of blackflies ascended from the corpse, buzzed around, settled down again.

The Ute, who had been taught to abhor dead bodies, did not approach.

She fought off a threat of nausea. "Is this . . . was this Mr. Gourd Rattle?"

"I don't think so."

"Mr. Ganado?"

The Ute tried not to breathe. "That'd be my guess."

"He appears to have been shot." Special Agent McTeague pressed the handkerchief against her nose, turned to the Ute, spoke through the linen square. "Charlie—do you have any idea who did this?"

"Ideas are a dime a dozen." Moon looked up at the sky. "But if I come up with anything worth mentioning, you'll be the first to know."

LILA MAE McTeague was dreaming about Frank Sinatra. Ol' Blue Eyes gave her a wink. Opened his mouth to sing. What came out was—*brrrriiiiing*!

The sleeper jumped, flailed about wildly in the darkness of her bedroom, managed to find the telephone. "Oh . . . uh . . . McTeague here." She was not entirely certain where *here* was.

"Good morning."

"Ch-Charlie?"

The deep voice boomed in her ear: "You sound half asleep—you still in bed?"

She turned over, squinted at the red numbers on the digital clock, groaned. "Do you know how early it is?"

"It is not early, Special Agent McTeague. It is almost five in the AM. Time to hit the floor, get your duds on, strap on that ugly 9-millimeter automatic pistol, go and do something useful for the citizens of the good old U.S. of A."

"Good idea." She yawned. "I'll hunt you down and kill you."

"That can wait. Was the corpse in the van Eddie Ganado?"

"It was." She frowned at the invisible man. "And you knew exactly what we'd find before you took me out there, so don't say you didn't." McTeague pulled the quilt up to her chin. "I bet you'd already found the van and his corpse. And I bet you put that padlock on the garage door."

"You'd lose both bets."

"Then how did you know—"

"I'd dropped by Ganado's place earlier. Soon as I parked my truck, I smelled his body."

"Without opening the garage door?"

"We rural folk tend to have better noses than city people. Probably because the air out here's so clean."

She yawned into the telephone.

"Tell me, McTeague—do you have any hot suspects in the Ganado homicide?"

"Do you?"

"I asked you first."

"No, I do not. But Stan and I are interviewing people who were acquainted with Mr. Ganado."

"Like the lawyer he worked for?"

"Of course. And that Apache character she represents—" McTeague closed her eyes. "My mind is so foggy when I first wake up—what *is* his name?"

"Felix Navarone. Would you like me to recite the date of his birth, his Social Security number, and the name of his favorite uncle?"

"Thank you, no."

"I'm relieved to hear it."

"I refuse to encourage show-offs who think they know everything."

"Not everything, McTeague. There's one thing I've never been able to fathom."

Anticipating a highly personal question, she smiled dreamily. "And what would that be?"

"The square root of minus nine."

"Mr. Moon, I believe that number dwells in the realm of the imaginary."

"I believe you're right, Miss McTeague."

"Don't you want to know what I found out from Felix Navarone?"

"Sure. What did he have to say about the Ganado shooting?"

"So far, nothing at all. Primarily because I have not been able to find him."

"From what I hear, Felix has been staying with his brother Ned. Him and Felix have a place over by Pagosa Springs."

"I am well aware of this," she said. "But Felix was not there when I went to call. And big brother Ned was not happy to see me. In fact, he threatened to break my head."

Moon's tone went deathly flat. "He actually said that?"

"I have omitted a few salty expletives. But yes, he did. And it seemed to me that he meant it. For a moment, I thought I might have to shoot him right between the eyes."

"Too bad you didn't."

She stretched, yawned again. "Charlie, I really appreciate your assistance in locating Eduardo Ganado's body—and Jacob Gourd Rattle's vehicle. You have been an enormous help in the investigation. So much, in fact, that my partner has concluded that I am an investigative genius."

Moon chuckled. "You must be really embarrassed."

"I just stuck out my tongue at you. Now I am going to hang up."

"After you do that, get dressed. If you leave your nice little house on Buttonwood Lane in fifteen minutes, you can be at the Southern Ute Police Department just about the time Wallace Whitehorse shows up and pours his first cup of coffee."

She fell back on the pillow. "You are *insane*."

"I must be—I've decided to scratch your back again."

Instantly, her feet were on the floor. "Same condition as before?"

"Right. Far as Stan Newman is concerned, you didn't hear this from me."

"Okay." She was hopping around, pulling on her slacks

with one hand. "Hold on a minute." The dancer bumped into a lamp, sent it tumbling to the floor.

"What was that?"

"I broke a lamp."

"You have got quite a temper."

"And don't you forget it. Now talk to me."

"Just a few hours after the Cassidy Museum burglary, Kicks Dogs showed up at my aunt Daisy's home, reported her husband missing. I put in a call to SUPD for some help in doing a preliminary search of Spirit Canyon. Jim Wolfe was just getting off the night shift, but he volunteered to respond to the call."

"I already know about that."

"Do you know Wolfe was wearing a raincoat over his uniform jacket? And that this raincoat had a zippered hood, fleece lining, and two big pockets?"

"The latest in men's fashion is not one of my strong points." She clamped the telephone between cheek and shoulder, buckled her belt, brushed a hank of hair off her forehead. "But no. I did not know that."

"That raincoat wasn't in Wolfe's apartment, or in his car. And he was not wearing it whilst he slept under the stones. Which probably means it's in his SUPD locker, with his other personal effects."

"This raincoat—it's important?"

"It might be. If you'd like to find some kind of connection between Officer Wolfe and Jacob Gourd Rattle."

She was buttoning a white silk blouse. "How do you figure that?"

I can't tell her about Oscar Sweetwater's videotape. "Ah— let's call it a hunch."

"Right." *Like your hunch about Gourd Rattle's van being in Eddie Ganado's garage.* "So what do I do with the late James Wolfe's raincoat?"

"Check the pockets."

"What should I expect to find?"

"Oh, the usual stuff. Stick of chewing gum. Coupla Tums.

Paper clip. Rubber band. Little bits of this and that. And maybe—an ignition key."

"What's so special about Officer Wolfe's car key?"

The tribal investigator told her that it was not. And also told her what.

CHAPTER FORTY-FIVE

IN THE SIDE POCKET

SPECIAL AGENT LILA MAE MCTEAGUE STEPPED SMARTLY ALONG the row of steel lockers, paused at number 14. A lined index card was Scotch-taped to the vented door. The neat script inked on the diminutive sign notified anyone who cared to know that this particular metal closet was assigned to one J. Wolfe.

McTeague stepped aside as Officer Daniel Bignight approached, brandishing a yard-long bolt cutter. He set the instrument's sturdy jaws on the hardened-steel shackle of a BullDog combination padlock.

Chief of Police Wallace Whitehorse imagined that he could read the FBI agent's thoughts, and considered it expeditious to respond to her unspoken question. "Our employees buy their own locks. According to regs, they're supposed to provide the combination or a spare key to my office. But you know how it goes."

The fed did not know "how it goes," nor did she care. McTeague had no interest in the cop-bureaucrat's commentary—she desperately wanted to check the pockets of the dead man's raincoat. But as one who was not supposed to have the least idea of what might be found among Officer Jim Wolfe's personal effects, she managed to suppress her excitement.

Whitehorse continued, "Some of 'em follow the rules, but some of 'em—like Wolfe—never quite get around to it. That's why I don't have the combination."

Danny Bignight grimaced as he muscled the handles on the bolt cutter. For a moment, it looked like either the impressive hardware or his biceps might not be up to the job. He set his jaw and grunted. There was a sharp *crack* as the shackle was cleaved.

The FBI agent watched Bignight work the broken padlock off the hasp. "I'll want photos before anything is touched."

Chief of Police Whitehorse nodded. *What does Miss Fancy Pants think we are—a bunch of bumbling amateurs?*

Danny Bignight dropped the heavy bolt cutters on his foot, muttered an untranslatable expletive in the Tiwa language, hopped around.

Oblivious to the unfortunate man's pain, McTeague and Whitehorse made a visual inventory of the open locker.

Hanging on a rusted metal rod were two wrinkled blue shirts, an SUPD uniform jacket, a black fleece-lined raincoat. In the bottom of the space, a Houston Oilers' visored cap, a pair of well-shined black boots, a few paperback novels, three unopened packs of mentholated cigarettes, a Leatherman tool, a .32-caliber Browning automatic pistol in a canvas holster.

"Must be Wolfe's personal piece," Whitehorse said. *He shouldn't have kept his private gun in his locker.*

"Photograph and bag the firearm," McTeague said to Bignight, who was rubbing his instep.

Though he took his orders from Chief of Police Whitehorse, Daniel Bignight understood the unwritten rules that applied to working with the Bureau. He followed her instructions. After the pistol was properly disposed of, he took several photographs of the locker—including a close-up of the movie-star pinup on the inside of the door where Wolfe or a predecessor had taped a magazine photograph of a pretty lady who was long since dead. Perched on the tiled edge of a turquoise-blue swimming pool, she wore a modest yellow bathing suit and a seductive smile. The SUPD cop read the caption. "Lana Turner," he muttered. *Wonder who she is.*

Whitehorse scowled at the Pueblo Indian. "Let's get on with it, Danny."

Special Agent McTeague waited with the best imitation of

patience she could muster, leaving the removal of the contents to Bignight.

The Leatherman tool.

The books.

The boots.

The baseball cap.

The cigarettes.

And on and on and on.

Finally, Wallace Whitehorse removed the items of clothing from the locker, placed them on a folding-leg card table that had been set up to display the meager effects of the recently deceased Officer Wolfe.

McTeague managed to maintain a detached, professional air. *Surely they won't forget to—*

They did not.

Bignight pulled on a pair of skin-tight rubber gloves, removed objects from the jacket pockets: a soiled handkerchief, a package of cherry Life Savers. He repeated the procedure on the raincoat. He placed each item on the card table, took appropriate photos.

The FBI agent stared at the specimens. Not precisely what Moon had predicted, but not far off. A small Swiss army pocketknife with jet-black handles. A half-full pack of cigarettes. A book of matches from the Mountain Man Bar and Grille. Seventy-eight cents in coins. Three plastic toothpicks. A small bottle of over-the-counter eyedrops.

And a worn brass key.

Danny Bignight proceeded to insert the potential evidence into plastic bags.

She tried to sound nonchalant. "What's the key for?"

Both policemen looked at her. Both shrugged.

She put out her hand like a blind beggar reaching for a few pence.

Bignight gave the fed the Ziploc bag.

Lila Mae McTeague studied the contents. "Looks to me like an ignition key."

"Yeah," Whitehorse said in a monotone. "An ignition key." *So what?*

"That's what it looks like," Bignight said. "But it's not for one of the department's units." He squinted. "This key is old and worn."

The chief of police slipped on a pair of rimless spectacles, leaned to inspect the brass artifact. "Officer Wolfe drove a Subaru Forester. But that's no Subaru key."

"I have a hunch," McTeague said.

The pair of Indians gawked at the enigmatic fed.

She flashed a smile. "Let's go out to the holding yard where you stored Mr. Gourd Rattle's Dodge van. See if the key fits."

Hunch, my left hind leg. Wallace Whitehorse's eyes narrowed. *She's got some inside information. And she ain't gonna tell us zip.*

Daniel Bignight held a quite different opinion. *This lady is as smart as she is good-looking.*

HIS COURSE set for the Gourd Rattle van, Special Agent Stanley Newman marched across the graveled holding yard with all the enthusiasm of a brand-new ROTC cadet. McTeague was there, flanked by the SUPD top cop and one of Wallace Whitehorse's underlings. Newman gave Chief of Police Whitehorse a perfunctory nod, ignored Daniel Bignight altogether, shouldered up to his partner. "If you'd let me know where you were going this morning, I coulda met you here."

"It was just some routine stuff." McTeague avoided his penetrating gaze. "I thought one of us should be present when the SUPD checked out Officer Wolfe's locker." She omitted to mention that she had suggested the action.

Newman rubbed his fingers along the prickly bristle of an unshaven jowl. "You should've called me." That was standard operating procedure. Your partner didn't go gallivanting off without at least letting you know where and why. Not unless your partner knew something and was up to no good—like trying to grab all the credit for herself.

"I got up at the crack of dawn," McTeague said. "Didn't want to wake you."

Her partner grimaced. "This really stinks."

"Look, Stan—I don't intend to apologize for—"

"I mean the van." Newman sniffed. "Still smells like dead meat." *And you don't fool me for a minute.* "So what've you got, hotshot?"

She smiled at the Pueblo Indian. "Officer Bignight will demonstrate."

Daniel Bignight put the key in the ignition, turned it. He grinned at Newman when the engine started. "And it's no accident. We already run a check with the manufacturer. This is the key that come with the van when it was brand-new."

"Great," the fed growled. "Any of you people gonna tell me where you found Mr. Gourd Rattle's ignition key?"

Wallace Whitehorse told him.

Newman arched both bushy eyebrows. "No kidding—in Officer Wolfe's coat pocket?"

"Raincoat pocket," Whitehorse said. He gave the white woman a suspicious look. "We were about to bag it, when Special Agent McTeague realized the key might be important."

"That's right." Danny Bignight hoped to endear himself to the handsome woman. "I was about to pack the key away with some other junk from Wolfe's pockets, and she said, 'What's the key for?'"

Stanley Newman rotated to face his partner, gave her a knowing look. "Is that a fact?"

She tried to stare him down, felt a warm blush creeping up her neck, looked away. "It appeared to be an ignition key. But Chief Whitehorse was sure it wasn't for a Subaru, which is what Officer Wolfe drove. So we decided to try it on Mr. Gourd Rattle's van."

Thinking the pretty woman far too modest, Bignight chimed in, "That was Agent McTeague's idea too. I never would've thought of it—that Jim Wolfe would have been carrying Jacob Gourd Rattle's van key around in his pocket." He shook his head in a go-figure expression.

The chief of police blasted Daniel Bignight with his blackest stormcloud grimace, made a jerking nod. The boss departed, with a chastened Bignight trailing behind.

Stanley Newman grinned at his partner. "I am really impressed. First you find the Gourd Rattle van, with Eddie Ganado's shot-up body inside. And now—now you find the Gourd Rattle van key in the recently deceased Ossifer Wolfe's coat pocket."

"I got lucky." *Lucky that Charlie Moon is helping me.*

"You are way too modest, McTeague. In fact, I am so happy with the job you're doing that I'm going to buy you a serious breakfast."

She tried hard to look pleased.

CHAPTER FORTY-SIX

SUSPICION

WITH THE FASTIDIOUS SKILL OF A NEUROSURGEON, SPECIAL agent Stanley Newman sliced his stack of lavishly buttered whole-wheat pancakes into perfect quarters. Satisfied with the result, he proceeded to subdivide these pointy portions into eighths. He poured on a generous helping of thick, maple-flavored syrup. The fed tasted the sweet result, pronounced it satisfactory. He shot an amused look at his partner. "How's your eggs, McTeague?"

She salted the subject of his inquiry. "I will know when I have tasted them."

Newman watched her lovely face. "Now we know Jim Wolfe was definitely connected to Jacob Gourd Rattle—why else would he have Gourd Rattle's van key in his pocket?"

Now she peppered the sunny-side-ups. "Raincoat pocket."

"It could be an important detail." He saluted her with his fork. "Thank you for correcting me."

"You are welcome."

Newman used a paper napkin to wipe syrup off his chin. "Officer Wolfe had that ignition key because he'd drove Gourd Rattle's van at least once. I wouldn't be surprised if Wolfe was behind the wheel on the night when Gourd Rattle left his wife in the canyon to freeze to death."

McTeague took a sip of hot tea. "Which is the same night the Cassidy Museum was burgled."

Wheels turned in Newman's head. "Maybe Wolfe and Gourd Rattle did the heist."

"Which, with one of them being a Native American and the other an employee of a Native American tribe, puts the museum caper in Bureau jurisdiction."

"Caper?"

"Sorry, Stan. I could not help myself—I have always wanted to use that word."

"I hope it is out of your system." He speared a defenseless sausage link. "You know what bothers me?"

"Of course. Why did Officer Wolfe still have Mr. Gourd Rattle's van key in his raincoat pocket?"

"Yeah. Why would he carry around this incriminating evidence—why not ditch it?"

"Perhaps," she said, "because Wolfe had driven the van shortly before his demise."

"Sure," Newman said. "Our rogue cop pops Eddie Ganado with his trusty six-shooter, loads the corpse into the van, stashes it in Ganado's garage. Wolfe is out of our jurisdiction, but we need to get our hands on Jacob Gourd Rattle."

"I'd like to have another chat with Mr. Gourd Rattle's wife about her .22-caliber pistol," McTeague said. "See if she sticks to her story about her husband carrying it around. While I'm at it, I'll ask her how many keys they had for the family van."

"Sounds like a good plan, Agent McTeague. May I come along when you interview this oddball who calls herself Kicks Dogs—that is, if you don't mind having your partner's company?"

She wrinkled her nose at the sarcastic man. "Tag along if you wish."

The grease-loving gourmet impaled a second sausage on the tines of his fork. As he chewed, Newman gave the woman across the table a long, penetrating appraisal.

McTeague poked a fork at an egg that stared back at her. She dispatched the egg, made a valiant effort to ignore the irritating man.

He leaned forward, squinted at her.

She shot him an annoyed look. "What?"

"I am pondering about something."

"I am trying to enjoy my free breakfast." She pointed her fork at a dark corner of Angel's Cafe. "If you must ponder, do it over yonder."

He appeared to be hurt by this remark. "You don't wonder about what I ponder?"

"Not one-millionth of a minuscule." She took a dainty bite of whole-wheat toast. "I would much rather know why moss prefers to grow on the north side of trees."

"Very well, if your feminine curiosity must be satisfied." He pushed his breakfast plate aside. "I am pondering about whether my partner is an extraordinarily smart cop—or just plain lucky. Or," he added with a sly expression, "something else altogether."

She smiled at his homely face. "You know what they say."

"I think I did once upon a time, but it has slipped my mind. Please remind me."

"It is better to be lucky than smart."

"This remark does not address my question."

"Technically speaking, Stan—you have not asked a question."

"May I?"

McTeague shook her head. "I would strongly advise against it."

"Okay. Fair enough. But let's *pretend* that I pose you a question."

"If you must indulge your masculine fantasies."

"What if I was to ask, 'Would Lila Mae McTeague hold out on her partner?' "

She gave him a frosty look. "Is this some sort of veiled accusation?"

Newman threw up his hands. "Oh heavens no, it is more like a hypercritical question."

"Hypothetical." She frowned. "At least I think that's what you mean."

"Whatever. But here's the deal. What if I was to ask if you

knew—before you got to SUPD headquarters this morning—
that the ignition key to Jacob Gourd Rattle's van would be in
Officer Wolfe's coat pocket."

"Raincoat pocket."

He ignored this. "If I was to ask such a direct question, I
wonder if you would give me a straight answer."

"Here is a hint—your life is destined to be overbrimming
with titillating mysteries." She dipped her toast in his coffee
cup, spilling dark liquid into the saucer.

Newman watched this assault on his beverage with minimal amusement. "Then you wouldn't tell me?"

"Tell you what?"

"The answers to my hyperthermal questions. Did you got a
tip from an informer? And if you did, how did this anonymous
tipster know the key was in Wolfe's coat pocket? Answer me
that."

"I do not entertain hyperthermal questions—they tend to
give me a fever." She avoided his gaze. "Now let us cease this
dawdling about, and finish our morning meal."

"Okay." He consumed the soggy remains of the pancakes.
Finished off the remaining sausage link. Drank his tepid coffee. Belched. "That was a fine breakfast. But I can't help wondering how Charlie Moon knew the ignition key was in
Wolfe's pocket."

She dropped her fork.

"Hah—I saw that!"

"Saw what? The thing just slipped out of my hand."

"Then explain why you blushed like a beet when I mentioned the tall, dark, conniving tribal investigator?"

"Well, pardon me." She tossed the toast away. "Maybe it
was because I am embarrassed that my partner is such a . . . a
goofball!"

"Goofball—is that the best you can do?"

"For the moment."

"We both know you blushed because you're being decep-
tive with your partner, who is loyal and true and faithful."

"That sounds like a description of a long-eared hound."

"That's right—try to change the subject. But I got a nose

for this sort of thing." He touched his ear. "So you don't need to tell me nothing."

"I am highly impressed, Stanley. Your knowledge of anatomy almost equals your uncanny grasp of the English language."

"Go ahead—laugh if you want to."

"Ha-ha."

"It *was* Charlie Moon, wasn't it?"

Her face burned. "I will not respond to your feeble attempts to learn the identity of any confidential source which I might or might not have."

Stanley Newman slapped his thigh. "I *knew* it! I bet he started being your 'confidential source' that night when you two was on your front steps." *Oh no—why did I say that!*

She got up from the table. "What—you were spying on us?" *Me and my big mouth.* "Hey, it was just a lucky guess."

"Stanley Newman, you are a *disgusting* man."

"That may be." He grabbed the check, shook it at his partner. "But I'm right, ain't I—Charlie Moon is your source?"

"Let me get this straight." She put her hands on her hips. "You think I am so incompetent that if I just happen to show up at the right place at the opportune moment, it must be because . . . because . . ." *Because Charlie Moon pointed the way.*

"I never said you was incompetent." He assumed his most earnest expression. "In fact, I think you're very competent. And pretty smart."

"Call me ungrateful, but I do not choose to accept this as a compliment."

"Okay, Miss Ungrateful." He jabbed a thumb at his syrup-stained tie. "Hey, I'm the dumb one. If I lean on Charlie Moon, he clams up. I should know better, but I keep doing the same stupid things year in and year out. But you—you are a cat of a different stripe. You blink the big eyes at poor ol' Charlie, he gets a serious case of testosterone poisoning, spills his guts to you." He chuckled. "With my good looks and your brains, Lila Mae—we could make one terrific team."

Special Agent McTeague made her right hand into a fist.

Took a hard look at her partner's nose. *It would cost me my job. But it might just be worth it.*

He backed up a half step. "Don't do it."

"Give me one good reason. Even a so-so one."

"Try this: It would look really bad if a tough guy like me got decked by a lady."

"What *kind* of lady?"

"A really good-looking lady?"

She shook her head.

"A really good-looking lady who is a first-rate cop?"

Lila Mae relaxed. "That'll just barely get you off the hook. For now."

"Charlie's sweet on you, ain't he?"

Despite herself, she smiled. "If he was, what's it to you?"

"D'you like him?"

She turned away. "Do you? Like him, I mean."

He thought about it. "Yeah. Sure I do."

"Why?"

"I've known Charlie Moon for goin' on fifteen years." Newman gave his partner a strange, almost fatherly look. "Ol' Charlie, he'll kid you from here to the Pecos and back, and he'll do his level best to swindle his best buddy in a bet—but he'll never flat-out lie to you. Matter of fact, that skinny Indian is a real straight arrow."

"Is that so?"

"You bet your garters, McTeague. And he's peaceable, too—Charlie'll avoid a scrap if he can. But just last year, that Ute took on two of the meanest drug-running thugs you ever saw—whipped both of 'em half to death with his bare hands. But if Charlie finds a little teensy moth in his house, fluttering around a candle, he won't swat it."

She smiled at this. "He won't even kill an insect?"

"Nope. He'll take that little bitsy moth outside, say some encouraging words—and turn it loose to fly away."

"He sounds rather gentle for a lawman."

"Charlie, he'd rather raise alfalfa and cows than be a cop. But in a pinch, there's not a man alive I'd rather have backing me up. And from time to time, he sees things most of us can't. But for some reason, he don't like to tell me about it."

There was a long silence.

She took a deep breath. "Just for the record: If it should happen that I get a tip from a source who prefers to remain anonymous, I will do my very best to do the right thing. Which is to say I wouldn't tell you in a hundred million years. Not if you got down on your knobby little knees and begged me."

He patted her on the back. "You're a good cop, McTeague." Newman smirked. "But if a Ute tribal investigator whose name I won't mention should ever offer you any under-the-table information—"

"You would expect me to take advantage of him." *Which is exactly what I've done.* "Squeeze the source dry so the Bureau can take all the credit. And I should not feel the least bit guilty if this helps my career along."

"Of course you shouldn't. Feel guilty, I mean."

"Not even if using the informant makes my sleazy partner look good?"

"Goes without saying." Newman laid a fifty-cent tip on the table, removed a twenty-dollar bill from his wallet.

"Thanks anyway, Stan, I will pay for my own breakfast."

He snorted, pointed in the general direction of Washington, D.C. "Look, McTeague—it's a slash-and-burn world out there. Full of ruthless felons, sleazy politicians, and do-nothing bureaucrats. You and me, we're federal cops. It's up to us to get the job done for the taxpayers. And from time to time, that means breaking some eggs."

Her smile was brittle. "You know what you are, Stan?"

"Yeah. I know." He straightened his soiled tie, buttoned his jacket around a slightly bulging midriff. "But I am also the senior agent on this here team, so don't you even think about saying it out loud."

CHAPTER FORTY-SEVEN

SATISFACTION

CHARLIE MOON PARKED THE F-350 ON A WEED-CHOKED DIRT lane that terminated within a few yards of Felix and Ned Navarone's home. A crude sandstone chimney supported one end of the unpainted structure, the outstretched limbs of a blighted elm appeared ready to catch the other. Over the years, a garish assortment of red, blue, and silver steel panels had been nailed onto the peaked roof, which capped the shack like a party hat on a corpse. The metal shingles rattled in a sudden gust of dusty wind.

A well-worn path cleaved a way through sage and chamisa to an outdoor privy that was only a dozen steps from a side door. A mud-splattered Jeep was parked under a dead pine, parts of a disassembled Honda racing motorcycle were scattered about on the front porch. There was no sign of Felix Navarone's 1957 Chevrolet pickup.

The tribal investigator considered how pleasant it was to make a call with no weighty goal in mind. *From time to time, a man needs to get out and do something that won't accomplish a thing. Just for the fun of it.*

Half-rotten porch steps squeaked and sagged under his step. A coyote hide was nailed on the wall; it was still green enough to attract a swarm of tiny wasps. The door was decorated with a chalky steer skull. The Ute rapped his knuckles on the unpainted birch.

There were creaks as someone of considerable bulk

walked across the floor. One of the toughest-looking human beings Moon had ever seen opened the door. Outfitted in tire-tread sandals, soiled green corduroy pants, and a brown felt shirt—the flat-nosed, square-headed man was six and a half feet tall. The behemoth had arms like elephant legs, a torso the size of a fifty-five-gallon drum. Matted black hair hung well past the Apache's broad shoulders. He was chewing a mouthful of meat, had a greasy butcher knife in his paw that evidently served as an eating utensil. He scowled at the man on his porch, who looked vaguely familiar. "Who're you?"

"A dedicated public servant." Charlie Moon smiled. "It would be a total fabrication to tell you that I am here on behalf of the CCPCC."

He stopped chewing. "See-see-what?"

"Colorado Citizens for the Preservation of Common Courtesy." Moon tipped his hat to demonstrate the art. "I allegedly have the honor to be the chairman for the south-central region, which includes Archuleta County."

The massive fellow swallowed his food. "I never heard a any such outfit."

"Then you might want to fan through our monthly newsletter—the *CCPCC Review*. It is complimentary to paid-up members, seven dollars a copy to the general public."

The heavy brows curled into a suspicious scowl. "You here to sell me some magazines?"

"We can discuss the *CCPCC Review* later, and the unlikely possibility of enrolling you as a provisional member of our organization. But first I must verify that you are the person I am here to see." Moon checked a blank page in his pocket notebook, looked at the beetle-browed monster. "Are you Mr. Ned Navarone?"

A puzzled nod.

"Take some time to think about it—you absolutely sure?"

A thoughtful pause. "Yeah. That's my name."

"Then I have business to conduct with you."

Ned rubbed the butcher knife across the belly of his shirt, leaving a trail of grease. "What kinda business?"

"Mr. Navarone, it pains me to bring this up, but I am

obliged to inquire—did you recently threaten physical harm to a lady who came to your door?"

"Huh?"

"Did you say you would break the woman's head?"

The bruiser, who threatened citizens at every opportunity, frowned at the sky as he tried to recall the particular event. His attention was diverted by a small cloud that resembled a pork chop.

"It was within the past two days," Moon said. "She's a long tall Sally. Works for the government."

The huge man grinned, exposing a mouthful of teeth the color of ripe corn. "Oh—that white FBI Nazi broad?"

You should not have said that.

Ned pointed the butcher knife at the alleged regional chairman of the CCPCC. "She wanted to know where Felix is."

Moon's face radiated childlike innocence. "Felix who?"

"Felix Navarone—my brother. That FBI Hitler's Sister was here looking for him."

You've gone and done it again. "I am not here about your immediate family, Mr. Navarone. It is your lack of courtesy to Agent McTeague that brings me to your door."

The massive man stared blankly at the visitor.

"But the CCPCC docs not rush to judgment—our organization takes into account the various reasons and root causes for unseemly behavior. We realize that there may have been mitigating circumstances."

"What?"

Moon explained, "It's possible you were in a bad mood when you threatened to break the lady's head. Maybe you were suffering from acute indigestion. Or a bad toothache."

"Nah." Ned waved the butcher knife. "Wasn't nothin' like that. She just ticked me off."

"Even so, I expect you would welcome a chance to make amends. So look upon this as an opportunity to make things right between you and that nice lady who works so hard for Uncle Sam."

The man's dark eyes narrowed. "This some kinda joke?"

Moon shook his head. "We of the CCPCC never jest about

the need for good manners. This is very serious business indeed." He produced a one-page document from his jacket pocket. "For your convenience, I've brought a typewritten apology for your signature."

The Apache cocked his head. "A what?"

"A sheet of paper. You sign it to say you're sorry."

Ned was not a subtle man. His glanced at his butcher knife, then at the tall man's throat.

Moon pressed on. "It is written is simple English, suitable for a person who has completed the third grade with a D-minus average. Shall I read it to you?"

He pointed the ten-inch blade toward Moon's red pickup. "You get offa my place before I slice your—"

The Ute cleared his throat and recited the single sentence: " 'I, Mr. Ned Navarone'—that's you—'wish to apologize to Special Agent McTeague for my rude behavior.' " He pointed to the bottom of the page. "There's a place for you to sign—right there on the dotted line. If you don't know how, just make your X and I'll witness it for you."

A low, dangerous growl began to rumble somewhere deep inside the huge man.

Moon tried to look disappointed. "Shall I take it that you refuse to sign the formal apology?"

The outraged knife wielder launched into a series of loud and vivid obscenities.

Moon waited until the verbal storm had abated. "I am forced to conclude that you are not sufficiently repentant." The tribal investigator fixed the Apache with a flinty stare. "So you might as well forget about a membership subscription to the *CCPCC Review*. You will have to purchase it by the copy, at seven bucks a pop."

Ned Navarone brandished the butcher knife under the Ute's nose. "I am gonna cut you up into little chunks and feed you to my hog."

The Ute shook his head. "You are not allowed to do that."

"What?"

"It is strictly against the CCPCC rules to feed a paid-up member to a swine," Moon explained. "I admit that this is not common knowledge, but I keep it under my hat." He removed his John B. Stetson, offered it to the Apache for a close inspection. "See if you can read the fine print on the sweatband."

Ned Navarone was holding the hat, staring deep into the dark well of black felt. This is why he never saw it coming.

WHEN THE sun had gone to rest in the west, and a silver moon was sailing along the crest of Plum Ridge, Ned Navarone regained what passed for consciousness in one of his limited capacity. He was in a sitting position, his back propped against the front door. A half dozen of his corn-yellow teeth had been shucked and were scattered about the porch; a bloody eye was swollen shut. He was wearing the chalky steer skull for a hat. With the orb that still functioned, he looked through the bovine eye socket, saw something protruding from his shirt.

It was the butcher knife—sticking out of his chest. *I've been stabbed right in the heart—and I can see my head bone from the inside.* He stared in rapt wonder. *I must be dead.* He made a gurgling sound, gingerly touched the knife handle— it fell off in his lap. There was no blade. *It must still be inside me.* He rubbed at his chest. *Funny, though—I don't feel nothing there.*

Charlie Moon had snapped the blade off in a crack between the planks.

Ned closed his eyes, tried to remember what had happened. Bits and pieces of the confrontation began to come back to him: *Some guy knocked on the door—tried to sell me a magazine prescription. I guess when I wouldn't buy, he must've hit me with a sledgehammer or somethin'. There oughta be a law against pushy salesmen.*

THE AWAKENING

CHARLIE MOON sat straight up in bed. *What was that?*

The telephone rang again.

He snatched it up, jammed the wrong end against his ear. "Yeah?"

The faint voice spoke in his mouth: "Hello—hello?"

He reversed the instrument, jabbing his eye with the stubby antenna.

Now the woman's voice was in his ear: "Hello—are you there?"

He rubbed the sore knuckles on his right hand. *Ned Navarone's head must be full of cement.* "Where else would I be?"

There was a smile in her voice. "You sounded startled." A pause. "I hope I did not wake you."

The digital clock on the bedside table informed the man that it was twelve minutes past four AM. He eased himself back on the pillow, stretched his long legs out on top of the quilt. "Wake a hardworking rancher—at this time of the day?"

"You were already up?"

"Us country folk sleep barely two hours out of every twenty-four. I have already made a batch of buttermilk biscuits from scratch, pitched three bales of alfalfa hay to the work horses and a peck o' cracked corn to the Dominiker hens."

"That is very unkind of you."

"The horses and hens did not complain."

"You know what I mean. You woke me up with your phone call; I was trying to get even."

"You'll have to try harder."

"Do you have any suggestions?"

"I'll try to think of something." He yawned into the telephone.

"Goodie—I knew I woke you up!"

"No you didn't." *The phone did.*

"Then why are you yawning?"

"I am bored?"

"No, that wouldn't do. And you should not lie to me, Charlie Moon."

"From time to time, I might exaggerate—but I would never tell you a lie."

So I've heard. "That is gratifying to know."

"It is also gratifying to know you was laying there flat on

your back, eyes big as saucers, not able to sleep—wanting to talk to your favorite cowboy."

"Don't kid yourself." *How did he know?* "I called to tell you that a slug found in Mr. Ganado's remains was in sufficiently good condition for our forensics experts to identify the pistol that shot it. I'm talking about Officer Wolfe's service revolver. Which is hardly surprising in light of the fact that Wolfe had possession of the Gourd Rattle van key, and we found the van with Ganado's body inside."

"Hmmm."

"Charlie, what does that 'hmmm' mean?"

"Oh, not much. It's kind of a filler when a feller can't think of a thing to say."

"Don't you give me that."

The silence fairly sizzled.

"Tell me!"

"McTeague, there are some things a modest man prefers to keep to himself."

"Charlie, you are beginning to get on my nerves."

"That's because you're wound up way too tight. But I know what'd make you feel lots better."

"Strangling you?"

"The pleasure from that would wear off in a week or so. What you should do is say something nice to me."

"Okay." She sighed. "Thank you for the tip."

"Tip?"

"You know very well what I mean—alerting me to look in the late Officer Wolfe's raincoat pockets for the ignition key to the Gourd Rattle van."

"Oh, that. You are welcome, McTeague."

"And I suppose your excessive modesty will prevent you from telling me how you knew?"

"You got it."

"Strangling still sounds like a good idea. You are a very annoying man."

"Don't think it comes easy. I took a six-week mail-order course."

"Good night, Charlie."

"Good night, Irene." He dropped the telephone into its small cradle, rolled onto his side. On the other side of the window-pane, the night was thick with darkness. Within minutes, Charlie Moon had fallen deep into a dreamless sleep.

CHAPTER FORTY-EIGHT

THE CLIENT

DURANGO ATTORNEY WALTER PRICE SHOULDERED THE LOBBY door of the Price Building with all the enthusiastic aggression of a seasoned NFL linebacker, glanced at the platinum watch strapped on his wrist, vaulted up the stairs three at a time, twisted the porcelain knob on the outer office door at precisely 8:58 AM. He very nearly bowled over Miss Weiss, who was waiting near the threshold.

"Ah—excuse me." Price removed his hat, exposing a neatly groomed head of silver-gray hair that was the envy of every bald man in Durango.

"Good morning, sir." She had something in her hand.

He placed his hat on a tasteful teakwood rack. "What is this?"

"Your mail."

"Impossible. The post does not arrive until eleven-twenty."

"This was a special delivery." She held the smile inside her mouth.

"How very odd." The attorney accepted the dirty white envelope, held it gingerly between immaculately manicured finger and thumb, turned up his nose. "It is soiled."

"That is probably because I stepped on it."

He frowned at the woman. "Why, pray tell, would you put your shoe on a piece of office correspondence?"

"I did not see it on the floor. Before I arrived at seven thirty-four, someone had slipped it under the door."

He noted that there was neither stamp nor return address. Someone had printed "W Price" on the envelope. "This is really quite irregular." He gave the thing back to the secretary.

"Shall I open it for you, sir?"

"If you must." He hung his topcoat just under the hat.

Miss Weiss applied a singled-edged razor blade to the envelope, removed a page of cheap lined paper. "Sir, I believe you should read this."

The attorney snatched the page from her hand. Squinted at the block-printed words:

> I got the Casidy stuff. I saw the rich woman on the TV. She can have it back for the milion $ but I wont have nothing to do with no too bit lawyer. If Charly Moon will act for me Ill prove I got the stuff. You want to deal put an ad in the papers an say you want to buy some spotted dogs. The kind that ride on fire trucks.

Yellow Jacket

Walter Price tossed the note onto his secretary's glass-topped desk. "This is truly appalling."

"Yes, sir. When I saw how insulting this person was to your profession—"

"The spelling, the grammar, the punctuation—absolutely atrocious."

"What do you intend to do, sir?"

"It is no doubt some sort of sophomoric hoax. And even if it were not, I would never associate the firm with such a . . ." He could think of no adequate descriptor.

"No, sir. Of course not." Miss Weiss allowed herself just the hint of a smile. "Not even if Jane Cassidy would be eternally indebted to you for helping her recover the family's stolen property."

"Hang Jane Cassidy and all her kith and kin. I detest the woman."

"Yes, sir. It is not like the firm needs to woo a wealthy client."

He glared at the woman. "Miss Weiss, are you being impertinent?"

"Only a wee bit, sir. It adds a bit of spice to my otherwise humdrum life."

"Very well then. Carry on."

"Shall I file the Yellow Jacket note?"

"If you wish. But do not think that I will not stoop to dealing with common burglars. Or, for that matter, with Jane Cassidy."

"Of course not, sir."

Walter Price barged into his spacious corner office. "Get me some coffee."

"Before or after I call Mr. Moon?"

"After."

CHARLIE MOON was at the kitchen table, listening to a string of complaints from his foreman. Pete Bushman's negative narrative was interrupted when the downstairs telephone in the Columbine headquarters rang.

Knowing it would rattle his employee, Moon ignored the nerve-jangling sound.

Bushman sat though seven rings, began to grind his remaining teeth. "Ain't you gonna answer that?"

The boss took a sip of sweet coffee. "Do you think I should?"

The foreman banged his fist on the table, yelled through his whiskers, "Shoot yes—this is supposed to be a bidness we're runnin' here. That could be McDonald's callin'. Or Burger King. Or one a them big supermarket chains."

Moon went into the parlor, put the plastic instrument against his ear. "Columbine." A momentary pause. "Sure, I'll hold for Mr. Price—if he don't take too long." A longer pause. "Hi, Walter. What's up?" A very long pause. "That's an interesting piece of mail you got. But ten to one it's some kinda joke." He listened to the lawyer's response. "Walter, I don't want to get mixed up in anything to do with the Cassidys. That cranky woman's already hired and fired me—and she's never paid me a dime for my time." Moon counted off the seconds as Price made his case. "Well, go ahead, talk to her if you want to. But I'm not making any promises." He hung up the phone, returned to the kitchen.

Despite an earnest effort to eavesdrop on the boss's conversation, Pete Bushman had heard nothing but a few muffled mumbles. "Well, who was that?"

"Some lady who said she was a buyer for some company called Krugers. Or something that sounded like that."

Must've been Krogers. The foreman's face went pale under his sunburned skin. "What'd she want?"

"From what I could tell, she's interested in buying some beef."

"Oh my goodness—what'd you tell 'er?"

"Told her I'd never heard of no Krugers outfit. But that if she'd send some credit references, the Columbine might consider doing some business with her. But I don't think she will."

Bushman felt his stomach knotting up. "Why not?"

"She hung up on me."

The light began to dawn. "Charlie—would you be funnin' me?"

Moon's face split into a mischievous grin. "Would a muskrat musk?"

CHAPTER FORTY-NINE

THE APOLOGY

CHARLIE MOON ROLLED OUT OF BED WHEN THE BIG DIPPER
was scooping the last few stars from the sky. The ice-cold
river was splashing over black basalt boulders. To the south,
ripples in Lake Jesse glittered in the galactic glow. The peaceful, sweet-smelling morning on the Columbine had all the
makings of a fine, soul-satisfying day.

The Ute made a deliberate decision to enjoy these precious
hours. He had a brief but serious talk with his dog, walked
down the lane to stand on the Too Late bridge and watch the
darting rainbow trout.

After a few minutes of smiling at the fish, he stopped at the
foreman's house to enjoy pleasant conversation and a fine
breakfast with Pete and Dolly Bushman. The kindly woman
had made enchiladas rancheros with green chili, refried
beans, and flour tortillas buttered with the genuine article. Between bites, Pete reported a fair stand of grass on the four sections north of Pine Knob. All it needed was "a couple inches
more rain, and it'll grow so high we'll be losing calves in it."
On cue, puffy clouds were already piling up a mile high over
the Misery and Buckhorn ranges.

Moon returned to the ranch headquarters, took a seat at the
fireside, and turned on the radio. According to the stockman's
report broadcast from the Grand Junction station, the price of
beef had gone up four cents a pound in the last week.

He closed his eyes. Smiled. *What could go wrong on a day like this?*

THE TELEPHONE in the foreman's house rang. Dolly Bushman answered it. "Columbine Ranch."

A now-familiar voice barked back at her.

The foreman's wife sucked in a deep breath before responding. "It's not my fault if Charlie don't call you back— I gave him all of your messages." The amiable woman listened patiently to the expected complaint. "If he don't answer the phone at the big house, it's most likely because he's got better things to do . . ." *Than talk to the likes of you.* Dolly's eyes popped. "You're out at the main entrance?" *I'll let the boss deal with this.* "Well, I suppose you might as well come on up the lane." She pressed a button to unlatch the gate.

CHARLIE MOON was relaxing before a crackling fire of split pine. The owner of the spread was reading the yellowed pages of a book Will James had written in 1929, *Lone Cowboy: My Life Story.*

Had it not been for a singularly annoying banging on the door, the ranch headquarters would have been soothingly silent.

Her voice screeched like a falcon falling toward its prey: "Charles—I know you're in there. Now open this door!"

He enjoyed another paragraph.

The determined woman kicked at the heavy door with her open-toed shoe, yelped with pain.

The Ute smiled at the near-miraculous account of Will finding Smoky again after the stolen animal had been missing for years. *That hard-case cowboy sure did love that ol' horse.*

She called out in a childlike whimper. "Charles, I believe I have injured myself."

He took a sip from a mug of very sweet, very black coffee, heard a happy bark from Sidewinder.

There was an immediate response from his female visitor: "Get away from me you horrid, filthy beast!"

Moon marked his place with a two-dollar bill, put the book aside, got up from his rocking chair.

Another round of barking.

"Charles, I demand that you call off your nasty dog!"

He unlatched the door, took note of his hound, eyed the shiny black Cadillac parked by his dusty F-350, smiled at the white woman on the porch. "Look who's come to visit—the rich lady who fired me."

Without waiting for an invitation, Jane Cassidy brushed past him. "Do not attempt to be snide, Charles—it does not become you." She limped across the dark parlor, plopped down on a leather couch near the massive granite fireplace.

"Make yourself right at home," he said. "Have a seat."

Her lips parted in a snarlish smile. "Sarcasm is not your long suit."

Moon glanced back at the Caddie, where Bertie sat behind the wheel. "Shall I ask your nephew to come inside?"

"Certainly not. I had to listen to Bertram whine and complain all the way here. Leave the little insect in the car."

He closed the door, sat down beside her. "Could I get you something to drink?"

She patted her hair into place. "A stiff shot of bourbon would do nicely."

"I was thinking more like coffee."

"I was thinking more like eighty-proof alcohol."

"Can't help you there."

"A glass of wine, then. A crisp, flinty Chardonnay would do nicely."

"Don't have any of that."

"Do you have a Grignolino port?"

The rancher admitted that he did not.

Her voice betrayed a hint of alarm. "Surely you have a wine cellar."

He shook his head. "We keep potatoes and onions and rutabagas down there."

"You must be joking."

"Only about the rutabagas."

"Oh well, I suppose a Bavarian beer will suffice. Do you keep Reissdorf Kölsch?"

"Nope." He grinned. "But I could call my foreman, see if Pete's got a six-pack of Bud in the fridge."

"That is *not* funny." An ugly suspicion was beginning to form in her mind. "Charles, I hate to sound accusative—but are you some kind of temperance freak?"

"I'm some kind of alcoholic."

"Oh, of course," she murmured. "I suppose all of you Indians tend to drink too much." Generously deciding to dismiss her host's shortcomings, Jane Cassidy held her palms out to the warmth of the dancing flames. "Aren't you going to ask me why I came all the way to this dreadfully remote and dusty place to see you?"

"Nope."

She turned to make round eyes at the Ute. "You're not?"

He shook his head.

"Why?"

"I don't want to know."

"Charles—that is positively . . ." She searched for the word. "Discourteous."

"And even if I did, there's no point in asking. You're going to tell me anyway."

She sniffed. "Well, if you take that attitude, I may not tell you a thing."

He tilted his mug, took a long drink of coffee.

She shot him a venomous look. "I may just get up and leave without saying so much as another word."

That'll be the day. Moon picked up a copy of last week's *Southern Ute Drum.*

She glared at the flames licking the bark off the pine logs. "The least a guest can expect is a little conversation."

"Beef prices are up." The rancher turned a page. "Four cents a pound."

She flung her arms up. "Well, wa-hoo!"

"Those of us poor souls who must work the land for a living care about such things as beef prices. And the cost of nails and horseshoes and baling wire."

"Oh blast you and your smelly cattle." Jane Cassidy resigned herself to the distasteful but inevitable task. "I suppose you expect an apology."

"No." Moon suppressed a grin.

"Well, you shall have one anyway." She avoided looking at his face. "I regret my behavior during our previous encounter. I was . . . well, in a somewhat snappish mood when you called. I should not have questioned your competence, or your advice about the best course of action for ensuring the recovery of my stolen property." Tapping a finger on her knee, she waited for an agonizingly long three seconds. "Well?"

"Meteorologist in Denver says we're in for a hard winter."

"Is that all you have to say?"

"I sent you an itemized bill. And not for the two hundred dollars an hour you agreed to, but for just a quarter of that. You never paid me."

"Money, money, money." She clutched her purse tightly to her bosom. "Is that all you ever think about?"

He considered this question with some care. "No. I also think about all the hours I spent trying to get your property back. I think about my unpaid bills. And if there's any time left over, I think about the unjust way some rich folks treat those less fortunate than themselves."

She sighed. "Well, if it is any comfort—I am deeply sorry I fired you. As of this moment, consider yourself back on the payroll."

Moon shook his head.

Her mouth gaped. "You are refusing to be rehired?"

He nodded.

"But why?"

"Working for you was no fun. Neither was it profitable."

A lengthy silence grew tense.

"Charles, there must be some way to settle our differences."

The Ute stared at a feathered war club mounted above the mantelpiece.

She wrung her hands. "Oh, I really must clear my conscience."

He turned a page in the *Drum*, smiled at the obituaries. "I can only spare you a few hours."

Jane Cassidy took a deep breath, held it as long as she could, then: "I am willing to confess that . . ." This was very hard. "That you were quite right."

"Right about what?"

"About how to recover my property."

He laid the paper down. "Aha."

"Oh please, spare me your triumphant 'aha'—it is most annoying." She examined a row of painted fingernails.

"Walter Price has agreed to represent an anonymous scoundrel who calls himself Yellow Jacket. This individual claims to be able to return the items stolen from the Cassidy Museum—in exchange for the exorbitant reward you persuaded me to offer."

"Sounds like things are beginning to look up for you."

"I happen to know that Walter Price has informed you of the fact that this felon will only make the exchange if you act as his stand-in."

Moon folded his hands over his silver belt buckle, closed his eyes.

Jane knotted her hands into pale fists. "Must you be so annoyingly taciturn?"

No response.

"Charles, you simply *must* cooperate. Otherwise, this horrible Yellow Jacket person may dump our family treasures in the river."

"Why should I care?"

"That is a very mean thing to say." Jane Cassidy found a laced silk hankie in her purse, dabbed the pink textile at her dry eyes. She leaned close to the tribal investigator. "Besides, I would feel much more confident if you were there with me."

"There where?"

"At Walter Price's office in Durango. That is where the exchange would take place. A representative from my Denver law firm will be present. And Bertie, of course. I really do want you there to protect my interests, Charles. After all—this million-dollar-reward thing *was* your idea." She watched the Indian's closed eyes. He seemed to be mulling it over. The rich woman played the only card she had. "I will of course pay you well for your time."

He opened one eye. "How much?"

She told him.

Charlie Moon shook his head.

"Do you have a figure in mind?"

He did. And told her.

"Charles—you cannot be serious!"

"And I get paid up front."

"Well, really—surely you trust me to keep up my end of the arrangement."

"Miss Cassidy—you cannot be serious."

"That is very cruel." She dropped her hand into a sweater pocket, found the willow ring the Ute had braided for her. "But of course you have me over the proverbial pot."

"Barrel."

"Whatever. But I agree to your conditions. Now do you promise to help me get my property back from this Yellow Jacket scoundrel?"

"Not till you make things square between us. You still owe me for time and expenses."

"Well, of course I had anticipated that small matter." She searched her purse. "Here is your check."

He held the slip of paper at arm's length. Released it. Watched it fall to the floor.

"What on earth are you doing?"

"I want to see if it bounces."

"Charles!"

He watched the inelastic landing. "It looks to be okay, but I am obligated to remind you that passing bad paper is a serious offense."

"Oh, phooey! Now *please* call Walter Price, tell him that you'll help me get my stolen property back."

The Ute leaned back, stared at the beamed ceiling. "There's one last thing."

"What?"

"That morning you fired me, you insulted Sidewinder."

"Who?"

"My dog. And his feelings are still hurt. So on your way to your Cadillac, make your apologies." He added, "Loud enough so I can hear."

"Charles, you are a horrid brute."

He heard the angry pop-pop of her slippers going across the oak floor, the crashing bang of the heavy front door. Then she opened it again.

Her quavering voice drifted into the parlor. "Nice doggie—sweet doggie. Come to Auntie Jane."

Completely taken in by this sinful deception, Sidewinder whined with pure joy.

"There, there, you like to have your pretty head rubbed, don't you." *Filthy, smelly beast.*

Satisfied, Charlie Moon opened the Will James book, removed the two-dollar bill. He began to rock and read. *This is good. After all his travels and trials and troubles in the city, ol' Will is finally heading back to cow country again.*

CHAPTER FIFTY

SNYDER MEMORIAL HOSPITAL

THE NOTICE THUMBTACKED TO THE DOOR WAS DIRECTLY TO the point: NO VISITORS EXCEPT IMMEDIATE FAMILY.

Charlie Moon knew for a fact that Ralph Briggs had no immediate family—which would deprive him of visitors altogether. Furthermore, the Ute reasoned that he was probably the antiquarian's closest friend, which was surely a passable substitute. Thus justified, he pushed the door open.

A stack of pillows propped Ralph Briggs up in his bed. His pallid face looked up at the towering man. "Why, Charles—it is nice to see you." He raised an eyebrow at the object in Moon's hand. "How prosaic—you brought the patient a flower."

"Patient? I'd heard you was dead—I brought this posy to lay on your chest." Moon approached the bed, hung his black Stetson on an IV stand. "But for a corpse, you look fairly presentable."

"Do not make jokes; I have had a terribly traumatic experience." The antiquarian pointed to a bandage on his chest. "My surgeon tells me that I am fortunate to be alive."

"Well, we'll see about that." The Ute pitched the lily onto the bed. "You never know—life can hold some nasty surprises."

Ralph Briggs inspected the flower. "It is frightfully wilted. Where did you find it—in a florist's trash bin?"

"Even better than that. That fancy pansy was in a Coke bottle down at the nurses' station. They said it'd been in room two-twelve till right about midnight, which was when the previous owner left all his worldly cares behind. Word is, the poor old guy expired from something highly infectious."

The sickly man grimaced, tossed the lily aside.

The Indian reached into his coat pocket, produced a small paper bag.

Briggs raised a hand to make a feeble protest. "Oh, please—not another gift."

Moon placed it on the antiquarian's lap. "I brought this just in case you bellyached about the first one."

The sick man accepted the offering with a wary look. Inside the bag was a fuzzy object. "What is this—a colony of stump fungus run amok?"

"It's a rabbit."

"If you say so. It looks a bit, well—scruffy."

"It is a rabbit that has seen some hard times."

Briggs turned up his nose at the stuffed animal. "Tell me this is not one of those battery-operated monstrosities that hops around and tells off-color jokes in a falsetto voice."

"Nah, he doesn't do none of that stuff. But you can talk to him and he won't talk back—Little Bunny Buddy is a good listener."

The sick man sneered. "Little Bunny Buddy—how sickeningly sweet."

Moon took the fuzzy rabbit facsimile from Briggs, placed it on the telephone table by his bed. "So how're you feeling, tough guy?"

"Dreadful. My chest feels like someone drove a railroad spike through it. And from time to time I still cough up clotted blood."

"I'm sorry I asked."

Briggs played with the tightly stitched corner of a green bedsheet. "Just yesterday, Bertie Cassidy stopped by to inquire about my health."

"That was thoughtful."

"Bertie is an old and dear friend." Ralph Briggs shot a quick look at the tribal investigator. "He informs me that some mysterious person who calls himself Yellow Jacket has contacted Walter Price—and offered to return the valuables taken from the family museum in exchange for Jane Cassidy's substantial reward. But the deal will fall through unless you agree to act as go-between."

"Yeah," Moon said. "That's about the size of it."

"Bertie also tells me his aunt is pleading with you to take on the job, but that you have been resisting."

"What do you think, Ralph—should I help Jane Cassidy get her stuff back?"

"It is not for me to say." Briggs gave his visitor a solemn look. "But I would advise you to treat the proposed exchange with due caution."

"You figure I could get burned—messing with this Yellow Jacket character?"

"That is a most likely outcome." With some puffing and grunting, Ralph Briggs managed to get up on one elbow. He took a sip from a glass of iced tea, pointed at his visitor with a plastic straw. "Even though you are used to dealing with dangerous felons, you could get in over your head. Mark my word—whoever has the burgled valuables is not only dangerous, he is also devilishly clever."

Moon looked doubtful. "From the note Yellow Jacket wrote, Walter Price has this bird figured as—and I quote, 'a charter member of the Illiterati.' "

"Do not be fooled by such a simple ruse—that is undoubtedly what the clever fellow wants everyone to think. In my estimation, you are dealing with a first-class criminal mind."

"I guess you could be right." Moon helped himself to a cookie from the patient's dinner tray. "You have any idea who it is?"

Briggs responded with a listless shrug.

"Smart money would figure it's the same Gomer who called you on the phone before you got shot. I kinda hoped that by now you might've remembered something that would help me to—"

"No, no, no!" Briggs closed his eyes and groaned. "As I have told the FBI, the state police, and Scott Parris—I can barely remember the call from that coarse person who claimed to have the Cassidys' stolen property. Since the trauma of the shooting, my mental and emotional condition has been very delicate."

"Sorry. Guess I shouldn't have brought it up."

"Apology accepted." The pale man collapsed onto the pile of pillows. "So—do you intend to help Jane Cassidy conclude her deal with the felon?"

"That kinda depends."

"On what?"

Moon closed the door to the private room, came close to the bed, lowered his voice barely above a whisper. "I think I've got things figured out."

There was a glint of interest in Briggs's eyes. "Do you know who Yellow Jacket is?"

"Way I see it—Yellow Jacket is a decoy. I've got bigger game in mind."

Briggs frowned. "What on earth do you mean?"

"We've been friends for a long time, Ralph—so I'm going to tell you something." Charlie Moon glanced at the closed door, then at his old friend. "There's a lot more to this museum burglary than meets the eye."

"Please explain."

"What's important," Moon said, "is not identifying Yellow Jacket. Or even finding out who burglarized the Cassidy Museum."

Briggs was startled by this assertion. "It is not?"

Moon shook his head very deliberately. "What matters is *why* it was done."

"Charles, this is all very confusing. Now please tell me what is going on."

"I can't let you in on all the details right now, but if things play out like I expect—I'll be able to blow the whole scheme wide open."

"When?"

"When Walter Price shows Jane Cassidy the Yellow Jacket loot."

Briggs stared at the Ute as if he had never seen his face before.

Moon kept his voice low. "Don't ask me why, but I have a hunch that the coins Yellow Jacket has are fakes. Which is one of the things you told me might happen."

The antiquarian's eyes grew large. "You believe the scoundrel would attempt to pass off counterfeits on the Cassidys?" Briggs did not wait for a response. "But that would never work. Bertie would spot a substitution in an instant."

"That's what I figure too. But if those coins turn out to be duds, I'll have the masterminds who're behind the museum burglary dead to rights."

"Excuse me—was that a plural?"

Moon nodded. "Way I got it figured, there are exactly two of 'em."

"You don't say!"

"Yes I do."

"Gracious—do you know who they are?"

Moon seemed a bit uneasy. "Only one for sure. But once number one is jugged, it won't take ten minutes to get the name of number two."

Briggs stared at the Ute. "Are you absolutely certain about this?"

"I can't be one hundred percent sure till Jane Cassidy's expert examines the coins. But if they're counterfeits, I'll be able to put the finger on those birds." Moon looked very pleased. "Then I'll be able to collect the whole reward for myself."

"I don't understand. How could you possibly—"

"About a week from now, Jane Cassidy's offer does a reverse. At midnight next Saturday, it'll be too late for the thief to turn in the real loot and collect the reward—the million bucks will be paid to the fella who provides Miss Cassidy with enough information to put the felons in the jug." Moon put his thumb on his chest. "And that fella will be me. Not only that, I won't have to lift a finger. I'll just turn my evidence over to the FBI and let them do all the heavy work."

"Evidence?"

He looked long and hard at the man on the bed. "Can you keep a secret?"

Briggs nodded eagerly.

Moon removed an object from his shirt pocket. "You know what this is?"

Briggs hesitated. "It appears to be a wooden box. Cedar, I should think."

Moon admitted that this was so. "You want to make a guess what's inside?"

A shrug. "Something important, I suppose."

The tribal investigator tapped his finger on the lid. "Inside this box is all the hard evidence I have to blow the Cassidy Museum burglary sky high. Put at least two people in Uncle Sam's jailhouse."

"Charles, it is not as if I have played no part in this drama; I have been seriously wounded by a vicious criminal who is probably connected in some way to the Cassidy Museum burglary. This being the case, I demand to know what is going on."

"Once this thing is settled—no matter how it plays out— I'll make sure you get to see what's inside this box." Moon hesitated. "If you're dead sure you want to know."

"I most certainly do." The antiquarian chose his words with care: "I have heard you out. Now, I want you to listen to what I have to say."

The Ute leaned closer. "You have my full attention."

"You are not behaving like yourself, Charles. You seem to me to be in, well—a vindictive mood."

"You're right about that." Moon gave him a narrow-eyed look. "But I've got my reasons. The way I see it, the criminals who set up the museum burglary may not have actually pulled the trigger on that .22. But one way or another, the rascals are responsible for you getting shot."

"Well, I must say that I am touched that you consider my misfortune to be so—"

"Which is just the way things happen sometimes. Here today, dead tomorrow. But what I can't forget is this: You getting shot and me coming close to getting plugged is why my woman left me." The Ute raised his hand, made a formidable fist. "For a thing like that, a heavy price has to be paid."

"Yes." Briggs blinked. "I see what you mean."

Charlie Moon gave the patient a worried look. "You look

all pooped out—I'm afraid I've overstayed my welcome." He placed the Stetson on his head, examined his image in a mirror on the wall, made a slight adjustment to the tilt of the brim, approved of what he saw. He shot the pallid man on the pillows a final glance. "I hope you're up and around real soon."

Ralph Briggs watched the tall man vanish, listened to the hollow click of his boot heels fade away down the long hallway.

The antiquarian turned off the bedside lamp but did not feel like sleeping. For quite some time, he stared at the fuzzy rabbit.

Little Bunny Buddy stared back.

In the dim half-light, he could have sworn that the artificial creature winked at him.

CHAPTER FIFTY-ONE

THE RETURN

DAISY PERIKA HAD JUST SCOOPED UP THE LAST SPOONFUL OF green-chili posole from her soup bowl. She was at peace, and thinking about getting into bed. In an instant, with no warning, a bone-rattling chill came over the tribal elder. After the shakes subsided, she turned to stare at the door. Without knowing why, Daisy found herself pulling on a yellow woolen shawl, turning the doorknob, stepping out onto the rickety wooden porch. Like one lost in a dream trance, she gazed at the trio of Pueblo women squatting on Three Sisters Mesa.

Daisy knew that something was very wrong.

She did not know what.

While the sky turned crimson with the sun's blood, the shaman stood watch, wondering what sort of wickedness was coming her way. Whoever or whatever it was, it had no right to be in this sacred place, or to disturb her peace. The old woman gripped the porch railing, set her jaw. *I am getting sick and tired of this.*

AN HOUR later, and not so far away, another wary female creature was alert and watching. The famished cougar was crouched under a scrub oak in Snake Canyon, muzzle resting between her paws. The very soul of patience, she waited for a deer to pass by.

AS IT had been on that other most singular night, so it would be again.

The land was bathed in a sea of pale moonlight.

Ever so slowly, an avalanche of clouds rolled off the mountains, spilled into deep sandstone chasms between the mesas. Icy mists bejeweled every piñon and juniper needle with glistening droplets.

With a sudden start, the big cat detected something unexpected. She pricked her ears, triangulated the location of the source. The predator looked up into the mists, blinked amber eyes. Something was up there. It was descending into the canyon . . . but not along the rocky trail. Though partially concealed by the moonlit mists, it was apparent that the intruder was floating in midair.

Muscles tensed along the mountain lion's rangy frame. She felt a tingle of elemental excitement, but not a trace of fear. This was something she had witnessed once before, and the beast was certain that she was not threatened by the *presence*.

As the bigcat watched, a puff of wind separated the mists, a silver sliver of light illuminated a spot on the canyon floor just below the Witch's Tongue. Like a plump droplet of water slipping along a blade of grass, the intruder seemed to be suspended on the narrow shaft of moonlight.

CHAPTER FIFTY-TWO

THE EXCHANGE

ENTHRONED LIKE AN IMPERIOUS POTENTATE BEHIND HIS MAG-
nificent cherry desk, Walter Price was in his element and lov-
ing every moment. The attorney tilted his finely sculpted head,
made ready to preside over the small congregation.

Jane Cassidy was perched on a moose-hide sofa, her
emerald-green dress bright against the soft brown leather. The
wealthy woman's attorney seated himself beside her, taking
care to neither rankle his wealthy client nor wrinkle his three-
thousand-dollar suit.

Standing quite still in a corner of the room, Bertie Cassidy was doing a passable imitation of the teak coat hanger
at his side.

Arms folded across his chest, Charlie Moon stood before a
heavy oak door, effectively blocking the entrance to a sound-
proofed conference room.

Walter Price pressed the red button on his desk intercom
station, spoke crisply to an unseen employee. "No calls, Miss
Weiss." The attorney got up from his chair, clasped his hands
behind his back, directed his words to Jane Cassidy: "You are
absolutely certain that you do not wish to have the exhibits examined by a team of independent experts?"

"That would be an unnecessary expense," she said. "Bertie
and I have discussed the matter. We will certainly know
whether the items to be presented are our property."

Price glanced at her lawyer, got a barely perceptible nod.

"Very well then. I assume that everyone present is fully informed of the purpose and protocol of these proceedings."

"You need not be so pompous, Walter," Jane said. "You're not a judge yet."

Price's face flushed beet red.

The ruthless woman continued. "I for one am *painfully* aware of the fact that I have come to your tastefully furnished office to determine whether this anonymous felon you represent—this Yellow Jacket—has produced the property stolen from the Cassidy Museum. If this is the case, I'm willing to redeem it for the sum of one million dollars." She turned to glare at her legal counsel. "So let's get on with this farce."

The Denver lawyer exchanged glances with his esteemed Durango colleague, made a mental note to apologize later for his client's unseemly behavior.

Jane Cassidy was not finished. She screwed her pale face into an ugly scowl. "We should be able to wrap this up pretty quick if this so-called Yellow Jacket—whom I presume to be the filthy night crawler who burgled my museum—is not trying to pull a fast one. I want *all* of the stolen property returned. And it had better be in good condition. Otherwise, I'll sic the law on the blackguard." She leaned forward, clutching her purse. "Will you communicate this outright threat to your client, Walter?"

Walter Price returned her stare. "Even as you speak, your pithy statement is being recorded on the audiotape—I daresay this will be sufficient evidence of your intention. But do take note of the fact that my client's identity is unknown to me." He glanced at the Ute. "Mr. Charles Moon has some measure of communication with Yellow Jacket. If he should have the opportunity, and wishes to do so—he may convey the gist of your comments."

All eyes focused on the Ute tribal investigator.

Moon, who was wearing his wooden-Indian poker face, made no reply.

Walter Price cleared his throat. "After I placed the requisite advertisements in the classified sections of a half-dozen local newspapers, the person who prefers to be known as Yellow

Jacket got in touch with Mr. Moon. Subsequently, Mr. Moon was able to take possession of certain items, which said Yellow Jacket represents as the same material that was illegally removed from the premises of the Cassidy Mus—"

Jane Cassidy threw up her gloved hands. "Oh for Jupiter's sake, Walter—will you skip all the stuffy legalese and get on with this third-rate show?"

The steely-eyed attorney managed to control his temper. "Very well, Jane. The conditions are spelled out in some detail in the agreement your legal counsel has already read. But here is the executive summary. If the property which I am prepared to present is accepted by you as that which was stolen from your museum, you agree to accept the property forthwith—and immediately render a cashier's check in the sum of one million dollars as a recovery fee. You also agree to take no action whatever either to identify my client or to assist the authorities in so doing. In the event that my client should ever be arrested and charged in connection with the theft of these particular goods, you agree to use all resources at your disposal to defend my client in any court of law where my client may be prosecuted. If you should not honor any detail of your part of the covenant, I will certainly sue you on behalf of my client."

The rich woman rolled her eyes. "Walter, I have already signed ten copies of your mind-numbing document, and each one has been witnessed and notarized. Now when do I get to see the stuff?"

The Denver attorney coughed.

Jane turned to him. "What is it, Harold?"

He smiled apologetically. "As your legal counsel in this matter, I merely wish to point out that if the objects presented do not suit you in any way—you are under no obligation to pay a dime."

"Quite correct," Walter Price said. "But the other side of that two-edged blade is this: If for any reason you decide not to accept the valuables, you shall leave all of the property in my possession." A malicious expression twisted the attorney's face. "Which will automatically result in other legal procedures quite outside the scope of the current agreement."

Bertie surprised everyone by speaking. "Do you mean that our—that the materials would be turned over to the police?"

"I am not at liberty to say precisely what such procedures would be." Walter Price spoke with almost no discernible movement of his thin lips. "But if it turns out that this Yellow Jacket person—or anyone else—is attempting any sort of fraud, I shall do everything in my power to see that justice is done. Which would begin with a detailed analysis by recognized experts of the items allegedly stolen from the Cassidy Museum. If there has been any attempt to substitute items of lesser value, I shall pursue the matter to the utmost legal limits."

"Great," Jane Cassidy barked. "Now let's see the loot!"

Price nodded at Charlie Moon. The tribal investigator stepped away from the door. The attorney took a shiny brass key from his vest pocket, unlocked the entrance to the conference room.

Inside was a long, varnished table.

At the far end of the table, a uniformed security guard stood at rigid attention. The hard-faced man had a semiautomatic pistol holstered on his belt. Closer-by stood a tall, thin, gray-haired woman, immaculately dressed in a black silk dress and black spike heels. A single strand of pearls was suspended from her neck. Walter Price's office manager was considerably more intimidating than the armed man. She stepped to one side, made a sweeping gesture to draw their gazes to the display on the table.

There were three cardboard boxes; each had once contained precisely twenty-four cans of Aunt Nancy's Chicken Gumbo Soup.

Price smiled affectionately at the elegant lady. "Thank you, Miss Nelson. You may return to your normal duties."

She moved across the carpet without making a sound.

The tough-looking guard remained at his post.

Walter Price reached into a box. He removed a transparent plastic bag, placed it on the table.

At the sight of it, Jane Cassidy shrieked, "My cameos!"

Price allowed himself a supercilious smile. "Take your time, Jane. Make certain these are the identical items taken from your museum. Again for the record, you have the right to bring in experts of your choice to verify the authenticity and condition of each item."

The Denver attorney nodded. "Yes, you must be quite sure that—"

"We don't need any experts," she snapped. "Bertie and I are intimately familiar with every piece that was stolen." Jane Cassidy snatched up the bag, held it up to the sunlight filtering through the office window, then clasped it to her breast. "Oh— dear Momma's precious Italian cameos—" She plopped down on a wooden chair. "I am so, so happy." She turned to wave at her nephew. "Come here, Bertie—come and see."

He came to look over her shoulder. "Yes, isn't it wonderful."

The Denver attorney muttered in her ear, "Is every piece there?"

"I believe so." Jane Cassidy opened the plastic bag, spread the assortment out on the table. "I don't recall exactly how many there were, but this seems to be the lot."

Walter Price coughed to get their attention. "And now we come to the most valuable portion of the stolen goods—the rare coins. Every piece has been meticulously cataloged and compared to the list of stolen items. Needless to say, the match between catalog and list is perfect. And please note that the coins are still in the original display folders, just as they were taken from the museum."

Each of the folders was sealed in a plastic evidence bag.

Jane was still clasping the hoard of antique jewelry to her bosom. "Bertie will have a look at them. One old penny looks much like another to me, but my nephew knows these coins better than anyone."

Jane's nephew took a seat at the table. Folder by folder, he examined the displays of large copper cents. Liberty caps. Draped Bust. Turban Heads. Coronets. Braided Hair. Mint-condition Flying Eagles, Indian Heads, bronze Two-Cents, Silver Three-Cents, Nickel Shield-Type Five-Cent pieces, a variety of half dimes, Capped-Bust quarters, Flowing-Hair half dollars. Most dazzling of all were the glistening Liberty

Seated and Morgan silver dollars. An atmosphere taut with suspense permeated the attorney's office as Bertram Eustace Cassidy peered at the plastic-covered displays.

Eventually, Jane would have no more of it. "For goodness' sakes, Bertie—are you in a trance?"

The small man turned with a start. "What?"

Jane managed a saccharine smile. "Dear Bertie—you do love your shiny little coins, don't you? But these overpriced lawyers are waiting to hear what you have to say."

Bertie seemed puzzled.

The Denver attorney approached him with a studied gentleness. "Mr. Cassidy, are these coins the ones stolen from the family collection?"

Jane Cassidy's nephew stared across the room at the tribal investigator. He flexed his fingers, rubbed his plump hands together. "It would appear that—"

Charlie Moon smiled at him.

Jane jerked at her nephew's sleeve. "Well?"

Bertie removed a crisply folded linen handkerchief from his shirt pocket, mopped at his forehead. "Yes. These are the coins that were taken from our family museum."

Walter Price was unable to conceal his relief. "Are they all there?"

Bertie nodded.

"And in the substantially same condition as when they were stolen?"

"Yes, yes." Bertie tugged at his collar. "They are in perfect condition."

Forgetting himself for a moment, Walter Price beamed at the odd little man, clapped him on the back. "Well, then. I'd say that does it." *There is nothing left to do but collect the money.*

AN HOUR later, Walter Price was alone with Charlie Moon. Armed couriers had arrived from the bank; the Cassidy check had been exchanged for six canvas bags of cash.

Relaxed now, the attorney removed his jacket, rolled up his

white silk sleeves. He stood at a window, watching the afternoon traffic. "Now all we have to do is get the payment to my anonymous client." The various niggling details caused him to frown. "There are several issues to be dealt with, but you should convey to Yellow Jacket that he must take complete responsibility for payment of taxes. My sole responsibility is to see that my client is paid in the manner previously agreed to." He glanced uncertainly at the Ute. "Which means that you are going to be responsible for transporting a very considerable sum of cash. I hope you have made suitable arrangements—for security, I mean."

Moon nodded. "That's been taken care of." Six Columbine cowboys—all armed to the teeth—were waiting outside to escort him back to the ranch. It was not really necessary, but the hardworking men would enjoy the outing.

Walter Price seated himself behind his desk. "I must say, Charles—in spite of the fact that your reputation is without blemish, I am nevertheless impressed that this anonymous person is willing to trust you with such a large sum. The point is this: I cannot help but assume that my remarkably shy client—even if he is not directly connected to the burglary—has something to hide. And such persons are not generally noted for their trusting nature."

Moon eyed the bags of greenbacks. "The way I figure it—this Yellow Jacket character must've not had much choice."

Walter Price nodded thoughtfully. "Yes, of course." He hesitated. "There is something I wish to ask you. But it is merely to satisfy my curiosity—you are certainly not obligated to reply."

Moon waited.

"This person who calls himself Yellow Jacket—I assume he provided the usual hand-printed notes to communicate with you. But have you ever seen him face-to-face?"

"You mean like right now, me looking at you, man-to-man—in the flesh?"

The attorney nodded. "Yes, that is precisely what I mean."

"No," Moon said.

"Charlie, do you know who Yellow Jacket is?"

The Ute looked at the clever attorney for a long time. "Are you sure you want me to answer that question?"

Walter Price smiled. "I believe you just have."

MIDNIGHT

KICKS DOGS was quite soundly asleep, dreaming of something that had never happened in her unhappy childhood. In this sweet fantasy, a kindly man gave her a shiny half dollar for ice cream. She ran away before he could take it back. Jacob Gourd Rattle's wife was roused from her peaceful slumbers. Not by a sound—merely by a sense that someone was *out there*. She clutched the covers to her chest and yelled, "Who's there?"

There was, of course, no response. There never is.

I must've imagined it. She got out of bed, wrapped a tattered bathrobe around her thin body, switched on the outside light, looked through the windowpane—and saw something on her porch. A parcel. This would have frightened a soul who conjures up images of cruel pranksters and lunatic bombers. Not Kicks Dogs. The package seemed to speak to her. What it said was, *Come and get me.*

Without another thought, Kicks went and got it.

Though she wept in spells, and laughed, even offered thanks to God—the ecstatic woman would not find sleep again that night.

She spent all the wee hours counting crisp new greenbacks.

CHAPTER FIFTY-THREE

MCTEAGUE'S TRIUMPH

CHARLIE MOON WAS HELPING A COUPLE OF THE COWBOYS shoe a skittish mare. The wild-eyed animal had already kicked a plank out of her stall; now she laid a hoof on the rancher's thigh. When his cell phone demanded immediate attention, Moon was happy for an excuse to take a break. He limped out of the barn, leaned on the corral fence. "Yeah?"

"Charlie, it's me."

He was unable to smile. "Hello, McTeague. What's up?"

Her voice crackled with excitement. "You will not believe it."

"I am fairly gullible—try me."

"Can't talk about it. Not on an open line."

"Let me get this straight—you called long distance just to tell me you can't talk to me on the phone?"

"If you want to know what's happened, you will have to saddle up and ride, cowboy."

"Where to?"

"Three Sisters Mesa. Get here soon as you can."

She found the grave in Snake Canyon. "I'm on my way."

"I'll be looking for you." She hung up.

He stared at the barn where the horse was still kicking sparks, half-wished he had not answered the telephone.

WHEN MOON braked the big red pickup to a stop on Three Sisters Mesa, he counted six SUPD units, all with emergency lights flashing—and one gray government-issue Ford sedan. SUPD chief of police Wallace Whitehorse was involved in an intense conversation with Special Agent McTeague, but the Northern Cheyenne was doing far more listening than talking, mainly punctuating the FBI agent's comments with grunts and nods. Whitehorse noticed Charlie Moon's approach but deliberately ignored him until Moon was within arm's length. Even then, he acknowledged the Ute with an almost imperceptible nod. *Charlie Moon and Oscar Sweetwater are thick as thieves—I bet the tribal chairman sent his big-shot investigator out here to see if I know how to do my job.*

Special Agent McTeague offered the new arrival a curt, professional greeting: "Good afternoon, Mr. Moon."

Mr. Moon touched the brim of his hat. "Yes it is." *I hope.*

McTeague gave the tribal investigator a nod. Leaving Wallace Whitehorse behind, she headed off at a brisk pace toward the edge of the cliff, where several SUPD uniforms were gathered. She stopped well short of the cluster of Indian cops.

Charlie Moon glanced back at Whitehorse, who was watching them like a hungry hawk. "What's going on here?"

The FBI agent looked very pleased with herself. "Believe it or not—I have finally managed to make some progress without any help from you. SUPD dispatch had a call from a tribal member this morning. The caller had been out looking for a few stray cattle, and he'd noticed some apparently suspicious activity on Three Sisters. Officer Blue Clay responded. He found that vehicle." She pointed at an archaic pickup half hidden by a cluster of scrub oak.

Moon turned. "That looks like Felix Navarone's fifty-seven Chevy."

"That's because it is." She nodded to indicate the gaggle of policemen at the edge of the Snake Canyon cliff. "Officer Blue Clay also heard some groaning. He took a look over the edge of the cliff, there was a half-dead guy down there on a ledge."

"Felix Navarone, I presume?"

"None other. The Apache was stranded on a shelf of black rock that sticks out from the cliff wall." She frowned with the effort to remember. "It's called the Witch's Something-or-other."

"Witch's Tongue."

"Oh—right."

Moon looked over her head. "Stranded? How'd that happen?"

"Search me. We don't know how he got onto the ledge in the first place, much less how he got stuck there. He didn't have any climbing gear, and we had to call in Mountain Search and Rescue to rappel down and tie him on a stretcher. It took an hour to get him onto the top of the mesa. Navarone was suffering from shock and exposure, so we couldn't get anything out of him that made any sense. Only some mumbling about how his *power* had failed, and something about a ghost. He was obviously delirious."

Moon nodded.

"The suspect might have used a rope to gain access to the ledge." She watched the Ute's face, but read nothing there.

"Felix Navarone had a dislocated shoulder from his fight with Jim Wolfe," Moon said. "And even at his best, I doubt he'd have been able to make that descent with a rope. Much less climb back up again."

"Good point," she said. "In any case, there was no sign of any type of climbing gear, so it was apparently removed by a second person. It was almost certainly someone Navarone knew who stranded him on that ledge."

Moon looked around. "So where is the poor devil?"

"He's been transported to the hospital in Durango, where he'll be kept under guard twenty-four seven. Once he's dismissed, SUPD will hold him for trespassing on restricted tribal lands. That will give us some time to sort out what's going on." She paused. "You might like to know what I found on the ledge."

He grinned. "You rappelled down there?"

"Sure." Agent McTeague shot him an indignant look. "What do you think—I'd let the boys have all the fun?" She unzipped a pouch pocket on her jumpsuit, produced a small, tagged plastic evidence bag.

Moon leaned to have a closer look. "A cameo."

"Looks like the thieves left one behind." She smiled at the

lovely antique. "I'll show it to Jane Cassidy. But it has to be part of the valuables burgled from her museum."

"I expect you're right. You find anything else on the Witch's Tongue?"

"No. Whatever else was there is gone." She started to address the major issue that was on her mind, decided to put that off. Instead: "Why don't you ask me if we found anything at the *bottom* of Snake Canyon?"

He had been expecting this. "Okay. What'd you find down there?"

"Unless I'm badly mistaken, the Gourd Rattle campsite."

Not being able to look the federal cop straight in the eye, Moon gazed over her head. "So they weren't in Spirit Canyon."

"They were not. And that's not all we found."

"The suspense is unbearable."

"A grave."

Moon tried to look surprised. "Occupied?"

"Sad to say—yes."

"Anyone I know?"

"Forensics will have the last word, but it appears to be the mortal remains of Jacob Gourd Rattle."

"Agent McTeague—you are a marvel. An outstanding example of the Bureau's finest." She did not seem overly pleased with this compliment, so he kept sliding down the slippery slope. "And it was thoughtful of you to call me."

The tall, strikingly handsome woman fidgeted, leaning first on one shapely leg, then on the other. "I wanted you to be here with me." Her voice took on a hard edge. "And share my small victory."

"Don't be modest, McTeague—this is a big break in the case." He realized that something unpleasant was missing from the scene, took a second look around. "Where's Stan Newman?"

"In Dallas. Applying for an opening on the bank-robbery detail."

"Hope he gets it." Moon sat down on a ponderosa log, patted a spot beside him. "You have done a full day's work, McTeague. Take a break. Relax your bones."

The woman who had just rappelled a hundred feet down a precipitous cliff eyed the proposed seat with no little apprehension. There were undoubtedly all sorts of fuzzy spiders, fire ants, poisonous scorpions, and the like lurking under the dead bark.

Sensing her concern, Charlie Moon removed his denim jacket, draped it over the log.

She sat down beside him.

He noted that for a federal cop, she smelled good. Like peach blossoms.

She gave him a sideways glance. "Charlie, you have a reputation for being rather clever."

He grinned at his scuffed workboots, which smelled of horse manure. "It's all hype."

"I know. But I'm quite impressed with how you knew that the ignition key for Jacob Gourd Rattle's van would be in Officer Wolfe's raincoat pocket."

"Aw, shucks—I didn't know for sure." He kicked at a stone. "It was just a hunch."

The FBI agent sprang to her feet. "Hunch my butt!"

Moon got up from the log. "Excuse me?"

"Don't give me that oh-so-innocent look. You knew all along that Felix Navarone was mixed up in the Cassidy burglary—and there's no telling what else you're still holding back." Her eyes narrowed to reptilian slits. "You may have even known about the Cassidy loot being hidden on the Witch's Lip."

"Tongue."

"Stop correcting me."

"Okay. But why would you think I'd know anything about the Witch's *Lip*?"

She stamped her foot. "Don't *do* that!"

"You seem to be just the least bit tense, McTeague. If I've done something that displeases you, tell me what it is."

McTeague took in a deep breath, began to count to ten. She did not make it past three. "Surely you did not think you could represent this thief who calls himself Yellow Jacket without the Bureau finding out about it. Sooner or later, one way or another, you are going to tell me what I want to know. So make it easy on yourself."

He pretended to be confused. "I'd like to help you out, but I don't know anything about any Mellow Jacket."

"*Yellow* Jacket!"

"Are you correcting me?" He grinned.

McTeague clenched her teeth. "Charlie, don't you *dare* do that again."

"Okay. You want to know all about Yellow Jacket?"

"You know I do—now let's talk!"

"Sorry. You'll have to talk to Walter Price."

The FBI agent thought she had him cornered. "Mr. Price is representing Mel—ah, Yellow Jacket. He is not representing you, therefore you cannot hide behind an alleged attorney-client privilege."

"I hate to disappoint you." Moon said this with a sad look. "But the fact is, Walter has been my legal counsel for some years now. And he has strictly advised me not to say a word about any alleged legal transaction that may or may not have occurred between the Cassidys and an anonymous person known as Yellow Jacket. And I never go against my attorney's advice; otherwise Walter would have a half-wit for a client."

She started to make a snappish reply, clamped her mouth shut.

He squatted to pick a crimson paintbrush. "McTeague, even if I was able to help, it wouldn't be right to deprive you of the suspense of the hunt and the joy of discovery. Not knowing what you're going to find is one percent of the fun." He offered her the plucked wildflower.

She slapped the blossom out of his hand, made a fist under his nose. "You tell me what else you've found out about all these felonies, or so help me I'll knock your—"

Moon stuck his chin out. "Take your best shot, tough lady. But if you break my jaw, I want you to know that I'll regret it till my dying day."

"Oh—you make me *so* mad!"

He grinned. "Even your mean little frown is pretty enough to make a man's heart skip two or three beats."

She blushed, glanced at Wallace Whitehorse. The sly chief of police was watching them out of the corner of his eye. "Don't fool around, Charlie—I'm on duty."

"And your eyes remind me of those big blue flowers that sprout up in snowy alpine meadows—"

"Stop it!"

He gave her a wounded look. "McTeague, are you peeved at me?"

"*Peeved* is hardly the word. I am very, very *angry* with you."

Charlie Moon watched her turn and walk away.

CHAPTER FIFTY-FOUR

EPIPHANY

DAISY PERIKA HAD WASHED THE DISHES AND WAS NOW DRY-ing them. While she attended to this chore, the tribal elder's thoughts were on the events that had recently transpired in Snake Canyon—and not two miles from her home! From what Charlie had told her, the police did not have enough evidence on Felix Navarone to hold him. The rascal who had surely murdered Jacob Gourd Rattle would have to be turned loose. Even though Jacob wasn't much to brag about, it galled her to think that an Apache could slay a Ute and not pay the price. *But there's no use in worrying—what can I do about it?*

When the answer to that question came to her, she dropped a saucer. It shattered on the floor, sending shards in all directions.

Ignoring this small calamity, the old woman hurried to the place where she kept the oversized, high-power cellular telephone her nephew had given her years ago. She dialed the number she knew by heart. After seven rings, she heard the familiar voice on the recorded message.

"This is the Columbine Ranch. Leave your name and telephone number and—"

Daisy banged her fist on the wall. "Answer it right now, you big—"

He did. "Hello."

She shouted into the mouthpiece, "When they found that white man's body, did they—"

"Whoa!"

"Don't talk to me that way, you big jug-head—I'm not one of your horses."

"Of course you're not. But slow down to a trot." There was a grin in Moon's voice. "Now what's all this about a body?"

"I'm talking about that white policeman that worked for the tribe."

"Jim Wolfe?"

Daisy Perika gritted her teeth. "How many *matukach* wear the SUPD uniform?"

"Good point. What about his body?"

"When that FBI woman found it under that pile of rocks, was there a piece of turquoise on it?"

He stalled. "On it where?"

"Around his neck. On a leather string."

"I don't know."

"Well, don't just stand there like a fence post—go and find out!"

"Could you tell me why it's so important?"

"What kind of a policeman are you?"

"The part-time kind. At the moment, I'm helping the Wyoming Kyd work out a way to ship three dozen head of beeves to Kansas City—"

"Forget about that cowboy nonsense. Find out about the turquoise pendant."

He sighed. "You're not going to tell me why."

"And when you find out, let me know. You know where to find me—I won't be in town kicking up my heels at some honky-tonk. I'm an old woman stuck out here by myself and I don't hardly ever go nowhere unless somebody feels sorry for me and gives me a ride." With that, she pushed the End button.

Full of hope, she swept the fragments of the saucer into a dustpan.

Twenty-two minutes later, Daisy's telephone rang. She snatched it up. "What?"

"There was no turquoise pendant on Jim Wolfe's corpse," Moon said in her ear. "Or in his apartment. Or in his locker. Or in his car. Or anywhere else that we know of."

The tribal elder grinned. "Good."

"Now will you tell me why—"

"Listen close, and I'll tell you what you have to do. Find out if that Apache that got stranded on the Witch's Tongue has the dead white man's turquoise pendant. Unless you're more interested in selling cows than finding out who murdered one of the People." The tribal elder hung up on her nephew. With the murderous Apache in mind, Daisy hummed a happy tune—"In the Jailhouse Now." That was where Felix Navarone needed to be.

CHAPTER FIFTY-FIVE

THE EXHIBITION

THE SOLEMN ATTORNEY FROM THE FEDERAL PROSECUTOR'S office felt somewhat ill at ease. For one thing, the mean-looking old woman seated across the kitchen table from him was rumored to be some sort of witch. For another, the towering tribal investigator was standing behind him. And Charlie Moon had not said a word since introducing the fed to his aunt.

The lawyer unbuckled a worn alligator briefcase, produced a stack of twelve color prints, pushed them across the table to Daisy Perika. "This is merely for a preliminary identification. Please take your time." He watched her face with considerable anticipation, but was unable to read anything on that wrinkled parchment.

The old woman slipped on a pair of wire-rimmed reading spectacles, examined the first image, the second, the third, thumbed her way through the assortment of digitized images. There were a variety of turquoise pendants, most looked like they might have been purchased recently in Durango. A few looked like the older stuff one sees in a pawn shop or Navajo trading post. On occasion, she would move a photograph back and forth to find the optimum focus. On the picture labeled "Exhibit Nine," she froze.

The lawyer leaned forward, expectation fairly dripping off his chin.

Daisy removed her eyeglasses, tapped a finger on the print. "That's it."

The fed had been holding his breath. "Are you willing to be legally deposed to the effect that this ornament was the property of the late Officer James Wolfe?"

She looked to her nephew for guidance.

Moon translated. "You ready to swear on a stack of Bibles that's Jim Wolfe's pendant?"

"Sure." She pointed at the photograph. "He wore it around his neck. Most people didn't know it was there, because he kept it under his shirt." Her mouth crinkled into a sad little smile. "It was a kind of good-luck charm."

The lawyer sensed a potential problem here. "Mrs. Perika, if the pendant was always under his shirt, how would you be in a position to know—"

"Because I doctored him," she snapped. "That white SUPD cop was all cut up after he had the run-in with that crazy Apache that jumped out of a tree on him."

He jotted a comment into a small notebook. "By the term *Apache*—are you referring to Mr. Felix Navarone?"

Daisy nodded.

The somber lawyer turned to the tribal police investigator, allowed himself a smile. "When he was admitted to Mercy Medical Center in Durango, Mr. Navarone had the pendant depicted in Exhibit Nine on his person. With your aunt's sworn statement, we should be able to convict him of the homicide of Officer Wolfe." He took a long look at the photograph. "I wonder why Mr. Navarone bothered to take such a trivial thing from his victim."

Moon's eyes were asking his aunt the same question.

Daisy Perika avoided her nephew's flinty gaze. Unlike Charlie Moon, Felix Navarone was a traditional Indian—the Apache would have immediately recognized the famous Hasteen K'os Largo pendant.

The lawyer shook his head. "I mean—it was such a foolish thing to do."

The tribal elder smiled at the Harvard graduate. "Oh, you know how covetous some people can be. Felix must've took one look at that pretty lump of stone hanging around that white man's neck—and he had to have it." *Just like me.*

· · ·

HAVING HAD no response to the messages he had left on Lila
Mae McTeague's answering machine, Charlie Moon dialed
the Durango FBI office.

The telephone was answered on the third ring. "Federal
Bureau of Investigation."

The Ute exchanged greetings with Special Agent Stanley
Newman, tried to sound as if his inquiry were of almost no
importance. "Uh—is Agent McTeague around?"

Newman snorted, reverted to his New Jersey accent:
"What's it to ya?"

"Well, I thought I might have a word with her."

"She's powdering her nose, Chucky." Newman made a
toothy possum grin. "But even if she was here, she wouldn't
give you the time of day."

"She still mad at me over this Yellow Jacket business?"

"Sure. But don't take it too hard, big guy. McTeague is one
of them high-strung dames."

The tribal investigator said his good-bye, hung up.

Stanley Newman was startled by his partner's sudden appearance. The tall, strikingly good-looking woman leaned on
his desk, eyed him like a kingfisher eyes a minnow. He
showed her his palms, spoke with the feigned innocence of a
wide-eyed choirboy. "Hey—what'd I do?"

"Since when do you take my telephone calls and discuss
my personal life? And what's this 'high-strung dame' stuff?'"

Newman switched to his ugly-bulldog face. "Lissen here—
I ain't no easygoing Charlie Moon, so don't think you can
push *me* around. I'm the silverback gorilla in this office—I'll
take any calls that come in and say whatever I feel like to
whoever's on the line." He poked a stubby finger at her. "And
if I see a dame who's wound up way too tight, what should I
call her—pleasant? Agreeable? Sweet? Nice?" He bared his
teeth to produce a hideously nasty grin. "High—strung—
dame," he said.

Special Agent McTeague reached for Newman's favorite
coffee mug—the green one with ATLANTIC CITY—1988 sten-
ciled on the side. "If a ceramic object such as this happens to

shatter, what should one call the pieces—shards? Fragments? Flinders? Smithereens?"

The bulldog face paled. "Hey—don't you dare—put that down!"

She did. It hit the floor hard. "Flinders," she said.

CHAPTER FIFTY-SIX

GRANITE CREEK PD

STANDING AT A SECOND-STORY WINDOW, CHIEF OF POLICE Scott Parris watched Betty Lou ease up to the curb. He turned to his desk, pressed the Speak button on the intercom. "He's here." He listened to the response, nodded at the unseen communicant. "Okay, if that's the way you want it. I'll buzz you when it's time."

PARRIS GAVE his best friend a hearty handshake. "Hey, Charlie—thanks for coming over on short notice."

"You're practically welcome." The tribal investigator looked around the spacious corner office. "So what am I here for?"

Granite Creek's top cop pointed at a white cardboard box on the conference table.

The Ute gave it a wary look. "What's in it?"

"Three guesses."

"Disgusting piece of road kill?"

"Dang," Parris said with genuine regret, "I should've thought of that."

"Okay—fried chicken from the Mountain Man Bar and Grille?"

The chief of the Granite Creek PD shook his head. "Better still."

Moon leaned close, sniffed. "Sugar and spice." He frowned at his buddy. "You brought me all the way into town for a snack?"

"Hey—you got a problem with that?"

"Nope." The Ute opened the box, helped himself to a still-warm jelly-filled pastry.

Scott Parris seated himself behind the desk, gave the tribal investigator a curious look. "Okay, Charlie—now tell me what'n blazes has been going on."

"Well, let me gather my thoughts." As the rancher converted the rich confection into sweet satisfaction, he concentrated his gaze on the slowly rotating blades of a ceiling fan. "About a week ago, a cougar took a calf over by Pine Knob. Last night, a couple of the new cowhands got into a nasty scrap over a hand of Texas Hold 'Em. One of the players got carved up some, the one that knifed him hit the road. There's a fine little ranch next door to the Columbine that's been put up for sale and my foreman thinks I should buy it and—"

"You know what I'm talking about, wise guy."

"Do I?"

Parris tapped a finger on his temple. "Remember who I am—and what is my noble calling in life."

"You mean like hassling jaywalkers and fixing parking tickets?"

"Besides that."

Moon looked to be completely bumfuzzled. "Could you give me a hint?"

"I'll tell you straight out—the shooting of Ralph Briggs."

"That incident has never left my mind. As you may recall, I was there at the time."

"So let me in on what you've been up to."

"Could you be more specific?"

"Okay. Here's specific. What got you interested in one Mr. Eduardo Ganado as a prime suspect in the Cassidy burglary? And why didn't you tell me?"

"I will address the first question."

"What about the second one?"

"I choose to pretend I did not hear it."

The chief of police felt the burn of acid in his throat.

Charlie Moon opened the grease-spotted cardboard carton once more with gusto, selected a heavily glazed doughnut. "I began to feel somewhat antsy when I went to visit Eddie Ganado and he came out to meet me with a shotgun. He claimed he'd had a prowler, but I guess he must've been worried that I'd found out he'd shot Ralph Briggs and was intending to put the cuffs on him. And while I was there, I realized he'd lied to me about how his hair got pulled out by the roots." The Ute gourmet tasted the sugar-crusted toroid, judged it to be more than adequate. "That wily Navajo had spun me a wild yarn about how a big pine was leaning toward his house, claimed he was using a chain saw to cut the tree down when the infernal thing grabbed him by the hair, yanked most of it out."

Parris was troubled by the image. "This guy actually expected you to believe a tree deliberately pulled his hair out?"

"I may well have been mistaken," Moon said. "But it was my impression that Ganado was referring to the chain saw."

"Oh—right. And you did not find this anecdote to be entirely plausible?"

"On the contrary, it was a fairly solid story. But when I stopped by Ganado's place, I did not see a fresh pine stump in his yard—or a pine left standing that could fall on his house. And on toppa that, he did not have a propane tank."

"Whoa, cowboy—you've done rode off and left me. What does a propane tank have to do with the price of pickled peppers?"

Moon gestured with a crescent of doughnut. "If Ganado does not have propane, he is doing his cooking and heating by more traditional means. Which means he'll store up all the wood he can collect before winter sets in. So if he takes down a pine tree in his yard, he'll cut it up and put in on his wood pile to age for a while. But all Ganado had stacked against his garage was cottonwood—and not half enough of that to get through December."

"Okay, so he lied about the chain-saw business. But that still doesn't suggest that he'd caught his hair in—" Parris bit off the rest of the sentence.

The tribal investigator grinned. "Caught his hair in *what*?"

"Never mind."

"There was another thing," Moon said. "Ganado had these funny-looking scars on his face. They were round, about the size of dimes—and white. They looked like burns to me. But I couldn't figure how he could've got them from a chain saw."

Our heavy hitter is swinging wild. "And what did you deduce from this?"

"At the moment, I would rather not say."

"Hah—on account of you don't have the least idea *how* he got his hair yanked out!"

"You misunderstand." Moon's expression radiated a pure, childlike innocence. "I will not say because—I am cursed with excessive modesty."

"Hah."

"You already said that."

"Okay Mr. Humble Pie—then tell me as much as excessive modesty allows."

"Well, there might be some small thing I could mention." The Ute put a Styrofoam cup under the spigot on a coffee urn, pressed the lever down. "Ganado's spiffy Pontiac convertible—which he'd already told me was the only wheels he owned—was getting badly spotted by sticky tree sap. This would not have happened if he'd parked it in the garage. And Ganado was very fussy about that car."

"So you figured Ganado had moved his Pontiac out of the garage so he could hide Gourd Rattle's van inside."

"Eventually, the thought did cross my mind," the tribal investigator said. "Where did you get these fine doughnuts?"

"New place around the corner. Fat David's Gourmet Bakery and Small Engine Repair."

"Sounds like David is a man of multiple talents." The Ute took the last bite.

Parris took note of the Seth Thomas clock on the wall. "Charlie, there is something I almost forgot to tell you. Something that will make you happy."

"Happiness is a good thing." Moon licked his fingers. "You have my undivided attention."

"Largely as a result of your aunt Daisy identifying Jim Wolfe's turquoise pendant, Mr. Navarone's attorney has plea-bargained her client for two cases of voluntary manslaughter—Jim Wolfe and Jacob Gourd Rattle, of course. Just yesterday, Felix Navarone made his formal confession."

"This is news to me—and the kind I like to hear."

Parris beamed at his friend. "Would you like to see my very favorite new TV program of the season, produced and directed by the United States Department of Justice?"

"Navarone's confession? How did you get the tape so fast?"

The white man blushed pink. "Uh—it was hand delivered to me just this morning."

"Hand delivered to you by who?"

"By *whom.*"

Moon pondered the pithy grammatical issue. "You sure about that?"

"Not in an absolute sense." But the criticism had distracted the Ute from his question. Parris had the VCR control unit in his hairy paw. "You don't want to suffer through the recitation of the plea agreement, how Mr. Navarone agrees to tell the truth, the whole truth, and nothing but the truth—in exchange for fifteen years in one of Uncle Sammy's finest slammers. I will fast-forward directly to the good stuff."

The tribal investigator seated himself in a comfortable armchair. "Let 'er rip. I am primed and ready to be highly entertained."

DOWNSTAIRS, AND situated immediately beneath the grand office of the Granite Creek chief of police, was a mildly oppressive cafeteria, furnished with a long dining table flanked by an assortment of gaudy plastic chairs and a half-dozen vending machines that—in exchange for silver-plated copper coins—offered up such delicacies as Dr Peppers, Milky Ways, and Moon Pies. At this hour, it was empty of GCPD employees. A single lonely soul paced back and forth, occasionally pausing to sip at a cup of acidic black coffee—and count the minutes.

CHAPTER FIFTY-SEVEN

ALMOST TRUE CONFESSION

SCOTT PARRIS THUMBED THE FAST-FORWARD BUTTON, WATCHED the VCR's digital counter advance. "That should be about the right spot." The chief of police pressed Play. The whining videotape jerked to a near halt, began to rotate at a more sedate rate.

The scene displayed on the Sony color monitor was of an antiseptic-looking room on the third floor of the Federal Building in Denver. The single camera had been set up to frame the conference table in the precise center of the screen. Seated on the viewer's right was the Apache, outfitted in a neon-orange jumpsuit. Felix Navarone was protectively flanked by his legal counsel; the thin-faced young woman wore a robin's-egg-blue suit, rimless spectacles, a thin smile. The left side of the table was occupied by the lumpy form of a middle-aged assistant United States attorney. He had a pencil in his hand, a sour look on his face. On the table in front of him were three stacks of documents, a glass of water, a yellow legal pad. He was speaking to the accused in a bullfrog-deep voice.

". . . AND SO you understand, Mr. Navarone—you must respond to all of the questions with the truth—"

The defense counsel interrupted: "The truth *to the best of his knowledge.*"

The federal attorney nodded. "Of course. But quite aside

from responses to direct questions, it must also be clearly understood that Mr. Navarone will not make any statement that is intended to misinform or otherwise mislead this investigation into the potentially deadly assault on Mr. Ralph Briggs, the deaths of Mr. Jacob Gourd Rattle, Mr. Eduardo Ganado, and Southern Ute police officer James Wolfe." He fixed Felix Navarone with a soul-chilling stare. "Furthermore, any relevant omission on your part will be seen as equivalent to deliberate lying, and will be considered sufficient grounds to break the terms of the plea agreement your counsel has negotiated."

Navarone turned to his attorney with a worried expression.

"Just tell the truth," she said.

"Let me make it crystal clear." Sour Face delivered the words in a cold I'd-just-as-soon-hang-you monotone. "If the Department of Justice should conclude that you're not entirely on the up-and-up, the plea-bargain deal is history. Forget the fifteen years max. Nothing you say here can be used as evidence, but you go to trial on two counts of first-degree murder." The federal attorney sketched a hangman's noose on his pad.

The prisoner stared at the grisly cartoon, nodded dumbly.

The defense attorney aimed a silver-plated ballpoint at her heavy-jowled counterpart. "I wish to go on the record—I am advising my client that he is not to address *any* issue unless he is absolutely certain about the facts. So do not attempt to trip him up with questions that will be looking for speculative responses."

"So noted." Sour Face tried to look pleasant. The effect was that of a fox grinning at a cornered rabbit. "Mr. Navarone—tell us what happened."

The prisoner seemed uncertain. "Where should I start?"

"Whose idea was it to break in to the Cassidy Museum?"

Navarone glanced uncertainly at his attorney.

She adjusted the spectacles onto the bridge of her nose. "My client wishes to state that he and Mr. Eduardo Ganado are the sole persons responsible for the burglary of the Cassidy Museum."

Sour Face glanced at Navarone. "That right?"

The Apache hesitated, then nodded. "Yeah."

The fed consulted a document. "In an earlier statement, you suggested that another person provided helpful information about the general lack of security at the Cassidy Museum—and encouraged you to burglarize it." He directed a cruel smile at the felon. "Do you now wish to withdraw that statement?"

"Yeah, I guess so. I sure don't want to queer the deal we made—"

"Our position on that matter is quite clear," the defense counsel snapped. "Because my client has no material proof of any alleged third-party involvement in the burglary, he prefers to make no statement on the issue. We do retain the option of addressing this issue in the future, should events warrant."

Felix Navarone was quite obviously confused.

His lawyer leaned to whisper in his ear.

The Apache nodded, said to the federal attorney, "I'm not claiming that anybody but me and Eddie Ganado had anything to do with the heist."

Sour Face had dotted the *I;* he had one more *T* to cross. "Was your brother, Mr. Ned Navarone, involved in any way in any of the crimes for which you are accused?"

"Nah." Felix Navarone grinned. "Ol' Ned ain't smart enough to tie his own shoes. I'd never let my big brother know what I was up to."

SCOTT PARRIS stopped the tape. "Felix Navarone tried to bargain himself down to five years by implicating Ralph Briggs in the Cassidy Museum burglary. So Felix must be the guy who called Ralph a few hours after the theft—and when Ralph refused to set up an exchange with Jane Cassidy, threatened our buddy." Parris shook his head at the stationary image of Felix Navarone. "Lying scum bum. I wish they'd put him away for life." He restarted the VCR.

THE FEDERAL attorney was making cryptic notations on his legal pad. "Please go on, Mr. Navarone."

The Apache continued in the casual manner of one telling

a friend about a recent fishing trip. "That night when me and Eddie drove up to the Cassidy place, it was dark as the inside of a crow's gut. I parked in some bushes. Eddie got the crowbar from behind the seat, broke through the glass on the museum door, reached through and opened the latch." He paused to smile. "It was no sweat—like opening a can of sardines."

The thief described the mundane details of the burglary, the jolly late-night drive to Three Sisters Mesa. And then Felix Navarone began to hesitate.

The federal attorney was glaring at the prisoner.

Engrossed in his memories of that night, Felix Navarone seemed almost unaware of the fed. "While Eddie kept a lookout, I stashed the loot on that ledge that sticks out from the cliff like a Ubangi's lip. Those Utes call it something else. . . ."

"The Witch's Tongue," the federal attorney said in a helpful tone. "For the record, Mr. Navarone, I understand that you do not wish to reveal how you were able to gain access to this rather precipitous ledge."

As expected, the response came from the prisoner's attorney: "That is correct. The precise means by which my client got onto the so-called Witch's Tongue is not relevant to these proceedings. He has admitted to his involvement in the burglary, and the fact that he concealed the stolen items on the ledge."

Having already agreed to this omission in the testimony (on grounds that it involved certain Native American "cultural issues") the federal attorney nodded. "So noted."

"STOP THE tape."

Scott Parris complied with the tribal investigator's request.

Charlie Moon leaned forward, stared hard at the frozen image of the Apache.

Parris eyed his enigmatic Indian friend. "What is it?"

"After he was dropped back in the jug on the murder charge," Moon said, "Navarone bragged to some of the other prisoners that he'd *flown* onto the Witch's Tongue. And I'll bet that's what he told his lawyer."

Parris's mouth crinkled into a merry grin. "Then how come

he got stranded there—why didn't he just flap his wings and fly off again?"

Moon's smile felt stiff on his face. "Felix Navarone told some of his fellow jailbirds that his magic was turned against him while he was on the Brujo's Tongue—he lost his ability to fly. At least for the time being."

"That's not the dumbest thing I ever heard," Parris said. "But it's somewhere up there in the top ten."

"I'm sure the Apache expects a big-medicine tale like that to make a serious rep for him behind the walls." The Ute pointed at the prisoner's image on the television screen. "But look at his eyes. Navarone is scared."

The chief of police turned to take a long look at the television. "I expect he's frightened about going to prison."

Moon shook his head. "It's more than that." *He's scared of whoever it was that left him on the Witch's Tongue. That's why he won't talk about how he got onto the ledge or how somebody made sure he stayed there. He's worried that same person will come back. And stop his clock for good.*

Parris pressed the Play button.

FELIX NAVARONE eyed the fed's glass of water.

The U.S. attorney took note of this. "Want something to drink?"

"Could I have a beer?"

The fed laughed out loud, the defense counsel smiled.

Even Navarone seemed amused at his request. "Then how about a Coke?"

"Sure." Sour Face raised an eyebrow at the opposition. "Anything for you, counsel?"

"Coffee would be nice. With cream."

The fed nodded to someone off camera. The courtesies disposed of, he asked the prisoner why he and his partner had selected that particular hiding place.

"We figured it would be the perfect spot. Almost nobody ever goes into Snake Canyon."

The latter assertion piqued the fed's curiosity. "Why is that, Mr. Navarone?"

The Apache stared at the pitifully ignorant white man. "It's a very bad place."

"I see." Sour Face penciled *Bad Place* on his yellow pad. "What happened after you had hidden the stolen property on the ledge?"

The prisoner shrugged under the loosely fitting orange jumper. "Well, me and Eddie Ganado are about to leave the mesa when we hear—uh—someone coming. Turns out it was Jacob Gourd Rattle. Ol' Jake, he must've saw the light from our Coleman lantern. Anyway, Jake yells, 'Who're you two yahoos—and what're you doin' here?' Me'n Eddie, we're so freaked we don't say nothing. Then Jake, he shakes his finger at us and says, 'You're not Utes—you got no right to be on Ute land.'" Felix Navarone ducked in an attempt to avoid the U.S. attorney's stare. "I couldn't tell you exactly who threw the first punch. It might've been Jake, it might've been Eddie."

"But it certainly wasn't *you*." There was a sarcastic smile on the fed's face. "And just for the record, you are not claiming self-defense in the Gourd Rattle homicide."

Navarone's counsel responded, "My client is merely stating that he does not remember who initiated the unfortunate altercation."

"So understood." The fed nodded at the prisoner. "You may continue."

"What happened," Navarone said, "was Eddie bopped Jake upside of the head—knocked him right off the ledge and down into Snake Canyon."

"KING KONG," Moon said.

Parris turned to his friend with a quizzical look. "What?"

"The lady under the spotted lizard may've been a little bit drunk, but Kicks Dogs wasn't quite asleep and she wasn't altogether dreaming. She saw King Kong fall off the Empire State Building. Heard him hit the street with a *thump!*"

The chief of the GCPD shrugged. "Whatever you say."

ON THE video display, Felix Navarone continued his narrative.

• • •

"When he knocked Jake off the edge of the mesa, dopey old Eddie tripped over his own feet and fell down and banged his knee on a rock. He was limping some, but he followed me down the trail into the canyon to check on Jake. Right off we could tell that nasty old Ute was dead. Eddie says, 'Felix—we gotta get outta here.' I says, 'Look, this Ute must have a camp around here someplace. And unless he walked ten miles in or rode a horse, he must have some wheels up there on the mesa, 'cause that's the only way to drive in.' Then I searched Jake, and found a car key in his pocket. 'When he turns up missing,' I says to Eddie, 'those Ute cops will send some people out to look for him. Maybe somebody knows he's here, maybe not. But either way we'll be a lot better off if there's no sign left of his camp. And we gotta move his car a few miles up the road.' Eddie says, 'Yeah—we need to make it look like Jake was somewhere else.' I say, 'Eddie, I'll hide Jake's body someplace. And if I can find his camp, I'll clean it up so nobody'll know he was in the canyon. While I'm doing that, you go up on the mesa and look for his wheels.' Eddie complains some about his knee, but says he guesses he can make it back up the trail if he takes his time. So I give Eddie Jake's car key and that's what we did. After Eddie hikes back up onto the mesa, it didn't take him very long to find Jake's clunky old Dodge van. And it didn't take me but a coupla minutes to find the place where Jake was camped. It was right there in Snake Canyon, and not far from where he landed when he fell off the mesa. But this is the strange part—Jake had dug a big hole where he'd set up camp, and he'd covered it up with a buffalo robe. It looked like a grave." Felix Navarone's face twisted into a puzzled expression. "Maybe he *knew* he was gonna die that night." He turned to his lawyer. "Sometimes they do."

She nodded, as if this made perfect sense.

The Apache proceeded with his confession: "Anyway, I put Jake's body in the hole and covered it up with rocks and dirt and smoothed it over real nice. Right then, it starts to snow, and it's about time for the sun to come up. So I picked up his

gear and lugged it up the trail to the top of Three Sisters Mesa.
I found Eddie, and we stashed Jake's stuff in his Dodge van."

PARRIS STOPPED the tape, turned to eye the tribal investigator.
"You have any idea why Mr. Gourd Rattle dug a trench in
ground?"

Moon got up to refill his coffee cup. "Like the Apache
said—it was a grave."

"Grave for who?"

"Jacob dug it for himself."

"You figure he intended to commit suicide?"

"No." Moon stirred in six spoons of sugar. "Jacob went
into Snake Canyon on a vision quest. He must've needed
some kind of healing. The pit is used to 'bury' the visionary's
body—this is supposed to encourage the soul to go free. And
the man seeking the vision must be alone. That's why Jacob
sent his wife away."

"If you say so." Parris glanced at the video monitor where
the talkative Apache was frozen with his mouth gaped open.
He pushed the VCR Play button. Navarone's affliction with
electronic lockjaw was instantly cured.

THE VERBAL deposition was interrupted when a tough-looking
young man brought a tray to the table. There was coffee and
cream for the defense counsel, a Cherry Coke for the prisoner,
a bowl of Ginger Snaps for anyone who wished to indulge.
After the Justice Department employee disappeared off camera, Sour Face tapped his pencil on the table, waited for the
prisoner to take a couple of swigs of the sugary drink. "So
now you had possession of the dead man's vehicle and his
camping gear."

Felix Navarone's head bobbed in a nod. "Right."

"Did you find any weapons in Mr. Gourd Rattle's vehicle?"

Navarone got the go-ahead nod from his lawyer. "Yeah,"
he said. "Eddie found a .22 pistol in the glove compartment. It
was wrapped in a rag."

The federal attorney reached under the table, produced a
transparent evidence bag, pushed it across the table. "Mr.

Navarone, is this the firearm your partner found in Mr. Gourd Rattle's van?"

A shrug from the Apache. "Looks like it."

"Who took possession of this firearm?"

"Eddie did." An amused shrug. "That Navajo liked guns."

The fed withdrew the evidence. "You have already stated that your intention was to leave Mr. Gourd Rattle's vehicle and camping gear at some distance from the general area where his body and the stolen goods might be found."

"That was the plan all right." The prisoner seemed to be reading the fine print on the Coke can. "But sometimes things don't work out the way you expect." The videotaped felon paused to shake his head, grin at the beginning of his long string of bad luck. "It was stupid, I guess, but we never thought of Jake having somebody with him in Snake Canyon. It was two or three days later we heard about his woman waking up the next morning and finding her old man gone. I guess the snow must've covered up his grave by then. If Kicks Dogs hadn't reported him missing—things might've turned out all right for me and Eddie."

CHARLIE MOON snatched the VCR control off Parris's desk, pressed the Pause button.

Annoyed at this unseemly appropriation of his "clicker," the chief of police glared at the presumptuous Ute. "Why did you do that?"

"It must be all the sugar and caffeine—I seem to have lost some of my excessive modesty."

"I sense that you are about to make a brag."

"I would rather make a buck."

"I don't doubt it. Give it your best shot."

"Felix Navarone is about to tell us how Eddie Ganado lost his hair." Charlie Moon grinned at Parris. "But you know that, 'cause you've already seen the tape. I, on the other hand, am not an overpaid administrator who waits to hear a confession. I am a real, working cop who has to figure out what's going on *before* the bad guy spills his guts."

"And you're telling me you know."

"If the price is right."

A smile crinkled the corners of Parris's mouth. "Are you suggesting a wager?"

Moon's grin got wider. "You bet."

"Very well, I think I will." Parris reached for his billfold, emptied it of bills, laid all his money down.

The Ute took a look at the attractive stack of greenbacks. "How much is that?"

The chief of police assumed a superior expression. "I am so sure of winning that I did not bother to count it."

Moon hesitated. "At the moment, I am a little short of hard cash."

This produced a smirk on the white man's face. "Go ahead—backwater if you're having second thoughts."

"Will you take my IOU?"

"Natch. Now tell me—how did Mr. Ganado lose his hair?"

"It was those little white spots on his skin that got me to thinking. It looked to me like Ganado was splashed with something hot."

"Splashed?"

"As with a liquid. The kind which—when it's under pressure—has a boiling point well in excess of two hundred and twelve Fahrenheit degrees. Naturally, this varies with the concentration of antifreeze."

Parris looked glumly at his money, said a silent good-bye.

Moon was very pleased with himself. "Way I figure it, either Felix Navarone or Eddie Ganado was driving Jacob's van away from Three Sisters Mesa when it broke down. But it must've been Eddie that stuck his head under the hood, trying to see was wrong—and Eddie's hair got caught in the fan belt. Aside from getting scalped by an engine—"

"What?"

"Not Injun—*engine*."

"Oh."

"Like I was saying, aside from getting scalped by an internal combustion engine, that poor accident-prone Navajo got his head banged pretty hard against the radiator about six dozen times before Felix Navarone could shut off the motor and—"

"Take my money, Charlie. But please—don't say another word about how the Navajo lost his hair."

The Ute picked up the stack of greenbacks, resisted the impulse to count them.

Parris snatched back the VCR controller.

THE ELECTRONIC facsimile of Felix Navarone helped itself to a digitized representation of a cookie and began to talk. "What happened was this. I got the van key back from Eddie, cranked up the old Dodge. Eddie gets in my pickup—he follows me on that little road off of Three Sisters Mesa. But we haven't gone a quarter mile when that stinkin' Dodge coughs and dies on me. There's big boulders on both sides of the road so Eddie can't get around the van with my pickup. Well, there we are—stranded with Jake's van blocking the lane. We can't just walk away and leave the dead man's van and my truck behind it. We're in ten kinds of trouble if we can't get Jake's old box of bolts started again. Eddie, he gets out of my pickup and goes around to the front of the van. I pull the latch and he pops the hood. At first, Eddie says, 'I can't see nothing wrong here.' Then he says, 'Hey, Felix—I think I found the trouble. Try it now.' So I cranks the engine and I hear this bang-bang-bang. I thought for sure we'd throwed a rod—but it's Eddie's head bopping on the radiator. He yells bloody murder, I shut off the engine. But by that time, he was bunged up pretty bad. Turns out a big hank of his hair has got caught in the fan belt."

Neither of the lawyers was able to suppress a smile.

Navarone shuddered at the memory. "It was awful. Eddie has cuts and burns all over his face and a bunch of his hair is wrapped around the fan shaft and the pulleys on the generator and I don't know what else. His blood is splattered all over the engine. He's not yelling now and I think maybe he's dead, but after I cut his hair loose with my Buck knife, he's not only alive—he's really mad at me for taking so long to shut off the engine." Navarone shook his head and snickered. "He starts cussing and chunking rocks at me. I laugh so hard I fall down in the snow. After a while, Eddie runs out of swear words and he can't find any more rocks to throw, so he sits down on the ground and starts to cry. Blubbers like a baby. I says, 'Eddie, get a hold of yourself—we got to figure out what to do. Way things are now, we can't leave this van anyplace where it'll be spotted. If the police find it with all your blood and hair on it— they'll know you killed Jake Gourd Rattle.' He says, 'You are in this too.' I say, 'Eddie—you're the one who bopped Jake and knocked him off the cliff.' He says, 'Felix, it don't matter who bopped Jake—we're in this together.' And I tell him that the police will be able to do tests on the blood and hair and trace it straight to him. He says, 'They'd better not, Felix—or your goose gets cooked right along with mine.'" Navarone took a sip of Cherry Coke. "Because his head is all bunged up, Eddie don't know what to do. So I say, 'Eddie, we'll take Jake's van to your place and hide it there while we clean it up real good, so there's none of your hair or blood left on it.' Eddie sees the sense in this, and says, 'Right—we will *detail* this old rust bucket!' So we take Jake's van to Eddie's place, stash it in his garage. We was awfully tired by then, so we decide to clean it up the next night and then get rid of it. Eddie was still in a ugly mood, so I thought I'd drive back to the place I share with my brother Ned over by Pagosa. But later on that day, when I was coming back to Eddie's place to help him get his hair and blood offa Jake's van—I got stopped at the roadblock."

PARRIS PRESSED the Pause button, turned to eye the tribal investigator.

The Ute had counted the take. *Eighty-six dollars. Not bad for a few minutes' work.* He folded the wad, put it in his pocket.

"Go ahead," Parris said. "Get it said."

"You sure you won't mind?"

Moon's victim nodded.

"Okay. Here goes. 'You are an easy mark.'"

"Charlie—mark my word. Your time is coming."

"That's what you've been telling me for about a dozen years now."

"Let's change the subject." Parris's wallet felt as thin as tissue. "I heard a rumor that you tipped off the FBI. Told 'em about the ignition key they found in Wolfe's raincoat pocket."

The tribal investigator frowned. "Who told you such a thing?"

"Stan Newman. He thinks you were trying to help his partner along, probably because she's prettier than he is."

"A ninety-year-old warthog that slobbers is prettier than Stan is."

"You'll get no argument from me," Parris said. "Stan admitted he was guessing."

Moon was relieved to know that McTeague had not revealed her source.

"Don't hold out on your best friend. Did Newman guess right?"

The Ute nodded.

"So how'd you know about the key in Jim Wolfe's raincoat pocket?"

"At the roadblock, when Felix Navarone jumped out of that tree onto Wolfe, a passerby was making a videotape, which fell into the tribal chairman's hands. I watched a part of it over and over, one frame at a time."

"And?"

"And while Wolfe and Navarone were rolling around on the ground, I saw Navarone slip his hand into Wolfe's raincoat pocket. Way I see it, the Apache should have been way too busy to be *picking* the cop's pocket. So it got me to wondering—what'd Felix have on him that he wanted to get rid of so bad that he'd run from the state police, climb up a tree, then jump off the limb to assault an SUPD officer? I recalled that it was when the state cop asked him for the *ignition key* that Felix got spooked. He would've had no reason to get panicky about giving the Smokey the key out of his truck. So I figured he had somebody else's ignition key in his pocket. And Jacob's van was missing from Three Sisters Mesa." He grinned. "Pretty good, huh?"

"Nobody likes a show-off." Parris restarted the video of the Ganado confession, fast-forwarded to the point of interest.

"At first, I wasn't too scared by the roadblock," Felix Navarone said, "because there's nothing in my pickup to connect me to the museum heist or to Jake's killing. But when that tough-looking state cop asks me for the ignition key, I remember that I still have Jake's van key in my pocket. I figure if these cops frisk me and find that key, I am dead meat and cold bones. So I make a run for it, hoping to toss the key before they can catch me. But I see them hot-footed cops is gaining on me and I know I can't make it into the brush where I can throw the key away without it being noticed. So I *have* to climb that tree. And while I'm out on that cottonwood limb, I have me a little time to think. What I think is, If I can jump onto one of these cops, maybe I can plant the key on him. Once I do that, there'll be no way they can prove I ever had Jake's van key unless I've left some fingerprints on it, but that's the only chance I have. So I jump on that white cop who is working for the Ute police. And while we're rassling, I slip the key into his coat pocket. That white man was one dirty fighter—I thought he was gonna chew my face off before those other cops finally pulled him offa me." Felix Navarone rubbed at his bitten nose, which still had not healed.

THE CHIEF of police thumbed the Pause button, shook his head as he spoke to the wall. "I am always saying it, and I'll say it again—with some training, Charlie Moon would've made a fair-to-middling police detective. But he is probably better off raising beef."

The Ute raised his coffee cup to salute this observation. "Thank you and amen."

Scott Parris checked his wristwatch. "During our brief intermission, you will have precisely ten seconds to gloat."

Charlie Moon had barely heard his friend's voice. The woman had slipped back into his consciousness. He wondered where she was right now. What she was doing. And . . . *Does she ever think of me?*

AT THAT very moment, the object of the lonely Ute's thoughts was in Harford County, Maryland. She was standing on the grassy bank of the Little Gunpowder. A warm flower-scented breeze skipped over patches of pink lady's slipper and wild columbine, brushed through leafy branches of hickory and oak, caressed the woman's dark hair, tossed the blue cotton skirt about her knees. Miss James was remembering the man who had named a lovely alpine lake after her. *I was a fool, and weak. I should never have left him.* The lovely lady stooped to pick up a stone. The plum-sized lump was deep red, veined with blue—and heavy as her heart. She tossed it into the water. Through eyes moist with tears, she watched concentric waves blossom away from the splash. *But I am not so foolish now. And every day, I grow stronger.* She smiled at the woman on the surface of the stream, made her reflection a solemn promise. *As soon as I am able, I will go back to Charlie.*

The rippling doppelgänger did not return the smile. *But will he want you?*

CHAPTER FIFTY-EIGHT

THE LADYSMITH

UNNVERVED BY THE UTE'S PECULIAR SILENCE, PARRIS RE-started the videotape.

THE FED turned a page on his legal pad. "Mr. Navarone, I have a few questions to ask you."

The Apache shot a sideways glance at his lawyer, got the go-ahead nod.

"First, did Mr. Eduardo Ganado take the firearm stolen from Mr. Gourd Rattle's vehicle to the home and business of Mr. Ralph Briggs with the intent of causing bodily harm to Mr. Briggs?"

Defense counsel's response was predictable and immediate: "Object. My client has no way of knowing what Mr. Ganado's intent may have been."

The Justice Department attorney had given it his best shot. "Mr. Navarone, please tell us what you know about the shooting of Mr. Briggs."

"Well, like you already know—I was in the Ute jail in Ignacio when it happened. But a couple of days before the shooting, Eddie stops by to visit me and I tell him—"

The federal attorney interrupted. "For the record—this was Mr. Ganado's *first* visit to you after you were arrested at the roadblock?"

"Sure. Eddie don't dare show up at the jail till he gets that job working for my lawyer—but he wants to get me out of the jug soon as he can."

"What was the big hurry?"

"It was like this—while I'm in the Ute jail, Eddie tries to get his hair off of the engine belts and pulleys in Jake's Dodge van. But it ain't no use, some of it is stuck tight. And cleaning off Eddie's blood is lots harder than we'd thought. So Eddie figures he'll have to burn the van, but he'll have to take it a long way from his place so as not to raise any suspicions. But if he does that, he won't have any way to get back home except maybe thumb a ride. Poor ol' Eddie is still crippled up from his fall in Snake Canyon; what he needs is somebody to drive another car to where he'll burn the van, so he'll have a ride back home. But the only person he can trust to do that is me, and I'm in the Ute lockup in Ignacio. Also, Eddie thinks I've still got the key to the van."

Sour Face allowed himself a small smile. "And Mr. Ganado thought it unwise to pay his partner in crime a visit in jail?"

"Sure—Eddie don't want the cops to make a connection between him and me. But one night when he's looking at the newspaper, Eddie sees this Durango lawyer's employment ad, and he comes up with a plan." The Apache smirked. "Eddie knows from talking to my brother Ned that this same lawyer is representing me—and she's also looking to hire a legal aide. The ad says she needs someone who's qualified to work with the local Native American population. Next day, Eddie shows up, pitches her a big line about what a hard worker he is, how many Indians he knows—and just like that he gets the job. This gives him a perfect excuse to visit me in the Ute jail, which he does right away. When Eddie tells me how he's stuck with Gourd Rattle's van, I says, 'I'd like to help you, pal—but there's no telling when I'll get outta jail.' And I also tell Eddie about how I called Briggs about an hour before I got stopped at that roadblock and how Briggs has flat-out refused to act as middleman between me and the Cassidys, and even threatened to put the cops on me." He glanced at his attorney, got a warning look. "We are worried about that feisty junk

dealer, so I tell Eddie to go talk to that tall, skinny Ute cop—
Charlie Moon—see if he'll testify that Wolfe has roughed me
up. Well, from what Eddie knows of Charlie Moon, he don't
think it'll work. But he don't have no better idea, so he drives
up to the Columbine Ranch and catches Moon just as he's
leaving. And Eddie was right: Moon won't buy what he's selling. But while Eddie is talking to him, that Ute cop gets a telephone call—from Ralph Briggs!" Felix Navarone's eyes
burned with hatred. "Briggs is setting up a meet with Moon so
they can talk about the Cassidy heist. Eddie figures that two-
faced junk dealer is gonna rat me out to the Ute, and Eddie
knows that if I go to the joint, he'll go with me. Eddie showed
up that night to shoot the both of 'em—Briggs and the Ute.
Eddie had it all worked out—he brought along the pistol we
found in Gourd Rattle's van. He was able to nail Briggs with
the first shot, but some crazy woman starts screeching and
that big Ute comes crashing through the window like getting
shot is the last thing on his mind. Eddie drops Jake's .22 pistol
like he'd planned to do—and manages to slip away in the dark
and get back to his car."

THE CHIEF of police shut off the tape, turned to the tribal investigator. *I wonder if he's come back from wherever he was.*
"You want to watch any more of it?"

"Maybe later," Moon said. "What does Felix Navarone
have to say about the run-in with Jim Wolfe?"

Parris worked his way through a written transcript of the
confession. "Here it is." He ran his finger down the page, refreshed his memory. "On the afternoon Navarone is sprung
from the Ute jail, he heads out to Eddie Ganado's place to
help his buddy get rid of the Gourd Rattle vehicle. The plan is
they'll hot-wire the van, Ganado will drive it to some remote
spot. Navarone will be following his partner. Soon as they
torch the van, they'll hightail it back to Ganado's place. But
they realize that taking the stolen vehicle out on a public road
is fairly risky—even in the middle of the night. So they decide
to scout out an out-of-the-way location for the big event. Kind
of a dry run. Felix Navarone cranks up his old Chevy pickup,

and with Eddie Ganado on the seat beside him they head off into the night. And what do you know—they haven't gone but a few miles when Eddie looks in his rearview mirror, thinks he sees a car pull out of some brush and hang a tail on him. He's not sure, because there are no headlights. Ganado turns around, watches until they hit a patch of moonlight—tells Navarone it looks like a Subaru. Navarone says that could be Wolfe's car, and decides to take this opportunity to deal with Wolfe once and for good. So he putt-putts along while Wolfe follows, then makes a turn toward Butterfield Mesa. Navarone parks his pickup in plain sight, and him and Ganado get out and split up—waiting for the SUPD cop to play out his hand. It's Eddie Ganado that eventually spots Wolfe—which turns out to be serious bad luck for the Navajo. Officer Wolfe empties his pistol into Ganado, and hides his body under a pile of rocks. But it's pretty dark and Wolfe has shot most of Ganado's face off—he's apparently convinced he's killed Felix Navarone. At least that's what the Apache says. He claims he heard Wolfe call the dead man 'Navarone.' "

Moon interrupted the monologue. "Could I make a guess?"

Parris looked up from the transcript. "As long as it don't cost me anything."

"Here's how I see it—after Wolfe is gone, Felix Navarone removes the stones, stuffs Eddie Ganado's body in the back of his old pickup, drives back to Ganado's place, transfers the Navajo's remains to the Gourd Rattle van, which is locked up in Ganado's garage. After this, maybe Navarone heads for Pagosa and the nice little place he shares with his kindly brother Ned."

Parris nodded. "That's close enough." He found his place in the written account of the confession. "Later on, Navarone claims he drove over to Ignacio, parked down the street from Jim Wolfe's apartment building. Late at night, he took a look through Wolfe's apartment window. Risky thing to do—it's a wonder Wolfe didn't shoot him."

Moon shook his head. "There's no point shooting a man you've already filled full of holes and buried under a big pile of rocks. You expect him to be sufficiently dead already."

"Good point," Parris said. "Poor fella must've thought he'd seen the Apache's ghost."

"That's why Wolfe went to my aunt's home—to get some corpse powder to sprinkle on the body. But when Wolfe shows up where he'd left the body under the rocks, there's nothing there."

Parris shook his head at the image. "Boy—can't blame the poor bugger for being spooked!"

"Did Felix Navarone admit to murdering Wolfe—and putting his body in Ganado's grave?"

"Call it voluntary manslaughter," Parris said. "Navarone claimed he went back again—to 'have a talk' with Wolfe." The GCPD chief of police snorted at this self-serving fabrication. "According to the Apache's version of the story, he thought it would be too risky to walk right up and knock on Wolfe's apartment door, so he needed to work out a way to get Wolfe to come outside without knowing who was there. And Navarone came up with something fairly clever. You'd never guess what he did."

Moon shook his head. "I know what you're up to."

Parris's face was a gilt-framed picture of innocence. "What?"

"You're trying to get your money back. You hope you can suck me into another bet."

"I wouldn't even think of such a thing." Parris's blue eyes twinkled. "But if you want to take a guess without risking any cash—go ahead. Give it a shot."

"You sure you want me to?"

"Sure. But if you guess right, it'll give me a bad case of heartburn."

"Pardner, I would not want you to suffer severe gastric distress on account of me."

Parris looked out the window. "Go ahead. Get it out of your system."

"Okay, here's my guess. Felix Navarone banged on Jim Wolfe's Subaru, which set off the theft alarm, which makes the horn go toot-toot-toot. The apartment manager heard the horn, and she heard Wolfe's door bang when he came out with his pistol in his hand. Wolfe didn't see anybody around his car, probably figured it was some dumb kid who'd caused the nighttime commotion. About the time he got into his Subaru to reset the alarm, Navarone must've slipped up with a rock in his hand, conked him on the head hard enough to crush his skull. Navarone stashes the dead cop in the back of his fifty-seven Chevy pickup, hauls the body out to Butterfield Mesa—right to the spot where Wolfe had buried Ganado—sticks Wolfe's pistol barrel into his mouth and covers him up with rocks."

Scott Parris found a bottle in his desk, downed a couple of Tums.

"Sorry," the Ute said.

"You were only partly right." Parris tried to smirk, looked like someone who had just swallowed a tablespoon of castor oil. "Navarone did not conk Wolfe with a rock—he hit him with a *brick*."

"Well, that sure blows my notion all the way to Kingdom Come." Moon watched his friend crunch on a third antacid tablet. "This really bothers me."

Parris shot the Ute a barbed look. "Navarone using a brick?"

"Besides that."

"What?"

"For his so-called confession," Moon said, "Felix Navarone—who has committed a cold-blooded, premeditated murder—gets off with fifteen years. And if he builds up enough good time, he could walk in ten."

"It is the American Way of Justice, my friend." Parris put the Tums bottle into a desk drawer. "Something else nags at me. I can understand why Felix Navarone buried Mr. Gourd Rattle in a grave the dead man had dug himself—the hole in the ground was right at hand, so it was a convenient thing to do. What I can't figure out is why Navarone would go to all the trouble and risk to transport Jim Wolfe's body to Butterfield Mesa, just to stash him in the same spot where Wolfe had piled some rocks over Eddie Ganado."

Moon nodded. "Did Felix offer any explanation?"

Parris belched, felt marginally better. "Navarone's attorney claims her Native American client was performing an old Apache cultural practice. According to her, Felix Navarone was 'closing the circle' on his enemy." *Whatever that means.*

Moon was beginning to think about hearth and home. "That sounds like something Navarone cooked up for his lawyer."

Parris cocked an eye at the Ute. "So you don't buy it?"

"Not for two cents on the dollar. My guess is that Felix Navarone put Jim Wolfe's body in Ganado's grave because it struck him as a hilarious thing to do." Moon allowed himself a thin smile. "Some of those Apaches have a peculiar sense of humor."

Parris consulted his watch. "Okay if we take a break now?"

"Fine with me." The lanky Ute got up to stretch.

Taking care not to be noticed, Parris pressed the buzzer button on his intercom. In response, a yellow light on the panel blinked twice. The chief of GCPD scooped up a handful of papers. "Uh—I got some things to do down the hall, Charlie. I'll be back before you know it." He hurried away, closing the door behind him.

The Ute had not missed his friend's monkeying around with the desk intercom station—or Scott Parris's reluctance to say who had brought the videotape all the way from Denver this morning. Charlie Moon stood with his arms folded across his chest, listening with great interest to the silence. Presently, he heard faint creaks as someone walked up the stairs outside the chief's office. The door opened silently on oiled hinges.

Standing with his back to the door, the tribal investigator knew who it was. He tensed. "Go ahead. Do it."

The newcomer stared at the tall man. Reached out. Ran a pointy fingernail down his spine.

Charlie Moon turned.

Special Agent McTeague smiled. "How was that?"

He smiled back. "Lila Mae, you do a pretty mean scratch."

SCOTT PARRIS approached his office. *Seems awful quiet—maybe they've gone.* He turned the knob, looked through a crack in the door. The chief of the Granite Creek Police Department felt cheated. *I've been working with the feds for a good twelve years now, and I like to think I've done a pretty good job. Two or three times I've got a slap on the back or a "Way to go, Scott." But in all that time, no FBI agent has ever hugged and kissed me.*

CHAPTER FIFTY-NINE

THE SACRAMENT

DAISY PERIKA WAS SEATED ON AN UNCOMFORTABLE CHAIR IN the rectory parlor. Preferring to avoid the priest's penetrating gaze, the Ute elder looked down at the weak cup of coffee in her hand. "So, how are your retirement plans going?"

Father Raes Delfino sipped at a cup of tea sweetened with honey. "I am reliably informed that the bishop has found a replacement."

Daisy did not inquire about the new priest because she did not care to know a thing about him. It would be some enthusiastic young smart aleck, all filled up with big long words and years of book learning. The old woman tried to make her next question sound like small talk. The trembling voice betrayed her. "Have you found a place to live?"

The Jesuit nodded.

Daisy shot him an accusing look. "It'll be a long ways off, I expect."

Probably not far enough. There was a merry twinkle in the cleric's eyes. "Shortly before I'm ready to make my move, I will pay you a call. Tell you everything."

The cantankerous woman shrugged, as if she did not care where he went.

"Daisy, I have known you for quite a long time. I do not believe you are here to discuss my retirement plans."

She squirmed in the chair. "Well—there is this one thing."

Aha. "And what would that be?"

The old woman grimaced. "It's been a long time since I've been . . . to confession."

Father Raes almost spilled his spicy-sweet tea. He set the translucent china cup on a matching saucer. Only last year, Charlie Moon had requested that holy sacrament—and for a most peculiar reason. And now Daisy. *Will God's wonders never cease?* The cleric found his tongue. "Yes. I suppose it has been. A long time, I mean."

Daisy strained with the mental calculation. "It was way back when old Father What's-his-name was here—the one who wheezed when he talked and had a big red mole on his nose. And Mole Nose was here before Father Martinez, who was still a couple of Fathers before you." She nodded to agree with this vague assessment. "And it wasn't long after my third husband died, so it must've been sometime around 1962." She shifted in the chair again, grunted. "Let's get to it."

The holy man looked to heaven for mercy. When there was no response, Father Raes Delfino made a halfhearted attempt at escape. "Perhaps you would prefer to wait until my replacement arrives."

The repentant woman shook her head. "Got to be right now." The old warhorse gave him a defiant look. "But I won't go into that little closet—it gives me the spooks."

"Very well. Under those special circumstances, I suppose we may proceed with less formality. Now to begin with—"

"It's not like that last time, when everybody thought my third husband fell off his mule, and that his death was an accident." She leaned forward. "The truth was—"

He raised a hand to silence her. "Presuming this sin has already been confessed in 1962, it is not necessary to repeat it."

"Then you're only interested in what happened lately?"

"Technically, we should discuss any sins since your last confession." *God deliver me from hearing all of that.* "But let us begin with whatever is most burdensome to your soul."

"Well, there's hardly anything that bothers me overly much."

He could not help smiling.

"But a while back . . ." She looked down at her wrinkled hands. "I took something that wasn't mine."

The priest raised an eyebrow. "You committed a theft?"

"You sound like a cop," she snapped.

"I beg your pardon, Daisy. But stealing is a very serious sin." He thought he knew the answer but was required to ask. "Did you return the stolen property to the rightful owner?"

"Not exactly."

Father Raes put on his most stern expression. "Daisy, forgiveness can hardly be expected until there is true repentance. And that requires restitution."

She thought of a mitigating circumstance: "I was *thinking* about returning it, but before I could, he came and stole it back."

Father Raes closed his eyes. *Dear God, give me strength.* "Why don't you tell me the whole story."

She did.

At the end of the tale about Hasteen K'os Largo's horned-star pendant and the murdered white policeman, and how it had all turned out "all right" because she had helped the authorities convict the Apache who murdered Officer Wolfe—the priest fixed her with an astonished look. "This is quite a remarkable account."

Having unconsciously interlaced her fingers, Daisy seemed on the very verge of prayer. Her voice crackled with fear. "Will I have to do penance?"

"Of course."

Imagining the dire possibilities, she cringed.

"But before we discuss that, there is something that you must understand."

The old sinner waited.

"Daisy, you must learn to love God—not the things of this world." The priest's voice was full of compassion. "The time eventually comes when we are compelled to depart from this mortal body." He looked past her at something neither he nor she could see. "And when we go, we are obliged to leave everything behind."

CHARLIE MOON had wasted hours searching the broad crest of Three Sisters Mesa. His happy hound had well spent the same interval scaring up cottontails and chasing every butterfly that fluttered by. The shadows were stretched and diffuse; both man and beast were ready to call it a day—when just a few paces from the edge of the cliff that hung over the Witch's Tongue, in the slanting light of the afternoon sun, the tribal investigator spied a fluffy wisp of something on the very tip of a yucca spike. It was a tiny hank of wool. Yellow wool. And a peculiar kind of yellow at that.

A few yards away, Sidewinder sniffed and whined at a narrow crack in the mesa floor. "What've you found, another rabbit?" Moon went to scratch his hound behind the ear. There was no rabbit. And because there were hundreds much like it, this particular fracture in the sandstone was hardly noteworthy. Except for the fact that a green piñon branch had been stuffed into the small crevice. The Ute removed the small piece of brush, stared at precisely what he had been searching for—a rolled-up bundle of nylon cords. He knew who had hidden it here. This was a highly significant piece of evidence. *By rights, I should tell McTeague about this.* But knowing that he would not—*could* not—Charlie Moon replaced the piñon branch over the hound's discovery. He walked away, Sidewinder trailing along behind. "You're a good old dog," he said to his fuzzy-faced friend. "How about a big chunk of prime beef for dinner—and some fried chicken livers?"

The canine gourmet licked his lips.

CHAPTER SIXTY

AMAZING GRACE

MONTHS PASSED WITH A PAINFUL SLOWNESS, LIKE OLD MEN walking uphill. A dry summer was replaced by a drier autumn. Cottonwood and aspen leaves crinkled into crispy gold, fell away to drift in the cool breath exhaled from the mouth of *Cañon del Espiritu.*

Every day, every night, Daisy Perika got a little older. A little wiser.

Every day, every night, she prayed for God to remove from her the burning desire for the K'os Largo pendant.

Every day, every night, she loved God a little more—earthly treasures a little less.

And it came to pass that she was blessed.

One fine October morn, while she was dozing on her lumpy little cot, the weary woman heard an automobile pull up near her trailer and stop. *Maybe it's Charlie.* Daisy got up to look through the bedroom window, saw an old, rusted-out Chevrolet sedan. She squinted at the license plate. *God help me—it's a whole carload of Okies!* But what were they doing here? She considered several possibilities, settled on what seemed the most likely. *I bet the dust bowl has come back and they've hit the road to look for work.* She retreated from the window, hoping and praying that they would go away. Her hopes and prayers were pointedly ignored. There were squeaks on the porch steps, a tentative knock.

I'm not here. Ostrich Woman closed her eyes and stood quite still.

Patiently, persistently, the knocking continued.

I might as well get this over with. Prepared for an unpleasant confrontation, she jerked the door open, found a grizzled-looking old white man standing on her porch.

He took off his new straw hat, smiled most pleasantly, and said, "Excuse me, ma'am—I don't know if we've found the right place. Might you be Mrs. Perika?"

Somewhat reluctantly, she nodded.

He tapped the hat brim on his chest. "I am Tobias Wolfe—father of Jim Wolfe."

Daisy took another look at the Chevrolet Impala parked a few yards away. A woman who looked about the same age as Tobias was staring at her from the passenger seat. *This must be the dead man's mother.* A slender youth leaning on the car looked enough like Jim Wolfe to be his brother. She found her voice. "I'm sorry about what happened to your son."

The other man approached the porch, climbed the steps to stand behind his father.

Daisy Perika eyed them both, knew what she must do. "Would you like to come in?"

Tobias Wolfe shook his head. "Oh no, ma'am. We would not want to impose ourselves on your hospitality. We just came to tell you how thankful our family is to you for helping the government convict the man who murdered our oldest son. If you hadn't treated Jim's wounds that day he had the fight, and took notice of that little blue stone he wore under his shirt—why, his killing might never have been solved." He turned to look at his wife in the Chevrolet. "And we'd never have been able to find peace of mind."

Daisy's face burned with shame. "I didn't do all that much."

"What you did meant a lot to us." As he put his hand in his coat pocket, the grateful man smiled at this remarkably modest woman. "Me and the wife, we got this property of Jim's last week by registered mail. It was legal evidence for a while, but now they don't need it no more. And seeing as how you have a connection with the thing, we thought you might like to have it. So we came all the way from Talequah, just to give it to you personal." He stuck out a knobby, work-worn hand. In his callused palm was the K'os Largo pendant.

The Ute shaman felt electricity tingle up and down her spine. All her good intentions vanished; every atom in her body lusted after the rare treasure.

"Go on," Tobias Wolfe said. "Take it."

She looked at the younger man. There was a smile, a nod.

The tempted Christian closed her eyes. Talked to God.

The puzzled old man waited with the patience characteristic of his kind.

Having made her decision, Daisy was able to lay her burden down. She looked through tears at Mr. Tobias Wolfe. This was not an ordinary pendant, she told him. It had belonged to a famous Navajo medicine man who died many years ago. It was probably worth a lot of money. Mr. Wolfe could sell it. Or keep it, in remembrance of his son.

He gave her a bewildered look, stuck his hand out even farther. "You sure you don't want it?"

Miraculously, she did not.

Daisy beamed a hard look at the kindly *matukach*. "Now listen to what I've got to say, because I won't put up with no argument. You people come inside while I make you some coffee."

"Well, I guess if you put it that way . . ." The old man nodded his assent, made a gesture to his wife, who got out of the car and approached the Ute woman's home. And so it was that three members of the Wolfe clan experienced the hospitality of Daisy Perika's kitchen. For hours on end, they talked about the son who had been murdered. He had always been a good boy. Daisy Perika provided Tobias Wolfe and his wife with oatmeal-raisin cookies and strong coffee. The shaman did not offer any refreshment to the young man. It would have been quite pointless.

And would certainly have startled his parents.

CHAPTER SIXTY-ONE

A DONE DEAL

CHARLIE MOON LOOKED THROUGH THE NORTH WINDOW, SAW Pete Bushman down at the riverside corral. He stepped out onto the porch, gave his foreman a wave.

Bushman was busy and did not want to be bothered. "What is it?" he yelled.

Moon yelled back, "Got some news."

Convinced by years of hard knocks that all news is bad, the bearded, bowlegged stockman approached the boss with an air of dread. "What is it now?"

Charlie told him.

For a breathless moment, the foreman stared in disbelief. "You did—you really *did*?"

Moon grinned. "Signed the papers this morning."

Bushman jerked his tattered hat off his head, threw it into the air, let out a screeching yelp that startled the horses in the corral and a flock of blackbirds passing by. "Ya-hoooooo!"

The owner of the Columbine feigned a look of disappointment. "From time to time, Pete, it would help if you could manage to show a little bit of enthusiasm."

THE DEALER

SEVERAL HOURS later, Charlie Moon was on the telephone, having an unpleasant conversation with the owner-manager of Happy Dan's Custom Trucks and Vans.

"So," the rancher mumbled, "the first payment on the F-350 is due."

Happy Dan confirmed that this was true.

"And remind me, Happy—how much does that come to?"

He was told the sum. To the very penny.

Ouch. "That much?"

Happy Dan reminded the Ute that this was a zero-down-payment, zero-interest deal. And the pickup was practically one of a kind.

"It's a great truck, but my budget is kinda strained right now." Moon hated to say it, but it had to be said. "Maybe I'd better let you take it back."

The cheerful salesman hated to tell his customer this, but there was a stiff penalty for return of the vehicle. Check the contract.

The rancher had a copy of the document on his desk. "I didn't see anything about a penalty."

Happy Dan directed him to page 16, subparagraph II-A.

Moon turned the pages, squinted. "That's so small I can't read a word of it."

His visual acuity was hardly the issue, the dealer informed him. The important fact was that Moon had put his John Henry on the agreement.

"If I can't come up with the monthly payments, I sure as heck can't afford the penalty."

Finding this remark hilarious, Happy Dan laughed in Moon's ear. After regaining his composure, the businessman suggested that the rancher get back to him. Soon. Pointed out that he could have one of his flunkies out there to pick up the pickup before Moon could say the machine's digitized name, which was Betty Lou. With that cheerful threat, Happy hung up.

Immediately, there was a knock.

Moon turned to stare at the door. *Surely not . . .*

CHAPTER SIXTY-TWO

METAMORPHOSIS

BUT OF COURSE, IT WAS NOT A REPRESENTATIVE OF HAPPY Dan's Custom Trucks and Vans who knocked on Charlie Moon's door. Even so, the rancher was surprised to see this particular person standing on his porch, and the sleek black Cadillac parked under a naked cottonwood branch.

Bertram Eustace Cassidy considered the Ute with a grave expression. "Charles, we must talk."

The rancher opened the door wide. "Come inside."

"No." The unexpected caller pointed at the river, slipping effortlessly over black boulders. "We shall go down there." Without waiting for a response, Bertie led the way.

Pulled along by his curiosity, Moon followed.

Bertie stopped on the rocky bank. For the first time in his life, the soft, bald, city-bred man hooked his thumbs under his belt. To punctuate this excess, he spat on the ground.

Moon wondered what was up, and posed the question to his guest.

"Charles, I am highly dissatisfied with my life. I do not have a serious profession. I have neither a wife nor a home of my own. Even the automobile I drive belongs to Auntie Jane." He fell into a dark silence before picking up his monologue. "This being my sorry condition, I have decided to be finished with it all." He left the grim suggestion hanging by its neck.

The Ute squatted at the river's edge, watched the setting sun's crimson reflection dance on the rippling mirror.

The visitor seated himself on a basalt boulder. "I have decided to shuffle off my superficial persona—to expose the shining inner self. I shall be transformed, from despicable caterpillar to splendiferous butterfly."

Moon sensed that a response was expected. "Sounds like a good move."

"I am gratified to know that you approve." Bertie's round face broke into a grin; the effect was that of a small pink melon splitting. "Because for the metamorphosis to be ultimately successful, your cooperation will be required."

The Ute turned to give Mr. Cassidy a suspicious look. "Would you run that by me one more time?"

Bertram Eustace Cassidy met the Indian's flinty gaze without flinching. "I will need your help."

Moon played for time. "I don't know much about caterpillars or butterflies."

"That was merely a transitional metaphor. The more concrete fact is—I wish to become exactly what you are."

Moon cocked his head at the pale man. "You want to be a Ute?"

Bertie threw up his hands. "Of course not—am I a silly child? Why on earth would I wish to become a feather-bonneted, spear-chucking, drum-beating aboriginal? I mean, that is the most ludicrous, most . . ." He ran out of words.

Charlie Moon took it all in stride. "The tribe will be very disappointed."

Bertie set his jaw. "I shall attempt to make my intentions perfectly clear. I want—no, I *hanker* to be a cowboy."

The stockman smiled. "You're joshing me, right?"

Bertie shook his shiny head. "In my entire life, I have never been more earnest."

"Well, Earnest—it's still a more-or-less free country. Buy yourself a big Tom Mix hat and a knobby-kneed cayuse and go galloping across the plains. Get falling-down drunk on rotgut whiskey. Play crooked poker with shifty-eyed villains." The Ute added with a twinkle in his eye, "And shoot yourself some bloodthirsty, feather-bonneted, spear-chucking, drum-beating aboriginals."

"Please, Charles—do not patronize me. I mean to be the real McCoy—a dusty, dirty, rip-snorting, grit-in-my-craw cowboy."

Charlie Moon got to his feet. The sun had settled easily into the saddle on Dead Mule Notch and was about to ride away. "Bertram, it is one thing to play at being a motion-picture cowboy. But being a real working stockman, that is another thing entirely."

"I realize that. During the past few weeks, I have researched the subject exhaustively."

"Good for you. But you can't learn a trade like cowboyin' by reading books."

"I am willing to start at the bottom, work my way up."

"You willing to shovel manure twenty hours a day?"

"If called upon, I will wade up to my knees in the stuff."

"How about doctoring sick horses that kick you in the face for your trouble. Sleeping in a drafty, flea-infested bunkhouse with a dozen smelly cutthroats that snore loud enough to drown out a tornado. Drinking muddy water six yards downstream from a bloated steer. All this for a few dollars a day and cold beans. And did I mention riding fences in sixty-mile-an-hour sandstorms?"

Bertie's eyes glinted. "Riding across the *lone prairie* on a noble steed? Why, I would do it for nothing."

Moon realized that drastic action was called for. He turned, pointed to the corral where a gimpy old cowhand was saddling up a decidedly ignoble steed. "You have any idea who that is?"

Bertram Eustace Cassidy shook his head.

"I call him Robert Finnegan. Most of the hands call him Sissy Bob."

Bertie blushed to hear such a shameful name. "Why do they call him that?"

"It's because of something that happened a long time before I owned the Columbine." The rancher hesitated. "But I guess it would not be right to tell you about it."

"Oh no, you *must* tell me!"

"All right, then—if I must. About thirty years ago, on a

blustery day in March, Robert was working alone on the low, marshy section over by the Buckhorns. With no warning at all, the white stuff started to fall real heavy. Now, snow didn't bother him none, so he just kept at his job—which was setting a line of cedar fence posts. Things was going along fairly well when something really terrible happened. It pains me just to think about it." The storyteller paused as if he might not be able to continue.

Bertie clenched his hands into fists. "What?"

"He stepped on a rusty old bear trap that'd probably been there for sixty-two years or more." The Ute's expression was deathly grim. "Faster'n a woodpecker's peck, Robert's left foot got snapped half off."

Bertie cringed. "That is absolutely *ghastly.*"

"You took the words right outta my mouth." Moon went on with his narrative. "That trap was chained to an iron spike that was driven into the ground, which was froze solid at the time. Robert couldn't get to his tools, and he didn't have a folding knife in his pocket, so he had no choice but to take drastic action." He waited for Bertie to ask him, "What did he do?"

"What did he do?"

"He used his teeth."

"His *teeth?*"

Moon nodded. "Robert gnawed his foot off just above the ankle."

Bertie blanched as if he had been slapped in the face. "That is simply astonishing. Even if a man had the raw courage to do such a thing, I would not have thought that he would be able to get his mouth that close to his foot—"

"Robert was a lot younger then, and a good deal more supple."

"Well, that is really the most amazing, almost unbelievable—"

"Yes it is. After Robert had chewed himself outta the bear trap, he dipped the bloody stump in a bucket of hot tar."

"Why did he happen to have hot—"

"For coating the bottom of the fence posts." Moon picked up the pace: "After that, Robert tries to get onto his horse. But his mount gets spooked by all the blood and tar, and off he canters, clippity-clop, clippity-clop." He paused to admire his way with words. "After he cusses that horse from here to breakfast, Robert breaks off a willow sapling and makes himself a crutch. What he has in mind is to hobble all the way back to the Columbine headquarters. Now, this was no small thing to do. On the way, he has to wade through eight or nine icy streams, cross over any number of steep ridges and deep arroyos—and all this during the worst blizzard this country's seen in eighty years. And by now the snow is a yard deep, three or four times that much in the drifts." As he contemplated such an admirable feat, the Ute's dark features took on a rapt expression. "This is a hike of twenty-five miles. But ol' Robert is tough as a fifty-cent steak; he makes it back alive."

Tears pearled up in Bertie's eyes. "I am almost too moved to speak."

"Did I mention that a pack of starving timber wolves trails him half the way home, and Robert beats one of 'em to death with his crutch?"

Bertie shook his head.

"Well, he did just that." Moon pulled down the brim of his hat, hoped Bertie would remember to ask.

After a puzzled frown twisted his brow, Bertie asked, "But why do the men call him Sissy?"

"Oh, that." The Ute looked toward the corral, where the crippled old cowboy was loading a few hand tools into a saddlebag. "Robert might not want me to tell you."

"Well, I certainly would not want to hear any scandalous gossip." Every cell in Bertie's body ached to know.

Moon lowered his voice to a conspiratorial tone: "You'd have to swear not to ever repeat it to a living soul."

Bertie crossed his heart.

"When Robert got back and told the other cowboys what'd happened, the fellas in the bunkhouse thought it was another one of his jokes. See, he was a big cutup—always pulling chairs out from under the boys, dropping bear-sign in the Mulligan stew—clever pranks like that. So they took a doubtful look at that twenty-pound gob of tar at the end of his leg and figured his foot was still in there. While five or six of 'em held ol' Robert down, the others began to pull that tar boot off." The storyteller assumed a pained expression. "And when they did, I guess it must've hurt something awful. Anyway, when the tar finally popped loose, ol' Robert sorta yelped."

"Yelped?"

Moon nodded. "And that's why they call him Sissy Bob."

"But—how *awesomely* unfair!"

"Maybe. But it's what a cowboy comes to expect."

"Gruesome and unjust though it is, your account of the old cowboy's tragic self-amputation does not discourage me in the least from pursuing my chosen vocation. Much to the contrary, I am all the more convinced that riding my pony on the wide-open range is the only life for me."

The Ute shook his head. "Bertram, I'm sorry to say this—but you might as well forget it. You don't have any applicable skills. There's not a stockman in the world that'd hire you on."

The small man set his jaw. "There is one."

"And who would that be?"

"You."

The rancher shook his head. "It will never happen, Mr. Cassidy."

"*Au contraire, Monsieur Lune*—it will happen. And within the hour."

Moon's interest was aroused. "What've you got in mind—some kinda bribe?" He hoped it would be hard cash. And plenty of it.

Bertie shook his head. "What I have in mind is vicious, filthy—blackmail."

Moon laughed in his face. "Is that a sure-enough fact?"

"You can bet your boots and saddle."

Despite the seeming absurdity of the man's threat, Moon felt an uneasy coldness settle in his gut. "You figure you got something on me?"

Bertie glared at the Ute. "I am morally certain that you, sir, have committed a flagrant piece of flummery."

Moon requested clarification.

"By some means, you discovered the location of the loot

burgled from the Cassidy Museum. I do not know how you got the stuff off that precipitous cliff ledge—but by some method or another, you most certainly did."

Moon tried to smile, botched the job. "You been smoking Jimsonweed?"

"Oh, bosh and piffle—I am onto you and you know it." Bertie gave him a very odd look. "And you will not deny it."

The Ute turned his gaze to the remnants of the sunset. The sky above the Misery range was on fire.

Moon's accuser cleared his throat. "I surmise that soon after you recovered the Cassidy valuables, you brought them to my aunt. Your intention was to return her property with no thought of asking for a reward." *That is the sort of man you are—a genuine straight shooter.* "But when you arrived, Auntie Jane was even more rude than usual. She shrieked and screamed herself hoarse—and the old witch fired you on the spot." Bertie watched the Ute's frozen profile. "That was when you decided to collect the reward. Not that I blame you, of course." His round face took on an expression of pure adoration. "It was, in fact, that single bold act that caused me to admire you more than any other living human being. To wit—"

"To what?"

"Please do not criticize my manner of speech. This is my account, I shall tell it in the manner that suits me."

"Sorry. Go right ahead."

"To wit—you scribbled that barely legible note to your lawyer with your own crafty hand." He pointed at Moon. "You, sir, are Yellow Jacket!"

The accused gave Bertram Eustace Cassidy a dark look.

"Charles, I know what you are thinking. You're thinking, He doesn't have any proof."

I'm thinking I oughta throw you in the river, laugh, and clap my hands when you go bobbing downstream like an empty jug.

"But I do not need proof—not the kind required in a court of law. All I need do is plant some doubt about you in Walter Price's mind. Your attorney is a very mean-spirited fellow. If Walter should come to harbor a suspicion that you snookered him into helping you fleece my aunt out of a fortune—he would make your life utterly miserable. And you know that I am right."

In an effort to roll this issue over to the left side of his brain, Moon tilted his head. "Let me get this straight. If I don't hire you on at the Columbine, you're sayin' you'll make trouble for me with my legal counsel?"

"Indeed I am." Bertie stiffened his back. "And I most certainly shall."

"I am surprised at you." Moon watched a cutthroat trout slice the river's shimmering surface. "Spreading inflammatory tales about a man is a low-down thing to do."

"Sticks and stones will shatter my bones, but words . . . et cetera."

Moon noted that there were several sizable stones close at hand. And a big stick.

Bertram Eustace Cassidy rubbed his pudgy palms together. "So—what do you say?"

Charlie Moon looked down his nose at the miniature blackmailer. "Making threats may be how things are done where you come from. But it is not the Cowboy Way."

This hurt, but Bertie stood his ground. "I don't give a hoot about the Cowboy Way. If you do not hire me on, I will tell Walter Price that you flimflammed him."

"No you won't."

Bertie's eyes goggled. "I won't?"

Moon's face was hard as steel. "Not if you value your life."

Miss Cassidy's nephew felt a delicious surge of fear. "Do you intend some kind of physical violence to my person?"

"I did think about dropping your sorry carcass into a tub of boiling pig fat. But there's lots better things to do with lard—and a better way to handle an ornery cuss like you."

"That sounds very much like a threat." Bertie assumed a lopsided Billy the Kid sneer he'd once seen on the silver screen. "Whatever happened to the Cowboy Way?"

"That is for *one hundred percent* cowboys. It is true that I raise beeves and wear a John B. Stetson hat. But deep down, I am a sure-enough redskin—the kind who will stop at nothing to get even with his enemies." Moon grinned wickedly at the little man. "You mess with me, I will turn you over to a certain party who is not as meek and mild as myself."

The small man stared owlishly. "Who?"

The Ute had never looked so savage. "I will tell Auntie Jane on you."

Bertie's skin took on a chalky-gray complexion. "Tell her *what*?"

"How you and Ralph Briggs set up the museum burglary."

"That is utterly absurd. Why on earth would I—"

"Because your aunt made up her mind to insure the Cassidy collection."

"You are shooting in the dark."

"Let's see if I hit what I'm shooting at." He aimed a finger at Bertie, cocked it with his thumb. "You knew the insurance company would send a passel of experts to examine and appraise every piece in the museum—and find out that most of those rare old coins weren't so rare anymore. And they weren't even old."

B. E. Cassidy looked as if he might faint. And fall back in it.

Moon hammered away without mercy. "They weren't even real coins, were they, Bertram? They were junk your partner provided to replace the good stuff he'd been selling off for you."

Bertie saw no option but to tough it out. "You are bluffing."

"I am holding aces and kings. After your aunt fired me, I had some time to think. And I thought I'd show the stolen coins to a collector down in Santa Fe who is a world-class expert. This noted numismatist told me they were all modern castings."

"So what if they are? That proves noth—"

"When I visited your buddy Ralph Briggs in the hospital, I told him that if Yellow Jacket's alleged pennies, half dimes, and silver dollars turned out to be duds, I'd be able to tell Jane Cassidy that a pair of slickers had set up the museum burglary—and name names." Moon grinned at his victim. "Do you see where I'm going?"

Bertie did see. He did not like the destination.

"I figured that if Ralph was your partner, he'd tip you off that I was onto the counterfeit scheme—and tell you to make sure Aunt Jane didn't bring in any experts to check out the Yellow Jacket loot. And about two minutes and ten seconds after I left his hospital room, he dialed your telephone number and did just what I'd hoped he would."

Bertie was shocked at such underhanded subterfuge. "You were listening to our conversation?"

"Not me. It was the rabbit."

Bertie looked perplexed.

"I brought Ralph a toy rabbit to keep him company. But this was not your regular run-of-the-mill toy cottontail. This bunny had a microphone in his mouth and a tape recorder in his belly—the voice-activated kind. I've only got Ralph's side of the conversation, but he mentions you by name half a dozen times."

"Isn't that illegal? I mean recording a conversation without permission—"

"The tape won't have to be played in a courtroom, Bertram. But if a certain rich lady by the name of Jane happens to get a microcassette in the mail and she pops it into a player and hears Ralph Briggs talking to somebody by the name of Bertie about how Charlie Moon is onto their scam and how Bertie had better make sure his aunt don't hire a qualified numismatist to check out the substitute coins"— Moon paused to take a breath—"because that's what that Indian cop is hoping for, I expect that'd get the job done."

Bertie stuck a pair of little fingers into his ears. "I absolutely refuse to hear another word of this."

Moon pulled one of Bertie's fingers out of a small, pinkish ear and spoke into the orifice: "Yessiree—when Auntie Jane finds out her favorite nephew has been selling off the family heirlooms, Bertram is in big, bad trouble. Even if I tell her it was Ralph Briggs that came up with the notion of arranging a burglary to get rid of the counterfeits."

Bertie unblocked the other ear. "You think me incapable of such a clever plan? I deeply resent that."

"Sorry if I hurt your feelings. But there's no doubt at all it was Ralph who talked Felix Navarone into stealing the fake stuff you'd leave out of the vault." He eyed the curator of the Cassidy collection. "Navarone was supposed to turn the loot over to Ralph for a set price. And once Ralph had his hands on the stolen goods, he would've made sure nobody ever saw the counterfeit coins. I expected he would've melted 'em down, made himself a nice pair of bookends. Then the both of you would've been in the clear."

Bertie attempted a snort. "That is an uncommonly amusing theory."

Moon grinned at his singular audience. "But no matter how hard we plan, things always go wrong. This time, just about everything turned sour. First of all, Felix took Eddie Ganado on for a partner—and Ganado was even greedier than Felix. When this fine pair of felons had a look at what they got away with, they must've decided that whatever Ralph Briggs had offered to pay for the loot wasn't nearly enough. But when Felix called the antique dealer on the phone and demanded more money, Ralph was not willing. This irked Felix no little bit, so he threatened to tip off the police about how Ralph is the brains behind the burglary." Moon shook his head. "This was a big mistake on Felix's part. That antique dealer may not look it, but our Mr. Briggs is not an hombre to mess with. Ralph called Felix's bluff. He'd take his chances with the law, stack his word up against the Apache's. But just in case Felix does rat him out, Ralph tells me about the call from the burglar. He even tells me some of the truth—that when he refused to deal with the caller, the thief got all hot and threatened to tell the police that the well-known antique dealer is up to his ears in the burglary. If Felix ever tells his story to the authorities, this makes me a first-rate witness for Ralph." Moon eyed his adversary. "Are you still with me?"

Bertie shrugged.

"Well, I'll leave out the part about how Eddie Ganado overheard me talking to Ralph Briggs on the telephone. Figuring Ralph was going to hire me to hunt down the thieves, Ganado dropped by that night and took a pop at Ralph with Jacob Gourd Rattle's .22. And if Miss James hadn't yelled, Ganado might've nailed me too."

"I regret that deplorable incident," Bertie said. "I detest violence."

"Me too. Especially when I'm on the receiving end." Moon flipped a pebble into the stream. "You've been a bad boy, Bertram. And your aunt Jane is a mean and spiteful lady. If she finds out you are responsible for all this trouble and expense, she will make your life miserable. And you know I'm right."

The white man's mouth gaped in the manner of a hooked carp. There was a choking gurgle, but no distinguishable words emerged.

The western sky was stained with swaths of shocking pink and deep purple. The Ute watched a fat moon rise over the wide valley. "How much did you and Ralph Briggs get for the coins you've been selling?"

Bertie sniffed. "I have been wondering how much of my aunt's one-million-dollar reward money you were able to keep. After Walter Price took his cut off the top."

"You first."

"Oh, very well. The total take for the coins was just under eight hundred thousand dollars. Ralph's fee was thirty percent."

Moon offered his financial report. "Walter Price took fifteen percent and some expenses."

B. E. Cassidy did the calculations in his head. "So you netted somewhat under eight hundred and fifty thousand dollars."

"Somewhat." Moon had delivered quite a tidy sum to Kicks Dogs, who would never know from where the greenbacks came. The balance had gone to purchase the Big Hat Ranch. It was, he thought, money well earned and spent.

"You did quite well, Charles. I'm surprised Walter didn't take half."

"You ended up with quite a nice piece of change yourself, Bertram."

"Not really."

"What happened—you blow your whole wad in Vegas?"

"Alas, it was much worse than that. After you separated Auntie Jane from her million, the old witch was absolutely determined to insure the Cassidy collection. Ralph and I were back to square one—as you have so aptly pointed out, the appraisers would have spotted the counterfeit coins, and quite possibly exposed what Ralph and I had done."

Please tell me that you did what I hope you did.

He did. "Ralph and I were compelled to purchase the counterfeit coins from my aunt."

Moon was thunderstruck with delight.

"The purchase was indirect, of course. I told Auntie Jane that Ralph Briggs had been approached by a wealthy Japanese collector. It took some time to persuade her to part with them, but I finally convinced the old hag that the coins had been more trouble than they were worth. Though it was very difficult for him, Ralph came up with almost half the purchase price. This was a great help, but I have only about ninety thousand dollars left in my account." Bertie was close to tears. "But the question is, Where do we go from here? I have something on you, you have something on me."

"Looks to me like your standard Mexican standoff."

The Man Who Would Be Cowboy sized up the situation and came to a drastic conclusion. "Charles, I wish to state that I am withdrawing my threat to make trouble for you with your hateful and vengeful attorney."

"Okay, Bertram. Then I guess I don't have any need to tell your aunt what you and Ralph Briggs was up to."

"Sadly, I am back where I started." Bertie took off his jacket. "I have nothing left to live for." He grunted as he pulled off his expensive wing-tip shoes. "In case you are mildly curious about how this shall end, I intend to throw myself into the depths of the river."

"Bertram, the stream is running low. You won't drown right off—you'll get beat to death on the rocks."

The pale man unbuttoned his canary-yellow silk shirt. "Forgive me the vulgarity—but quite frankly, I don't give a gnat's extraordinarily tiny excretory orifice how I shall expire." Effecting a theatric gesture, he tossed the costly garment aside.

"Well, there's *me* to think of."

Bertram unlatched a mother-of-pearl belt buckle. "You?"

"Sure. I'm the poor fella who'll have to wade in and pull

your cold, blue, water-wrinkled body outta the stream. You'll look like a prune that sprouted arms and legs." Moon's expression suggested an acute attack of nausea. "It'll be so disgusting, I won't be able to eat my supper."

"I do regret the deleterious effect on your appetite. But there is no reason to alter my course." Tears of self-pity filled his eyes. "Besides, no one will miss me."

"Oh, I doubt that."

He gave the Ute a wet, squinty look. "Will you regret my passing?"

Moon nodded. "Life won't be the same without you. I'll be upset for several minutes."

"That is quite touching. Nevertheless, I am obliged to jump into the river." He stepped out of one leg of his blue suede trousers.

"Wait—hold on there!"

Bertie paused. "If you have something to say, please get on with it. I am beginning to feel unpleasantly chilly and prickly."

"Put your pants back on."

"Why should I?"

"Because I can't stand to look at those shorts you're wearing. They've got little baby ducks on 'em."

"Is that all?"

"No, there's some teddy bears too."

"Oh, pshaw! I mean—is that all you have to say?"

"Step back into your britches, Bertram—I'll give you a job."

This could be a trick. "What kind of position do you have in mind?"

"I don't know exactly. We'll work something out."

"Will I get a horse to ride?"

"Sure. You can pitch your saddle on a nice little brush-tail mare we call Sweet Alice." *She's already crippled up three good riders.*

Bertram Eustace Cassidy drifted off into a glassy-eyed rapture. His words were as from one lost in a lovely dream: "Charles—may I tote a .44-caliber Colt six-shooter?"

"You can tote a brace of mortars for all I care." *With any luck at all, he'll fall off the horse and shoot himself.*

He stepped back into the breeches. "Charles?"

"Yeah?"

The chilly man buckled his belt. "I must make a confession—I really wish I could have succeeded in blackmailing you."

"You are a really nasty fellow, Bertram. A natural-born felon and cutthroat."

He slipped into his shirt. "It is apparent that you agreed to hire me on because you feel sorry for me."

"Well, if I ever did, I have got over it. As a matter of fact, if you want to strip buck naked and jump in the river, go right ahead. I won't pull your body out—your sorry carcass can float all the way down to the *Golfo de California*." Moon turned away. "I'm going back to the house."

Carrying his shoes, Bertie minced along behind the Ute. "I wish I had been able to effectively carry out my threat—extort you out of something more tangible than a job. I should like to have had something that was really important to you."

"Like what?"

"Oh, I don't know. Your favorite quarter horse. A perfectly balanced Winchester rifle. A section of prime grazing land. Something really *special*."

Charlie Moon stopped in midstride. "Bertram, if you're going to be a cowboy, you've got to learn how to keep your mouth shut for hours at a time. You could start practicing right now by not saying another word for a whole minute."

"Of course. Certainly." Bertie's brow furrowed into a frown. "I almost forgot. There is one more thing."

"What?"

"When you visited Ralph in the hospital, you showed him a small wooden box—which you claimed contained all of your evidence on the museum burglary. He was quite rattled by this mysterious assertion, as was I when he told me. In fact, that cursed box was a major reason I did not reveal the fact that the Yellow Jacket coins were counterfeits. I could have, you know. No one could have proven that the thieves had not made the substitution . . . unless . . . Charles—I want know what was in the box."

"Why should I give two hoots about what you want to know?"

"You needn't be so testy. Besides, as I am to be your employee, there should be some level of trust between us. Think of it as a gesture to prove your goodwill."

"I don't have any goodwill left for you."

Bertie stamped his bare foot. "Charles, I simply *must* know!"

"Then ask your partner in crime."

"Ralph Briggs has the box?"

"He should. I sent it to him a coupla days ago." The thought made Moon smile.

CHAPTER SIXTY-THREE

THE BOX

AT PROMPTLY HALF PAST THREE, THE UNITED STATES MAIL was delivered to The Compleate Antiquarian. Among the assortment of bills, advertisements, magazines, and catalogs was a small parcel. It had an illegible return address, a crisp Durango postmark.

What could it be?

The possibilities were titillating and practically endless.

With all the enthusiasm of a hopeful child on Christmas morning, Ralph Briggs used a sixteenth-century Florentine dagger to slit the brown paper wrapping. What he found inside was a surprise—the tribal investigator's little cedar box. Taped on the lid was a handwritten note from the Ute.

The message gave him pause.

THE AFTERNOON dragged on.

Perilously close to bankruptcy, ego terribly wounded, the antiquarian sat alone in the half-light of his immaculately appointed office. In a vain attempt to soothe his jangled nerves, he sipped straight gin from a crystal goblet. For the forty-ninth time, he read the enigmatic note:

Ralph—
    I made you a promise, so here it is.

But take my advice and do NOT open the box.
Set fire to it—burn it to ashes.

C. Moon.

He was afraid to flaunt the sly Indian's advice. Something bad would be inside. But he could not endure the rest of his life without knowing. Moon had assured him that in the box was the sum total of the hard evidence on the Cassidy Museum burglary. Enough, apparently, to send two respectable citizens to prison—*if* the stolen coins had been identified as counterfeits.

Minutes passed like snails in low gear.

A lemon-tinted sun fell behind the willows.

Twilight arrived with an expectant hush.

It must be done. He held his breath, gingerly pressed the button under the brass latch.

The spring-loaded lid yawned open.

Ralph Briggs frowned at the contents—five playing cards.

A three and a nine of spades.

Five of clubs.

Seven of hearts.

Jack of diamonds.

It took a few irregular heartbeats for understanding to dawn on the unfortunate man. The tribal investigator had shown his hand—his *nothing* hand. Briggs sat in stunned silence, stared at the mocking display. *Moon was holding trash. He had no proof that Bertie and I planned the burglary. It was another empty bluff—and I folded!*

Enraged, he drove the Florentine dagger through the jack of diamonds, impaling it to the Chippendale mahogany desk that heretofore had not the slightest blemish.

Oh no—what have I done?

Ralph Briggs clenched his hands into fists, beat them on the mutilated Chippendale. *I will get you for this, Charlie Moon. Just you wait and see.*

CHAPTER SIXTY-FOUR

MONTHS LATER

THE COWBOY TURNED THE BIG TRUCK INTO THE CHUCK-wagon drive-up, expertly nosed it into a space between a pair of small sedans.

Spotting the killer pickup, the carhop made a mad dash and was outside before the shining red behemoth had lurched to a rocking stop at station 10. Within a few strides of the F-350, Shirley Spoletto was unnerved by the sudden realization that Charlie Moon was not behind the wheel. In fact, there seemed to be no one at all in the cab. And then she saw the cowboy hat, its peak barely even with the top of the steering wheel. Shirley approached the vehicle with the righteous suspicion of a woman who was expecting a prince but has been offered a warty-skinned frog. The gum-chewing waitperson looked into the open window.

The lean cowboy wore faded jeans, a partially unbuttoned blue flannel shirt. His hands were scratched and callused from hard work. The face that looked back at her from under the sweat-soaked Stetson was sunburned, the blue eyes merry. "Howdy."

She sized up the half-pint. "Howdy yourself." Shirley remembered her current profession. "What'll you have?"

He winked. "What've you got, dream of my heart?"

Having heard a hundred better lines, the footsore carhop rolled her eyes. "Route 666 burgers, Tater Tots, hot fudge sundaes, and so on." She pointed at the sign. "It's all wrote down there."

The fellow touched the brim of his hat. "You want to see something awesome?"

Her eyes narrowed dangerously. "You do something obscene—I'll punch you right in the snout."

He removed the Stetson, exposing a head that—except for a brown horseshoe of fuzz set snugly above his ears—was as bald and pale as a peeled white onion.

She jumped back. "Ugh—what is that?" It appeared to be some kind of horrible disease.

"Look closer, my golden-tressed wench."

"You watch your smart mouth." Shirley leaned forward for a better look, clasped a hand over her mouth. "Eeeeew!" She had once seen a similar case on her favorite documentary television show, and knew right away what it was. "You got a lotta little blue brain-eating worms wriggling around under your skin—I saw that very same thing on *X-Files!*"

"Not so," said the cowboy. "It is a work of manly art. A hairy-faced Picasso in Pueblo applied it with carefully sterilized needles and organic ink." He tapped a finger on his skull. "Surely you recognize the famous subject that has been so skillfully depicted upon the epidermal canvas of my spherical member."

"It's only a tattoo?" Somewhat relieved, the carhop leaned closer still. "It better not be somethin' dirty, or I'll poke a thumb in your eye." She stared long and hard, finally shook her head. "What's it supposed to be?"

The owner of the artistic work made no attempt to hide his shock at her ignorance. "Why, it is obviously a map of Lower Mesopotamia—as it would have appeared in the latter portion of the sixth century, B.C."

She gave the bubble gum a good chew. "I think it's gross."

"Your words cut me to the marrow. This was a very expensive tattoo."

"Well, if it cost six bits, you paid too much. I still say it's a bunch of worms." She snickered. "Maybe they're tryin' to look like hair."

This suggested another approach: "Listen, toots—d'you know what leads to male pattern baldness?"

She thought about it. "Some kinda geek gene?"

"A natural assumption for one of your stunning limitations, but you are in error." He puffed up his chest. "The root cause of the dearth of hair on my head is—excess *testosterone*."

"Hah." She smirked. "That's a good one."

"A pithy rejoinder, my golden-haired Aphrodite erudite, but the baldness-testosterone correlation is a scientifically verifiable fact, and you can look it up if you are so inclined. I can quote to you a list of scholarly references in such reputable sources as *The New England Journal of Medicine*, *Archives of Endocrinology*, *The National Enquirer*, and *Soldier of Fortune*—all of which I have memorized for just such occasions as this." He smirked right back at the long-legged blonde.

Somewhat taken aback by this verbal onslaught, Shirley took a moment to regain her natural composure. She glared at the man with worms on his head; her words bore the unmistakable sting of accusation as she tapped the Ford's glistening fender. "Where'd you steal this fancy truck?"

"This magnificent product of Mr. Ford's Kansas City, MO, assembly plant and Happy Dan's Custom Trucks and Vans was a virtual gift. From a generous friend."

"Sez you. I happen to know for a fact that this F-350 belongs to Charlie Moon."

"Not anymore, missy. She is mine now."

"Oh yeah—how'd she come to be yours?"

"Charlie happens to be a buddy of mine—he gave her to me."

"He'd never do no such a thing." Shirley's eyes glinted dangerously. "I flat-out don't believe a word you're saying."

"Next time you see Charlie, ask him yourself. All the equity he had in the vehicle, he generously transferred to me—all I had to do was take over the payments." He placed the wide-brimmed hat back over Lower Mesopotamia, casting that unfortunate land into a darkness that smelled sourly of perspiration. "Would you care to examine the registration?"

Ignoring this challenge, she leaned on the door. "I happen

to know this truck has a name. If a man knows the name, he can start 'er up without the key."

The driver cleared his throat, then: "Go, Betty Lou."

The V-8 engine rumbled to life. Settled down into a throbbing, feline purr.

Jeepers—it really is his truck.

Sensing his advantage, the driver hurried to build on it. "Despite my scruffy appearance and low-paying job, I am a man of some means."

The long-legged kitten felt a purr coming on. She hung her elbows inside the cab. *He is a cute little bunny rabbit.* "My name is Shirley, Worm Head—what's yours?"

The cowboy grinned. "Cassidy, ma'am."

"Hah—I think I've heard a you." She blew a sticky pink bubble, which popped in his face. "You must be *Hopalong* Cassidy."

"Ol' Hoppy may well have been a distant relation of mine." He sniffed to demonstrate his distinct displeasure at the thought. "But I am not cut from the sort of cloth that those fancy movie-star cowboys are made. I have gravel grit in my craw, greased lightning in my draw, and I can whip my weight in wildcats. To sum it up, I am a sure-enough woolly-booger with spurs on."

Having rarely met any other kind of man, Shirley was tolerant of liars and braggarts. "Is that the honest truth?"

"The hard-case cowboys at the ranch—they call me by a descriptive nickname."

She asked what.

The driver of the big red pickup truck told her what.

Shirley giggled. "You kidding me?"

"No, ma'am." The Columbine cowhand tipped his hat. "Butch Cassidy is who I am."

CHAPTER SIXTY-FIVE

DUE RECOGNITION

WHILE HE LISTENED TO HIS INVESTIGATOR'S REPORT, THE tribal chairman deftly tied a tiny blue hummingbird feather onto a long-shanked hook. When Charlie Moon had finished, Oscar Sweetwater put the trout lure into a small plastic box. "That's it?"

Moon nodded. "Felix Navarone is doing his fifteen at a federal jug in West Virginia. Jacob Gourd Rattle's wife has gone home to North Carolina." He glanced at the clock on the wall, remembered his obligation. "I'd better be rolling on down the road. Aunt Daisy is expecting me."

"Tell her I said hello." The old man got up from his desk, gave Moon a stony look. "But before you leave, there's something I want you to see."

Moon clamped the John B. Stetson on his head. "What would that be?"

"Follow me."

Charlie Moon followed Oscar Sweetwater out of the chairman's musty office, down the dimly lighted hallway, out of the tribal headquarters building, across a neatly kept lawn, under the branches of a leafy maple.

At the edge of the parking lot, the elected leader of the Southern Utes stopped at a newly painted-off space. A sturdy wooden signpost was at the curb. The sign was wrapped in shiny red paper; this covering was secured with a blue ribbon that blossomed into a festive bow. "Remember what you asked for?"

Moon stared in amazed disbelief. His request for a private parking space had been a joke. This hard-nosed old politician didn't have a sense of humor. "Look, Oscar, you didn't need to—"

The chairman raised his hand for silence. "You've been doing good work for the tribe. And I guess I'm not too good at letting people know how much they're appreciated. I figured this was the least I could do." He gazed expectantly at his part-time employee. "Well, ain't you gonna undo the wrapping?"

Moved by this unexpected kindness, Charlie Moon tore the crimson paper off. Atop the square pine post was a thick set of cedar boards. The assembly was two feet long, almost a foot high. On the side facing the parking space, a gifted craftsman had etched deep letters into the wood: RESERVED C MOON.

C Moon swallowed the lump in his throat. "Thanks, Oscar. That's really nice."

"There's more inside. Open it up."

The tribal investigator noticed that the sign board was hinged on one end; he pulled on the other. There was more inside. A glistening silver parking meter.

The flag was showing red.

Oscar Sweetwater had been waiting for years to line this smart aleck young buck up in his sights—and pull the trigger. As he saw the look of astonishment spread across his victim's face, the marksman knew he'd nailed him good. Oscar laughed so hard he had to lean on the parking meter for support.

Charlie Moon watched the chairman haw-haw and gasp and wheeze. *Silly old geezer.*

CHAPTER SIXTY-SIX

THE SHAMAN'S NEW FRIEND

THE LEAN MAN TOWERED ABOVE HIS AGED AUNT. THE MIS-matched pair made their way along a deer trail that meandered among boulders, scrub oak, and clumps of yucca spears. Aside from the occasional scuffing sound of boot or shoe, they enjoyed a companionable silence that melded into the vast stillness in *Cañon del Espiritu*.

Finally, Daisy Perika decided to speak to her nephew. She watched his long shadow—spoke to it, as if the sliver of darkness were an extension of his soul. "Did you know that some of the People think you was the one who stranded that Apache on the Witch's Tongue?"

The talking drums never stopped. "Do they, now?"

"It is bad manners to answer an elder's question with another question."

Moon allowed himself a smile. "Is it?"

"Don't get sassy with me." Daisy tapped him on the shin with her walking stick. "But whenever I hear that kind of gossip, I set 'em straight. I say, 'Don't you go accusing my nephew of doing something like that.' "

"Thank you. I appreciate your vote of confidence—"

"It don't have anything to do with confidence. I *know* you didn't do it."

"How do you know?"

"Oh, I have my ways." She smiled. "Sometimes I see what

happens with my own eyes. Other times, them that sees things come and tell me."

Moon thought he would let that dog sleep.

The tribal elder stopped to lean on her oak staff. She stared at the shadow's head. "You want to know who's been telling me stuff?"

"It depends."

"On what?"

"On whether the person in question is still within the reach of the law."

She thought about it. "Not the kind of law you're talking about."

I thought so. Charlie Moon put an arm around her shoulders. "I bet I can guess."

"Try."

"Okay. Jacob Gourd Rattle's ghost rose up from the grave. He comes and talks with you."

She shook her head. "Jacob's spirit hasn't been around to see me yet." A pause. "But another one has."

Moon hoped she would not tell him.

"It was that *matukach* who worked for our Ute police department."

He felt a sting of surprise. "Jim Wolfe?"

The shaman nodded. "Back in October, he came here with his father and mother."

"His parents are dead too?"

"No. Last time I saw 'em, Tobias and his Okie missus was warm as you or me."

"What were they doing here?"

"They came to thank me for helping put their son's murderer in the penitentiary." *And to give me something, Some nights I wake up wishing I had took it.* "But when his folks went back to Oklahoma, Jim Wolfe stayed here with me. We're good friends now."

Charlie Moon did not want to hear it.

Daisy was determined to tell him. "Jim has told me lots of things, and some of it's pretty strange."

Her nephew was not surprised.

"Like about that time when you told him not to let the nickel fall off the whiskey glass, but it happened right after you left the saloon—and he never did get it out of the crack in the floor. Jim said that was when his luck started to go bad." She watched her nephew's face. "Does that make any sense?"

He had no answer to that.

"All the time, he tells me, 'I should have listened to Charlie Moon. Charlie always gave me good advice. He is a smart one. But me, I have always been dumb as a stump. Dull-witted as a barnyard turkey, stupid as a—'"

Moon heard the words fall out of his mouth. "Sack of dirt."

"He said you'd say that." She sat down on a ponderosa stump, laid the oak walking stick across her lap. "Anything you'd like to pass on to him?"

Wishing there was a way to make amends for things done and things left undone, Moon thought about it for a long time. The aged woman could serve as his confessor. "I'm sorry about the way things turned out. And I wish I'd helped him a lot more than I did." He smiled at his aunt. "You can tell Jim that."

She responded with a prideful smugness. "Tell him yourself."

The unbeliever felt a clammy coldness creep over his skin. "You're kidding."

"No I'm not."

Moon felt extremely foolish, but had to ask. "Where?"

"He's been right beside you since we left my trailer."

He took a cautious sideways look.

"No, on your left."

He turned his head. "I don't see anything."

"I didn't expect you to." She reached into her pocket, found a lemon drop. "For a *matukach*, Wolfe isn't all that bad. I sorta like him."

"Right." Moon grinned. "But what do you say when he's not around?"

Daisy Perika popped the candy into her mouth. "I'm the only real family you got left." She looked off into the canyon mists, watched a very old lost soul do a macabre dance before a faded petroglyph of a horned snake. "While I'm still here in Middle World, you should treat me with more respect."

"I'm willing to give a try."

She gave him a sly look. "Start by telling me about that package in your coat pocket."

The Ute produced the paper-wrapped parcel. "This is what's known in our traditional culture as 'men's stuff.' So, seeing as how you're a member of the female gender, I should not let you see it. If I break one of the old rules, I might get a headache when the sun goes down."

The shaman glared at her nephew. "Let me see it, or I'll fix you so your brain starts to ache while there's still daylight."

"Let's make a deal."

"I'm listening."

"That's the deal—all you can do is listen. So pay close attention, and tell me what it is." Behind her back, he wrapped the loose end of the leather cord twice around his palm, let the flat-bone piece attached to the other end fall to his ankle.

Slowly at first, Charlie Moon began to swing the thing.

The thin slab of bone began to sing.

Vooooom.

Daisy shook her head.

Louder: *Vooooom.*

"No," she muttered.

Louder still: *Vooooom!*

Moon was enjoying the demonstration. "Jacob Gourd Rattle brought a bullroarer to Snake Canyon; probably to call the spirits of wind and thunder."

"Put it away," the shaman said.

"It's just a noise-making toy—"

Somewhere up there, a heavy rumble of thunder. A damp gust of wind swept down the canyon.

Charlie Moon ceased his demonstration of the groaning board. But only to make his aunt feel better.

By cosmic coincidence, silence and stillness returned to *Cañon del Espiritu.*

Daisy Perika heaved a sigh of relief.

Her nephew looked up at the thin slice of clear blue sky.

The unseen thunderhead was probably somewhere over the mesa. And unexpected winds were always rolling down these canyons.

Knowing the gist of his thoughts, Daisy shook her head. *Fools never learn.*

Moon seated himself on the ground near his aunt.

In a vain attempt to find a more comfortable position, the weary woman shifted her rump on the stump. "I know how you got down onto the Witch's Tongue." There was a mischievous twinkle in her eyes. "And how you got back up again."

"I guess Wolfe told you about that too."

Daisy shot him a crafty look. "He says you used that electric winch—the one on your fancy new pickup truck."

She's guessing. But a mighty good guess it was.

"By the way—whatever happened to that big red truck?"

He felt the merest twinge of guilt. "Somebody else needed it more than I did." *And could afford it more than I could.*

CHAPTER SIXTY-SEVEN

AN OLD, SWEET SONG

THE CATHOLIC PRIEST GOT OUT OF HIS WORN-OUT BUICK, eyed the Expedition with the Columbine logo painted on the door. *So Charlie Moon is visiting his aunt.* Father Raes Delfino peered through his bifocals at Daisy Perika's trailer home. As he climbed the porch steps, the visitor reached for the Logo suspended from his neck on a silver chain. He whispered a prayer for the old woman, another for her nephew.

He tapped on the door. *I will let Daisy know that Charlie has provided me with a quiet place to live.* A fine little cabin near a lake. The priest knocked again. *I wonder where they could be?*

As was so often the case during the course of these blessed days, the answer *came* to him immediately. He turned, stared at the yawning mouth of Spirit Canyon. *Perhaps I should wait here until they return.* Again, the holy man touched the crucifix. *But that might be a long time.*

DAISY PERIKA pointed to a place across the canyon where the cliff was honeycombed with pits and caverns. "You know who's over there."

Her nephew did know. Daisy was referring to his mother's bones. The remains were concealed behind a carefully crafted wall of sandstone. Charlie Moon had put her there, and every year without fail—during the Moon of Dead Leaves Falling—he came to maintain the vault. This mother's son could not find his voice.

"That's where I want you to put me—someplace close to her." Daisy blinked her tired old eyes. "But seal me in good so the varmints don't come and chew on my bones." She gave the young man a sharp look. "You hear what I'm saying?"

A nod from the nephew.

"And tell the women that fix me—I want to be put away in my purple dress. The one with the silver threads stitched into the collar."

He managed to make some words. "That'll be some time yet."

"And if Father Raes is still alive—I want him here when you put me away. He can say some good words over me, sing a song or two. But if he goes before I do, you bring some other Christian minister out here." Another steely glare. "I want you to promise me you'll do what I say."

Moon tugged the brim of his Stetson down, hiding his eyes in the shadow. "I'll see to it."

"Good. Then I'm ready to go." Daisy gripped the walking stick with both hands, got to her feet with a painful grunt. "That feisty little priest is supposed to come by later today, so I guess I'd better be home when he shows up—just so I can twist his tail." Daisy firmly believed that her fondness for Father Raes was a deep secret.

But Charlie Moon knew that the old woman loved the priest. The angels in heaven knew it.

"He's going to retire," she sighed. "And move away somewhere."

"That's what I hear."

They resumed a slow pace toward the mouth of the canyon. Daisy Perika grimaced at a sharp pain in her hip, stopped to lean on her oak walking stick. "It's a long way home."

Her nephew nodded. "But you'll soon be there."

"I wish I was there already. I am *so* tired."

Charlie Moon looked at the cloudless sky, where something circled. Too big for a raven. He thought it might be a hawk.

Daisy also looked up, shaded eyes dimmed with age. *I am in the shadow of His wings.* Feeling stronger, she tugged at Moon's sleeve. "There's one more thing."

Her nephew was not surprised. There always was.

"What's going on between you and that white woman?"

"Which one?"

She groaned. "How many are we talking about?"

"Less than three."

"I want to know about the one whose first name you won't tell me."

"Miss James?"

Daisy nodded.

"She's gone." *And won't be coming back.*

This satisfied the old woman—until she counted to two. "But you have a new girlfriend?"

"I don't know if I should tell you."

Daisy made a menacing gesture with the oak rod. "If you don't, I'll whack you so hard you'll forget your middle name." To emphasize this threat, she gave him a gentle tap.

"I don't have a middle name."

"See, it's working already!"

"What do you want to know?"

"Everything."

"That's quite a lot." He smiled down at black eyes set deep in the wrinkled face. "But I'll tell you about one fine day on the Columbine—a day I spent with this good-looking woman."

She snorted. "Another *white* woman."

He ignored this. "And as we rode along on our nags, me and this pretty lady heard something. It was a man, in the log cabin by the lake. He was singing an old, old song."

Daisy trudged along, pegging at the ground with her walking stick. "What man was this?"

He shook his head. "You are not supposed to ask."

Seeing how much fun her nephew was having, Daisy played along. "Can I ask what old song?"

Moon smiled at the memory of his epiphany on Three Sisters Mesa. "For quite some time, I wasn't sure myself. But later on, I had an inspiration."

"Hah," she said. "That, I would have liked to see."

"Then I will demonstrate." He closed his eyes, concentrated for a moment, then pointed at a spot just above his hat. "Did you notice that lightbulb right up there—and how it just flashed?"

She nodded. "It was a tiny one—the kind a sickly firefly has in its tail."

"Even so, it was enough." He raised his arm to salute the Three Sisters. They were sitting as still as stone, hanging on his every word. "At that very moment, I understood Kicks Dogs' dream about seeing Jacob climbing up a moonbeam."

Another snort. "Silly white woman."

"But it was not a dream," Moon said. "And Jacob was not climbing a moonbeam."

"I know it wasn't no moonbeam." She could not help bragging. "And I know what he *was* climbing."

"I hope you're not going to tell me Jim Wolfe told you."

"I won't say he did, because he didn't." The shaman grinned. "I have other ways of knowing stuff."

"I know you do." The tribal investigator gave her an odd look. "And so do I."

His aunt stared straight back at him. "What do *you* know?"

"I know about the ladder."

Daisy looked away, muttered, "What ladder?"

"The nylon-rope ladder Felix Navarone and Eddie Ganado tossed over the edge of Three Sisters Mesa, so they could climb down to the Witch's Tongue and hide the Cassidy loot. But they let it fall all the way to the bottom of Snake Canyon. Which is why Jacob Gourd Rattle was able to climb up and confront that pair of thieves—and get himself killed for his trouble."

She shrugged, as if to say, *Oh, that ladder.*

Charlie Moon watched her shrink under his gaze. "When Navarone came back to get the Cassidy coins and cameos, he used his rope ladder again. But he was a few days too late; somebody had already been there and took the stuff." Yellow Jacket allowed himself a satisfied smile. "But that Apache's bad luck had just got started. While he was down there, looking for the stuff he'd stashed, somebody pulled the ladder up—left him stranded on the *Uru-suwã-ci Agõ-pi.*"

It took her a dozen heartbeats to muster up the courage;

what finally passed her lips resembled a mouse's squeak: "You have any idea who pulled the ladder up?"

"Yes, I do." Moon's eyes twinkled. "Near the edge of the cliff, stuck on a yucca spike, I found a little piece of wool. Yellow wool." He added, as if it was an afterthought, "Greasewood yellow."

Daisy's greasewood-dyed shawl suddenly weighed her shoulders down. The shaman closed her eyes, looked as if she might slip away from Middle World.

The sworn officer of the law smiled at the ill-tempered old soul. "A little hank of wool doesn't prove that a particular person stranded Navarone on the Witch's *Agō-pi*—just that she was in the vicinity." He patted his aunt on the shoulder. "Anyway, I expect she didn't intend to leave that Apache out there long enough to die."

The Daisy made a grim face. *Don't bet the farm on it.*

"Matter of fact," he added, "I think she had one of her friends call the SUPD dispatcher about a suspicious truck somebody'd left on Three Sisters Mesa—so the tribal police would rescue Navarone."

She opened her eyes, looked longingly toward the mesa, as if memories of happier times might be hidden up there in the mists. "It's too bad all those people had to die."

Moon followed her gaze. "They didn't have to die—they made wrong choices. Eddie Ganado preferred stealing to living by honest work. Jim Wolfe cared more about getting even with Felix Navarone than staying alive."

Charlie always tried to make sense of things, but Daisy saw her chaotic world through a darker lens. "What about Jacob Gourd Rattle—what mistake did he make?"

"Jacob?" Moon thought about it. "Well, I'd say he picked the wrong ladder to climb."

"What do you mean?" She squinted at her enigmatic nephew. "There wasn't another ladder—was there?"

"Sure." Moon's dark eyes sparkled. "There's always another ladder."

This annoyed the crotchety old woman no end. "That don't make any sense."

"I sense that you are a doubter." While Father Raes was still far away, Charlie Moon had seen him coming up the canyon. "If you are ready, I will demonstrate my point."

"I'm ready as I ever will be," Daisy grumped.

Indeed she was.

The happy man threw his head back, boomed out in a voice that could have shattered stones,

We are climb-ing, Jacob's Ladder—

Startled to hear her nephew sing so loud, the old woman laughed.

But Daisy was far more astonished to hear Father Raes's response:

Every round goes higher, high-er!

The elder called out in a raspy, cracking voice so lovely it pierced the hearts of angels,

Sinner do you love my Je-sus?

The priest's voice filled the canyon:

If you love him—why not serve him?

The rhythm of the hymn vibrated in willow limbs.

Blissful syllables ricocheted off ancient stone walls.

All manner of feathered bird, furry beast, scaly reptile— even lowly invertebrates—the whole multitude took time off from their sundry tasks to listen and wonder.

The trio's voices were heard by a three-toed woodpecker. A long-tailed vole. A collared lizard. Even a six-legged juniper hairstreak—a lowly creature of whom hardly anyone ever speaks.

Like the precious days and hours, the song proceeded along its way.

To here, there, and forever.

It mattered not that the vacuum of interstellar space cannot carry sound. Unfettered by lesser laws, the joyful words went forth to Brother Sun, Sister Moon, and well beyond the silent warp of space to penetrate that sly illusion called Time.

So far above them
So very near
Where life and light are eternal
Silver feathers on silver wings
rise up on the wind-song
Soar higher . . . higher

Keep reading for an excerpt from
the next Charlie Moon mystery

SHADOW MAN

AVAILABLE IN HARDCOVER FROM
ST. MARTIN'S MINOTAUR AND JAMES D. DOSS

GRANITE CREEK, COLORADO

AS THE ACCUMULATION OF MANY WINTERS PRESSED HEAVILY upon her, Daisy Perika had become set in her ways. The Ute elder was a contented recluse; the mere thought of being far away from her little home at the mouth of *Cañon del Espiritu* made her shudder. On those occasions when she took a meal in town, Daisy preferred Angel's Diner in Ignacio or Texas-Bob's Barbecue in Durango. But here she was—almost a hundred miles to the north, in Granite Creek—seated at a fancy, linen-covered table in the Stockman's Hotel Restaurant. The shrunken woman was flanked by two sizable men—Southern Ute Tribal Investigator Charlie Moon and Granite Creek Chief of Police Scott Parris. It would have been perfect, except for the fact that FBI Special Agent Lila Mae McTeague was seated directly across from Daisy, who had noticed how the pretty white woman was eyeing her nephew. Worst of all, Charlie was eyeing her right back. Daisy's face was set like granite. *I'll just pretend that she's not here.*

The table's delectable centerpiece was a three-layer strawberry jam cake, its inch-thick pink icing dotted with dozens of red candles. While they watched, Daisy opened her birthday presents.

Charlie's gift was a satellite telephone. It was astonishingly small, and came with a nylon cord so she could hang it around her neck like a pendant.

Daisy Perika muttered her thanks for the gadget, which she

thought resembled a fancy dog collar. When her nephew demonstrated how the thing worked, she grumbled that she could barely make out the tiny labels by the brightly colored buttons, much less read the script on the narrow little gray strip that served as a monitor.

Charlie assured his aunt that he had programmed in all the numbers she would need for an emergency. At the press of this button she would get 911, that one would ring his ranch land line, another one his cell phone. Wearing his now-pay-attention-because-I-am-dead-serious expression, he made it known that he expected her to wear the high-tech communications device all the time. Even when she was taking a bath. Especially when she was out walking in the wild canyon country around her home.

She solemnly vowed that she would, and immediately dismissed the promise from her mind.

Scott's gift was an ebony cane; the head was a hand-carved soapstone owl. This would be nice for going to church, she told him. Daisy had a special affection for the white man, who was her nephew's best friend. She reached over to pat the *matukach* on the arm.

The FBI woman had brought her a lovely parcel—wrapped in embroidered white cotton, tied with a ribbon of Japanese silk. Daisy discovered a lovely Spanish shawl inside, gave it a once-over. *It's probably a Chinese knockoff.* While everyone watched, the shameless old woman found the label, squinted hard at it. Barcelona. *Well. I guess she's trying to impress me.* Which just went to show how calculating and sneaky these man-hunting white women could be.

A Portuguese waiter with the willowy frame of a bullfighter appeared, touched each candle on the cake with a butane wand. Completion of this operation took quite some time.

"Oh, my—look at that." The flames danced in Daisy's eyes. "There's way too many to blow out."

Lila Mae smiled. "Then let them burn."

Daisy pretended not to hear.

The FBI agent felt the slight. It was her face that burned.

By nature oblivious to petty thoughts or malicious intentions, Moon looped a long arm around his shriveled aunt. "Time to wake a wish."

The ancient woman closed her eyes, shook her gray head. "Oh, God—I wish I was eighty again."

This produced a roar of laughter from the men, a brittle smile from Lila Mae.

Charlie Moon sliced the cake, passed ample portions around.

Daisy dug right in.

Lila Mae barely touched the rich dessert.

Sensitive about the tightness developing lately under his belt, Scott Parris left half of his helping behind, but pecked wistfully at the remains with his fork.

Moon, slim as a whip-snake, completed his wedged section, and helped himself to a second serving of the sugary confection.

The second hand on the wall clock went clickety-click.

Old times were recalled, mostly-true stories were told.

During a momentary lull, the waiter brought a silver decanter of steaming coffee. The caffeine-rich beverage triggered further remembrances, even more audacious anecdotes.

In an attempt to break through Daisy's defenses, Lila Mae offered up an account of her sixth birthday party, and a tiny white kitten with a "little pink bow" around its neck. Her father, she recalled, had presented the gift in a root-beer mug. Birthdays were a special time. She flashed her sweetest smile at the Ute elder.

The wicked old woman yawned in her face.

Even Charlie Moon noticed this. He shot his aunt a warning look.

This mild rebuke merely annoyed the birthday girl. *Why did Charlie have to invite that pushy woman anyway? I wish he'd brought along one of my friends instead—like Father Raes Delfino. Why didn't he do something nice like that?* These thoughts produced a deeply satisfying pang of self-righteous pity.

As if he had heard her secret wish, Charlie Moon passed his aunt a small package. "I almost forgot. Father Raes asked me to give you this."

Daisy turned the birthday gift over in her hands. The parcel was wrapped in plain brown paper, tied with a stout length of twine. "Why didn't he bring it himself?"

"He left the Columbine a couple of days ago," Moon said. "He's going to spend a month in Italy."

Daisy sniffed. "I didn't know there was any shortage of priests over there." She borrowed Moon's steak knife to cut the string, unpeeled the wrapping. "It's a little book," she said. And indeed it was. The gold-leaf title on the scuffed leather cover was *The Little Flowers of St. Francis—Illustrated.* The pages were worn from many turnings. She squinted at the yellowed flyleaf where someone had written in blue ink, now faded: "To our Dear Son Raes Delfino on the occasion of his sixteenth birthday."

This must have been very, very precious to him. Tears filled the Ute woman's dark eyes. She thumbed through the book, stopped at a woodcut print—St. Francis Praying on Mount Alverna. Daisy was drawn in by the simple sketch. *I wonder if that's what the man who talked to birds really looked like.* As the shaman blinked in disbelief, the black-and-white drawing seemed to take on extra dimensions. Branches on bluish-black spruce trees shivered in a chill breeze, a puff of cloud drifted across a sapphire sky, the grass under the saint's knees was green and wet with pearly dew. The man from Assisi turned his head toward the woman who held the book in her hands.

Daisy's mouth gaped. *What on earth . . . ?* In the blink of an eye, the saint's countenance had changed. This face was someone she knew. "Father Raes," she muttered, and heard Moon's voice come from somewhere far away.

"He said to tell you he'd be here in spirit."

The tiny version of the Catholic priest gave the old back-slider a heart-piercing look.

Panicked, Daisy tried to shut the book. The covers were like welded sheets of iron; they would not move. Her hands trembled. She whispered: "What do you want?"

The others at the table were staring at the peculiar old woman. The general consensus was that she must be reading from an interesting passage.

She watched the elfin apparition shake his head, heard his voice say: "Daisy, Daisy. Every morning, every night, I pray to God for your soul. The angels in heaven weep for you." With this pronouncement, the phantom priest collapsed into nothingness, the scene on the yellowed page reverted to the simple woodcut of the kneeling saint.

The small volume slipped from her hands.

Daisy understood that God expected her to do something. She knew exactly what it was. The penitent sinner resisted for a painful moment before she looked across the table at the FBI lady. "Uh—I guess I forgot to thank you for the scarf." She strained hard to get the words past her lips. "It's very nice." *There—that should make God happy.*

It made Lila Mae McTeague happy. She beamed at the unpredictable Ute woman. "I'm so glad you like it."

"I sure do." Daisy pulled the exquisite covering over her head. "I'll wear it to the next funeral I go to." She breathed a melancholy sigh. "And that probably won't be too far off. Most of my friends are almost as old as me and they're dropping dead like flies at the first hard frost." Another possibility suggested itself to her. *Or maybe some of them will be coming to say good-bye to me.*

Barely three miles away, at another expensive eatery, two other diners were working out their entwined destinies.

THE STOCKHOLM Room at Phillipe's Streamside Restaurant was filled with soft amber light, joyful strains of Brahms' Festival Overture—and a congregation of happy patrons.

Just beyond the green-tinted windowpanes, a small patch of night was gaily illuminated by a string of Chinese lanterns. Because the evening was chilly, the man and the woman had the Streamside Patio to themselves. A combination of effects conspired to make this a uniquely romantic spot—the lusty roar of Granite Creek's rolling waters, a low mumbling of thunder over the cloud-shrouded mountains, the hooked horns of a crescent moon, the winking flicker of a sugar-sprinkle of stars.

The lady in black dress and pearls picked at the roasted remains of a freshly slaughtered chicken, tastefully nestled in a deathbed of wild rice and damson plums.

The well-dressed man with the forked beard relished his pork roast, caramelized onions, and buttered new potatoes flecked with a pox of chopped chives. It is true that Manfred Wilhelm Blinkoe gave the lady an occasional appraising glance; equally true that Amanda Anderson seemed barely aware of his presence.

Their tables were separated by a dozen paces.

It was just as well.

Manfred had a very attractive young wife at home, and serious business on his mind.

The lady diner was down on men in general, having just left one behind.

Somewhere on the far side of the stream, a tawny wood-rat scuttled among the dry leaves.

On a craggy cottonwood branch, a saw-whet owl spread her white-spotted wings, launched herself aloft. This *aegolius acadicus* had her yellow eye set on the sliver of silver moon, harbored in her breast the happy ambition of landing there.

Like the robin-sized owl, the woman was entertaining optimistic thoughts. For example, that she had reached the pinnacle of a successful career, had more than sufficient funds in the bank to purchase a spacious condo in Aspen, a fine house in Santa Fe. Better than that, she finally had more than sufficient evidence to divorce her lying, lecherous leech of a husband. To top it all off, she was still a fine-looking woman, well on the sweet side of fifty, and in perfect health. As she raised a long-stemmed wineglass to toast her excellent prospects, Amanda had enormous confidence in the future.

There was something else she had.

Seven seconds to live.

The short-timer felt the man's gaze tingle on the side of her face, turned to return the brazen stare. If she had not moved, the soft-nosed bullet would have struck her in the left temple, barely two centimeters above the ear. As it was, the crimson entry wound appeared on her forehead, just under the line of her hair—as if a magnanimous genie had placed a precious ruby there.

There was no pain.

There was . . . nothing.

SCOTT PARRIS was halfway home from Daisy Perika's birthday party when a sudden shower of rain rattled on the windshield. There was a blurred flash of lightning in the east. He counted the seconds until a rumble of thunder tumbled off the mountains. *That was about a mile and a half away.* He smiled in the darkness. *A fine dinner with good friends, and now a rainy night—just the thing for a good sleep.* This pleasant thought was interrupted by an unpleasant vibration in his shirt pocket. Only a half-dozen souls had his private number. The chief of police pulled over to the curb, frowned at the digits on the display. *That's Doc Simpson's cell phone.* He punched in the number, waited.

The medical examiner's voice crackled in his ear. "Scott—where are you?"

"On my way home—how about you?"

"I'm at Phillipe's. Enjoying my sweet little niece's wedding reception."

Simpson sounds like he's had a couple of drinks. "Good for you—give the lovely couple my best wishes for a long and happy life."

"I've already done that." A pause. "Scott—would you do me a big favor?

"Maybe." Parris hung a Cheshire grin in the darkness. "If it don't have anything to do with lending you money."

"I'd appreciate it if you'd come over to Phillipe's. Right now."·

"Tell me what for."

"I'll tell you when you get here."

Silly old goat. "Why can't you tell me what this is all—"

"Park on the south side, next to the kitchen entrance. But don't come inside—walk around back, to the patio. I'll be waiting for you." The telephone connection went dead.

The chief of police did a tight U-turn on the newly wet street, popped a couple of antacid tablets between his teeth, swore he'd retire before this time next year. *If I win the lottery.*

SCENE OF THE CRIME

THE LONG strings of multicolored lanterns cast a bizarre tint of unreality onto the restaurant patio, where a large red-and-white table umbrella sheltered the remains from the rain. Scott Parris could not shake an absurd, nagging conviction that this ugly display had been staged for his benefit. It would turn out to be a setup for one of the medical examiner's tasteless jokes. Any second now, the woman in the black dress and pearls would sit up, smile at him, wipe the tomato paste off her face. Doc Simpson and Phillipe and the bearded guy he didn't recognize would start laughing their heads off. "April Fool," they'd say. "We sure had you going there!" But the first of day April was gone with the melted snows that swelled the roaring stream.

He took a few steps away from the small gathering, dialed dispatch on his cell phone. After appropriate orders had been barked out, the Granite Creek chief of police approached the umbrella, knelt on one knee. This had been a handsome, upper-class woman. The pearls would be the real thing. Another real thing was the small hole in her forehead. The lead bullet had expanded, so the exit wound would be at least an inch wide. He knew this because a yard away there was a half-dollar-size fragment of skull, shiny with a smear of brain tissue, a long hank of dark hair attached to a flap of scalp. He braced a hand on his knee, got to his feet with a grunt. "Give me the short version."

Dr. Simpson shrugged under his rented tux. "The brief account is the only one I know. I'm inside, enjoying the reception. Phillipe comes over, gives me a nudge and a look. I follow him down the hall, through the kitchen, out the side door by the Dumpster. He tells me something horrible has happened, brings me around here." He pointed his chin at the body. "I find this lady. Just like you see her. She's dead, of course." Simpson continued in a professional monotone, as if he were talking to his microcassette recorder. "The lesion on the forehead has the appearance a small-caliber entry wound. Probably a hollow point, from the damage evident at the exit." Anticipating the question forming on the policeman's lips, the medical examiner jerked his head to indicate the second diner. "There was only one other person on the patio. A Mr. Dinko. He's a dentist."

"Orthodontist." The man stepped forward. "And the name is *Blinkoe,* Manfred Wilhelm Blinkoe."

The experienced policeman calibrated the witness in a single glance. About five-eleven, hundred and eighty pounds, a good fifty-five years old. Probably closer to sixty. Nearsighted, judging by the thick spectacles. The man's outstanding physical feature was a forked beard. "What happened here, Mr. Blinkoe?"

"*Doctor* Blinkoe, if you please."

Parris tried again. "What happened here, Dr. Blinkoe?"

The man swelled with a deep breath. "Because the wedding reception had booked the main dining room, the lady and myself were dining on the patio. She was seated there." He pointed at the table nearest the corpse's feet. "I was just over there, at the table by that, garish blue flowerpot." Oblivious to the light rain, he looked up at the dark sky, as if he saw something there.

"Did you know the victim?"

Blinkoe glanced at the corpse, shook his head.

Parris crossed his fingers, hoped for a 'yes.' "You happen to get a look at the shooter?"

"Sadly, I did not."

It had been too much to hope for, but the policeman felt a surge of heartburn.

As if hoping to please the public servant, Blinkoe added quickly. "But I did hear the gunshot."

Well, that's something. And something is better than nothing. "Just a single shot?"

"Yes. It was merely a little pop." The witness pointed toward the river. "And it came from directly behind me. From across the stream, I should think."

Parris stared at the tangle of brush on the opposite bank. It made sense. A hundred assassins could hide in that small, dense forest. Fifty yards beyond the thicket was a little-used county road where the shooter could have parked his car.

Blinkoe continued. "As chance would have it, I happened to looking directly at the lady when I heard the shot—I and saw the bullet wound appear in her head. For a moment, she merely stared"—he goggled his eyes to imitate the victim's blank expression—"then, she toppled out of the chair. Kerplop." He made what was evidently intended to be a 'kerplopping' gesture with his hand. "I was quite startled, of course—one never expects to see such a terrible thing. I immediately took cover behind the big blue flowerpot by my table. When I was convinced there would be no second shot, I approached the body and placed my finger on the lady's neck, just under the jaw. There was not the least hint of a carotid pulse. Having determined that the victim was dead, I entered the restaurant and summoned Phillipe."

The owner of the business nodded. "As soon as I was informed about the incident, I came to see for myself." He stared in amazement at the corpse. "There she was—exactly as Dr. Blinkoe had reported. By remarkable good fortune, the county medical examiner was inside, a guest at his niece's wedding reception." He made a slight bow to Dr. Simpson. "Naturally, I requested that he come outside at once and examine the body." He added hastily: "If there had been any sign of life, I would have summoned an ambulance. But sadly, there was no need. I conferred with Dr. Simpson, and we thought it advisable to be discreet." He glanced at the series of large windows that framed the ongoing celebration inside, added unnecessarily: "The wedding party has not been informed about this tragedy." He looked hopefully at the chief of police. "After all, what good would it do to disturb my happy guests with such terrible news?"

Straining to hold his temper, Parris addressed his remark to the surviving diner. "Do you recall what time was it when you witnessed the shooting?"

Manfred Blinkoe shrugged. "I did not look at my watch. But I would estimate that the poor woman was shot—oh, about twenty-five minutes before your arrival."

Twenty-five minutes! Parris ground his teeth. "Someone should have dialed nine-one-one immediately."

Phillipe recoiled as if he had been struck by a snake. "But the woman was dead—what good would that have done?"

The professional lawman did not expect much from citizens whose experience was limited to running high-priced restaurants or fixing smiles that still had some personality. But the county medical examiner should have known better. "If one of you had called the emergency number right away, told us somebody had been shot on the patio, the department would have had uniforms all over the area within three minutes flat. We would've stood a fair chance of nailing the shooter. By now, the guy has had time to drive halfway to Durango. Or Leadville. Or Gunnison."

The ME withered under this attack.

Feeling mildly sorry for the old man, Parris turned his cold stare on Phillipe. "Here's the deal." He pointed a sausage of a finger at the man's chest. "You go inside and tell your guests that nobody leaves the joint."

Deeply wounded by the deliberately crude characterization of his four-star establishment, Phillipe gave the gastronomic Neanderthal a look of utmost disdain and pity.

Parris barely restrained himself from grabbing the businessman by the collar and shaking his teeth loose. "Do it right now. Or I will."

The restaurateur retreated with an inaudible mutter that suggested that Parris's parents had never enjoyed the benefits of matrimony.

Dr. Simpson sidled up to his friend. "I'm sorry, Scott. I should've made the emergency call." He tried to grin. "Guess I may've had two or three martinis too many. And even when I'm sober, my old brain don't function like it did twenty years ago."

Parris patted the ME's stooped shoulder. "Sorry if I snapped at you guys. A murder in my jurisdiction kinda puts my teeth on edge."

Feeling at least partially absolved of his sin of omission, Simpson turned his attention to the corpse. After shaking his head at what had been a lovely woman, he covered the body with a vinyl tablecloth. Only the lady's feet protruded, and her left arm.

The chief of police was staring at the fingers on the dead woman's hand. There was no wedding band. But there was a pale white circle on the tanned skin where one might have recently been.

The orthodontist cleared his throat. "Excuse me."

One of the woman's red high-heels had slipped off when she fell from her chair. Parris was mesmerized by the exposed foot. "Yeah?"

"I am, needless to say, not an expert in murders and such." Annoyed that the policeman did not look at him, the witness unconsciously clenched his fists. "But if you will indulge me, I believe there is a distinct possibility which you may not have considered."

"Consider yourself indulged." Just under her big toe, there was a dime-sized hole in the silk stocking. *I wonder if she knew about that.*

Blinkoe raised his voice. "I believe the bullet was intended for me."

As he turned his head to glare at the witness, Parris almost jerked his neck out of joint. "Why do you believe that?"

"Well, for one thing—the shot came from behind me."

"Yeah. I remember you said that. Is that the only reason?"

There was a hesitation. "I have a very strong feeling that I am the person who was supposed to die tonight."

He has a feeling. *Great.* "Look, I understand you've been through a traumatic experience, but—"

"I doubt that you understand *anything* about what I've been through." The man's eyes seemed to bulge from their sockets; the startling effect was magnified by the thick spectacle lens. "Have you ever been shot at?"

The former Chicago cop felt the bad memories come flooding back. "Yes, I have." *More than once.*

Blinkoe blinked. "Oh—well yes, I suppose you would have been. In the line of duty and all that." He flicked a tiny piece of wet lint off his cuff. "That is one thing. But let me tell you, Sheriff—it is not the same when you are sitting in your favorite restaurant."

Scott Parris's blue eyes twinkled. "Yeah. I can see how that's enough to put a man off his feed. But the point is, you weren't hit." He glanced again at the corpse's bare foot. "It was this lady that got shot dead."

Blinkoe shook his head. "Nevertheless, I am virtually certain that the unfortunate woman was not the murderer's intended target."

"Dr. Blinkoe, take it from me. Any guy who can place a slug dead center in his target's forehead—even from just on the other side of the stream—is an expert marksman. If he'd had the bead on you, you'd be stone cold dead." He pointed at the corpse. "And I'd be talking to this lady about what happened when *you* got popped."

The witness assumed a stubborn expression. "I think I may have moved just as he fired the shot."

"Then the slug must've passed pretty close to you."

"Well, yes—I suppose it would have."

"Did you get nicked?"

"Well, no. Of course not."

"Did you hear a chunk of lead go zipping by?"

"I did not." Blinkoe bristled at this hard-headed cop. "But I tell you—that bullet was meant for me!"

Parris glanced at his wristwatch, wondered when the first GCPD unit would arrive. "Dr. Blinkoe, can you think of anyone who hates you enough to shoot you?" *Aside from me.*

Blinkoe struggled to return the lawman's bold stare. "Every man has his enemies—I suppose I have my share."

"Okay. So give me a name—and a motive."

The supposed victim finally averted his gaze. "I am not prepared to speculate on such matters."

Why does my only witness to a homicide have to be a nut-

case? The policeman managed to retain a thin veneer of civility. "Then what do you want from me?"

Blinkoe canted his head, stared intently at the starless sky—as if the answer might be concealed in that dark space beneath the heavens. "I don't know. Protection, I suppose."

Parris closed his eyes, gently massaged the lids with his fingertips. "Witnessing a killing at close range is a nasty experience. Makes a man stop and consider his mortality." *Makes some of 'em downright goofy.* "But I expect you'll feel a lot better after a good night's sleep."

"Thank you for this halfhearted attempt to cheer me up. But what if you are wrong?" Blinkoe glared at a Chinese lantern as if he could not fathom what on earth the vulgar contraption was. "What if the murderer strangles me in my sleep? Runs me through with a rapier? Poisons my morning tea?"

Parris's patience had fallen below the quarter-tank mark. "Then you'll be dead."

The citizen scowled at the public servant. "I *beg* your pardon."

Regretting the unprofessional retort, the weary chief of police made a final attempt to get through to this stubborn man. "Dr. Blinkoe, if you won't tell me anything specific about who might've taken a shot at you—or why someone might want you dead—there's nothing much I can do." *But what* am *I gonna do with this guy?* Like most eureka moments, this one seemed to come from nowhere. Parris proceeded with a wary caution. "Maybe you'd feel more comfortable having someone else look into it." He managed to look quite sympathetic. "Someone not connected with the police department."

Blinkoe's expression was an unhappy mix of bald-faced astonishment and acute pain. "You don't mean like a—a gumshoe?"

Parris maintained an earnest expression. "Nowadays, we call 'em private investigative consultants. PICs for short."

"PICs—really?" Blinkoe pulled at the left cusp of his beard. "I suppose it is not a totally absurd notion." He gave the cop a hopeful look. "Could you recommend a private investigative whatever—a PIC—who is both highly capable and very discreet?"

"Well, let me think about it." Granite Creek's top cop tilted his head back, pretended to consider a bushel of gumshoe-fruit hanging on a massive willow tree. Eventually, he nodded as if he had shaken the right one loose. "Yeah. I believe I know just the guy."

Anticipating such an outcome, Blinkoe had produced a small leather-bound notebook and a gold-plated fountain pen. "Please give me his name."

Cocked and loaded, Scott Parris gave him both barrels. A name. A telephone number.